The First Lamp

April 2009
To Sandy,
Your light is
a blessing to those
around you. You
are so loved.
Cathleen Hulbert

ISBN: 1-4392-1741-6
ISBN-13:9781439217412

Visit www.booksurge.com to order additional copies.

The First Lamp

A Story of Cosmic Illumination

Cathleen Hulbert

Dedication

This book is dedicated to my mother and father,
to my brother, Michael, and my nephew, Andrew.
You are my light.

Contents

Acknowledgements

I would like to thank those who inspire and nurture me as a writer. This includes family, friends and other wise teachers. I also cherish the support of the tail-wagging companions who sat at my feet and kept me company during hours of otherwise solitary writing. Phoenix was the brightest star among them.

My parents, Albert and Micheline Schoppenhorst, my brother, Michael Schoppenhorst (the book's first editor), and my nephew, Andrew Schoppenhorst, have readily welcomed Kalah and her world into their hearts. They have accepted my role as a storyteller with humor and grace. It takes a special group to take this kind of "time-traveling" in stride. I could never have risen to the challenge without their support. My friends also are wonderfully open-minded and creative. In particular I want to thank Karen Thurston, Julie Herron Carson, Kitty Hulbert and Angie Matthiessen for reading the story as it unfolded and enhancing it with their editing skills and wisdom. I am indebted to many other friends who are not named here. They kept me moving forward by loving me and simply believing in "The First Lamp."

I extend a very special "mahalo" to Roz Rapozo, a co-founder of the World Turtle Trust, for her encouragement and graciousness in helping to ensure that the conservation activities and themes in this book ring true. Around the globe, conservationists like Roz are caring for our wounded planet. They deserve our attention and gratitude.

I deeply appreciate award-winning photographer William Tan for sharing the exquisite image on the cover. His talent and generosity supplied a timely infusion of energy that was crucial to the completion of this project. Likewise, the dedicated people at BookSurge have empowered me to move forward with their professionalism and innovations in publishing.

And this expression of gratitude would not be complete without acknowledging my favorite author and storyteller, Richard Bach. His rich books, among them "Jonathan Livingston Seagull," and most recently, "Curious Lives," have taught me to be true to the creative voice within. Inside this novel other writers are named and quoted. Bach and all of these spiritually brilliant men and women have guided my path. Their courage has inspired my own.

It is also important to thank those who have not always resonated with this story. Your responses have challenged me. Thank you for helping to me to sharpen my skills as a listener and as a communicator. You, too, have guided the manifestation of this book and its message of unity.

Along the way nature has given me opportunities to open my mind and heart. The ancient creatures of the sea, most notably sea turtles, are survivors of planetary changes that the human race cannot begin to comprehend. I hope we are not the one challenge that destroys them! Our future is tied to theirs and in protecting them we are saving ourselves. My friends the dolphins remind me to play and to move through life honoring the rhythms of the planet. The whales, magnificent in size and dignity, have helped me to put my human agenda in perspective. The winged ones keep me looking up, not just to the sky but to my own higher consciousness as well. Together I join Kalah and her clan, both modern and ancient, in thanking each reader for reaching out to connect with the innocence, joy and spiritual power of Aloha.

Cathleen Hulbert

Foreword

This book has its own spirit. From the time it pushed itself into my awareness as a story wanting to be told, I experienced it as a collection of friends. Some of them are very old and familiar friends with a deep sense of the divine. As I wrote "The First Lamp" I often felt angelic energy around me. And it would not surprise me to learn that one of my more persistent muses had wings. Human beings have always learned spiritual lessons through stories. I just happened to be sending out a signal that I was ready and willing to write. I encourage you to do the same. We all have an imagination that can serve as a portal for the Holy Spirit.

Like the great turtle within this novel, "The First Lamp" carries a message of eternal love. Writing it all down has had a profound impact on my life. I have not always known about the plight of sea turtles. I have not always taken the time to truly investigate what I can do to help endangered species. Likewise, it was not until a few years ago that I felt a deep need to connect with Hawaiian culture and the healing quality of Aloha. As I shaped the book the book was shaping me into someone with a burning love for Hawaii, someone who now recognizes the truth about the needs of Mother Earth. Her future is our future. The ancients understood this holy Oneness of things. My prayer is that I continue to understand it a little more each day and that you will, too. Together we will write new stories.

I am deeply grateful that the spirit of Hawaii reached across the country and touched my life while I was working as a social worker in an Atlanta children's hospital. Skeptics might call this a "reach" of another kind. No matter. Spirit will work its wonder on them as well. On some level high above my conscious mind, I know that it all makes perfect sense. Like Sarah in this book, I learned so much about human goodness while living in New York City. It is a city that I will always adore. As a microcosm of the world, New York allowed me to witness just how regularly diversity can transform itself into brotherly love. And so it felt very natural to synthesize the ancient, illuminating lessons of Aloha with New York City's colorful and edgy brilliance. Both provide an opportunity to witness humanity at its best.

Thank you for opening yourself to this story. Sarah and Kalah, the twin flames in the book, are in some ways aspects of me. You might also recognize them as aspects of you. So, too, with the others: Porter and Gabe, Kai and Aunt Twylah, Uncle David, Makani and most of all, young Pablo. (He is the holy Child in us all.) As you read this book, you might see yourself in the characters' ups and downs, triumphs and setbacks and their sometimes silly human behavior. Perhaps the parts of them that you most chafe at represent aspects of you that want to be acknowledged and healed. Above all, I hope this story will make you laugh. The levity that laughter brings is liberating. As Kalah says, "If you knew how much you are loved by Spirit it would break your heart. It would break your heart wide open and you would be free."

Cathleen Hulbert

October 2008

The First Lamp

By Cathleen Hulbert

"The truth in you is as radiant as a star, as pure as light and as innocent as love itself."

— A Course in Miracles

CHAPTER ONE

Choices

Sarah threw the book and screamed.

The scream started in her gut, pushed through her aching chest and emerged from her throat like the roar of an injured lioness. As this pain was released into the ethers it merged with a multitude of other screams, cries and unspoken heartaches, the greatest of which came from the planet herself. But this was unknown to Sarah.

Momentarily shocked by the sound of her own fury, she fell back on the couch. Finally, it had come to this: one explosive protest to punctuate months of frustration and confusion. It all started when she went on a quest to understand what had become of her life. After months of therapy, Sarah had turned to books. They were cheaper than New York City shrinks and less likely to have her committed.

Now her mind shot back to the crowded Manhattan bookstore where she first cradled this book in her hands. The author's face radiated peace. She wanted that peace. So she purchased the book with its shining author on the cover. She was tired of playing the damsel in distress and ready for a valiant and heroic explanation of why her life was upside down. Squinting, she decided that if this particular writer were placed on the back of a white horse he could possibly look like a knight. She went back to her apartment and forgot about dinner as day slipped into dusk. And as evening stretched lazily into night she felt herself relaxing and taking comfort. His words filled her up. It was her spirit that needed to be fed. Sarah sensed that she was getting ready to start a new chapter in more ways than one. She stood up to stretch and get a glass of water. She fluffed the pillows before settling back on the couch. It was then that she came face-to-face with the words that would change her life. The book had opened her heart to the possibility of radical healing. Now it issued a challenge that could be summed up in three words: extreme personal responsibility. Her stomach tightened as she read:

"Consider the possibility that you are an architect of this mad version of reality that you call your life. You are probably reading this book because you have found yourself to be a player in a world that makes no sense. Looking for someone to blame, you might have avoided examining your own part. You are not alone. Our shaming culture encourages finger pointing as a survival technique. But consider your creative power as a child of God and ask yourself if you truly are a helpless victim or rather a constant creator, along with the rest of us. If you have come this far you must now resist the temptation to see yourself as a tiny, helpless fish in a big sea. That is a fishy lie told by the guilt-ridden and falsely modest part of you, your ego. It is your turn to take responsibility for what you see around you. Think about it and be honest. How can you start a bigger change without first creating the changes you want to see within yourself? It is your choice, of course. Your whole life is built on your choices. And this whole world is built on our collective choices. Guess what? That's the good news."

"Are you nuts?" she asked. "That's the good news?" She kicked a pillow. "You need to take that back."

She turned the page. "Hell." He wasn't taking it back. Her vulnerability turned his blunt words into a sharp object that stoked her anger. And that is how the big scream was born. Still stunned by the sound of it, she brought her thoughts back to the present moment. She glared at the offender. The book now lay across the room in a crumpled heap. "You stay there!" she seethed. "This world is built on our choices? Haven't you ever seen an abused child or a neglected old person? Don't you watch the news?" She slid off the couch and sprawled on the floor, wanting like an angry toddler to protest with her whole body. With uncanny timing the light above her head flickered off and on, finally going out with a muted "Pop."

"Great," she thought, peering around the dim room. "Even the appliances want to keep me in the dark." She began to sob. Somewhere outside an ambulance honked as it negotiated traffic. The wail of its siren merged with her cries, sending mingled sounds of urgency and grief into the night air. It seemed that the more she felt the faceless enemy advancing, the more she searched the horizon for her knight. But if a knight had ever set out on a mission to save her, clearly he had taken a wrong turn and would never make it in time. Of that she was now certain. She pounded her fist on the floor, almost daring her downstairs neighbors to pound back. "I did not choose this mess," she shouted, still determined to set the writer straight. "I would have chosen far better than this." As if freed by this temporary crack in her mind, different aspects of her psyche began to express themselves. She heard the grieving widow and the uprooted Southerner who missed her family back home. She heard from that part of her spirit that felt like a fallen angel, irate with God for being an absent landlord and letting the world fall apart. The fearful Catholic student inside of Sarah, always trying to smooth the waters, immediately apologized to God for the fallen angel's brazen accusation. Then the social worker tried to comfort the worried Catholic kid, who was beginning to have an anxiety attack. She declared that it was fine, even appropriate, to be steaming mad. Sarah kicked the pillow again and looked upward. "Why do we have to suffer?" she demanded. "I'd like to know what you're thinking, God!"

Through it all, there was the ever-present journalist within, a remnant of her first career, reporting grimly that madness had overtaken the world. Sarah had roughly the same number of inner voices as anyone else. But tonight they were competing for the microphone. She listened for a while then grew tired of the noise and rolled over on her back, studying the cracks in the ceiling. Only her inner comedienne was utterly speechless, although Sarah managed to say, "Well, that was lovely," as she pulled herself up into a sitting position. She ran a hand through her long brown hair. For a moment the room seemed to grow bright. Puzzled, she looked around for the source of this light.

"Note to self," she said, exhausted. "Figure out what in the hell that was all about." She stood, reaching to turn on a lamp. Her eyes caught sight of an overturned glass, its contents spreading across the hardwood floor. The floor seemed to vibrate a little, coaxing the spill into a rounded shape with flippers. Uneasy, she grabbed a sweatshirt off the couch and threw it on the image, which had begun to look a lot like a turtle. She walked over to the book, kicking it a little with her toe. She half expected it to kick back. Studying the cover she looked the author straight in the eyes.

"Right, I chose this. We all chose this." Her moment of regret turned to disgust. The book landed in the trash with a thud.

CHAPTER TWO

Questions

Time was collapsing. The screams and protests of another place were making their way to Kalah's world. Urged on by a force she did not yet understand, she moved quickly up the path that led to her prayer place on the mountain. She was surefooted. She took a leap and landed on a rock that jutted out from the cliff like a wing. For a moment Kalah stood, her arms outstretched, and gave thanks to the ancestors who were the guardians of this place. She sat down and reached into the pouch at her side, feeling past small shells and flowers until she found the whalebone comb that was a gift from her teacher. Touching it, she felt a surge of emotion. Kalah held the comb up to the sunlight and studied it. Then a question came to her. It was a question about the perspective of the whale.

Wanting to calm her emotions, she guided her thoughts out to the sea. This was good medicine when she felt confused. "Where your attention goes, so go you," her teacher, Mama Hanu, would say. Whether she swam with her body or with her spirit, the sea was refreshing and attentive to her feelings. Relaxing, she felt a smile forming on her lips. She closed her eyes, entering with each breath more deeply into the world of spirit. There, Kalah imagined herself as a dolphin swimming in an ocean of calm. It was a comforting meditation and for a while she felt serene. But something began to tug at her, disturbing her reverie. The palm that cradled the comb had begun to ache and sweat. She opened her eyes, squinting against the light, and looked down at her hand. A deep hurt pushed into her awareness. She wondered when the great whale had lost its life to provide for her people. She imagined how it felt when it died.

Her thoughts moved next to the journey she would take to a new time and place. She was a sky-walker, true. But would her bones one day rest in the hands of strangers? Kalah raised the comb over her head, wanting suddenly to throw it into the sea. Her hand fell down on her lap. No, the whale was gone. Its bones could not be returned. She put the comb back into the pouch and stood up, lifting her face to the sun. She raised her palms toward the pale blue sky and chanted the prayer of her ancestors, asking for the wisdom required to chase away shadows. In her mind flashed a brilliant spear, humming as it passed. She felt guided to seek wisdom from Chief Ka-welo. Running down the mountain, she called out to the chief with her thoughts. She sensed his willingness to speak with her.

"But first you must find my hiding spot," he replied with his thoughts. She laughed. His humor always lifted her spirit.

"Good morning," she said, discovering him sitting on a rock by the sea. He was sharpening a spear. His white hair was loose today, resting on strong brown shoulders. He nodded and raised an eyebrow. "That didn't take too long," he said, his eyes smiling. He nodded approvingly. "You are getting better at finding me." Then he returned to his task, his voice more serious. "You have much on your mind today."

"Yes. You sense correctly, beloved chief. This whalebone comb that Mama Hanu gave me..." she paused to take it out of the pouch. "Is it also correct for me to consider it a gift from the whale, the bone, that is? What is the perspective of this whale? This is suddenly important for me to understand."

His gaze remained fixed on the image of a sea turtle he had carved into the spear. The turtle was a symbol of the Mother Earth and a beloved spirit guide of their village. She felt his mind touch hers and it was a comfort. She knew he was trying to understand.

"Did the whale give us the bone for that comb, or did we take it?" he asked. "That is the distinction you are trying to make?" She nodded.

"I feel troubled in my heart. Somehow I have never thought of this before. Surely the whale did not give us its body willingly," Kalah replied.

"And how do you know?"

"Because it must have been very afraid," she said.

The chief looked up at her. "Are you afraid?"

"I want to tell you that I am not." The wind blew her hair, which she shook from her face. She lifted her chin, expecting to be tested.

"But are you?" he asked more gently this time.

"At times I feel afraid." She searched his eyes.

"Yet you want to travel to the other place, even if you are afraid?"

"Oh, yes," she said, suddenly very certain of this.

"Why?"

She looked at him, feeling a dawn of understanding. "It is why I was born. It is the Great Spirit's plan!"

"So you go to serve Spirit? Fear will not stop you?" She nodded resolutely. Of this she was certain. "Then make no assumptions about the whale," he said. "Make no assumptions." He returned to his task and for a while they were both quiet. Again she held the comb up to the sunlight, blinking as she studied it. "So it is true," she asked, "that you have had many visions of my journey, you and the elders?" She knew the answer, but needed to hear it again. He nodded.

"We have seen much," he replied. "Your journey is magnificent."

"Still, a question now burns in me. When my part is complete, will my bones return?" She felt the crashing of waves in her heart. She held out the comb. "Or will all of me, including my bones, become a gift to the others?"

His face grew gentle. Putting down the spear he opened his arms to her and she fell into his embrace. "Yes, my beloved sky-walker," he whispered. "Your bones will return. And for now, that is all you need to know."

* * *

A full day passed.

She sat in her family's small boat, watching the waves that gently rocked it. Birds called. In the distance white plumes of sea water splashed against cliffs of lava rock. Kalah's hand touched the shell bracelet on her wrist, turning it in gentle circles against her skin. In his wisdom, Chief Ka-welo had sent her on a search for floating seaweed. He had presented her a newly woven net blessed for this sacred purpose. The bounty she brought home would be used for the village's next rite of forgiveness and release. She cast a net across the water and brought in the seaweed, adept at this skill even though it was a task normally reserved for men. Somehow it came easily to her and she did it with the chief's blessing. Tugging at the edge of the net, she remembered what he said the day before as they were parting company.

"I believe that your questions and your feelings mark the nearness of your journey. Fear is the weapon of the saboteur and this entity now believes more than ever that it has reason for worry. You have a remarkable gift when it comes to releasing your fears quickly. I am grateful for that." He had held her hands as he spoke. "We do not know the exact day or time that this journey will begin for you. When the moment is right, your spirit and the will of the Great Spirit will unite fully and you will be guided. What is here and what is there are only a short distance apart to the Creator of all there is." For three hours she pulled in the seaweed and freed it gently from the fibers of the net. She knew this action was symbolic. Forgiveness, be it of self or others, was a release from the net of guilt cast by the saboteur. At times she prayed. At times her thoughts scattered and she listened to the sounds of her village. She heard the chants of canoe builders, the laughter of children. Somewhere beyond the fields, in the depths of the jungle land, she heard the fall of a koa tree that would become a canoe. She heard women beating large pieces of bark into sheer strips of kappa fabric for ceremonial dress. She cocked her head suddenly. What else did she hear? What else could there be?

It seemed that someone was calling her, not with words but with a scream of pain. A warm gust came across the water, rocking her boat more vigorously. She looked up and saw a luminous cloud settling around her. She opened herself to this presence and felt only love. Melodious tones enveloped her, pulsing through her body, mind and heart.

"Take me there, Great Winged Being. I am in your service."

CHAPTER THREE

The Prophecy

Kalah landed in Sarah's apartment in time to see the offending book take flight. She watched Sarah in amazement, immediately comprehending her vulnerability and her volatility. She saw in this sister a human volcano in desperate need of a creative outlet. Her heart pounded. That aching scream! Could it have come from her? It had reverberated through Kalah's bones like an anguished cry from Great Mother. She knew this was bigger than one person's misery.

"It will be all right," Kalah whispered. She understood that Sarah could not yet see or hear her. But this would change. "If you knew how much you are loved by Spirit it would break your heart. It would break your heart wide open and you would be free."

This thought brought light. It filled her mind. Dizzy, she closed her eyes. She saw the gentle faces of Mama Hanu and Chief Ka-welo. She saw a vision of the chief throwing his spear. It was radiant against the black sky. It moved up and down in a wavy trajectory. Behind it trailed an endless thread of sparkling light. Then she saw Mother Turtle, that cosmic being from which all turtles spring into the material world. Their eyes met. Kalah felt calm.

Again she fixed her gaze on Sarah, whose sparkling embers glowed in the aftermath of her volcanic fury. She smiled, recognizing this turbulent sister as a vessel for the sacred flame of Great Spirit, a daughter of the fire Goddess Pele.

"Soon you will see me," she whispered. She looked around at the sharp edges and strange forms in this place where Sarah dwelled. The newness of it gave her a surge of excitement. At last the prophecy truly was unfolding! She saw a growing light above her and sensed a return to her own world. She placed both of her hands to her lips, blowing a kiss. Kalah then returned home as suddenly as she had left. With a gasp, she found herself sitting in her small boat, gently rocking in the teal waters of the lagoon bordering her village. She gripped the sides and looked into the water where her net still floated. It was full of seaweed. Out of the corner of her eye she saw the shining shell of a red turtle with markings of golden sunbursts on her back. "Hello, Honu'ea!" she said. "Mother Turtle was with me on my journey!"

Kei, her dolphin friend, glided past the turtle and broke the surface, resting a sleek head on the side of the boat. She gave Kalah a sidelong glance. "Oh Kei, it was amazing." She was interrupted by the voice of her husband, Makani.

"Kalah! Mama Hanu is asking for you!" he called over waves hitting the shore. She waved to him and pulled in the net. Kei slipped under the boat. Kalah saw her move toward deeper water. She felt a sense of urgency to speak with the elder who had first called her a sky-walker. Paddling, she remembered the story that had been told to her family. Mama Hanu had been given a vision of her sacred destiny just after putting the newborn Kalah to her mother's breast for the first time. She saw Kalah as a young woman surrounded by light. In her hands Kalah held a dark bowl with a bright rainbow light. A glowing spear pointed the way into darkness. Beside her swam Mother Turtle, who was traveling toward the destiny of her struggling offspring, threatened and barely surviving in a far-way time. As soon as this revered medicine woman received the vision, the chief was notified and the circle of elders gathered for ceremony. They asked Great Spirit what this daughter of their village would accomplish and how she should be prepared. After three hours of prayer and chanting, the same number of hours her mother had labored to give birth, the magnificent triangular form of *Ke-Ao Lanihuli* appeared before the elders with a burst of fiery light. The ancient symbol told them that Kalah was not only a sky-walker but a light-bearer as well, verifying what Mama Hanu had seen. It heralded a time when their daughter would bring fresh spiritual energy to people who had grown tired of living in fear. The elders bowed their heads in gratitude. They were deeply moved.

With the blessing of her parents, Kalah was taken under Mama Hanu's tutorial wing at age four, spending several hours a day with her teacher. She absorbed much about the healing arts and communicating with thoughts. Studying with other elders, she learned about the sacred art of slipping out of the body and seeing with the eyes of her spirit, far beyond what the physical eyes could see. But her journey would take her much further, the elders predicted. She would travel far into the future and eventually learn to take her body as well. She would do this to be a messenger and a guide. In this sense, they believed that her experiences would be far beyond the realm of the most experienced kahunas in the village. It was an aspect of her destiny that had less to do with training than with her strong connection to the universal life force, her abundance of sacred mana. The elders felt blessed and greater in their wisdom after contact with this girl. Kalah learned from all of the teachers in this circle, absorbing the sacred wisdom that they had to share. And in turn, they felt lighter as they taught her. The vibrations at their cores were elevated and the village shared in this spiritual harvest.

Their bright apprentice accepted the rigors of her training as if it were all a wonderful game. Even through adolescence she took in knowledge with the curiosity of a child eager to know the seen and unseen worlds. Mama Hanu urged her parents, and then her husband, to nurture and protect this innocence.

"Only with the trust of a child can one make this journey unharmed," she said. "For a heart of innocence trusts and obeys Great Spirit, pushing past fear and confusion. But the mind lacks trust and wants to take control. Mind is a gift. It has much to offer in this world and its questions are fruitful. But it does not know how to navigate the waters of the mysterious and the sacred. It does not know how to obey the One who knows the way."

Pulling her boat out of the water, Kalah now ran to Makani filled with wonder at what she had heard and seen. He stood tall, his hands on his hips, clearly admiring the graceful movements of his young wife. "I went to the other place. The journey, it has started," she said breathlessly, searching his kind eyes for a response.

"How are you?" he asked, studying her face with great tenderness. He put his arms around her. "You seem to be in one piece."

"Yes, I was only gone for a moment. At least that is how it seemed. But I know now where I will go on my journey. Can I share it with you later? Do you understand? If Mama wants me now, I should go." She turned toward her boat. "It is full," she said. "I was successful." He nodded and kissed the forehead of this woman he had known all of his life. He shared her respect for the wise woman.

"The tide is coming in. I will tie your boat and bring in the seaweed," he said, moving toward the water. She looked over her shoulder, laughing as she heard the rest of his thoughts, sent playfully from his mind to hers. "At least *one* of you I can tie down!" She threw her head back and laughed again as he dangled the rope from her boat.

"I should really get some of this for your feet!" he said out loud.

"Hush! I promise you will not need the rope," she said, dancing playfully on the sand before heading up the path on the east side of the mountain. But her feet did seem to glide above the ground as she hurried along. She shook her hands vigorously, hoping it would make her feel more solid and grounded.

"You have the right idea, child," she heard Mama Hanu say with her thoughts. "Get yourself firmly back in this world so we can talk."

"I'm coming. I'm coming. Please, Mama. My head is still spinning. I cannot run and have this conversation at the same time!" A bright lizard jumped off the doorway and a startled red bird fluttered into the air as she approached Mama's hut. She smiled at the commotion she was causing. It was not unusual. Holding such powerful mana within her being, Kalah often triggered swirling vortices of energy around her.

"What took you so long?" the elder exclaimed, slapping her knees and feigning impatience as she burst in and knelt down. "So!" she said, her eyes dancing. "What did you see?"

She rested her head on Mama's knee. She closed her eyes, recalling every moment of her time in Sarah's world. The two women sat quietly, breathing deeply and releasing. Mama nodded occasionally at what Kalah showed her with their thought connection.

"Yes," Mama said softly after a while. "I see her clearly. Like you, she is very spirited. Unlike you, she is very confused."

"Both are true," Kalah said, shifting her position to sit at Mama's feet. "Her world is very strange, but I understand her somehow. She is on the verge of great change. She has the potential to make a big impact." She paused, gathering her thoughts. "She is feeling her power more and more, and yet she is afraid of it. On some level she sensed my presence and took comfort in it. Otherwise she would not have allowed me to hear her thoughts and to know these things about her."

"Her name is Sarah," Mama said, her head cocked as if hearing something far away. "If you listen, her heart speaks to you even now."

"Sa–rah." The sound of it was foreign. "Well Sarah lives in a very noisy world!" Kalah exclaimed, her eyes wide. "It's like she lives in a jungle full of squawking birds! No wonder she cannot hear herself."

"Yes. That is the key. She cannot hear her *true* self. It is noisy in her world and noisy in her head. Her life has broken her sense of self into bits and pieces. She is trying to gather them up and feel whole again. But she does not know how. She does not know what to do with her own spiritual power. That is why she is angry." Kalah nodded.

"Did you know, Mama, that I would see that incredible light over my boat?" she asked the elder.

"Light is a central part of the prophecy, as you know. You were not alone. Great Spirit was with you. Turtle Mother was with you. Others were there, too."

Kalah nodded, feeling humbled. She was quiet and her teacher did not disturb the silence. She was happy that her student was remembering to balance the excitement with quiet time to reflect.

"And the spear with a wavy line of light behind it," Kalah said finally. "What do you think that meant?"

"Questions, questions!" Mama Hanu answered, playfully throwing up her hands. "It was your vision, daughter. How do you read it?"

"Well, let me think." Kalah said, holding the spear in her mind's eye. "It reminded me of a needle for sewing. Great Spirit is making something." The old woman threw back her head and laughed heartily, slapping her knees with weathered hands. Kalah couldn't help but laugh, too. It felt good.

"Yes, the Great One is always creating. Females love to create and within our hands the spears of men become tools of creation. It is perfect, more perfect than you realize. From Spirit's great vantage point, our time and Sarah's time are simply like separate pieces of cloth or different shells to arrange on a necklace. You know when you and your sisters make adornments you select materials that are very different, so that each will accentuate the qualities of the other. Isn't that what you love to do?"

Kalah nodded. She loved contrast.

"Ah, yes. Great Spirit is making something very grand. And you, child, are helping, an apprentice to the greatest Creator of them all." Kalah smiled radiantly.

"Now let us give voice to the prophecy," Mama said, "for the words we know hold the dance of the sacred opposites. She began to chant the words that came to her in a song when Kalah was seven days old.

"Our lives are the darkness and the light," she chanted. "The darkness will know its source. Our form is the vessel and the waves. The ship will know its course. Our story is told by the one who is silent. Turtle will find a voice." Mama sprinkled herbs on the fire, creating tiny stars.

"Now then," she said, suddenly waving her hands. "I sense that your fine husband is eager to speak with you. Go home! Come back and see me tomorrow when the sun is straight in the sky. I have a wonderful gift for you, a story." She took the young woman's hands and lifted her to her feet. In her presence, Kalah still felt like a small child.

"A story you haven't told me? I didn't know there were any stories left!"

"I haven't heard this one myself," replied the elder. She stepped outside to scan the heavens. "But I sure do feel it coming."

CHAPTER FOUR

Light

Sarah's daydream was broken by the screech of subway brakes. Gliding through tunnels and across vast expanses of urban landscape, she had slipped into a pleasing reverie. A circle of women had appeared in her mind, happy women gathered around a large piece of cloth. The oldest among them looked Hawaiian. She felt a powerful pull coming from this elder female.

The voice of the conductor brought her back. "Flatbush Station. End of the line." She stepped out quickly and hurried across the busy platform, spotting her friend, Gabe.

"Hi stranger. How was Phoenix?"

"I didn't see much of the city," he said, slipping a newspaper under his arm and giving her a kiss on the cheek. "I spent most of my time at the conference center with about 200 fellow shrinks. Scary thought, isn't it?"

"Hmmmm. Your head doesn't look like it got shrunk in the process," she said, looking him over. "If anything, your head looks a little *bigger* to me, Mr. Keynote Speaker." He laughed and rolled his eyes.

"Hey, can I help it if I'm in demand? I think a little ground-breaking work on brain injuries is sorely needed in our head-banging society."

"Speaking of heading-banging," she said, looking embarrassed, "I finally had that meltdown you've been prescribing, doctor. I had it yesterday."

"I'm sorry I wasn't here for you. Do you feel any better?"

She shrugged, wishing she hadn't told on herself.

"I actually screamed. I mean full-throttle." She searched his face. "Can you believe that?"

"Yes," he said, tugging on her ponytail. "I can believe that."

"Really?"

"Of course."

"Why?"

"Why not? People need to scream sometimes."

"I'm not sure the neighbors would agree with you."

He put his arm around her. "You can't be the first one to go primal in that building." She laughed, a little snort escaping through her nose. He usually teased her about it but he didn't this time. They hurried up the steps of the subway station. Cool breezes and city sounds flowed down to meet them. She sighed deeply as they made it to the top and rounded the corner, dodging pedestrians hurrying toward the station entrance. She felt safe enough to continue.

"Anyway," she said, recalling the previous night. "You missed quite a show."

"Trust me. I bet it was pretty mild as meltdowns go. You are a resilient and remarkable creature."

"Yesterday I was just a creature."

"Well, then learn to love the creature," he said, laughing.

"Is that what you discussed in Phoenix? Learn to love the creature within?"

"Among other things. I wish it had all been that interesting. But I'm serious, Sarah. Give yourself some credit. You're a strong woman."

"Thanks. I have to agree with you about that. And strong women should avoid marrying their pain."

"Pardon me?" He stumbled a little on the uneven sidewalk.

"One day I had this realization that I was getting too attached to my pain, you know what I mean?" She looked up at him, shrugging. "Hard to explain. But then it hit me. I said to myself, 'Sarah, go ahead and feel the pain. Mingle with the pain, talk to the pain. But don't fall in love with it, for God's sake. You have to know when to draw the line.' And for a little while I think I snapped myself out of my obsessing."

He nodded. "Interesting."

"It worked that time, but I can't always call in that wisdom," she said. "Pain has a strong pull. It can be very seductive. I'm not sure why."

"When you figure that one out, fill me in."

"Have you come close to marrying the pain, too?"

"Been there, done that," he said. "Thank God we didn't have kids."

She pinched him playfully. He smiled at her and they walked the rest of the way in silence, moving quickly along several blocks of housing and business fronts that were succumbing to urban decay. Adults and children moved in and out of the buildings. Some of the structures had once been beautiful and all had once been sound. But the energy needed to maintain them had been withdrawn along the way. Now they crumbled from years of neglect. Numb to the bleakness of these surroundings and shielded by the deepening bond between them, they entered the front doors of Mercy Medical Center, where Gabe worked as a psychologist and Sarah a social worker.

"Lunch?" he asked.

"I have a home visit. We've lost touch with one of our sicker kids. Let's try tomorrow if that works for you." He nodded, giving her a playful salute as they veered off in different directions. As she started to turn, the hospital lobby was transformed. There was a burst of light that sent something glowing through the air in front of her. A faint buzzing sound trailed it. She staggered and fell back, her heart pounding as if she had narrowly escaped being hit by a bus.

"What on God's earth was that?" she said. "Gabe! Hey, *Gabe!*"

He turned around.

"Did you see that incredible light?"

"What light?" he asked, looking around. He was smiling, his face suddenly radiant. She opened her mouth but no words came out. Seeing this he walked quickly across the lobby, the light around him intensifying as he got closer. She shook her head as if to shake off the sight. She swallowed hard, struggling to find her voice.

"I'm okay," she said, finally. "I think there was a power surge." She looked up at the exit light, which was flickering. "See? That's what it was."

"Well, call me if you need to," he said, looking uncertain. "Are you absolutely sure you're okay?"

"I am," she said, mesmerized by the light around his face. "I'm good."

Walking toward the elevator, she tried to dismiss what she had seen. Gabe is a great guy, she reasoned. There was nothing strange about a little extra glow now and then. And that burst of light didn't seem to rattle anyone else. In fact, it appeared to have shot through the crowded lobby unnoticed by anyone but herself.

"How could that be?" she thought to herself. "It was bright, really bright."

Rummaging through a virtual wardrobe of explanations, she tried on several but none seemed to fit. "I hope I didn't pop a blood vessel yesterday. Great. I finally get to scream and I pop something." She looked around, scanning the lobby. "No, I don't think that's it. Maybe I'm going crazy. No, if I were going to go crazy, it would have happened months ago. And somebody would have noticed by now."

She looked up, watching as little red numbers tracked the downward course of the elevator. She imagined how the unidentified flying object would play out on the evening news.

"A mysterious flash of light makes it way through a crowded hospital lobby. One employee says it might have been a UFO. But where are the *other* witnesses? More details at 11." The elevator doors opened and she stepped in. It was time to shift gears and become who they paid her to be: Sarah Ann Pierce, clinical social worker and emotional anchor for those who were losing it. Hastily, she stuffed images of the light show into her brain's deal-with-it-later file. She stepped out, trying to look focused and professional. Approaching her office she was stopped in her tracks by an unexpected display of creativity. Taped to the door was a child's drawing, a rainbow-colored spear trailing what appeared to be a yellow ribbon. It was signed, "Pablo."

She hurried down the hall to Pablo's room. "I love it!" she said, approaching his hospital bed. He reached his arms up to her and she gave him a hug.

"I dreamed it last night and drew it for you this morning. Miss Priscilla said she would put it on your door," he said proudly. The 7 year old, born HIV positive, now had full-blown AIDS. The hospital was becoming a second home.

"You had a dream about a spear?" she asked, sitting in a chair next to his bed. "That sounds interesting. What did it do?"

"It flew threw the air!"

"Well, yes. Silly question," she said. "But can you tell me more about your dream? It must be important if you drew such a beautiful picture so early in the morning."

"It had a glowing tail. I colored it yellow but that's not exactly how it looked. And it was flying right toward *you*! You were in my dream, too."

"I was? And it was flying toward *me*? Ouch! Did it get me?" she asked, wondering if Pablo was tired of all the shots and retaliating in his dreams. "Hey, did *you* throw that spear at me?"

"No, Miss Silly." He coughed. She stood up to pat his back. "It didn't poke you," he explained, sounding raspy. "It brought you light. It thought you needed some light." She was speechless. It was only 9 a.m. and already her day was developing an improbable theme: Light. Mysterious light. Light that flew through a child's dream, across a hospital lobby and right in front of her face. Sarah's deal-with-it-later items had been transferred into her mind's most urgent file, the one called deal-with-it-now, silly, *because what could be more important?*

"I think the spear worked really good," he said, bringing her back to the moment. "Because now you are shiny. Your face has light on it." She sat down abruptly like an obedient child, looking at his face through moistening eyes.

"Your face has light on it, too, Pablo." She was telling the truth. He was glowing. They sat together quietly, communicating without words. When he finally grew sleepy and closed his eyes, she tucked his blanket around him and slipped away. Sitting at her desk, she wiped tears from her face and studied the drawing. Twenty-four hours earlier her life had felt devoid of anything remotely mystical. Now, there was this *light.*

"I'm seeing love," she said, simply. She did not know the origins of this revelation. She only knew that it made perfect sense. It had been obvious for some time that Gabe's feelings for her were deepening. And Pablo was the essence of love. Surely this wise little boy had seen her feelings for him. Despite her attempts to keep some semblance of professional distance, it must have been written all over her face. She did a mental replay of the burst of light in the lobby. It reminded her of the eerie brightness that filled her bedroom one night when a lightning bolt shook the pavement just beneath her window. Other than setting off car alarms up and down the street, it did no real damage. It was a deeply humbling moment, the bigness of New York City momentarily dwarfed by the bigger power of nature. The worries of the day, which had been festering in her tired mind as she lay in bed, had vanished into thin air. Somehow it was reassuring to be reminded of who was in charge.

The light in the hospital lobby, much gentler yet equally humbling, had to be something good, she decided, if for no other reason than it was tied to Pablo. With that decision to accept the gift Sarah felt a deep shift, as if her soul lifted itself up and turned around to get another perspective on life. She was tired of pain. She was tired of ugly. She was ready to see something else. She was ready to see Gabe's shining face and Pablo's spear with the tail that brought her light.

On her way home she stepped into the bookstore, looking for a new journal. The universe was up to something, she told herself. It was time to start writing again.

"Yes everybody, it's me," she said, amusing herself as she entered the store. "It is big, bad Sara Pierce. Book-thrower." She imagined all of the books leaning forward and roaring *"Boooooooooo,"* as if she were the hated opponent in a battle between gladiators. She burst out laughing, immediately attracting the quizzical look of a store clerk.

"I need to call Mom," she thought. "She gets me." Thinking of her mother while standing in line, she recalled their last conversation on the phone.

"You ought to get back to your writing," her mother announced one evening after her daughter had described another typical week in New York. "When you were little, you wrote the best stories. Remember the one you wrote about Martians landing on top of the house? You got an A on that one."

"Hold everything. You mean that didn't really happen? I thought that was how I came to join our family." Her mother laughed, and she laughed, grateful for the comic relief.

"Seriously," her mother had said, before they hung up. "Send me something."

Sarah's thoughts were interrupted by the cashier's strained *"Next, please."* Judging by the woman's tone, Sarah had already missed one *"Next,"* maybe two. She apologized and stepped up quickly. Over the woman's shoulder she caught sight of a book with an island scene on the cover. She sighed, wishing she could beam herself to the South Pacific with her new journal, a straw hat and a beach towel.

"I'd rather be in Hawaii, she said, nodding toward the book.

"Amen," the cashier replied, her demeanor softening.

And then a new voice spoke inside of Sarah's already overcrowded head. It seemed to rise above the rest in the pecking order of inner voices. Speaking with kindness and authority it gave her some very direct advice.

"Speak up if that's what you want, girl. You might just get it."

CHAPTER FIVE

Drums

Sarah hurried home and slapped together a cheese sandwich without the usual lettuce, tomato and mustard. She didn't have time. She foraged through a drawer looking for a pen. Finding it, she headed for the couch. It had been a year and a half since she had kept a journal. She wrote:

Bless me, father, for I have sinned.

She was surprised at the words on the page. A flash of memory shot through her. She saw herself as a child sitting in a dark booth, preparing to begin the Catholic sacrament of confession. The process began with a description to the priest of how many days, weeks or months it had been since the last confession. It was followed by a list of sins committed during that time. The priest was usually kind. Sometimes she made up sins so that she would not disappoint him. But she was feeling more defiant than cooperative at the moment.

Bless me father for I have sinned. It has been 18 months since I wrote in my journal or anywhere else for that matter. I have not been expressing myself. Despite my vow to the contrary, I have not been using my voice. That's right, 18 months of self-imposed silence and I'm not sure if I'm about to start writing now! Okay, I'm sorry for my rotten tone. But I'm so tired of feeling bad about things. I'm tired of guilt. Maybe I haven't written because I haven't had much to say. Or maybe I've had plenty to say but I was mad at God and worried about what would come out if I expressed myself. But you know what? I think God can take it.

She put down her pen. She ate part of the sandwich, chewing vigorously with the energy of a new passion stirring within her. She closed her eyes, trying to replace the image of the confessional booth with the circle of happy women she had seen in her mind's eye earlier that day. Yes, she could see them now. She picked up her pen again. As if striking up a conversation, she wrote:

What are you sewing?

Her vision wasn't cooperating. They didn't seem to hear her.

Hey, if you're in my head, then why won't you answer? No response. *That figures. Speak up. Speak up, the wise voice says. Well sometimes I do speak up, but I'm not heard. Sometimes I find my voice, but certain people haven't found their ears. So what's the point?* She pushed hard on the pen. *So I ask you, what is the point?*

The image of the women faded as if a dark curtain were pulled to block her view. She wondered if her mind had pulled the curtain. Her hand began doodling. She drew a spear. It didn't look as friendly as Pablo's. She drew another spear, this one pointing toward a frantic-looking stick figure. She recognized the hair. It was her. Rapidly, she began drawing more spears, completing the trajectory until the final spear was almost at her heart. She swallowed hard, shaking her head.

"No," she said to herself. "No spears through the heart today. Pablo's spear brought you light. Remember?" She drew a big X over the menacing image and turned the page. She drew a rendition of a Hawaiian cliff. Then another spear appeared.

"Oh, good grief." It seemed that spears were waiting to come out of her pen whether she liked it or not. She created more spears following a new trajectory, this time heading straight for the cliff. She brought the final spear to land on the side of the mountain. She drew roots coming out of the tip, roots that went deep into the ground. Watching in amazement, she drew leaves on it, many leaves until it took the image of a tree. Apparently satisfied with the transformation, her busy hand now skimmed down to the base of the mountain and hurriedly drew an ocean scene, adding some fish and a turtle. It seemed that somewhere close by a drum had started beating. The beat was picking up. She looked around, then back at the paper. Her mouth was dry. She gulped down some water and studied what she had drawn.

"Honu," she said as she wrote the word beside the turtle.

She wondered what the word meant. She turned the page and began to write. She felt a part of herself floating above the scene. When she was finished, she leaned her head against the couch. Her heart was fluttering. The room was somehow light enough to read, although it was now dark outside and she had turned on no lights. She looked out the window. Why was that streetlight so bright? Again, the circle of women appeared as a living portrait inside her head. The vision was increasingly fascinating. It seemed to have a life all its own. Now the women's faces were starting to come into focus. She thought she saw her mother and her mother's sister, Twylah. The eldest among the circle, the Hawaiian woman, seemed to look right into her soul. The room they were in was large and open. It seemed to have no walls. She could see torches around them, seven in all, and a night sky filled with sparkling stars.

"Read to us," this elder seemed to say with her thoughts. "Read it out loud, what you have written. Speak with your powerful voice." Mesmerized, she obeyed, turning back the pages to begin. Before she started, she had a burst of insight.

"Honu!" she exclaimed. "Honu means turtle!" She saw the woman nodding. Sarah cleared her throat and began to read, surprised to hear a deeper voice that she hardly recognized:

"With the grace of a bird gliding through a watery sky, Turtle rises to the surface of the sea. She moves with beauty to the rhythm of beating drums. The drums give voice to the hearts of humans. With great power the drums call to the others.

"Lifting her head above the water, Turtle sees the spear that has blossomed into a tree. Her heart is full of gladness, for the hearts of human beings are healing. With great power, her spirit calls to the others.

"Turtle dips back into the deep where she can better hear the heartbeat of the planet. She feels the pulses and rhythms of creation and knows that Mother Earth is happy. Humans are waking up. With great power their voices call to the others."

She stopped speaking, the words on the pages of her journal now blurring through hot tears. "My God in heaven, where did this come from?" Suddenly exhausted, she leaned back and fell asleep. Her spirit was eager to join the sewing table with the other women. In the morning she would not remember how they had opened their arms and welcomed her and how they chanted together in heavenly harmony the words she had written. But deep in her soul she would begin to feel the flutter of change, a gentle acknowledgement that things would, in the end, be brighter. Her ship was now on course. The darkness within her would know its source.

Turtle was finding a voice.

CHAPTER SIX

Messengers

Sarah made it through the hospital lobby the next morning without any balls of light or cosmic spears coming at her, but as she stepped into the elevator her mind was still digesting the quirkiness of the light's latest appearances.

"Say, Dr. Johnson," she said nonchalantly as one of the doctors stepped in the elevator. "What are the early symptoms of a brain tumor?"

"Well, there are so many, I'm not sure where to start," he said. "Why? Is someone in your family feeling bad?"

"No, not at all."

"A friend having health problems?"

"Nope."

"Are *you* feeling bad?"

"Um, no. I'm feeling better than ever," she replied, suddenly wanting to drop the subject. She knew she wasn't sick. So stop with the morbid questions, she told herself. The doors opened and the doctor shrugged, stepping off.

"You're not giving me much to work with."

"I know. It's nothing," she said before the doors closed. Continuing alone to the ninth floor, she leaned back and confided in an imaginary physician, one who wouldn't judge or consult psychiatry. "You see, doctor, it's just that when I stepped out of my apartment this morning I saw a squirrel with a halo. It's very cute, actually. But things got even better when I got to Brooklyn because even the bums are starting to look like saints. As a matter of fact, I think I saw St. Peter and St. Paul standing on the steps of St. Mary's Church. What do you make of that? Oh, well, doctor. I can see that you're stumped. But that's okay. Because whatever it is, I think I'll keep it."

Arriving at her office, she stopped and stared in amazement at the new picture on her door. Her jaw dropped. Pablo had drawn an animal with a long bushy tail, sporting a bright halo.

"Pablo, I do love you, but I don't know if I'm comfortable having you read my mind." Walking to his room, a part of her wanted to laugh at the playfulness of it all. Despite her recent tirade she had always assumed that God had a sense of humor. Otherwise, how could human beings have one? Pablo was watching cartoons when she entered his room.

"Hi," she said. "Who's the very important critter?"

"You know," he said, his huge eyes sparkling.

"I do?" she asked, wanting to hear his explanation. "Let me think." She looked at the picture, then back at Pablo.

"Can you help me out?"

He sighed a little and gave her a look that seemed to say, "Work with me, lady."

"Okay, I'll give you just *one hint*," he said, nodding toward the drawing with a knowing look. "Look at its tail."

Sarah looked at the bushy tail. Part of the fur was missing.

"Gracie? From my porch?"

"Yep. It's the squirrel that eats seeds on your porch," he said proudly. "I dreamed that he is happy about the seeds you give him. And he says don't worry about his tail. It doesn't hurt or anything."

"It's a *he?* I guess I'd better give him a boy's name. Are you sure it's a boy?"

Pablo shrugged a little apologetically, as if to say, "I'm just the messenger."

"He doesn't really need a people name," he clarified. "God just calls him 'squirrel.'"

"Oh," she said. "That's good to know."

"Great," she added in her thoughts. "I'm the professional here. I'm pressing him about gender issues like he's the squirrel's official spokesperson." She took a deep breath and let it out. "Okay, Pablo, I'll be honest with you," she said, feeling that he could see right through her anyway. "This is kind of blowing my mind. How on earth did you know that I feed a squirrel with a hurt tail?" He looked at her with the gravity of a wise old man.

"Miss Sarah, my angel said that if I drew these things, it would help you know you're not crazy."

"This is supposed to *help?"* she blurted out, immediately feeling insensitive and ungrateful. "I mean, it does help, really, because.... yes... it's clear to me now that it's all *true.*

"Yes, it's all *true!"* she continued, wanting badly to succeed at damage control. "That exploding light thing yesterday and Gabe's shining face and the squirrel with the halo and then that spear. They're all saying to me, 'Hey, Sarah, lighten up! Open your eyes.'" She stopped. Pablo was staring. She was babbling.

"I love it. I'm in awe," she said, deciding that this would become her standard response to Pablo's drawings. "I am truly humbled that your angel wants me to feel better. Really. I can't thank you enough. I can't thank you both enough."

He smiled sweetly and began to wiggle a loose tooth in the front of his mouth. Satisfied that he was not hurt, she returned to her office, suppressing a giggle. "This just gets better and better."

At lunchtime, Gabe found her getting caught up on patient notes. He paused to study the drawing taped to her door.

"Great drawing, but I hope it's not Saint Squirrel's Day," he said. "I forgot to wear gray." She burst out laughing.

"No, you're fine. It's a long story."

"Well I have a surprise for you."

"Lay it on me. This has been quite an interesting day."

"I have a substitute lunch date for you."

"You don't want to have lunch?" Then she spotted a figure behind him.

"Hey! Who is that?" She stood up, trying to peer around him.

With Broadway-like showmanship, he stepped aside to reveal her godfather, Porter. "Oh my gosh!" Sarah shrieked in delight, jumping up to hug his tall form. "Oh my gosh! I can't believe it!" Porter leaned down and wrapped his strong arms around her, hugging her tightly.

"Believe it."

"My work here is done!" Gabe said as he walked away. Her arms still wrapped around Porter, Sarah watched him move in long strides down the hospital hallway.

"Thank you," she called. Gabe had met Porter at her husband's memorial service 18 months before. The two men bonded quickly in their efforts to cushion her profound shock. At the time both men expressed a strong sense that they had known each before.

"I didn't mean to boot him out of lunch," Porter said. "I wanted him to join us."

"No problem. He's like that. He and I can have lunch tomorrow. Look at you. Am I dreaming?"

"You're awake," he said, his eyes moist. She watched the beautiful light around him as he looked around her dingy office. It was not a pretty place. "That's quite a stack of papers. Can you get away for lunch?"

"If you want the best Jamaican chicken that Brooklyn has to offer, I'm taking you to Minnie's Café. If we leave now, we can beat the rush."

They walked out quickly. With skill that came from practice, she ducked a few people who might want to stop her for something. As they walked down the sidewalk she kept looking at him. Porter tightened his raincoat against the autumn chill and shook his head. "How do people keep their spirits up living in a place like this?" he asked softly, looking at the crumbling sidewalks and neglected buildings. Potholes gave the street the look of a war zone. "This has got to be depressing."

"It's depressing to be poor and depressing to feel forgotten," she said. "These streets turn into small lakes during a heavy rain. I see men pushing flooded cars on a regular basis. We even have leaks at the hospital and have to move patients to keep them dry. Funds are depleted because the hospital's foundation was literally crumbling. We were on the verge of having to close. It's something you'd expect to find in the so-called Third World. You'd never deal with this on the Upper East Side of Manhattan. I mean, never. But we all live in the same country, the same city, for God's sake. Is it any wonder people get angry?" She let out a long sigh of frustration. "Don't get me started."

"Maybe they should just tear it all down and start over," he said.

"Don't give anyone any ideas."

Entering Minnie's Café, their mood was instantly transformed. Though it had been a part of the neglected neighborhood for years, the café maintained an upbeat atmosphere, a reflection of the owner's Caribbean charm. Minnie spotted Sarah and greeted her warmly. Porter was rocking slightly to the lilting Reggae music as she approached.

"Minnie, this is my godfather, Porter Hudgins. He and my Dad have been friends since their Army days. Porter, this is Minnie. Careful. Her food is addictive."

The two shook hands and Minnie nodded to Sarah with a touch of mischief in her eyes.

"I see a definite resemblance," she said knowingly. She led the two to a booth, with Porter giving Sarah a quizzical look behind the woman's back. When Minnie had walked away, Porter whispered testily, "A resemblance? Please tell me she doesn't think you said I'm your *grandfather.*"

"No, no, she heard me right," she said, waving a menu at him playfully. "Minnie has four adopted children and she has raised several foster kids. She has this saying, 'Love ties are stronger than blood ties.' Anyway, she believes that when people have a family bond of any kind they take on each other's characteristics. Who knows what she saw with us? We probably flashed the same delirious grin as soon as we smelled the food."

He wasn't convinced. He held up a spoon, looking in its dull reflection. He slapped the underside of his chin with the back of his hand.

"Does it jiggle when I do this?"

"Stop!" she said, giggling. She always felt like a little girl when her godfather was around.

"Okay, okay, I'll stop being vain and get to the point," he said, his tone changing.

"There's a point?"

He nodded and settled back in the booth, studying her. She felt self-conscious and looked away, pretending to study the menu. Who was she fooling? She put it down and returned his gaze.

"So you came," she said softly. "You not only came, but you found the hospital and you found my floor and you managed to run into Gabe before you ran into me. So you could surprise me. Just like that."

"Very interesting how it all came together. It probably happened that way because I was on a mission. I zeroed in on you like a heat-seeking missile."

"Hmmm. Not sure about that analogy. I prefer to think of you as the cosmic pelican. You seem to swoop in and scoop me up before I even know you're around. That's quite a talent, keeping the element of surprise after all of these years."

She stopped, suddenly deeply moved by his uncanny ability to show up when he was most needed. "Did my letter freak you out?"

"In a manner of speaking, yes, it freaked me out. I've never heard you sound that depressed. I suspected that you probably needed to vent and writing me was better than alarming your parents. Hell, I don't blame you for questioning God. Given what you see every day, the bigger mystery is how you hold onto your faith at all. Not to mention your indomitable sense of humor. Which brings me to my motive in coming here. Yes, I needed to lay eyes on you. But there is something else. And of course I now see that the waitress is fast approaching, so I'll hold that thought."

"Boy. Cliff-hanger," she said. She ordered for both of them and they were again free to talk. "I want you to know quite honestly that I came to New York to talk you into leaving all of this," he said, his hands folded in front of him and his face serious, as if he were on a witness stand. "Yes, I had a motive for coming and a plan about how I would convince you to leave. I knew exactly what I was going to say and how my sales pitch was going to unfold. It involved taking you to a fancy restaurant. I came to remind you that you don't have to surround yourself with such painful images and experiences. You've paid your dues. And as soon as I saw you at the hospital I changed my mind completely."

"You did?" She took a drink of water. "Can we still go to a fancy restaurant?"

"You bet. Look Sarah, you are my only child," he said, repeating their private joke. He took her hand and looked at her with gentle eyes. "I've been worried, as have your parents. I guess I wanted to be the hero and fish you out of this place, pun intended." He made a swooping motion with his free hand to illustrate a pelican landing on an unsuspecting fish. "But when I saw you a little while ago, I had the strangest sensation, as if I were seeing you in a whole new light." He was silent for a moment. "Yes, it was like I was seeing who you really are and not just the vulnerable image of you that I'd been holding in my mind since Collin died." He paused, wondering if he had gone too far, too soon into the visit. "This time around, I see very clearly that you are not a victim."

He paused, searching her eyes for something. "I got a flash of insight that is very difficult to explain. And I'm not usually at a loss for words, as you know."

"I'm on the edge of my seat, here. What did you see?"

He shook his head, his gaze far away for a moment.

"It happened when I was standing behind Gabe, looking at you working so hard at your desk. In the blink of an eye I saw you not only sitting at your desk, but also engaged in a dozen other scenarios, all related to your work, as if they were happening at the same time. Don't ask me why or how I saw these things. It was sort of like a life review, the kind you hear about when people talk about near-death experiences. Only it wasn't my life I was seeing. It was yours.

"The gist of it is this. I saw you as a soldier. Every bit the soldier, engaged in a very serious battle."

"Me? Most people would call me a bleeding heart."

"A label given by those who have never walked in your shoes. I know a soldier when I see one. Hell, all of you are soldiers. You could choose to be somewhere else. But you squelch your fears and wade through the anger and the poverty and the danger to get to people who probably half resent you for having somewhere else to go at night. You do it to help people that most of us never bother to think about. Who am I to interfere with your choice?"

She was painfully aware of Porter's emphasis on *choice.* She wasn't used to her godfather talking like a seer and a mystic, but he was right. There was much about her life that she was certain she had not chosen, but welcome to the club. As far as she could tell, Pablo didn't choose to have AIDS and his young parents didn't choose to die from it. As brutal as her surroundings were, it was clear that she returned five days a week out of her own free will. There was something in it for her. There had to be. Sarah knew she was no saint.

CHAPTER SEVEN

Sending the Very Best

"I'm not sure I want to be a soldier, Porter. No offense to you and Dad, but being a soldier implies war. There's already anger here. And even if I were a soldier I don't know who or what I'd be fighting. How do you fight the injustices of history? How do you fight fear and disease?"

"On some level, I think you know."

She shook her head. "No really, I don't. I'm not playing dumb."

"Well, I can't speak for you and your purpose. That's between you and God," Porter said. "But I once heard it said that the best way to get rid of an enemy is to transform that enemy into a friend. You're doing that here, if fear is the ultimate enemy. Look. You're in a potentially menacing environment, facing exposure to disease and crime. And your face tells me something that your letter didn't express. On some level, maybe a very deep level outside of your awareness, you are at peace with this place, this experience. You're shaking your head, Sarah, but you have a twinkle in your eye." She looked away, smiling a little.

"Not always, I can assure you. I have my share of bad days."

"But you still feel driven by some higher calling? You continue to come to work each day, even when you are afraid? Fear does not stop you?"

She nodded. "That's right."

"So here you are," he said. "It appears that your sense of a higher purpose has overruled your fears. Look at you. You are absolutely beaming right now." She shrugged, feeling embarrassed.

"Don't you think that's quite an achievement?" he asked. "Isn't that the ultimate victory? To walk this walk unafraid? And to know that even if you do become afraid, you will walk it anyway? I know you're pretty used to all of this, but doesn't that sound the least big amazing?" She shrugged a little.

"I appreciate what you are saying," she said. "Really, I do. But I get to go home at night to a cushy apartment. And I've had many advantages, including an education at one of the best universities in the country. Yes, for whatever reason, I've chosen a tough job in a tough neighborhood, but the real heroes are the people who live here and hold on to their decency. They are exposed to the danger and the despair much more than I am."

"Excellent point and exactly what I've come to expect from you. But you're not ducking my praise that easily, young lady. I'm talking about you right now."

He raised a water glass to make a toast.

"Sarah, I have the utmost respect for you. You came here for a reason, a purpose. Somehow, as I watch you negotiate this world, I see very clearly that you are up to something important, and woe unto me if I interfere." He took a sip. "Now, having said that, if you do want to get out of here I will do everything in my power to help you leave. I mean that with the utmost sincerity. How's that for having it both ways?" She laughed. The main course arrived and she fanned the aroma toward her face.

"Leave? Are you kidding? Things are just starting to get good."

"Oh, really? Are you referring to Sir Gabe the Gallant?"

"No, I don't mean Gabe." She felt her cheeks redden. "I'm still a big wimp in the love department, too afraid of getting hurt again. And he's still recovering from his divorce."

He shrugged sympathetically. "Understandable."

She was hesitant for a moment, wondering if he would resume his worrying if she told him about the interesting twists of the last couple of days. "Better save it," she told herself. "Porter is deep, but he might not be ready for cosmic light shows and a psychic child who gets his art assignments from an angel." As she pondered these things, her godfather was having his own inner dialogue. What would Sarah say if she knew about the mysteries filling his life? The two smiled at each other, secretly sizing up the other's capacity to keep an open mind. Minnie appeared as soon as they were finished eating, quietly clearing the table. Sarah smelled the rich aroma of mint on her hands and commented on it.

"Okay, say no more. Let me guess!" Porter responded playfully. "Really, just let me have a little fun. Fresh mint. Let's see. Many New Yorkers have deep roots in the South. They like fresh mint in their iced tea. It's a comfort thing. Judging from Sarah's reaction, this is the first time she has smelled it on your hands. She's a regular customer, so it must be a recent addition to your menu. Am I right? Are you growing it on the property, somewhere out back?" He beamed.

Minnie's eyes widened. She nodded, studying him intently.

"Very impressive. You are right on all points. Either you're psychic or a detective."

"Close," he said, looking devilish.

"Porter, you're a banker," Sarah said, laughing.

"Banker, psychic and international spy," he replied, making his eyebrows dance.

"He just spies for Mom and Dad," she whispered loudly in Minnie's ear. "Say, Minnie, can you clear up a mystery that Porter *wasn't* able to figure out?" He kicked her under the table.

"Ouch! When you said you saw a definite resemblance with us, what did you mean?"

Porter winced.

"What I meant was the way you are both lit up. You're lit up like Christmas trees." Porter let out a sigh of relief. Sarah was intrigued.

"Lit up like Christmas trees? And that's good, right?" She was seeking validation. She already knew the answer.

"Oh, child it is quite good. Bright lights don't walk in here everyday, so I tend to notice." She looked knowingly at Sarah. "And you will notice more when you start using those eyes to see." Then she walked away.

"She knows something's up," Sarah thought. "She and Pablo must have the same angel." She watched the slender woman glide down the aisle, her graceful movements in perfect harmony with the music despite an arm full of dirty dishes. And she realized that Minnie was way ahead of her in the light-seeing department. Understanding this about a woman she held in such high regard had a deeply soothing effect. She felt herself releasing defensiveness, letting go of vague fears that there might really be something wrong with her. And with this flow of unexpected grace, she understood that Minnie's comments, coming so naturally from her heart, were a precious gift. The timing was no accident.

"She's a good woman," Porter said, sensing Sarah's unspoken respect.

"She's the best, Porter. Somebody up there cared enough to send the very best."

CHAPTER EIGHT

Dreams

Mama was right to send Kalah back down the mountain. She understood that her young student was not only a sky-walker, but also a man's wife. Makani could think of little but her journey as he returned to work with the other men on a double-hulled canoe they would navigate together. As she shared her memories with Mama up on the mountainside, images flashed through his mind as well. A growing worry blended with excitement and awe. The prophecy was true. That much was now certain. Using all of his self-discipline he brought his focus back to the meticulous work of crafting a vessel. But his mind drifted again and again. How could he be an anchor for her, he scolded himself, if he could not get himself anchored?

She sensed his turmoil and opened her heart to him, wanting to reassure her mate that all was well. Excitement made her heart dance. She felt a surge of energy surging through her spine. She wondered if her thoughts were actually soothing or if they were unsettling to him. Huge waves pounded against the cliff, making the sound of a mighty drum beneath her as she made her way down the path. She hurried past the great banyan tree, as familiar as an old friend, its many trunks sharing a single canopy of leaves.

She had to duck quickly under a thick vine that was sinking from the weight of white blossoms. She hopped over a coconut that had dropped in the path. She stopped to pick it up, thinking what a treat it would make. Then she rolled it aside and continued. She would look for it tomorrow on her way back. It would make a great gift for Mama Hanu.

On a typical day she would not have sought out her husband while he worked on the boats. It was a sacred task and crucial to the prosperity of the village. But this was not a typical day. Suddenly she felt a jolt of pain. She found him sitting in a clearing near the boat hut, a perturbed look on his face. Moments before, he had cut his hand with the carving blade. He was a master carver, as skilled with a blade as any man. So it was with great embarrassment that he watched Kalah approach just as his brother stooped down to wrap his hand. Shocked by the sight of Makani's wound, the younger Kini had impulsively grabbed a piece of cloth salvaged from the sail of a boat battered on rocks during the last big storm. The sail was to be repaired and used again in honor of three men who drowned.

"I do not like the feel of this. Cloth from a sail used to stop my bleeding," Makani said, his voice tight as she knelt down beside him. "This was carelessness. Am I bringing bad fortune?"

"You know better," she said tenderly removing the cloth and holding his wounded hand. She was not superstitious.

"Whether this cloth soaks up the wind or sea water or your blood, it all comes from the same Maker. Why do you think one is better than the other?"

He smiled. She had a way of putting things in perspective. She looked deeply into his eyes. "I know your fear. But it will be fine." The sea breeze caught her long hair. She held his injured palm in her right hand and cupped her left hand over it, calling on the ancient healing rays. Immediately he felt the warmth of this energy pouring into the injured place, just as she felt the energy flowing into the crown of her head from the sacred place where all good things are born. Minutes passed as she softly sang ancient prayers of mending and healing. In her mind's eye, she saw strands of radiant light pulling the wound shut. When she uncovered his hand the other men came forward to look, each hoping that the healing energy flowing from her would bless them as well.

"I am always amazed," Makani said. Where his skin had been open, it was now sealed shut with a faint pink line above his thumb. He rotated the thumb. "No pain." He bowed his head. They all sat in a circle, singing a chant of praise for the Great One who shared this healing gift with his children. Then Nui, their leader and teacher, announced very unexpectedly that it was time for a swim in the sea. He laughed out loud at their confused faces and motioned with a big sweep of his powerful hand for them to go. Like their chief, he was a tough taskmaster, but he also had a playful side.

"Go before I change my mind." The men got up and started running, laughing boyishly as they went. Kalah glanced longingly over her shoulder, wishing for a swim. She missed her romps in the sea with Kei. They were becoming rare.

She turned and hurried up the shoreline to the home of her parents, who also had plenty of questions. Word traveled fast in a place where barriers between loved ones were thin. "I am coming. Let me catch my breath!" she called out to them affectionately with her thoughts. She felt as if she had been traveling all day. In the evening, it was with great relief that she curled up with her husband, talking with him about all that had happened since the last setting of the sun. That night, as he held her warm body and watched her sleep in the light of the full moon, he found himself wondering when she would travel again and how long she would stay. He fought back other thoughts, fearful images that were vague at first, then growing sharper in his mind. He saw an image of his wife stranded in the other world, pounding her fists against an invisible barrier that would not let her return. In preparation for this time in their lives, the elders had counseled them about the dangers of succumbing to fear. He knew without a doubt that unacknowledged fear could do the most damage. Tomorrow he would share his deepest concerns with Nui and Malu, a healer and elder.

As he thought these things, Kalah was dreaming. She was walking with a group of women across a landscape covered by volcanic ash. Some of them were strangely dressed. She put ash in her palm and poked it with a finger. Pieces of it began to flutter, dancing like tiny feathers in the wind. She blew and they responded to her breath, collecting into the form of a red and white bird. The bird cocked its head and looked at her with great intensity. She saw fire in its eyes. She heard words: "Look homeward. The winged ones will return to guide you." She started to ask the women if they knew what this meant, but stopped and remembered to try and answer her own questions. The dream ended. Her eyes opened as Makani kissed her forehead. Sunlight surrounded his face. She rolled over and looked at him. He was brown and muscular from ceremonial dancing.

"My, my, I do have a fine husband," she said, resting her chin on her hand. "Why don't you come back here with me, where it's so comfortable and…" He was back in their bed before she could finish.

* * *

She arrived at Mama Hanu's hut just before noon holding two ceremonial leis made by her mother and the large coconut she found by the banyan tree. She cradled it in one arm like a baby.

"Come in, come in," the elder said. "Ah, thank you. This is quite a treat," she said, taking the coconut. Her face was soft and her cheeks full of color. Kalah put the red lei around her teacher's neck and the white one around her own, pausing to smell the sweetness of the delicate flowers. Mama poured water on Kalah's outstretched hands and poured water over her own. The rest she sprinkled over the fire, bringing steam. She took herbs from a pouch around her waist and sprinkled them on the fire.

Star-like flashes of light appeared here and there. Kalah felt her heart opening. She never tired of these little stars dancing over the fire. Mama said the sparks helped them remember that divine light was all around them, floating in the air and waiting to be seen. "These sparks are children of the fire. The fire is a child of the sun," Mama said. "The story that comes to us now is a story of eternal light. Sparks. Fire. Sun. Source. Each links us to the other."

Kalah nodded, her eyes bright with excitement. "Sparks. Fire. Sun. Source," she repeated. "Each links us to the other."

Mama motioned toward a woven mat on the floor and Kalah sat down. "Listen, child and receive this story. Hear it with your ears and hear it with your heart. Let it flow through you. Its meaning is greater than the words carrying it." Kalah sensed a powerful energy surging through the elder woman's solid frame. Mama stood on her toes reaching up as if she were a young child wanting something from a parent. She held herself in this manner for some time. Her young student marveled at her balance. Suddenly there was a flash of pulsating light, the power of it pushing Kalah back. She caught herself with an elbow and instinctively put one arm over her face to protect her eyes from the brightness. She dropped her arm and sat up in wonder when she saw that Mama did not wince or flinch. With a deep voice Mama Hanu began to tell the story.

"Great Spirit has many songs. Worlds have been created with these songs. Mountains have moved. Yes, oceans roar in harmony and suns flash into existence when Great Spirit's songs speak of light. There was a desire to share this immense creative power. And so it was a moment of profound joy when the most the tender of these songs created a child. A magnificent offspring, it was blessed with Great Spirit's gift of creation. This child sang, too, and divided itself into the first female and the first male, whom we now call Great Mother and Great Father. Free to explore the universe, they flew through space like mighty comets. They never completely left Great Spirit, who loved them both deeply. They remained attached with a shimmering thread of pure love. But they were granted great space and freedom in the cosmos and they practiced their ability to manifest glorious things with the power of songs."

Mama's eyes closed. She beamed with joy at the images she was seeing.

"They were such happy beings, these two. They existed in the eternal now and they could not remember an instant when they did not know each other. They were made from the One who has no beginning and no end. It is what they knew and it could have been enough. But they were playful and they were curious. Brimming with creativity, they decided to make a moment of surprise. They wanted to know the joy of meeting for the first time. So they decided that Great Father would slip away and hide for a while and Great Mother would wait. Mother already knew where she would go when it was her turn to hide. She would go to the nesting ground of First Turtle, the place where worlds and stars are born."

Mama Hanu stopped and drew in a deep breath. Again she nodded, indicating that she heard what came next. Kalah smiled, hugging her knees and waiting.

"Ah, yes. They needed to create *time,* something that does not exist in the eternal now. In order to have waiting, there must be a steady unfolding of events. So they imagined it and made it real, real enough for their game at least. Then Great Father slipped away. Mother waited, searching the cosmos. She wondered when she would see her beloved and how it would feel.

"Yes, she was happily looking this way and that when she spotted a wonderful image. Who was coming? It was not yet her beloved. It was First Turtle with a big smile on her face. Turtle motioned her head toward her back, where a glowing object lay. It was a vessel made of dark rock, a piece of this planet's birthing. Inside it danced a glorious rainbow light. 'It's a gift,' Turtle said, 'from your beloved. May it brighten your waiting.' Mother was enraptured! She recognized it instantly. The colorful light was his.

"Father could not bear to be completely apart from her, not even for a game of waiting. She held the glowing vessel tenderly in her hands and watched Turtle swim away into the starry universe. And then an amazing thing happened. As Mother's very core brimmed with gratitude for this gift, the dancing light in the vessel grew brighter and brighter. And as it cast its glow upon her face she became even more beautiful. Hiding in the cosmos, Father felt the light of his own being responding. For you see, the flame she held in her hands was still a part of the great light flowing from his heart. Feeling her joy, he became even more magnificent. And so when he slipped back into view, he saw that his gift had enhanced her beauty, as love always does. And to Mother he shone with an even greater brilliance. Their game was a great success, you see. For love transformed these two into new beings. In their newness they truly were meeting each other for the first time."

Mama Hanu paused, folding her hands over her heart.

"They wanted to go home to share this tale with their Maker. It was easy to find their way back. Their connection to Great Spirit was never broken." Mama paused, her hands resting contentedly over her heart. "This is the power of love and the story of the first lamp." She looked at Kalah. "This story is linked to the prophecy. As the children of Great Spirit awaken to the innocence of the first stories, this planet will become a vessel of matter brimming with the light of sacred love. What a wonderful gift it will make for Great Spirit! We will return home with our radiant planet glowing like a lamp in our hands."

Mama was quiet but she remained standing, as if she were still listening. Then she added, "The red turtle of our seas is a beautiful symbol of the Turtle who carried the first lamp," she said, nodding vigorously as this new knowledge filled her heart. "Yes, the shell of *honu'ea* carries images of sunbeams and sparkling light. That is why we love all turtles and in particular this one, with yellow and red colors on her shell!"

Tears streamed from Kalah's eyes. More time passed. Finally Mama bowed reverently to the ancestors around her and sat down. "We will take this story to the others and you will take this story to Sarah and her world," Mama said. "It is a story with many layers and great spiritual power. It will help bring sacred light to a world that has grown dim and tired." Kalah nodded.

"But there is something else. For you see," Mama continued, her voice suddenly tight with emotion, "My heart has received a knowing. In Sarah's time there are fewer turtles swimming in the ocean. The green turtles are very small in numbers and the red turtles..." Her voice trailed off. Her eyes went far into the future and she was given a vision.

"Mankind has robbed red turtle of her shell in numbers that are too great. Her shell is taken for adornments with no sense of balance or gratitude for the bounty. In truth, these humans have a deep hunger for light and beauty. It is an understandable but misguided quest that causes them to take so many turtles from the sea."

"Are they gone in that time?" Kalah asked, her heart pounding.

Mama replied, "Very nearly gone. Red turtle is all but gone in that time. She has so few places to lay her eggs. Human beings have not been paying attention."

"No! Not the turtles! They are our spirit guides!" Kalah stood up, remembering the anguished scream she had heard the day before. Perhaps it had come from the very soul of the earth on which they stood. She felt a sense of urgency to do something.

She put her face in her hands, trying to calm herself. Then she lowered her hands to her stomach, feeling a deep ache. Mama pulled at her hand and brought her gently down to the ground again.

"But the prophecy," Kalah protested. "Turtle must find a voice! Are we too late?"

"It is going to be fine," Mama said softly, echoing what Kalah had said to her husband the day before. "I must remind myself so that I can remind you. And you must know it in your heart before you can travel safely to that place again. I did not mean to upset you, child. One thing I know for sure. When the big story ends and Great Spirit has finished with us all, it is going to be beautiful. We have difficult lessons to learn, but there is no other possibility than a beautiful conclusion."

Kalah nodded, feeling relief. She raised her open palms heavenward and made a vow to help make the ending of the story beautiful. She got up and reached out to help her teacher stand. The women embraced, their foreheads touching. And each, looking so lovingly into the eyes of the other, saw the image of Great Mother smiling back with great peace and knowing.

CHAPTER NINE

The Challenger

New stories were treated like important guests arriving on short notice. An evening of food, music and ceremonial dances would be put together skillfully and quickly. This tradition called for nearly everyone in Kalah's village to drop what had seemed important and to begin flowing with the rhythms of celebration and spontaneity. It was deeply freeing. At any time their busy lives could be loosened from the moorings of the mundane. Their sense of a greater purpose was restored. For this they were always grateful.

The two women sensed the excitement building as they walked quickly down the mountainside. Chief Ka-welo, aware since yesterday that a new story was imminent, had gathered the elders before sunrise to begin the planning. Their happy anticipation had rippled out among the sleeping villagers, some sensing the shift before they were fully awake. Kalah scanned the sea from their vantage point on the cliff and pointed to a gathering of dolphins. Anticipation was brewing among them, too. She knew Kei was there. She allowed her thoughts to take her out to sea. She daydreamed of splashing with the dolphin, then dove with her thoughts down to the reef and watched the interplay of turtles. A young red turtle, more solitary than his green turtle kin, swam through a patch of sunlight in the water. His shell was even more magnificent in the light. Kalah knew in her heart that red turtle's gift would be the reason for his near disappearance from the sea. In that respect people of the future were not so different from people of her time, she thought. Human beings were not content with their own beauty and wanted to wear the best aspects of other species as well. She brought herself back to dry land, sensing that a growing number of whales, dolphins and turtles were moving closer to the shore. Tonight, when the new story was shared, powerful breezes would sweep the story out to them as they bobbed in the night sea. In whale and dolphin songs its mysteries would reverberate throughout the waters, ensuring that the essence of its message would be carried far and wide. Birds of the forests, always very chatty, would share it in their own languages as well. Even the insects were likely to get noisy.

Her thoughts shifted to the first story celebration that she could remember. She was a young child and ready to burst from the food and excitement. She remembered the impossibly loud burp that had slipped out of her mouth during a moment of prayerful silence. Her little hands quickly covered her mouth, but it was too late. She could recall every detail of the hilarity that followed when everyone, including the chief and his entourage of warriors, lost the battle to keep a straight face. Laughter had finally overtaken them all. The evening ended well, with the chief playfully pretending to burp then bowing to the little girl and acknowledging her power to transform a situation. He was like that, pulling wisdom from the most unusual situations.

She was brought back to the moment by the feel of Mama's hand on her arm. She had been so lost in thoughts of childhood that she was a little surprised to find herself a grown woman on her way to help organize a feast.

"What's wrong?" she asked.

The two stopped, studying each other's faces. Then she heard it, a cry of anguish. They nodded simultaneously. A deep sense of foreboding washed over her.

"Makani!"

Her heart pounded. She could feel it beating in her head, her chest and her palms. They heard it again. Then she saw him. In her mind's eye she saw her husband lying on a mat, his face twisted in pain. Never had she seen him struggle so, and yet the face of Nui, so close to his, remained calm. She saw Malu put his hands on her husband's chest, directly over his heart. Makani panted, as if giving birth. She felt a chill. What had entered him so profoundly? She remembered what her father had said the last time a new story was given. His brother, her uncle, had been overcome by a strange fear that he could not explain. When the heavens open and great spiritual light pours in, her father said, the shadows of fear and disharmony are angered and they look for ways to retaliate.

Makani's screams pulled at her insides. And yet there was something unreal about the force he was battling. She was torn between this insight, which she knew to be a higher level of truth, and the deep worry she felt for her husband. If he did not realize in his weakened state that he was battling shadows far less powerful than he, then they still had great power to torment him.

"He needs me," Kalah said, feeling a pressure to act growing within her. "Do you hear it? He is calling my name."

"He is in good hands."

"But listen. He is calling me."

"This is not your battle," Mama responded firmly. "The screams are his, but that is *not* Makani's voice you hear calling to you now." Kalah looked down at her feet, her eyes filling with tears. She heard her name. Could her teacher not hear it?

"This is your husband's battle with fear. Close yourself to it right now, Kalah. That part of him that is not suffering, that part of him that stands witness to this and knows the higher truth, wants you to seal off the connection. Listen and do it." Mama looked straight in her eyes. The force in her voice was building.

"NO!" Kalah was shocked with the anger in her response. Never had she talked to an elder that way. She looked down and tried to steady herself. "I'm sorry. But I cannot shut him out."

"Ask yourself why, then. Ask yourself why." The old woman's voice was much softer now. They stood on the path, facing each other. Finally, Kalah spoke.

"You have told me yourself, Mama Hanu, that the pains of one person represent the pains of all. So perhaps it is my battle, too."

Mama took her hand and gently pulled her closer. Kalah felt herself resisting. She wanted to run down the path leaving her teacher far behind. She knew her feelings were no secret. Mama looked gently into her eyes. Then Kalah saw the young woman that Mama had been. How beautiful. Her face was tender and lovely. Her heart was moved. These were the eyes that looked into her eyes now, the eyes of a young woman who had loved her own husband deeply. Mama drew in a deep breath and released it. The image slowly faded from Kalah's mind, but the power of it did not. Now she could listen.

"It is simply fear, Kalah. That is the enemy that seems to attack your Makani. You are correct. It is the same fear that could torment anyone, a lost and rageful entity looking for a home. But it has not found a home in you. It hopes that it has found such a dwelling place in Makani. It is a coward, this saboteur, always looking for one who is compromised. But you know, and you have known since you were a young child, that the saboteur never wins a battle against one as spiritually strong and as loving as your husband." They heard another scream, a sound of great torment. Kalah sat down on the ground. She put her face in her hands and began to cry.

"Why does he allow this? Why was he open to this torment?" she pleaded through her tears. She felt a scream building inside of her. Never had she felt so frustrated.

"It is his love for you that has created an opening. He worries for your safety as you go to a distant place. In his fear and confusion he feels you slipping from his life. He feels your unborn children disappearing from his world and all of his hopes and dreams threatened by the prophecy. That is why he is begging you to cut off the connection. Just for now. Let him work this out."

This time she heard it. Mama was right. The higher part of him was asking her to shut him out until the battle was over. It was the cunning voice of the saboteur that had temporarily drowned out this request, calling her name to confuse her and gain an opening. She knew it would only be for a short time. But in that time, she would not know what was happening to him. Even the soothing images of Nui's face would be lost to her. She had a flash of awareness that this was Makani's experience, worrying that he could not reach Kalah, could not see or protect her, when she traveled to the other place. She was filled with a deeper understanding of what had driven him to this state, how his own good judgment had faltered. They would both have to be strong. They would both have to trust that higher powers protected them. Mama bent down and stroked her hair.

Kalah lifted her face and wiped away the tears. She closed off the connection between herself and her husband. Before it was completely shut, she sensed his relief. Her decision, though difficult, had helped her husband and herself. This was a new level of understanding. She realized it would serve her well in the far-away place, where she would be tempted to battle illusions rather than to step out of the way so that divine wisdom could take the lead. In this respect fear had unwittingly made her wiser. She was grateful that Mama Hanu had been with her this time. In the other place, she would have to give herself wise counsel. "Fear, I understand you better now."

Mama pulled her up. She radiated admiration, amazed that this new insight had emerged with clarity during a moment of great crisis.

"I must apologize for the way I spoke to you," Kalah said, brushing herself off. "I honestly do not know where that came from." She wondered to herself if the saboteur had fleetingly entered her. Mama smiled broadly, love pouring from her eyes.

"I'm not unhappy that you found your own voice. I honor you for that, even if your tone was angry. Your anger was understandable."

"You honor me? But that is not how I have been taught to behave."

"Perhaps it took anger to push you past the edges of our teaching, past years of respectful obedience to your elders," Mama said, shrugging her shoulders to show that she was learning, too. "Perhaps you learned the lesson of obedience a little too well. We taught you how to obey, but ultimately obedience is best directed at the heavens, not at other mortals. And I heard your concern. It was not the saboteur speaking through you, Kalah. I know the difference." She motioned to start walking again. Mama felt joy building in the village and wanted to guide the younger woman toward it.

"Your journey has started," she continued. "This time calls for you to stand fully in your own wisdom and spiritual power. You are listening more to your own heart now and this is precisely the right time to do so. That is where you will hear divine guidance when we are not with you. In that respect, I also thank fear for the gift it brought you. You are wise enough to balance your inner voice with the wisdom that exists in others. Great Spirit trusts you. We trust you. And you have a right to make mistakes, just like the rest of us. You are being sent on this journey with your humanness fully intact. If heavenly spirits could do the task better, you would not have been given this part."

Tears rolled down Kalah's red cheeks, which were beginning to sting from the saltiness.

"We know the heavens are happy. It is time to celebrate," Mama said. Kalah took her hand and held it tightly. Then she brought it to her lips and kissed her teacher's hand, bowing in the process. Images of Sarah flashed through her mind, new images. She saw Sarah talking with a man, looking radiantly happy. Mama looked at her, seeing the same images.

"Beautiful," Mama said. "One of your companions of destiny is winning a battle with illusion. Your fine husband is winning, too. I can feel it in the wind." Kalah's eyes lit up. In her mind she saw her husband happy again. She felt relief pouring into her heart. They walked quietly for a time.

"Now, may I give you one more word of advice before I back off from all of this teaching?"

Kalah blushed, feeling sheepish.

"Of *course.*"

"As you go through this day, you might feel a tug to review the painful images you saw. But keep your focus on the story of the lamp. Your energy is best directed there. Your thoughts are powerful, more powerful than ever. What you focus on will gain power in this world. You will see it manifest. That is one of the messages of the new story." With that, they hugged and parted.

CHAPTER TEN

The Aloha Connection

Sarah entered Central Park a block from the Guggenheim Museum, where she and Porter would meet at 3 p.m. She had given him a key to her apartment. He would drop off his suitcase before meeting her. Three days had passed since she had last seen him. They had dined with Gabe at a French restaurant on Second Avenue before he caught an evening shuttle flight to Washington D.C. Porter promised more fun when he returned from his short business trip, including an adventure to Chinatown, where he was to have his first acupuncture appointment.

This announcement had surprised her to no end, but she decided to ask him about that later when they were alone. It seemed that her godfather, the straight-laced Houston banker, was going through a metamorphosis of his own. Before hailing a cab they had paused for a moment outside the restaurant, scouring the ads for a possible Broadway play. A colorful picture grabbed their attention. The Guggenheim was hosting a Chagall exhibit. The artist's painting, "Wall Clock with a Blue Wing," illustrated the page. Sarah looked closely, observing two lovers embracing inside the body of the tall clock. Its far-swung golden pendulum was moving toward them.

"This is where we'll start when I return," he said. "Deal?"

"Deal," she said happily.

He called a cab and got in. "I'll be back," he said through the window in his best "Terminator" voice. The vehicle moved away, blending into traffic. Now, with an hour to spare before they were to meet again, she headed for the nearby oasis of the Central Park water reservoir, weaving around joggers, skaters and people on bikes. Her mood always lifted as she walked up the twenty-two steps of the pebbled staircase to the circular path. Sparkling water, rustling trees and the chatter of seemingly misplaced gulls had their own magic. People brought their troubles there, whether they realized it or not. This water could cool the fires of city living. And the sandy path was an antidote to miles and miles of concrete, reminding those pilgrims on the path that Mother Earth was still beneath them. The birds spoke the language of this Mother, soothing human psyches with conversations about elemental things: water and wind and sunlight. It was no mystery then, why the place made her heart so glad. As she climbed the steps, she glanced at the golden bust of a former New York mayor peaking out through tall autumn flowers. A falling leaf paused on his smooth head then slid down. A brown bird landed and took the leaf's place, chirping sharply with a yellow beak that looked like wax Halloween lips.

"Hello, bird-ling," she said. "How are the loons treating you?"

The bird flew off. She continued up the staircase with light steps, then onto the path, swinging her arms and blending effortlessly with the other walkers and runners. The fall air was invigorating. The wind blew her hair and swept across her skin, a needed caress as she tried to unwind. She inhaled deeply, willing herself to release stress as she released the breath and stepped up her pace. It was working. She was feeling lighter. Sun pushed through clouds. She held up her face to receive its warmth. She had completed a circle and was half-way around the reservoir again when something began to shift. With no warning, a hand seemed to press the top of her head. She could feel the pressure quite intensely. Her crown responded immediately by warming up. At the same time a chill shot down her back. For a split second, she wondered if Porter had arrived early and found her here. She spun around, seeing no one.

"That's odd." Again she had the feeling of being touched on her head, this time the faintest caress drifting down her left temple. She stopped. The chill was coursing down her spine now and spreading across her shoulders and arms. She turned around. But she knew what she would find. No one was there. The flow of people on the path began to move around her now. She was aware that by stopping she had become an obstacle. She stepped off the path and leaned against a black wrought-iron lamp, feeling dazed. A few yards ahead were two rows of benches. Between them was the ornate white bridge that led to the tennis center. She fought back the urge to run across the bridge into a more familiar experience of tennis matches and mingling people. But the elements whispered to her. "Sit down, Sarah."

She walked toward the benches, reeling a little as if she were on a moving ship. As she approached, she noticed that one of the benches had been dedicated to a man's wife, whom he referred to as "Mrs. Wonderful." She paused, scanning the engraving on the dedication plate.

"That is so sweet," she said softly to the spouse who honored his wife with a park bench. Looking at the next one, she saw another engraved plate, this one making a dedication to "Mr. Wonderful." The benches were like an old married couple watching the parade of humanity go by.

"Come sit down with us," they seemed to say. "This is a magical place." Sitting down on the wife bench, she pulled up her feet and positioned her body to face the water. She stretched her legs and reached out to touch her feet, arching her back, which was now covered in perspiration. Then she sat upright again, wiggling her feet. With her right hand she held on to the bench. With her left, she rubbed her forehead. A runner slowed, moving in place for a moment.

"Are you feeling okay?" he asked. She thought he looked like a doctor.

"Yes, thank you," she said, touched by his concern. He nodded, hesitating a moment longer before continuing his run. She saw his light. It was a soothing blue mixed with a healing green. She watched a lone gull fly high into the sky, then soar back down toward his clan. She saw the bird's light, too. It was gold. She shook her head a little and blinked her eyes.

"You're not crazy, Sarah," she thought, wanting so to be a good friend to herself. "Someone was definitely there. We'll figure this out." Again, a touch. This time on her shoulder. She jumped. The chills rippling across her skin gave way to deep warmth like nothing she had ever felt. It spread from the base of her skull and down the back of her neck, flowing down her spine to her legs. She felt it surge out through the soles of her feet like water pouring from a hose. Then another wave of warmth began to build, taking the same course. It actually felt wonderful. She found herself waiting for more. She wondered if Collin was behind this turn of events. Her Aunt Twylah had a tendency to get visitations from those who had passed on. Sometimes these spirits gave her private information about the people who were starting to poke fun at her gifts. This had the gratifying effect of keeping jokes to a minimum. It had been a long time since anyone had accused Aunt Twylah of being crazy. And right now Sarah felt grateful for that. She sat quietly, waiting to see what would happen next. Then she felt the brush of a hand across her shoulder. She turned her head.

"Collin?" Her stomach knotted up. "Collin?" She was losing patience. If he had come to play games, she was going to let him have it.

"Collin, if that's you I'm going to kick your ass for leaving me," she said, her anger erupting. "You need to show yourself or say something right this minute!" A jogger was approaching. She realized that even if he were too far away to hear her, he could still see her lips moving. She had a reputation to maintain. She pulled out her cell phone and held it to her ear, hoping to look socially acceptable. "Collin? I'm sorry. I think we have a bad connection." Nothing happened. "Look, honey. I'm sorry about what I said. Obviously you're invisible and made of spirit, so I'm not in any position to kick your ass. I just need answers, Collin. And I need them now. Look, I know I sound harsh. But I'm sure you'll understand if I've *hardened* a little since you died." She heard the bitterness in her voice. It made her sad. She missed him and wanted him to know that, too. "Collin, please don't go away. I'm sorry. I'll be nice." She felt like a nut. If Gabe knew what she was doing he would start shrinking her head on the spot.

She sighed. "Yes. I hear you. And I do plan to get help," she said dejectedly to the silent phone. She started to put it back in her pocket. Then she heard it. It was unmistakable. A soft voice seemed to be coming from far away and moving closer on the wind. Then it was by her ear, whispering.

"Not Collin. *Ka-lah.*" It was feminine. Fumbling with the phone to keep from dropping it, she quickly put it back to her ear. A couple walked by deep in their own discussion. They were followed by a flurry of others, running and walking. Then the path in front of her was calm again. "Kalah?" Her mouth felt dry.

"Perfect."

"What's perfect?"

"The way you said my name. I had a harder time with yours." The voice was playful.

"Okay." Sarah said. "Give me a moment, here."

Silence. She was grateful for it. She wanted to say, "And don't talk any more, whoever you are." But she didn't mean it. That voice had power. She wanted to know the source of it. More joggers and walkers passed, but she was growing oblivious to them. Something was pulling her up the way water is pulled down a drain by gravity. She no longer felt the bench beneath her legs. She no longer saw the reservoir. Another surge of warm energy went through her, followed by stillness, blackness and then fire. She saw torches: three to her left, three to her right and one straight ahead. The one before her moved in a triangular motion. She saw a powerful hand holding the base of this huge torch, moving it with grace as if it were a light, fiery wand. Then the torch seemed to recede into the background and she saw three women performing a hula dance like none she had ever seen. Their hair blew in the wind. They were crowned with circles of white flowers and they were enacting something that to Sarah looked deeply sacred. Each took a foot and moved it back and forth in the sand, as if to make a groove. Their arms were folded, moving like flippers. Then the dancers' arms opened wide and they brought their hands together in front of their faces. They palms were held upward. They looked as if they were holding something, their faces radiant.

It was the most beautiful thing she had ever seen, a profoundly sacred scene bathed in sheer grace and natural elegance. Behind the women huge palm trees blew in the night wind. She heard the sound of drums and people chanting. She felt herself pulled closer and closer to the scene.

"This is familiar," she said softly. Then she was aware of her body again and felt adrenalin surging through her bloodstream. She looked around her. In the light of day the tall iron lamps circling the reservoir had mysteriously turned on. They glowed like torches. "Oh, my gosh. *Hawaii.* I wished for this. I said I'd rather be in Hawaii." The thought of having that much power over her life made her feel queasy. Panic broke in like a third-party caller with news of a disaster. Sarah struggled with herself, not wanting to return to her everyday perceptions but not wanting to get lost somewhere in between. The Hawaiian images grew more vivid, as if sensing her fear and vying for her attention. She saw one of the women in the scene step forward. She held herself so majestically. And yet she had the big open smile of a child. Something about her reminded her of Pablo.

"I am Kalah, a daughter of this village" she heard her say. "And this is the story of the first lamp." Sarah felt enraptured but continued to wrestle with fears that she was going crazy. Fear was winning this round. She fought to return to her place in the park as if fighting hard to awaken from a dream. It was a beautiful dream, a dream of a faraway place, perhaps a faraway time. But with all her heart she wanted to be back fully on the bench in Central Park. In a flash the reservoir returned before her. Or had she returned to the reservoir? She had no clue. She lurched back as if she had made a rough landing on a plane. Behind her she could hear the soft thud of tennis balls being served by the completely unsuspecting.

"My Lord. There is something wrong with me," she thought. "I do need a doctor." She felt light-headed.

"You are not sick," spoke the vision. It was that same voice. "I promise. I am so glad that you caught a glimpse of how we celebrate a new story. It is a very exciting time here."

"Who are you?" Sarah asked, feeling her emotions becoming more turbulent. With a shaking hand she put the phone back to her ear, but not in time. A man jogged by, trying not to stare but looking at her out of the corner of his eye. The young Hawaiian woman's face flashed again in her mind.

"When you calm down, you will be able to see me for longer periods of time," she said sympathetically.

"Calm down?" Sarah shot back. "Reality as I know it just gave way to a luau, and you want me to calm down?" She heard giggling.

"Is that what you call it?" she asked. "I mean I'm sorry if that's not the correct term." More stifled giggling. Clearly the woman was not offended.

"Oh, give it a rest," Sarah thought to herself. "You don't have to be politically correct every minute of the day." She turned to look back at the bridge, wondering again if she should make a 50-yard dash toward the predictable and familiar. But a deep sense of knowing filled her. No. Maybe it was all of those esoteric conversations with Aunt Twylah, but something was telling her not to be afraid. "Stay put, girl. You might learn something," she could almost hear her aunt say.

"Fine. I'm calming down," she said into the phone, a little defiantly.

"You know, I have had a lifetime to get ready for this. You have not," the woman said. "So you are doing well. Your mind is very open. Your curiosity is serving you, as it should. But your heart is still beating too hard."

"You mean this was planned? And how do you know my heart is beating hard?"

"It was planned. But not by me," Kalah replied, ignoring her latter question. She would have to remember that in Sarah's time people wanted to consider themselves separate from one another by walls of unknowing. Sarah could vaguely see her again, pointing heavenward with a grin so innocent and yet so mischievous that it transcended all cultures.

"It was planned by heaven?"

Kalah nodded.

"Is English your native tongue?" Sarah asked, suddenly wanting to switch from the spiritual to the mechanics of how they were communicating. Thinking about God right now made her feel too vulnerable. "I'm fairly certain we don't speak the same language, right? Or do we?" She was vaguely aware of the steady shuffle of sneakers and as more joggers passed her by.

"No. We are actually talking in different languages. And we live in very different times. I guess you would say that I live in your ancient past. You live in my distant future. The majority of people in your culture and mine believe in time and so we make it real, at least real enough to get along with our daily lives. I cannot explain it. But your time and mine, it is all the same to

Great Spirit. What you need to know now is that you are not going crazy. We do not have to understand all of this. We should just do what we are guided to do."

"You are definitely starting to remind me of Pablo," Sarah said, warming to her visitor. There was no reply. She sensed the woman was waiting for her to say more. "Pablo is a wise little boy at the hospital. He makes this incredible artwork. Oh heavens! Artwork. Chagall. Porter. I have to go now." She stood up.

"I know. I have to go, too," Kalah said. "I am in the middle of a very important ceremony." Sarah heard the sound of distant drums, then chanting. She got a final look at the young woman, her graceful hands making a rolling motion in front of her heart, then flowing out to the side. Kalah smiled and blew her a kiss.

"Aloha, my sister," she said. "Until we meet again, waves of love roll from my heart to yours." And in that fleeting yet eternal moment before they parted, the two women came together as one and shared a sacred vision. Kalah and Sarah looked across the sunlit waters of the Central Park reservoir toward the Guggenheim Museum and watched as its image was transformed into another white structure, an ancient domed hall that also housed great works of art. It was the Museum of the Art of Prophecy, a sacred place that was ancient even in Kalah's time. They both looked at it in amazement. Then the vision melted and the Guggenheim appeared again, vivid and beautiful against a backdrop of tall buildings. The consciousness of the two women gently split, parting as two rivers flowing away from a shared source. Kalah pondered all of this. Then she saw an image of the one whom Sarah called Pablo and she recognized him as a great being who had dwelled in that ancient hall of art.

CHAPTER ELEVN

Grace

Sarah's feet began to move now, taking her back on the circular path and into the flow with the others. She shook her hands, as if this would somehow make them more solid. She had another half-circle to go before she would be back at the park entrance near the museum. As she walked, a vision of Minnie flashed before her eyes. And she remembered her words of wisdom. Minnie said that you don't have to understand the mechanics of grace to benefit from it. You just have to receive it. She also said that the human ego hated heavenly grace and usually attempted to explain it away out of fear and envy.

"That is ego trying to feel superior to God," she had told her.

Sarah recalled her own response. "Who in their right mind would actually feel superior to God?"

"That is precisely my point. Who in their right mind? Ego is the crazy part of us, not the part of us that stays open to miracles." As Sarah made this connection between the two women, she was flooded with feelings of deep love. Her throat ached and she held back tears of joy. She stood at the top of the steps, looking at the sparkling reservoir. A part of her wanted to run back to the park bench and the beauty of what she had seen.

"It's all still inside of you." She recognized this wise voice. It was hers.

"Grace," she thought. "This is what it feels like when you're receiving it and you're actually paying attention." She was becoming wiser. Even she could sense that about herself. "Stay open to it," she told herself softly as she turned and left the park. "Stay open to the light."

Back in her world, Kalah also was savoring the shared gift of this connection. Holding her palms upward toward the heavens as she finished a dance of thanksgiving, she saw in her mind's eye this place called the Central Park reservoir resting in her hands. She saw the giant structures pointing toward the sky and the birds and the people moving with such purpose, their bodies surrounded by light. She saw her own memories of Sarah sitting on the bench, her long hair blowing and her bright eyes shining as they spoke. The rhythm of this place beat in her palms like a drum. She placed her hands over her heart, putting it all inside of her. It felt good.

Walking down the steps and away from the park, Sarah felt herself solidly in New York City again. And it did, indeed, feel good. There was nothing like the sound of honking cabs to get her grounded. She looked at her watch and laughed. She was known for being punctual and this was going to be no exception. "I should have been a mailman. Neither visions, nor voices nor the strange and unexplained can keep me from being on time," she thought to herself. "Does that make me compulsive on a cosmic scale or what?"

"Hey Porter!" She saw him on the steps and waved to get his attention. He opened his arms to embrace her.

"Ready for the clock with the blue wing?" he asked as he hugged her. "Do you suppose Chagall had theories about time-travel?"

"Oh, my God, Porter. Don't say that," she said, suddenly feeling dizzy.

"What? What did I say?" he asked with concern. He held her arm to steady her. "Are you feeling okay? You've gone pale."

"Yes, yes. I'm fine. Let's go in. I'll tell you about it all later," she said. "Things have just been a little weird."

"I know just what you mean," he said. "I keep dreaming about a Hawaiian healer dropping coconuts on my head. I wish he had my phone number instead." She laughed even as she caught the Hawaiian connection. They entered the Guggenheim and let themselves feel transported. Chagall's surreal creations granted permission to see things differently. Sarah breathed them in, wishing she could paint the incredible visions she had seen in Central Park. "Maybe this artist actually saw these things in his mind's eye," she thought. "He had an outlet. I need to find one."

* * *

In Brooklyn, Pablo sat at his grandmother's kitchen table, a box of crayons turned over in front of him. He was making his next gift for Sarah. His grandmother looked over his shoulder as she put a snack of cheese and fruit beside him.

"Mommy!" he said, using his name for her. "If I don't get sick soon will you mail this to Miss Sarah?"

"Well, I hope you don't get sick soon," she said, her stomach tightening. "Of course I'll mail it.

"That's a pretty fish," she said, fighting back tears. "And I like the color you chose for the water. Turquoise."

"Thank you, Mommy, but it's not a fish," he said. "It's a dolphin. And a teacher."

"A dolphin is a good animal. Very friendly," she told him, stroking his wavy black hair.

"Yes, very friendly," he agreed. "It tells me stories in my dreams."

The telephone rang before Gloria Mendez could ask her grandson and only surviving relative about the dreams and the stories. But she believed him and she was deeply intrigued. She knew Pablo had one foot on the earth and one foot in heaven. A devout Catholic, she cherished his connection to God, but hoped with all her heart that he would stay close to her for a long time.

* * *

In the darkness of the night sea, Kei swam peacefully with her dolphin family and clicked a tender note of enjoyment to those around her. The story of the first lamp was being celebrated on land. As she came up for air she could see Kalah moving fluidly with other women. The men had performed a dazzling dance, leaping in the air as if they were dolphins themselves. Makani had performed one dance by himself as the lead chanter told the story of his battle. It was a story they could all learn from, the chanter explained.

"Listen well to this story," he said. "For the next time it could be you facing the challenger." Makani told them how he had felt the pounding of fear's fists on his chest.

Then he felt it enter his body. He prayed for purification and was transported to another realm. In this realm, he stood to face an enormous wave roaring with all the might of the heavens. Nui the great navigator stood behind him, sending him courage in the face of it. And Malu did his part by speaking to the wave in a language that Makani had never heard. The wave roared back its response, but it did not harm anyone. As Makani felt himself overtaken by the great waters of purification, only his fears were washed away. He felt safe and clean.

Kalah listened, marveling. Then she and her sisters performed the sacred turtle hula before she stepped forward to tell the story of the lamp. In the sea, Kei listened with other sea beings. The story moved every being, opening all hearts to new light and new insight. Connected as they were to humanity, the dolphins and the whales understood the story from the human perspective. They also would be the first to understand its larger meaning. Deep in their spirits, they already knew that the lamp made of rock was a symbol of the planet, a planet that would one day hold greater illumination.

CHAPTER TWELVE

Coconuts and Meridian Lines

The two men stood over a dazzling map of the solar system, their fingers tracing a grid that crisscrossed the images of the stars and planets.

"What she's doing makes perfect sense," the older one said. "She is traveling along these meridian lines. She has entered access points on her side and on this side. The electromagnetic currents running through these meridian lines take care of the rest, getting her here in a matter of seconds. She has divine help, that's for sure. Only God could guide her through this journey!" The younger man studied the face of the other, clearly trying to take in the magnitude of what he was saying.

"You're not just talking about miles here. You're talking about a trip from the past to the present," he replied.

The older man nodded and continued.

"You could view these meridians as rivers or even highways. Instead of past, present and future, you simply have Point A, Point B and Point C. Einstein himself said that time was an illusion, that what we call the past, the present and the future are actually all happening at the same time."

The younger man broke in. "So you're saying that she's traveling along a sort of cosmic super highway, and it's as simple as that. "I wonder what the bumper stickers say out there." They chuckled. A woman's voice joined the conversation.

"I actually saw one. It said, 'All One Tribe, Born in the State of Grace.' Do you get it?" They turned to look at her. The younger bore a striking resemblance to Gabe.

Sarah sat up, startled. Those last words had come out of her own mouth, waking her up. She looked around, squinting. Porter was returning to the waiting room. Rays of sunlight shot through a long vertical window behind him, framing his silhouette in bright light. He turned to bow and say a parting word of thanks to his acupuncturist, a petite Asian woman with graying hair tied in the back. She returned the bow and smiled kindly. He closed the door and turned to Sarah, who now looked like a small child roused from a nap.

"Did you fall asleep?" He sat down next to her and patted the arms of his chair. "Comfortable. Thanks for waiting. It took longer than expected." He leaned back, looking deeply relaxed. He appeared to be in no hurry to leave the waiting room, which was empty except for the two of them. She studied his face. It dawned on her that the older man in her dream was Porter.

"I was dreaming one of those dreams that feel so real you can't shake it," she said. "I must have gone into a deep sleep very quickly."

"I nearly fell asleep myself," he said. "And that's with about fifty needles protruding from my forehead and belly. The acupuncturist told me I think too much.

Apparently it's just like eating too fast. I need to slow down and give myself a chance to digest things. I guess that makes sense."

"I can't believe that doesn't hurt," she said, wincing. They stood up, heading for the stairway. They were three floors up. The elevator seemed to be broken.

"It doesn't hurt a bit. In fact, it's incredibly relaxing. I can't explain it."

"Well, you were explaining a lot in my dream," she said.

"Really? About acupuncture?"

"Not exactly. But remember last night you were telling me about meridian lines of the body. You said that acupuncture removes blockages in the body's energy circulatory system, so that the life force – what'd you call it?"

"Chi."

"So that the chi can flow unimpeded and nourish the body," she said.

"Very good. You were paying attention"

"My dream was about meridian lines, but more like the lines you see crisscrossing a globe. Actually, they were meridian lines drawn across the solar system. Does that make any sense?"

There was a very long pause before Porter spoke again. She looked at him as they rounded the staircase. He had put on his poker face.

"What?" she asked. "Are you shocked that I was paying attention?"

"Not shocked about that," he said. "I'm only shocked because I had a very similar dream about meridian lines across the solar system."

They were about to step outside. She stopped and turned to face him, propping the door open with her foot and crossing her arms in front of her like a sentry. To those passing by, it looked as if she wanted to block him from leaving the building.

"When?" she grilled.

"Last night."

"Was someone pointing to grid lines on a map?"

"Yes. I was."

"No way! And who were you talking to?"

He laughed. "It's going to sound nutty."

"Try me."

"I was speaking to a kahuna I met when I was in Hawaii. It was many years ago. He's an amazing man, very kind yet a conduit for a very powerful energy. He told me I would return someday. Now he shows up in my dreams, sitting in a palm tree and throwing these little coconuts on my head. I didn't know he would be so persistent. I guess I'm a hard-headed student." Sarah burst out laughing, but stopped when she saw that he was embarrassed. Clearly it was more than a dream to him. This relationship was real and he was feeling like a dummy. "Well, what's that about? Does he want you to get a concussion?" She turned and they pushed through the doorway, walking out into the bright autumn light.

"No. He wants me to wake up, in the spiritual sense. At least that's what he keeps saying in the dream. This is no ordinary man, Sarah. When he shows up, it's a blessing and an honor. You pay attention."

"So when in the dream did you start talking to him about meridian lines?"

"After he stopped throwing coconuts."

"No seriously."

"I am serious. When he was through pelting me, he sort of floated down from the palm tree and we started walking along this path deep in the jungle. Next thing I know I'm standing in his home leaning over a table with a map of the solar system, and I start talking about how they resemble meridian lines on the body. He was nodding. He started to tell me something, but the dream ended abruptly before I could hear it."

"This is too much," Sarah said. She massaged her forehead, which felt tight, and looked around. "We have got to sit down and talk." They approached a restaurant, the Jade Palace Garden, and studied a menu taped to the window.

"Looks good," they said in unison. They walked inside and were seated. The smells in the place were tantalizing, the scent of fish, salty sauces and fried rice filling the air. They picked up the menus but couldn't drop the thread of their conversation.

"So I have a dream about meridian lines spanning the solar system and you have a similar one. What are the odds of that?" he whispered, looking around to see who was within hearing range.

"The odds are pretty good if you consider the theory you spelled out to me last night," she said. "And I'm pretty sure I wasn't dreaming then."

"What theory?"

"You said your gut feeling was that everything is connected, that the little universes we call daily life are intimately connected to that big universe we can't begin to comprehend. That's why there are so many so-called coincidences. You said every particle of the small stuff is a piece of the big picture, and like a seed, each tiny detail of life contains a blueprint of the entire universe. You also expressed the mind-blowing belief that our universe is a living entity with its own meridian lines. Hello! I'm still absorbing that one."

"It sounds a lot grander the way you said," he acknowledged. "I was rambling for two hours and you've just summed it up in a few sentences."

"Remember. I used to be a reporter," she said. "We have to boil things down on deadline. At least you know that I really was paying attention." He smiled. His eyes sparkled and she saw his light. It felt good to be in the company of someone who knew her so well and liked her so much. She decided it was truth-telling time. She needed to land this spaceship that was her life. And the universe was pointing to a brightly lit landing spot: Porter's mind. He could handle this. She knew it.

CHAPTER THIRTEEN

Guides and Allies

"Can we talk?" Sarah asked, suddenly feeling like a little girl again.

"Why little lady," if this ain't talkin' I don't know what is," he replied, John Wayne style. He poured them both some tea. They ordered and continued. She had so much to say, she could hardly breathe. Last night didn't seem like the right time to spill the beans about Kalah or any of the other events leading up to her appearance. But now it was all starting to feel like a dream. Sarah was afraid it would evaporate from her life if she didn't find the courage to talk about it. As she spoke, she realized that she didn't have to make sense of it all. That wasn't her job. The story of the lights and Pablo and Kalah and the visions in Central Park simply unfolded into a cohesive story. The more she spoke, the softer his face became, as if a heavy weight was being lifted from him. His eyes were tender and he laughed at the right parts, particularly how she used the cell phone to avoid looking crazy in the park and how she had threatened to kick Collin's ass.

It was a bittersweet laugh. The mysteries surrounding her husband's "apparent suicide" were a source of continued uneasiness for all who knew the couple. The deeply mystical moments she was describing sent ripples of chills down Porter's spine, verifying to him that something big was underway. They ate a delicious meal without really noticing how good it was. That was somehow appropriate. There was so much abundance in this moment that their systems couldn't acknowledge it all. Finally she drew in a deep breath and released it. She was trying to remember to breathe.

"That's it, Porter. And it's all true." She raised her right hand. "So help me God."

"I think that's exactly what God is doing," he said. She smiled and looked down, her eyes filling with tears of relief. It was what she needed to hear and she had no doubt that he was sincere. Porter wouldn't humor her if he had serious doubts about her mental health.

"Let me recite something to you that I memorized recently," he said. "I didn't know when I would share it, or with whom, but my instincts told me that the right time would make itself known. These words are from a book called 'The Mayan Oracle.' Here goes," he said. "I will offer you to the light of new beginnings. In myriad forms do guides and allies await, proffering strength and courage for your journey." She blinked at him in amazement.

"I will offer you to the light of new beginnings," she repeated. "It's perfect."

"I rank it right up there with Shakespeare and Whitman," he said. "And for some reason, I find it easier to memorize. A lady friend, Kate, gave me the book for my birthday last year. Sometimes I just open it up and point to a spot at random. The message always seems relevant."

"It's gorgeous," she said. "Do you know more by heart? Please tell me you do."

"Let me see if I can fish it out of my brain," he said. He cocked his head, trying to pull forth other passages he had tried to tuck away in his memory banks. Then he smiled. It was coming to him.

"Your new sense of purpose will draw to you..." he said, pausing. "Your new sense of purpose..." He closed his eyes. "Will draw to you, like iron fillings to a galactic magnet, loving hands to clasp your own, knowing eyes to reflect your heart's yearning, and the remembrance of a sacred song that you may sing together in the rapture of a shared dream realized." He beamed. His memorization skills had not failed him.

"Incredible," she said, enraptured. "You say it's from a Mayan oracle? What is that, exactly?"

"The full title is 'The Mayan Oracle: Return Path to the Stars,' and it was given to me as a set. There is a book explaining the mythic concepts behind a series of sacred Mayan-inspired symbols. It comes with a deck of cards, each with one of the symbols on it. They move my spirit. I believe they have deep roots in the collective unconscious. Some people use them for meditation. I use them more like cue cards that either stimulate me to think about things from a different perspective, or tell me that I'm on the right track. It's uncanny sometimes. The thoughts I'm thinking will be mirrored in the cards. I've heard it said that when this happens, our individual minds are simply connecting with the greater mind that is all around us."

"That's fascinating." She was leaning back in the booth, a faraway look on her face. "Porter, I'm realizing that there's a lot about you that I don't really know. I've had this image of you in my mind that was sort of two-dimensional. I'm the goddaughter. You're the godfather. Period. That's pretty childish."

"No it's not," he said. "I've encouraged that perspective and I've enjoyed it. But there's a lot more that I can tell you. And after your brave disclosure, there's a lot more that I *will* tell you. But not here. Not now."

"Oh, not fair, Porter! Not fair." She pretended to pout.

"I'm not holding out on you, girl. I'm just saying we can't keep this table all day." He motioned for the check. Her brain felt tired. Her intuition told her that Porter's wheels were turning at a rapid rate, but she could tell that he believed her. In fact it was a little unsettling how much he seemed to believe her.

"Let him breathe. Let him out of the box." Sarah recognized that voice. It was hers. She had spoken the words out loud. Fortunately he didn't hear. He was telling the waitress to keep the change. They stood up and walked out into the other-worldly-ness of Chinatown. With great success this world had been transplanted into another world called New York City. It never ceased to amaze her. Inside the subway station they joined the throng of others waiting for the next train, a train that would quickly and easily take them to a different world. She leaned over and whispered in his ear.

"Meridian Line."

"Pardon?"

"They could call this leg of the system the Meridian Line. Do you get it? Moving quickly and easily from one world to another? Sound familiar?"

His eyes brightened. He nodded.

"To our ancestors this whole concept of a subway system would sound far out, but here we are traveling from Point A to Point B in a matter of minutes," she said.

"It's not such a big leap to imagine time-travel," he replied. "You just have to know where to get on and where to get off." They laughed, enjoying the shared secret. And as they traveled home, she caught Porter looking at her and smiling. Whatever he was going to tell her, it was going to change the way she thought about him, that she already knew. But that was fine. She was going to take her own advice and let her godfather out of the box. It was clear that he no longer fit in that tight little collection of ideas she had held him in for so long. And something else was clear. When Porter stepped out of the box he was going to be moving in very long strides.

CHAPTER FOURTEEN

Darkness and Light

The phone rang as soon as Sarah and Porter walked in. It was Gabe with a funny tale to tell. "Do you have a minute?" he asked. "I have to tell someone this story."

"Tell me!" she said affectionately, wondering if the stars were somehow aligned so that everyone suddenly felt compelled to share an unusual story.

"Well I strained my back moving the TV, so I'm on the floor on my back thinking it would help. And it just seemed like a good time to try meditation."

"What? Hold everything. Dr. Gabe Mahoney was going to meditate? Hey, Porter! Now I know we're in The Twilight Zone!" Her godfather, who was hanging his coat, just nodded his head, as if to say, "I know. I know."

"For research purposes," Gabe said, not sounding very convincing. "It came up at the conference in Phoenix as a way to reduce stress and anxiety in hospitalized patients. Sort of like biofeedback, only more Zen."

"Right, of course," she said, giggling. "You were going to start meditating for research purposes. I'm following you. Go on." He had dished out plenty of teasing and knew he had it coming.

"Work with me here. I'm trying to branch out," he said.

"Okay. Sorry," she replied. "I'm listening."

"So, I'm wondering how to begin the whole thing, because I think I missed that part of the presentation," he continued. "I must have been getting coffee. So I start off with the standard tense/relax sequence."

"The standard tense/relax sequence?"

"You start at your feet and tense each muscle group, then relax it, and that's supposed to help teach the body to notice the difference between tense and relaxed. The squeezing is also good for the muscles. Anyway, it's working fine until I get to the top of my head. Ever try to tense the muscles at the top of your head?" he asked.

"No. I'm wondering if you're even supposed to."

"Well it doesn't *work!*" he announced. "So I'm thinking, okay, I'll just skip that part of my body and then I feel this 'whack!' on the crown of my head, really hard. I mean it hurt. And I roll over, kind of freaked out. And it's the dog. She had this stuffed blue bone in her mouth and she looked at me like, 'Was one time enough, Gabe, or would you like me to hit your head again?'" He paused, laughing at the hilarity of it. "My dog, the meditation trainer."

Sarah laughed with him for a moment, but the day's conversations were starting to blur together. Porter was getting hit on the head with coconuts. Then Gabe's dog somehow thrashed him on the crown at precisely the right moment. She was starting to get a headache. The laughter gave way to silence, which was rare in their conversations.

Gabe sounded deflated when he spoke again.

"I guess you had to be there."

"No, it's actually kind of amazing," she said, trying to get her second wind. "Because I've actually heard of these very revered Buddhist monks hitting their students on the crown of the head with a stick to assist them in reaching enlightenment. I think it was supposed to get them to focus or something."

"You're making that up and you're making fun of me. I'm going to hang up now."

"No, really, and Porter is nodding in agreement so I must not be totally crazy. Here. Say Hello to Porter. We had just walked in and I need to hit the bathroom." She handed Porter the phone.

"I'm going to go soak my head," she teased, holding her hand over the receiver.

The men were still talking when she walked back in the kitchen. Porter hung up shortly after her return. She made him a drink and they sat on the couch, making small talk about Gabe's conference and his first attempt at meditation. Finally, Porter seemed ready to start talking about himself.

"So," he said. "You want to know more about my life. I'll get to the point. Let me tell you why I was in Hawaii years ago. I was there on business. On assignment, actually, for the CIA."

Sarah's eyes grew wide. She would have been far less shocked if he announced that he was actually the first man on the moon. "What? You're pulling my leg, right?"

"Nope." He looked down self-consciously, his hands pressing at the creases in his pants. "No, I'm quite serious. You know me as a banker, which I am now. I studied international finance at Yale after I left the Army, which you already know. But for many years banking was my cover. I was an agent stationed in Asia and the South Pacific. I spent a good deal of time in Hawaii."

"Did Mom and Dad know this?" she blurted out, regretting the words as soon as they left her mouth. He was intuitive and he sensed her concern.

"Do you mean, did they know that when they chose me to be your godfather?" He was trying to hide it, but she could see that he was hurt.

"I didn't mean it like that. I was just wondering if they had this secret they've been keeping from me all these years.

But then, so have you. Ouch. I'm sorry. This isn't about me. I'm a jerk, Porter. I'm sorry."

He laughed.

"You're not a jerk. Maybe I'm the jerk for putting you on the spot. Who wouldn't have a moment's pause about having a godfather in the CIA. Sounds ghastly, even to me."

"It's a job, Porter, and an important one. Let's get past this episode of 'Sarah's Surprise,' Okay? I was surprised. Now I'm over it. Tell me more." Her voice was firm.

His story poured out. He had retired from the agency after two decades, then began his financial career in earnest, assisted by connections he had made at Yale. He excelled at what was supposed to be his first career. He hoped that the change would help him have a more normal life, but he never met someone he wanted to marry. Over the years he began a spiritual quest, bouncing from religion to religion, trying to find his way in a world that he already knew too much about. Ultimately, he realized he admired aspects of all religions, but didn't want an organization between himself and his Maker. He was looking for a one-on-one connection. He followed the threads of his spiritual longings and they led him to study the faiths of many cultures. Ultimately he found God most purely in the practices of some indigenous people.

"There are those in my family who have let me know about their deep disappointment that I've strayed from the religious fold," he said. "In other words, their religious *mold.* They call themselves skeptical about the things that I actually find most compelling, like the study of ancient spiritual practices. But my answer is this. If you're skeptical about every religion but the one you grew up with, you're not a skeptic at all. You're a frightened conformist afraid to have a spontaneous relationship with God. And if you'd rather see me as someone more likely to burn in hell than to fall innocently back into the arms of God, then you are no closer to the truth than I am."

"That kind of takes my breath away," she replied.

"In an odd way, working for the agency actually prepared me for a more mystical outlook, although that didn't come until much later," he said. "Spies dwell on the outskirts of what we would call everyday life. I realize now that I was drawn to the work because I've always been intrigued by the undercurrents. I mean most people tend to take life at face value, right? Things are what they appear to be and that's that. But when you're with the CIA you are trained to look beneath the surface of things, to be suspicious about the way things seem to be and to wonder what's really going on. In other words, you have to be a little nutty by everyone else's standards. Am I losing you?"

"Well, I'm having trouble envisioning you as a spy," she said. "But a month ago, I would not have thought of you as a mystic. Now I do. So I'm with you. You became accustomed to standing in two worlds, with one foot in everyday life, in order to blend in, and one foot in the undercurrents, searching for the truth about what was really happening behind the facades." She wondered where she was getting the energy to work through this. "Mystics and spies actually have a lot in common."

"That's very generous of you. There are similarities, in a shadowy sort of way. Mystics and shamans live on the fringes. People tend not to think about them until there's some kind of problem that feels way over their heads. The same goes for the CIA, I guess. People have this vague realization that spies are out there, but they don't think about them much until they're afraid an enemy is out to get them. Then they're happy to have people lurking in the shadows, as long as those shadowy people are on their side."

"I just can't see you lurking in the shadows," Sarah said.

"I have to remind you that sometimes I was the illusion for the other guy. I'd like to think that I was working for the right side. But to succeed I had to become a master of charades. I dealt in falsehoods when I had to."

"But who isn't a master of charades?" she asked, aware of the many facets of her own personality. "We have to be so many things to so many people it's amazing that we don't get lost in our own costume closets." They both smiled, checking each other's faces to get a reading. "Is it okay that I know? I mean about the spy thing?" she asked. She realized that he had never answered her question about how much her parents knew.

"It's okay that you know I had a job with the CIA. But that's about all I can tell you," he said. "I have many fascinating stories to tell and unfortunately most will go with me to the grave. But my experiences in Hawaii, and the great pull that place has on me now, are somehow linked to what is happening in your life. I'm sure of that."

Sarah's mind went to Kalah. She was glad she had talked to Porter.

"I wonder what Kalah's doing," she said suddenly.

"I have to tell you something fascinating about her name," Porter answered. "I have been holding back on this because I didn't want to overwhelm you. I don't know what it means in her world, but in Hawaii of the present time her name means Sarah."

"No way! I can't take this!" she said, helplessly throwing up her hands. "I surrender. I give up." She fell over on the couch and hid her face under a pillow.

"It's okay. Give up. Or better yet, wake up. That's probably exactly why you're being bombarded with coincidences, just like I'm getting pelted with coconuts," he said.

She poked her face out, released a little scream and hid it again. He could hear her laughing. "Talk to me," she said, her voice muffled. "I'm sure there's a great story here."

"There certainly is. A friend of mine had a darling little girl named Kalah, spelled K-a-l-a-h, after her grandmother, who was half Hawaiian and half German. They told me that among other things, her name means "keeper of the keys." I don't know about keys, but she sure was a ball of fire. I couldn't persuade your parents to name you that if you turned out to be a girl. Your mother was convinced that it would be mispronounced all the time. But I think your parents loved my need to play some part in your naming. They recognized that it foretold of a strong bond between us. So they researched the name and found that a variation of the name means Sarah. That's how you were named. You might also be interested to know that kala means both forgiveness and release in Hawaiian. There is even a type of seaweed called kala because it is used in ceremonies of forgiveness. The word means other things, too. You know me. I looked it up. It can mean release from bondage. The spellings are different, but the sound as it flows from the mouth is the same. I think that's key. So perhaps there's more to her name than that simple coincidence with my friend in Hawaii," he concluded. "To the Hawaiians, especially the ancients, words were chosen with great care because of their enormous power as they flowed from the breath. And many words had multiple meanings, which gave their storytelling great depth. To me, the name Kalah has the beauty of a bell ringing. It's a wake-up bell." He looked at Sarah's face. She had pulled the pillow away, enraptured.

"And I keep seeing that little girl, who actually reminds me so much of you." He studied her face a little longer, then his gaze drifted beyond her. She sensed that he was deep in thought. She threw the cushion on the floor. It was no use trying to suffocate herself, she decided. These mysteries were mounting a massive offensive against any resistance she might have left and they would follow her into the afterlife. This she knew.

"You look really sweaty," he added. "Do you have a fever?"

"I'm going to go stand in the shower. I'm okay. Just a little shell-shocked."

"Well, I don't blame you. It has been quite a day. I feel like taking a long walk. It helps me when I'm trying to put pieces of a puzzle together. On the way back I'll pick up something that we can eat for dinner."

"I was going to cook us a light meal this evening, but honestly, I don't have it in me. That would be wonderful, Porter." She stood in the shower, the warm water hitting her face. Then she sat down and leaned back, the water still falling. She might have drifted away in daydreams but the warmth was waning. She knew the water would soon be cold. Bundled up in a beach towel, her hair wrapped in a makeshift turban, she stood in her bedroom and looked out at the busy street. It all looked solid enough. But who was to know? Somewhere in Chinatown, she had dreamed of meridian lines. Somewhere in that incredibly realistic dreamtime, Kalah's travels made perfect sense to at least one man trying to explain it to another. And in Kalah's world, it probably made sense to everybody on the entire island. What if they all understood Einstein's theories a lot better than she did? What if Einstein was simply rediscovering some ancient wisdom that had been buried over time? She smiled at the irony. Her instincts told her that the truth of things was "discovered" many times, in many ways.

Porter left the next morning. Any fears they had about the sharing of secrets were diminished. They felt closer than ever. She sought out Gabe. They went to lunch at Minnie's and were seated at the same booth where she and Porter had talked. But she wasn't ready to open up to Gabe on that level. He was kind and deeply caring, but also highly analytical. The thought of presenting her mysteries to his so-called "rational" mind would be like putting precious documents into an automatic shredder. She shuddered at the thought. And yet she was dying to tell him. She realized that she wanted validation from him. If she told him and he understood, it would be like two sides of herself uniting. She watched him poking around in his salad, looking for the good stuff. Yes, there was a part of her that was just like him. How many times did men and women get polarized over matters such as these, she thought, when they were really made of the same stuff? She made a mental note to be on the lookout for her own internal shredder.

"It's a sneaky little machine," she told herself. "and so portable. No telling where it's hiding." A few days later, she received a card from Porter. On the front, a beautiful woman with long black hair was bursting out of a volcano. Inside, Porter had written in bold letters: *"I believe."*

He went on to explain that it was an image of the Hawaiian goddess, Pele, who was associated with fire and intense emotions.

"In Hawaii, people tend to be drawn to volcanoes rather than running away from them in fear," he wrote. "At least, that's the way it is now. No telling what kind of havoc Pele wreaked when the islands were newer." He also wrote about his return to life in Houston and elaborated on Kate, a neighbor with whom he had become "very close." She smiled to herself, happy that Porter was not lonely. He urged her to keep her courage and her faith in what was happening in her life. He counseled her to feel nothing but gratitude for the light coming into her awareness.

"The Mayans believed that this was the end time, but not in the sense of an apocalypse. Long ago they predicted that in this century, the old way of seeing life would forever give way to a greater vision and a closer relationship with God. Maybe the only thing that will end is our blindness. Wouldn't it be amazing if the so-called apocalypse amounted to no more than a collective release of our fears?"

She felt chills across her arms. He included another quote from the book.

"Remember, you are keepers of the spiral wisdom, as in the precincts of a temple. Give voice now to the sacred ancient/future ways, vessels for the divine fire."

He had written more but she paused, holding the card over her heart. "Thank you," she said, scanning the last words again.

"Give voice now to sacred ancient/future ways, vessels for the divine fire."

She felt another inflow of grace. How had she ever lived without this? How had she survived the loss of this precious connection? She shook her head.

"I've been crazy for most of my adult life," she said. "Minnie is right on about which part of us is out of touch with reality."

After a while, she opened the card again to finish reading what Porter had written.

"Kai says 'Hello. Hello and wake up!' He's the kahuna. He's back in my dreams with more coconuts. And I think he knows where you live, Sarah. I really think he knows where you live. Cover your head. Better yet, open your mind. Sweet dreams. Love, Porter."

CHAPTER FIFTEEN

The Vessel

Kalah had enjoyed the feel of Central Park. Judging from her brief encounter, it seemed to have its own spirit. The tall trees and the water were a refreshing contrast to the staggering cliffs and valleys of New York City. She wondered if dolphins and whales swam in the waters near this place. If so, what stories they must have to share.

And something else intrigued her. Sarah's face, when it wasn't contorted in pain, looked increasingly familiar. There was something in her eyes that reminded Kalah of her own people. It wasn't the color, for Sarah's were much lighter. Rather, it was the way she spoke with them. Despite Sarah's apparent consternation during their brief conversation, Kalah had seen a hint of laughter in those eyes, as if deep in her soul she found the situation amusing. She was thinking these things while Makani massaged her tired feet in their section of the family sleeping quarters. Was it only last night that they had stood before the entire village, giving voice to stories of darkness and light?

Kalah recalled the odd feeling of being in two worlds. The steady beat of the ceremonial drumming had eased her into a meditative trance. She could feel herself fully in the dance and yet a part of her was present with Sarah. She was deeply curious about how this could occur. She sighed and stretched. She wanted to sleep but her thoughts danced like a hungry butterfly moving from flower to flower. Pictures of Central Park flashed through her mind. She recalled the soft hues of Sarah's long hair and every detail of the materials she was wearing. So many layers! You could barely see her skin! And what was it that she held to her ear? It was too small and flat to be a shell. And why would Sarah want to hear the humming of a shell at such a time? No, her instincts told her that the object was a communication tool. She wondered when they had lost the gift of thought-sharing.

She opened her eyes when she felt the warmth of Makani lying next to her. He, too, was reflecting on a journey. This one had not yet been taken. The big canoe was nearly finished and soon he and his fellow mariners would be on their way. They would travel to the big island volcano, where the hot lava of new life mingled with the salty sea. It was the season of festivities, when conflicts between tribes were forbidden. It was the only time his people journeyed to the big island. He loved the trips. These moments of intimacy with the earth and her bubbling life force always stirred his soul. Thinking of this he turned his head to look at his wife. He wondered when they would have a baby. Mama Hanu had predicted that they would have three in all: two boys and a girl. He reached over and tickled her. She laughed and tried to wiggle away. It was good to be back in the moment.

"Were you busy today?" he asked.

"Yes. It was interesting. Lomi and I went to look for feathers. We took Mali," she said, referring to two of her sisters, one of whom was still a child. "The chief requested it. He said he is having bird masks made, one red and two white. We had trouble finding the red feathers. But finally there were enough." They were quiet. The chief had sent three sisters on a journey. It seemed like an ordinary request and yet it wasn't. Expert feather finders usually were sent, those who knew the habits of the birds and where to look for particular colors.

She closed her eyes, opening herself to any insights that might come. Nothing. She decided that she shouldn't try to guess the chief's motives for sending them on such a quest. And anyway, it was fun to be together. They had so much to talk about in those hours of searching. She released her questions and felt herself drifting into a light sleep. Immediately she had a vision. She was a bird flying above a boat filled with men. They were paddling across the vast expanse of dark blue sea, the swells of the water lifting and lowering their boat in a steady rhythm. They were headed toward the big island. She saw Makani and Nui. She saw the island puffing and surging with heat. Steam rose from the water in tall misty clouds. She flew ahead and watched red lava pouring into the dark foamy sea. The men saw it, too. She heard their excited conversation. She could see that they were not afraid. She circled the boat and Makani looked up, still paddling in unison with the others. He smiled at her. He moved his lips and she could see that he was speaking. She soared down to hear his words.

"I release you to the light," he said tenderly. Then he looked forward, his eyes focused on the island. His face was peaceful. She circled the boat another time and looked down again. Makani now wore a mask of a white bird's face! "The winged ones return," he said, looking up at her. She awoke with a jolt of energy rushing down her spine. Her eyes opened to the sight of Makani kneeling over her. She wondered how long she had been in dreamtime.

"Come with me," he said softly, his face radiant. "The chief is outside with our families. He said he has a gift." She propped herself up on her elbows, blinking. Then she stood up. She ran her fingers through her hair. She did not feel presentable, even though the chief was like a grandfather to her. Makani wrapped a large cloth around her. It was a deep blue kappa cloth with white water marks. She slipped it under her arms and tied it in front.

"You look beautiful," he said, placing a ceremonial circle of shells around her neck. He kissed her. Stepping out she was stunned at the sight. Makani's family and hers were standing around the family altar. They looked happy. Her little sister looked sleepy, but she gave Kalah a big grin, showing where a tooth had just come out in front. Kalah focused her gaze on the chief. In his hands he held a lamp, a black lava lamp shaped like a bowl. She knew from his expression that it was precious to him. The flame was unlike any fire she had seen, for it shimmered with the colors of the rainbow. She scanned their faces. When she looked again at the chief's face, she knew with certainty that the legends of his family line were true. In that moment, Chief Kawelo looked every bit the star being, a man whose roots stretched out into the cosmos. Waves of love poured from his eyes and many years seemed to have dropped from his face. His aura matched the aura of the stars. When he smiled he looked both kind and magnificent, as if Great Father himself gazed out from those dark eyes. He held her face with his eyes for a moment. Then he spoke.

"This lamp has been handed down in my family for many generations. It was made on a great land mass, most of which now rests at the bottom of the sea. This island is part of what is left." He paused. "This lamp does not belong to me. It does not belong to any human being. It belongs to all. The story of the first lamp signaled that it was time to pass this on to you, Kalah. It will serve your journey."

He extended his arms, offering it to her. With trembling hands she accepted it. "Thank you," she whispered. She felt the crown of her head open to accept a rushing flow of mana.

"Daughter of this village, we release you to the light," the chief said. "This lamp is a symbol of your powerful spirit. Look to it in moments of joy and in moments of darkness. It will show you the way. Nothing more is needed." He brought his hands to her face. The lamp light flickered between them.

"I warm myself at the fires of your perfection," he said, repeating his favorite blessing. Her heart fluttered. The chief took a step back. She turned to look at Makani, searching his eyes. There was no worry in them.

"I release you to the great light that took you once before, my love," he said. "When we are together again, we both will shine even more brightly." She bowed her head in prayer. Then she raised the lamp to the night sky. "See this sacred lamp and carry its image within your hearts. Cherish it as Great Mother cherished the first lamp. It is a symbol of truth. There is no separation between us and we are always connected to Great Spirit." With great reverence, she lowered the lamp. But she was drawn to look back up. The zenith star, a constant source of guidance to mariners, twinkled above them. She looked at the moon, its fullness just beginning to wane. And she had a revelation.

"The moon is much like a lamp!" she said, a touch of the child in her voice. "It is not so different from the one I hold in my hands. Not so different from the first lamp, given by Great Father. The moon comforts us when the sun has slipped away for a little while. It reflects the light of the sun, telling us that the sun has not gone too far. Whether you are standing on this island or standing somewhere very far away, we are all looking at the same moon. We are looking at the same lamp in the sky." She looked into Makani's eyes.

"Remember, Makani. Remember each night to look at the moon. It will brighten your waiting." With that, a brilliant cloud of light descended upon them. They heard the fluttering of great wings and she was gone. The arm of her mother now wrapped around Makani, whose body had softly lurched at the moment of her disappearance. It was a subtle movement, as if the ground had shifted under his feet. He stared into the emptiness of where she had just stood and sent his love to that place, knowing it would follow her as she traveled. It was all happening in perfect order, he realized. He could not have endured this experience had he not acknowledged and released the saboteur. They all looked at the chief. He held an expression of exquisite joy on his face. Walking to the place where Kalah had stood, he raised his arms and began to chant songs of thanks and safe travel. They all joined in.

Up on the cliff, Mama Hanu lifted her arms and sang as well, a well-wisher standing at the very gates to the sky. Within every cell of her being she held the image of Kalah's perfect journey. In her mind's eye, she had seen what they saw in those amazing moments around the family altar. And all across the village others also spontaneously lifted their arms and sang the chants of praise and thanks. Up and down their spines, they all felt the ripple of change that had flowed through the universe when the fabric of time and space opened and their sister was carried through.

CHAPTER SIXTEEN

Safe Landings

To Kei, who bobbed in the sea, it sounded like the whole island was singing, possibly even the whole earth. The dolphin saw in her own mind an image of the lamp, which Kalah held so tenderly in her hands, burning brightly and humming sweetly. She sensed that her human sister was moving incredibly fast.

Kalah was traveling far into the future, thousands of years beyond what she knew. And yet it seemed that she was not moving at all. She had been standing with her loved ones around the altar and then it appeared to her that they had disappeared. But she knew this was not the case. The flickering rainbow light in the lamp grew taller, as if reaching to see over the edge of the bowl.

The white light that surrounded her began to hum. More rich tones emanated from the vast being that carried her. In response, the flame she carried in her hands began to hum, matching the rhythm and tones of the larger light. It seemed to Kalah that they were talking to each other! She found herself humming along, matching the sounds of the two lights. Then she saw the form of a man stepping toward her from the light. He was very tall. His body was sculpted like the body of a warrior dancer. As he came into focus, she saw that he wore a mask. It was a white bird mask, which stopped just above his lips. He stood before her, radiating a powerful male energy. Smiling with great compassion and joy, he kissed her on her forehead.

"You are so loved," he told her with his thoughts. "The Father adores the Mother. You will help reunite them on your planet." Then he was gone. Sparks shot up from the lamp forming dazzling shapes in the air around her. The soft, rich tones sounding in her head began to form words. The words were not familiar, and yet they were becoming a part of her. Another language was being added to her own. Now she felt solid ground beneath her feet. She sensed the spirit of the place and knew that somehow she was on familiar territory. She was in someone's home. It was very spacious.

"Aloha." A handsome elder man stood before her. His face looked very kind.

"You are safe. Your arrival was expected," he said. "I am a time-traveler, too, although I have never journeyed as far as you have. But I understand and honor your journey. My wife and I will look after you. Her name is Hannah. My name is Kai'ilo. You can call me, Kai. We are greatly pleased to have you as our guest here. Our ancestors are pleased. Do you understand?" She nodded and smiled. Somehow she did, although she could not yet form the words for a response.

Kai told her that she was in Hawaii, very close in distance to the island she had left. While she was very far from the world she knew, she was still home in the land of palm trees and sacred hulas and the healing wisdom carried by the kahunas. This would comfort her and nourish her, he said, during her period of adjustment. She looked into his eyes. For a moment, she thought she saw the eyes of her own chief smiling back. She offered him the lamp. He held his hands over it and prayed. Then he took it with great reverence and placed it on a wooden table beside a low, colorful bed in an adjoining room. As he leaned down, she noticed two small totems that dangled from a cord around his neck. One was a turtle, carved from red coral. The other was a brown ball make of dark wood. He stood up and followed her eyes, touching the totems.

"Red turtle," he said, "the heart of our sea. Not many are left but they will endure. There is a plan for their survival."

She nodded. She was glad Mama Hanu had prepared her. Then he touched the little ball. He smiled. "This is part of the plan to save turtles. It's a coconut." With that he winked, but his gaze went past her. His playfulness brought a smile to her face. She felt herself relaxing. Perhaps he is a descendant of the chief, she thought. She looked over at the bed in the next room and wanted to sleep. The sun was bright in the sky and she could see from the window that they were near the sea. It looked inviting. But her body needed to rest. He handed her a cup of water and she drank heartily. "More?"

She nodded. She had not uttered a word but felt deeply understood. She sensed that she should sleep before trying this new language. He poured more water from a pitcher and she drank it. Then he bowed and motioned for her to lie down. She went immediately into a deep, restful sleep.

Thousands of miles away, a sleeping Sarah had been preparing for her own flight as Kalah was traveling through the cosmos. Sarah's body was heavy with the weight of slumber. But her spirit was alert and ready. It slipped out and began soaring. She felt so free, moving like a small comet across a canvas of black sky and white stars. She flew for what seemed like an eternity. Then black and white sky gave way to blue and white sky. She saw lush greenery. Suddenly a great light seemed to explode over her head. It was the same explosion of light that she had seen at the hospital. At first she had the feeling of being watched and she did not feel comfortable. Then she began to relax. She had the soothing sensation that she was actually being carried by this light. She looked up. Yes, she was being carried.

"Where am I?" she asked.

"Where would you like to be?" a voice asked. "It's your choice." She made a choice not to be afraid and her mood shifted. Somehow, it was easier here. Descending from flight, she landed gently inside a house. It seemed to reach up and draw her inside. She immediately saw two people talking. One was Kalah. She was talking to a man. His long white hair was pulled back. His strong features were chiseled, even regal. He wore crisp white clothes. She wondered if she should try to get their attention. But her eyes were drawn suddenly to an unusual lamp the man took from Kalah's hands and put on a table. A colorful flame looked over the lip of the bowl. Sarah smiled the way she would smile at a baby. Her attention was suddenly diverted by the man's words.

"Red turtle." He was pointing to something hanging from his neck. She felt out of place, like an eavesdropper, but also felt deeply curious. She shifted her attention to the lamp, but jumped at the next words she heard. "This is a part of the plan to save turtles. It's a coconut," he said, touching something hanging from his neck. He winked. Sarah felt busted. He was looking right at her.

"Oh, no! It must be Porter's kahuna!" she whispered to herself. Instinctively she touched the top of her head. She felt a blow.

"Ouch! That hurts!" she yelled, feeling mad. She did not share Porter's patience with this. She was ready to return fire with anything she could get her hands on. She looked around and realized that she was now sitting up in her own bed. She turned around to see that she had crashed against the mahogany headboard. She had given herself a good whack. A giggle popped out, followed by a laugh. Then more laughter built up in her belly. Sarah roared, falling back and nearly hitting her head again. She laughed with her entire body, until her ribs and stomach hurt. It felt like God was tickling her.

"Stop!" she giggled, like a child.

The alarm clock went off and her whole body jumped.

"Oh, Lordy. I'm awake! I promise." She grabbed the journal from her bedside table and began to write in terse telegram style.

Took a trip in my dreams. Saw Kalah. Saw a man. There was a flame in a bowl. It looked like it was happening now. It's the kahuna. I just know it. Must call Porter. If coconuts are part of the plan, Porter is part of the plan. I'll write more later.

She stopped and put the journal down. She picked it up again. *Almost forgot to mention. I saw the flash of light again. The darned thing is not only following me, now it seems to be carrying me around.* She stopped and scratched out *darned.*

"Sorry, God. I shouldn't complain," she said out loud. "It's beautiful. Whatever it is, I'll keep it." She paused and added one more line to her journal.

I don't think I can live without it.

CHAPTER SEVENTEEN

Invitations

Sarah stood up and stretched. She started her usual march to the kitchen, pondering turtles and coconuts.

"Coconuts," she said. "What is the symbolism there? Where is Carl Jung when I need him?" She turned on the coffee maker, still trying to answer her own questions. "Well, a coconut has a very hard shell. And it's kind of hairy. But tender on the inside, if you can pry the darned thing open."

"Hmmm. Sounds like a man." She scrunched up her face, trying to follow the thread of these things. "Hard on the outside, tender on the inside. Turtles have a hard shell, but turtles aren't hairy. At least I don't *think* they're hairy. Maybe they have some fuzz, but I doubt it. No, they're reptiles for Pete's sake." She shook her head. "Pull back, Sarah," she told herself. "Keep this up and you'll get lost somewhere scary where no one will ever think to look."

She got ready, going through the motions with great detachment. She almost walked out wearing one blue shoe and a black one. She rolled her eyes and marched back to the closet, trying to find a match for the blue one or the black one. In the dimness of her closet, the matches seemed to be hiding. She finally grabbed two other matching shoes that weren't right for the season. They were sandals. It didn't matter. The greater part of her was still with Kalah and the kahuna. He was becoming very real to her, too. She felt sheepish about wanting to pelt him, hoping there was no big punishment for that. She made a mental note to e-mail Porter as soon as she got to work. Settling into her subway seat she pulled out her journal and continued to write about the images now pouring into her mind. She wrote about everything she could remember since life had become different, including a young policeman she saw near her apartment, his face soft and radiant as a group of kids gathered around him.

Lots of people have light around their faces now. Or rather, I'm seeing it now. But I still did a double-take with this guy. The man is an angel. I know it. The kids were drawn to him like he had some kind of magnetic pull.

As the train came to a halt she tucked her journal in her purse. Walking from the subway to the hospital across blocks of crumbling sidewalk, she felt herself losing this connection to the mysterious. Red turtle thoughts began to drift away. She entered the hospital and made small talk with others on the elevator. She unlocked her office and stepped around some mail that had been pushed underneath the door. One envelope had a familiar name on the return address. It was from Gloria Mendez.

She opened it up and unfolded the construction paper, smiling at the dolphin. She examined the colorful seascape Pablo had drawn. Thoughts of turtles returned. She half expected to see one in the colorful drawing, given the boy's knack for tuning in. But she didn't find any. "Nearly gone," she heard the kahuna say as if he were whispering in her ear. She made a mental note to get on the web that night and start doing her homework. She wanted to see what they looked like. Maybe if they could figure it out, the kahuna would be happy and Porter would stop getting hit. She went about her day with turtles floating in and out of her awareness and in and out of conversations at the most unexpected time. In a meeting with other social workers someone started talking about a turtle. One had disappeared from his home aquarium.

"Where do they go when they disappear like that?" her co-worker asked. Sarah shook her head in disbelief. "I mean, one minute the little guy was there, and then he was gone!"

"Do you have a cat?" their supervisor asked.

"No. We have two finches, a hamster and the aquarium," the man answered. "And a 4-year-old boy."

"Oops," someone said. "Better check under the bed. Children keep their secrets under the bed." There was some chuckling around the room, but the last sentence resonated deeply inside of Sarah.

"Children keep their secrets under the bed," she repeated softly. "Why does that ring such a big bell? I know. It's because everyone keeps their secrets under the bed! That's what shadow is. The things we're trying to hide." The room was quiet. All eyes were upon her. She cringed, feeling embarrassed.

"That's really deep," the person sitting next to her said.

"Did I say that out loud?" she asked, wincing.

"Actually, that's an interesting topic: secrets and shadows," her supervisor said. "Maybe you can present on that sometime. Carl Jung's work about projections of the human shadow will give you plenty of research material. Make it relevant to what we are doing here. With AIDS in particular our culture projects a great deal of shame onto our patients." Sarah saw that she was completely serious. This surprised her.

"Okay," she said, softly. "I will." And that was that. The case of the missing turtle, and the shadow that might know its whereabouts, were put aside. It was a long meeting, heavy with details about the increase in pediatric AIDS cases. She thought of Pablo and made a mental note to call him and thank him for the drawing. She also wanted to know more about what inspired this picture. Back at her desk after lunch, the phone rang.

"Hi, dear. It's Mom," the voice on the other line said. Her voice was hoarse and unrecognizable at first. She sounded as if she had been crying.

"Mom. What is it?" Sarah's heart lurched.

"It's Uncle David, honey. He's sick. He just found out how sick." There was a pause. "He's got an advanced case of pancreatic cancer, Sarah. The doctors didn't want to make a prediction. But he pressed them. He's got about six months to live. Twylah called me. She's pretty torn up. I'm sorry I called you at work. But I had to talk to you. I'm so sorry for the bad news." She started to cry. Sarah felt a blow to her gut, as if she had been punched. Her thoughts raced. Fighting back tears she tried to comfort her mother, who had known Uncle David most of her life. He had lived in their neighborhood when her mother and Twylah were children. He and Twylah were engaged before they finished college. They had moved to the Gulf Coast of Florida, where they ran a restaurant called Mama Alligator. He was a great fisherman. He had taught her aunt to fish in the sea and bought a boat called The Misty Marlin. Sarah had enjoyed many happy times with them on the Marlin. Dolphins seemed drawn to it. Or perhaps they were drawn to Uncle David. He had a magnificent aura that Sarah could see before she started seeing other lights.

"Sarah, he wants to have a family gathering," her mother continued when she was able to speak again. "He wants to see everybody before the funeral. He says the funeral is for Twylah and the kids and everyone else, but his eyes won't be working too well by then. Those were his exact words. He wants to see us now." She laughed a little and blew her nose.

"That's a beautiful idea," Sarah said, trying to rally for her uncle. "When is everyone going?"

"We don't know yet. We're all scrambling to get something set up. If you fly to Atlanta we can drive down together. I think we'll need that time to prepare ourselves mentally. I don't want to be weepy the whole time."

"Just say when, Mom," she answered. "I have plenty of vacation time coming to me." They exchanged a few more words of comfort and said good-bye. Sarah felt herself wanting to reach through the phone to hold on to her mother. When she hung up she felt her mood plummet, as if her heart had been dropped from a tall building. She pushed her chair back from the desk and doubled over. The tears came out in a flood of grief, old grief mixed with new.

As sadness about her uncle overtook her, memories of Collin were awakened. "Suicide." That's what his death certificate said, but she still could not believe it. An apparently happy man, on top of the world in his career, had simply disappeared. A strange note told her that he would be late, that he had a "crisis" to work through. But the note was reassuring. "Don't worry too much. I'll deal with and I'll be back soon."

His body was discovered in a state park in a car filled with carbon monoxide. There was no other note, no explanation for why he would do such a thing. His calendar was full of plans. They were trying to have a child. Sarah had always suspected foul play that was set up to look like suicide, but she could not conceive of a motive. Collin was a journalist, but not the investigative kind. His "human interest" stories tended to make people feel good, not angry. No, the reasons for his death had gone with him to the grave.

And now Uncle David was leaving. Not another good man down. Not another family tragedy. Her sobs came in waves. After a while there was a knock at her door. She did not answer, but sat up, looking for tissues. She had forgotten where she was. The door opened a crack.

"Sarah?" She recognized the voice. Jo, a nurse, peered around the door. A look of shock flashed across the younger woman's face.

She stepped into the office and quickly closed the door behind her.

"What is it?" She knelt in front of Sarah, who was trying to dry her face with a sleeve. Tears were now rolling down her neck. Sarah looked through burning eyes at the radiant face of this woman, so tender and full of compassion. She felt waves of energy flowing between them. Jo was sending her something powerful, and she was deeply grateful for it.

"It's my uncle," she finally said, her voice cracking. "He's got cancer. It's really, really bad." She swallowed back a sob. "And I started thinking about Collin and I couldn't stop. I started thinking about the call I got when they found him in the park. And I lost it. I lost control. I am so sorry to be falling apart at work. I know we have a presentation to make, but I can't do it. I just can't." She shook her head. "I'm a mess."

"Not a problem. The presentation can happen another day. Can I get you a cold towel? What can I do to help?"

"Another angel," Sarah thought to herself as light poured from her co-worker's face. "My God, they are everywhere."

"You look really flushed. I'm getting you something cold for your face," Jo said, not waiting for an answer. As she opened the door, Sarah heard Gabe's voice in the hallway. He grew quiet. She knew Jo was telling him what happened. She felt embarrassed, imagining that this turn of events made her seem completely out of control.

"Sarah?" He knocked softly. "Can I come in?"

"Sure," she said, hoarsely. "You might as well see me at my worst." He came around the door and looked down at her. His face melted. She reached up for him as he bent down to embrace her. She rested a hand on the back of his head, feeling the softness of his hair.

"God, I'm so sorry," he whispered. They held each other until Jo returned. She pulled up a chair and pulled back strands of Sarah's hair, which were sticking to her face.

"By the way, you're an angel," Sarah said. "Has anyone ever told you that?" The nurse smiled, shrugging a little. "You would do the same for me. Now please go home and take care of *yourself* for a change. I'll let everyone know that you have a family emergency."

"Yes, another one," Sarah replied shaking her head.

Gabe stayed, sitting on the edge of her desk. She told him about her uncle's request to see everyone one last time.

"This is awful," she said. "But I have to say, it's a brilliant request."

"It really is. It's going be a gift to everybody involved."

Sarah put the cloth over her face. "I'm going to get myself together and go home. I'm useless."

"Would you like company tonight?"

"If I don't fall asleep as soon as I get home. That's usually how I deal with grief. Can I call you?"

"You bet," he said. They hugged again and he slipped out. She leaned back and closed her eyes, imagining Uncle David on his boat. He would find good fishing in heaven, she told herself. Twylah had talked to so many who had crossed over. They always told stories of incredible peace and great light. They had the same message, said in many different ways. "Don't worry. I'm doing well." Sometimes they added, "I miss you." Later that evening, her trembling fingers dialed Gabe's number. He answered right away. She could hear his relief when he heard her voice.

"I was tempted to call you. But I didn't want to wake you up."

"I'm awake. And I'd love your company."

"Have you eaten anything?"

"I ate some ice cream. But no real dinner."

"Can I bring you some noodle soup? I'll pick it up on the way."

"Sounds perfect," she said. She paused, her heart beating. "Gabe?"

"Yes?"

"Would you feel like bringing your toothbrush, too?" She winced, waiting for a response. She realized that they hadn't even had their first kiss yet. What a hussy, she thought to herself.

"My what?" he was quiet for a moment. "Oh! My toothbrush. You mean, as in staying over tonight?" She heard surprise, mixed with cautious optimism.

"If that's a brazen request, I'm prepared to chock it up to shock and grief. We can pretend I didn't ask. I need to be held. But I don't want you to feel like my teddy bear, Gabe. I'm not asking you to play that part. I already have one. He's ratty, but he's good." She felt herself sinking, as if each word she uttered was more ridiculous than the last. "You know, forget I even said it. Never mind. I've gone crazy." Exasperated, Gabe pushed his way through her anxious second-guessing. She was about to close a door he had been waiting for her to open.

"Stop talking yourself out of it!" he said, laughing. "I'm bringing my toothbrush. It's not a contract. It's a toothbrush. If you want to push me out the door, my toothbrush and I will slink on home."

Sarah smiled. The image amused her. "Oh, and you can bring anything else you want. Bring a change of clothes, or whatever. I mean unless you don't want to."

"Stop," he said, trying not to laugh. "I want to."

He was over within the hour. Sheepishly he tossed his duffle bag behind the couch, trying to look as if he hadn't. She took the food and kissed his cheek. There was a brief shyness between them, which evaporated quickly. They talked late into the evening about loss and life and grief and loving. He told Sarah more about his divorce. His wife had fallen in love with another man. She had remarried very quickly.

"I can't imagine anyone leaving you," she said sincerely. He blushed.

"It was pretty ugly. If she wanted an excuse for leaving me, I gave her plenty before it was all over. It wasn't my finest moment or hers. The worst part is that I never saw it coming."

"I know just what you mean," she said. They were quiet for a time, holding hands.

"Wow, it is already midnight," she said, finally. "Do you really want to stay?" He nodded and opened his arms. She leaned into the embrace, burying her head against his chest. They were quiet for a while. He kissed her forehead.

"Your hair smells good," he said. She looked up at him.

"Thanks. I took a shower. Just for you. Come on." She took his hand and led him into her bedroom. They undressed to their underwear, then felt shy again and jumped in bed, pulling the covers up to their necks.

"Awkward moment!" she said. "Awkward moment! Oh, my gosh. What do we do now? I can't remember."

"As I recall, you only asked to be held tonight," he said, rolling over to face her and propping his head with a hand. "I haven't heard any other requests, so I'm going to stick with that one." She curled up in his arms. She wondered if she should at least try to act sexy. She wondered if she remembered how.

"This feels good," she said. "Really good. Will you be mad at me if I fall asleep? I'm so tired I feel drugged." Her voice was growing hoarse with exhaustion.

"Your eyelids are growing heavy. You are getting very, very sleepy," he replied. It was too dark for her to see his big smile.

"Don't you ask me to bark like a dog for the audience, Mr. Hypnotist," she said softly. "Or flap my arms like a chicken. I'll never forgive you. Never, ever." She kissed him and fell asleep quickly, her spirit feeling peaceful. She wouldn't be taking any dreamtime journeys tonight. She was just fine right where she was.

CHAPTER EIGHTEEN

Cabs and Chariots

Sarah scanned the nearly empty café. She had taken a late lunch hour, hoping that business had slowed down and Minnie could join her for a meal.

"I know it's your restaurant, but can I buy you lunch? You have to eat lunch, right?" Minnie smiled, studying her face for a moment.

"I'd love to join you. It's been a long time since I've eaten lunch sitting down." They walked to the back of the café, settling into the most private booth.

"How are you?" Minnie asked, putting a bright napkin on her lap.

"I'm somewhat troubled. I need a little advice from someone I trust."

"I'm honored," Minnie answered. She waved for the waitress to take their order. Erma seemed surprised to find her boss sitting down. "May I recommend the blue plate special," she said, pointing to the menu and trying to sound serious. "The owner's recipe, you know."

Minnie looked at Sarah, who nodded in agreement. "Two specials and two iced teas, please," she said. Erma leaned down and whispered in her ear.

"You're not selling the place, are you?"

"Nothing to worry about," Minnie said. "Now quit being nosey."

"Well as long as you're not selling the place." Erma winked at Sarah and hurried to put in the order. "The boss is eating this, so make it good," they heard her say to the cook. Minnie winced and shook her head. "I didn't need to hear that. So talk to me," she said. "What's happening?" Sarah bit her lip before speaking.

"Well, remember when I was here with my godfather and you said something about using my eyes to see?" Minnie nodded.

"Well, low and behold I am doing just that. It's not something that happens because I try. It just happens. If you hadn't said that to me, about the light and using my eyes to see, I would have panicked a lot more. But when I start feeling uneasy about it I recall the things you've said to me and I feel better. So thank you. Your timing was perfect."

Minnie nodded. "You're welcome. And how do things look to you, now that you are using your eyes to see?"

"Well, I've been seeing this light around people, even animals. Especially animals." She lowered her voice to a whisper and looked around before she spoke. "Gabe's dog, Haley, has an actual halo. So do the squirrels."

Minnie burst out laughing. "And this surprises you? They're more innocent than we are." Erma approached with the iced tea.

"Well I don't expect everyone to understand," Sarah said a little defensively. "I don't want to sound crazy when I reveal this stuff, which is why I came to you."

"I know. I couldn't resist having a little fun. Go on."

"Really, that's all," Sarah said, clamming up. "I'm satisfied with telling you that much and having you understand. That's all I needed. So, that's enough about me. How are you?" Sarah realized that she was more comfortable being the understanding listener. Minnie wasn't letting her off the hook that easily. She scanned Sarah's face. "Have you received some bad news?" she asked.

Sarah was stunned. "Why do you ask? Did Gabe tell you?"

"No, he didn't tell me anything. I can see it in your eyes. Someone close to you is hurt or sick. That's why you feel troubled."

"That's amazing, Minnie. I can't believe you can see that just by looking in my eyes."

"It's not magic. It's just paying attention. And I know you very well. Who is it?"

"My Uncle David," Sarah replied, looking down. "He's got pancreatic cancer. The whole family's going down to Florida to see him. It's his idea. A reunion before the funeral, as he puts it. I can't tell you how much I love that man." Her voice started to crack. They were quiet for a time as she collected herself. Erma appeared with the food. She started to joke, but saw Sarah's face and remained quiet as she put the plates down.

"So here I am seeing this light and feeling a whole new kinship with God, and then I feel shot down again, like it's all so ugly," Sarah said finally. "I mean, it's not *all* ugly, but there's definitely too much ugly."

"You think his death is going to be ugly," Minnie said. "It can't possibly be compatible with that beautiful light you are seeing, right? And yet, what seems like darkness can lead us to our Source."

Sarah nodded, shrugging a little. "True. I can't tell you how many times I've heard people thanking God for pulling their loved ones from the jaws of death," she acknowledged. "Like God took that person right out of the hands of Satan. But there's always a little voice in my head wanting to address that contradiction. Did God pull your loved one away from something bad? How can that be if you think the final destination is heaven? I wonder if they even understand what they are saying. But there's never a good time to point that out, not in a hospital setting."

"We're a bundle of contradictions, we human beings," Minnie said. "We curse death when it's actually our chariot taking us home. Can you imagine our saying, 'Well thank God my dear husband missed that taxi! It was headed straight for the pearly gates! Whew. That was a close call!'"

Sarah felt a shift in her awareness, as if she were waking up from a dream. "I'm around death so much. I think that for the longest time some part of me has wanted to break through the grim images and see a brighter picture. And it would have helped so much, particularly when Collin died. But it's weird, Minnie. I have to examine myself and be honest. It's like I was fighting that higher awareness and intentionally keeping myself in the dark. I wonder why I chose to deny myself some relief, why I've chosen to deny others." She shook her head and took a bite, chewing slowly as she pondered this more. "It makes no sense."

"Don't be hard on yourself. When my loved ones are sick my first response is to think of death as a bad thing, too, particularly when there is suffering involved. It's human nature to fear death. It's just easier to get a clear look at these things when they are playing out in someone else's life. And I'll tell you another thing about seeing the light," she added softly. "Sometimes I pray for the Holy Spirit to fill me up and my prayer is answered. But the experience of having so much light in my soul actually puts me in a grouchy mood, not a peaceful one. How's that for a contradiction?" She took a sip of tea. "So that's my little confession to you."

"Is that a bad sign for us?" Sarah asked. "If the Holy Spirit fills you up and it puts you in a bad mood, well, that doesn't seem to bode well. Does that imply that the Holy Spirit is angry?" Minnie looked at Sarah and saw the worried Catholic kid peering out of her eyes.

"Oh, I'm not saying the Holy Spirit is mad," she said, laughing warmly. "I'm the one who gets grouchy when all of that powerful light comes into me. It's just my resistance to seeing things clearly.

There is a part of me that craves the light enough to beg God for it and a part of me that fights it when it comes. I'm like a grouchy little kid who doesn't want to wake up. Because waking up means a call to action. And sometimes I feel a little lazy, that's all."

"Oh," Sarah said, trying to follow her wise friend. "You're telling me you also have a little resistance to the truth sometimes."

"A lot."

"Okay, a *lot* of resistance to the truth sometimes, just like I do. This light-seeing business isn't always a picnic."

"Now you're with me. And bless your heart, you came in for a little reassurance and I took you on a wild ride through my way of relating to the Holy Spirit."

"It was a good ride, Minnie," Sarah said. They finished eating in silence, the kind of silence reserved for kindred spirits. "Is your family okay these days?" Sarah asked.

"Everyone's doing great. I'm grateful for the peace. We have a large, extended family, so there's not too much time in between illnesses and accidents. But for the moment, everyone is fine. By the way, I really enjoyed meeting your godfather. He's fascinating."

"What makes you say that? I mean he really is fascinating, but I'm curious about what you thought of him."

"My take is that he's a man with many layers, some of them quite deep. He has compassionate eyes. And his hands, they really tell the story."

"His hands?"

"He has very strong, rugged hands, like a sailor's hands, but the rest of him is very refined. So he has these powerful hands, but he moves them in a very light, refined way. Have you noticed the contrast? Does he sail?"

"I don't think so," Sarah said, trying to visualize Porter's hands. "It's funny that I can't answer that question. I've known him all my life."

"Well to me, his hands say that he's prepared to set sail. He's ready for a journey, and he's not afraid of hard work."

"Fascinating. I'll keep you posted on that one." Sarah looked at her watch. "Thanks for having lunch with me. The food was great and my spirit got fed, too."

"This feeds my spirit, too," Minnie answered. "I'm glad you came. Please come see me when you get back from Florida. Will you do that? I want to know how it went with your uncle. And you put away your wallet right now young lady."

Sarah hesitated, but buckled under Minnie's firm gaze. She put her wallet away. Minnie reached across the table and took Sarah's hands, holding them palms up toward the heavens. "Your hands also speak to me. They say that you've come to this earth prepared to receive something beautiful," she said. "I feel something brewing. Stay open. Will you do that?"

Sarah nodded vigorously. "I will."

CHAPTER NINETEEN

Clouds Parting

The flight was bumpy. Sarah curled up in her window seat and looked out. To the child in her they seemed to be soaring through a cloud kingdom with big, fluffy structures and a giant lake filled with sparkling yellow sunlight. She wondered if the plane, so big and so dense, was intruding somehow. Or were the wispy beings of this kingdom used to such things?

She closed her eyes, wishing she were a child again. If she were a child, Uncle David would have many years to live. Her thoughts moved to the letters in the pocket of her coat, which was draped over her like a blanket. She reached in and pulled them out. One was from Porter, the other from Gabe. Both men were eloquent and sincere in their heartache about her uncle's diagnosis. She knew Gabe's by heart. Her eyes scanned Porter's, which she had already read twice.

"Sarah, there is so much that I'd like to say. There is a part of me that still wants to bundle you up and carry you away to a safe haven, where loved ones do not pass away and children don't get hurt or sick. As your godfather, I want to take you to a place where you will be completely and entirely out of a job. No one will be suffering. Everyone will have what's needed. No one will need their hand held by a compassionate social worker. As I write this, it occurs to me that there is such a place. You and I both know it.

"Ironically, though, it's not a place you and I are longing for, at least not consciously. It's the place your Aunt Twylah calls 'the other side.' It's the place where your Uncle David is going. So why are we sad? I think it's the missing part that hurts so much. We don't get many phone calls or post cards from the other place. Not unless you're somebody like Twylah. I miss my father very much. He died while I was in college. I know you miss Collin and probably will for a long time. And I think you already miss your uncle. The mind moves forward like that sometimes, wondering how it's going to feel when things change. Yes, I think it's the missing part and the fear of the death process itself that causes us so much pain. If it weren't for those things, we'd all be celebrating. We'd be celebrating in a big way. I don't know David as well as I would like, but my hunch is that he's called you together to celebrate his life rather than focus on his death. And how do we know that he won't out-live us?

"We don't know what's waiting for us around the next corner. It could be the proverbial bus about to hit. This is not to make light of what David is dealing with. I am extremely aware that his news was not good. But deep in my heart I am wishing you a beautiful time in Florida with your family. David is being given a chance to say a quality farewell. Many of us won't get that opportunity. Death doesn't usually give six months notice. As your godfather, I will dutifully close with my spiritual thoughts on the matter. And it boils down to this: I think that when we finally shed our human skins and say good-bye to each other for a little while, we walk right into the arms of our angel kin. Perhaps there is a reunion of another sort being planned for your uncle on the other side. As I wrote those words, goose bumps formed on my arms and legs, telling me that this is true. I love you, dear. Porter."

She was amazed at the way his thoughts resonated with what Minnie had said. He closed with the words of the 23rd Psalm. Gabe's letter had ended with the same words. Funny, she thought, how both men had rebelled against the constraints of their traditional religious upbringings, yet both recognized words that were deeply imbued with the love of God. She read it again, her eyes filling with tears that overflowed and fell down her face.

The Lord is my shepherd; I shall not want.

He maketh me to lie down in green pastures; he leadeth me beside the still waters; He restoreth my soul; he leadeth me in the paths of righteousness for his name's sake. Yea, though I walk through the valley of the shadow of death, I will fear no evil; for thou art with me; they rod and they staff they comfort me. Thou preparest a table before me in the presence of mine enemies; thou anointest my head with oil; my cup runneth over. Surely goodness and mercy shall follow me all the days of my life; and I will dwell in the house of the Lord forever.

She stretched and repositioned herself. She touched Gabe's letter to her lips. Thoughts of him flashed through her mind. In the two weeks since he had first spent the night, they had deepened their bond and tasted the sweetness of physical closeness and first kisses. They were looking at each other in a new light and trying to learn to trust again. But as with this flight, there were bumpy stretches. Sarah was initially offended that he hadn't been more sexually demonstrative. Gabe finally admitted that he didn't want their first love-making to take place while her grief was so palpable.

"Well at the rate my life is going, you might have to wait a long time if you can't stand the presence of grief," she had said, feeling rebuffed.

"You don't understand," he had responded tenderly. "I *can* stand the presence of grief. And I am extremely attracted to you.

But having sex with you doesn't feel like the most chivalrous way to respond right now." They had mended that fence very quickly and moved on. They were friends first and would-be lovers a close second. They both knew that what she needed most was Gabe the friend. She closed her eyes, her heart feeling like a lost child. She thought of the mysterious black lamp and how its rainbow flame moved in the bowl like a child dancing. She couldn't shake the image. With this thought her heart called out in the darkness of her confusion. It did not call out for Porter or Gabe. No, it was Kalah she wanted now.

"Where are you?" she asked with her thoughts. She waited, but got no reply. "I'm afraid I'm going to lose you. I'm afraid that I'm doing something wrong and that I'll push you away. Don't let that happen." More thick clouds. The plane was surrounded by them, engulfed in white. "How can the pilot possibly know where he's going?" she asked herself. It hit her how much she trusted someone she had never met. She had a revelation. Like most revelations it came at a time when the cynic in her was about to seal her mind shut and batten the hatches.

"We can't see where we're going," she said to herself. "But we *trust* where we're going. All of us on this plane have taken a leap of faith. We filed inside this metal tube and strapped ourselves in, saying, 'Take us to Atlanta.' We can't see a darned thing but clouds, clouds and more clouds. Wispy surreal white stuff. But we all seem to feel quite confident about our destination. And we don't need any big explanations about how this plane works.

"So why is it," she asked herself, "that we trust the pilot more than we trust the Holy Spirit? Why can't I trust God like that?" She took in a deep breath and let it out slowly. The plane bumped and shook a little. Her heart fluttered. "Better not admit your faith issues when you're dangling in the air," she thought. But who was she kidding? God knew her inside and out.

"It's okay to admit you're a novice at genuine trust," she told herself. "I want to trust and God knows that. But I have to grow into trust, that's all." She folded the letters and put them back in her coat pocket. The captain's voice came on, telling them they were beginning their descent. It was rainy in Atlanta, he said, and 62 degrees. A flight attendant moved efficiently down the aisle, collecting trash. Sarah handed her a cup and waited for the important words that had not yet been spoken.

"Please return your trays to the upright position." She obeyed, feeling that only now were they free to descend. The animal part of her brain needed predictability. It needed commands that could be quickly and easily obeyed.

"What's that, Captain? Now you want me to get off this plane and drive five or six hours to the Gulf Coast and spend quality time with my uncle, who is dying? Well, okay. But this is getting a little tougher now. Can't we stick to the easy stuff? No? Well, it doesn't hurt to ask." She knew which "Captain" she was really talking to now. And she knew that she would, in fact, do what she was being asked to do. She would walk off the plane, look for her parents and make the drive to Florida. Her mother's face softened as soon as they made eye contact.

"There she is! There's Sarah!" She hugged both of her parents and walked with them to their car, pulling her suitcase behind her. For the first time in her life she had managed to travel light. She had no idea what she had actually packed and didn't really care. As long as she wasn't walking around stark naked nobody was likely to notice. They drove for several hours, talking most of the way. She felt herself starting to relax when they crossed the Florida state line. Just a couple more hours now and they would be on Twylah and David's big back porch, ocean breezes caressing them.

"Here's a letter from Porter," she said. "It's gorgeous. Be prepared to cry," Her mother reached back and took it.

"How was your visit with Porter?" she asked, unfolding the letter. "You haven't said much about it."

"It was incredible. I realized how little I've really understood him all these years. He's even more amazing and complex than I thought." Her parents were quiet. She read their silence and decided to answer the unspoken question.

"He told me he used to work for the CIA."

"He did?" her father asked. "I wasn't sure if he would ever get up the courage."

"Why did it take courage?" Sarah asked. "It's a job."

"Is that how you felt when he first told you?" he asked, studying her face in the rearview mirror. "That it's just a job?"

It was her turn to be quiet now.

"No," she replied sheepishly. "My first thoughts weren't so positive. And my second thoughts were about you two. I felt a little betrayed. I wondered how long you had known."

"Yep. That's my girl," her father said, laughing. "Porter knew you'd react that way. That's why he couldn't figure out whether to tell you or leave it alone." She could tell that he was smiling. She wondered if he had been a spy, too. The idea was way too strange and it quickly evaporated from her thoughts.

"I wonder why he decided to tell you now," her mother said. Sarah shrugged but didn't answer. This didn't seem like the right time to talk about time-travelers and light and a kahuna with coconuts.

"Oh, my, he's brilliant," her mother said. She was reading Porter's letter. "Listen to this honey." She read it out loud. Sarah opened her purse and started fishing around for Kleenex. "Here, Mom." Her mother reached back without looking and grabbed the tissue. She wiped the tears from her face.

"That's incredible," her father said. "And it makes so much sense. Now do you understand why we wanted him to be your godfather? No one else would do." She could see her father's eyes in the mirror. They were moist with tears.

The hard rain was easing to a drizzle. Sarah felt butterflies in her stomach. "I don't feel as sad as I thought I would," she said.

"I think Porter is right. This is supposed to be a celebration. When are John and his family arriving?"

"Your brother is probably going to beat us there," her father answered. "And Twylah and David's bunch are already there. Allison flew down early to spend some time with her parents. Scott left straight from work and brought the kids last night. Clara and Matthew are so tall. They are nine now! It seems like yesterday that the twins were just starting school. They look so much like Allison. Here take a look at this photograph."

Sarah studied it and saw her cousin and Uncle David in the faces of the twins. "I love their eyes," she said. "Very soulful."

"I agree. They are old souls. Uncle David said Clara is really into fishing, particularly deep-sea fishing. Matthew is more into snorkeling. Twylah got him an underwater camera. She thinks he has a gift in that area. Maybe he'll end up being an artist like her."

"So we're the last to arrive? Now I do feel nervous," Sarah said, shifting the subject as her thoughts settled on her uncle.

"Why?"

"We only see the entire family when it's a very special occasion. I'm feeling overwhelmed by it all."

"It's an absolute miracle that everyone could come on such short notice. It helps that it coincides with the Thanksgiving weekend," her mother said.

Sarah closed her eyes. Her heart called out to Kalah.

"Where are you? Have I lost you?" And then her heart jumped and did a flip inside the walls of her chest. Behind closed lids she saw her beautiful face. It was shining.

"I'm here," she said softly. "I'm right here. Keep your focus on the heavens and you will not suffer." Sarah opened her eyes. She heard excitement in her mother's voice. They had arrived. How did that happen? It seemed that only a minute ago they were still more than an hour away. She saw her aunt and uncle coming out of the house. Her uncle walked more carefully than usual, but his face was beaming and happy. She saw her brother walking behind them, his arm around his wife. They all stood in the gravel driveway, hugging and holding each other. Then she caught site of John's face as he gazed skyward. He pointed. "Look! Look! It's an absolutely gigantic rainbow!" One leg of the vast arch seemed to stand on land and the other over the water, a bridge between worlds.

Looking at the heavens, they all smiled like children.

CHAPTER TWENTY

The Ship's Course

Kai was visible from the kitchen window, a large straw hat on his head. The thunderstorms were subsiding and there were branches to pick up. Kalah walked outside and knew what Kai was thinking. She asked, just to be sure, if the storms had something to do with her arrival. Never had she seen such lightning, which crossed the sky horizontally in great streaks. And the thunder made the ground shake, moving things on the shelves in Kai and Hannah's home. He answered her question truthfully.

"Yes, I think they have something to do with your arrival and the vortex that was created when time folded," he said. "I know that your power and the power of the lamp are much bigger than we might imagine. But I believe these storms are purifying. They are washing away thoughts and energy that resist the changes you bring."

Kalah nodded, thinking of Makani's experience with the great wave of purification. Hannah came out with cups of cold water. Kalah told them her husband's story. Fascinated, they hung on every word. It was still amazing to them that she had come gifted with an ability to speak their language. She explained the tones and sounds that flowed over her during her transition to this time.

It was then, she said, that she learned their words. It was all part of the plan. Instinctively upon her arrival, Hannah and Kai had put away the television, fearing its words and images would be too troubling to their young guest. When Kai was curious about weather and current events, he would go sit in his car and turn on the radio. He excused himself now to check on the weather. The women went back inside.

"Good news," he called from the driveway. "I think the purifying is finished for now!" Kalah went to the window and grinned at him. Then she returned to her task. The women were mashing poi root to make a sauce. Kalah licked a finger, the sweet aroma bringing back memories of home. It was a staple in her time, too, but she usually was not present for the pounding and mashing. She was intrigued by this role reversal between men and women. In her village, men did the cooking and women tended the gardens, she explained. Hannah said she loved the idea of men taking responsibility for all of the cooking. She was familiar with this ancient tradition.

"But I do love to cook," she added. "And Kai is happiest when his hands are in the soil. It's therapeutic." Kalah cocked her head, trying to grasp the full meaning of the term. "That means it is good medicine for our bodies and our spirits. It gives our minds a chance to rest as our hands take over."

Kalah nodded. "I understand. That's how I feel when I'm swimming." For the most part she was blending easily into their daily lives. She sensed that this was the most appropriate thing for her to do. Kai had talked about a period of adjustment, both for her and the people whose lives she was touching. Concerned about her comfort and her mission when she first arrived, he had gone deeply into prayer, asking his spirit guides what he should do to assist her.

"Nothing unusual," was the casual reply from the cosmos. He went more deeply into prayer, thinking he might have misunderstood or had not asked the question in the right way.

The same words were repeated several times just to make sure he got it. Sheepishly, he shared this with Kalah. He wondered if he was losing his touch.

"Hah!" she had replied, laughing with relief. "I got the same answer! But how can I possibly do that. Everything I'm doing here is unusual!"

She was teasing. She was actually quite intrigued by their modern conveniences and wondered why Hannah had stopped using them. Electricity made sense to her, she explained, because it followed the same principles as the flow of sacred mana in the human body. "You should not change your ways because of me," she said. "It doesn't feel right." But Hannah was not so sure. What if all this newness was a distraction to Kalah? What if they all needed to adopt a simpler way of life?

"Better not take any chances," she had told herself. If putting away some of the gadgets would assist with the spiritual evolution of the planet, so be it. Hannah put the vacuum cleaner in the kitchen closet and bought a new, sturdier broom to use on the floors. She would shake out the rugs by hand or beat them with the broom. The blender and the toaster were tucked away in the pantry. She found she did not miss them.

As the two women were talking about these things, Kai walked by the kitchen window. Only the top of his hat was visible. Seeing the triangular tip moving by, Kalah was reminded of a dolphin gliding through water. Her mind shifted to Kei. How she missed swimming with her friend.

"Mama Hanu says I'm part dolphin," she said, nibbling on a spoonful of poi that Hannah had given her. "And I think she means that. She checks sometimes to see if my back fin is coming in!" She reached back with an arm to feel along her spine.

"No. Nothing yet," she said, smiling.

"Well, I'm from the shark family," Kai said, curling his lips to look fierce as he looked at them through the open window. "Look at my kill. These poor vegetables never saw me coming."

"You are very funny," Kalah called. "You remind me of home."

"Good. That's the greatest compliment you could give me," he said, walking through the door and shedding his shoes. "But I should not really joke about the shark. He has powerful energy. He is not my family's guardian spirit, but I know many who embrace him. *Carefully.*" At this, Hannah looked from her husband to Kalah. She reached across the table, gently squeezing her hand.

"Thank you," Hannah said, her heart drinking in the amazing sight of this adorable young woman eating purple poi sauce at her kitchen table. The plain modern dress she wore did not take away from her striking beauty. "I don't know if I have ever properly thanked you. You have traveled far from home to be with us at a time when your own life was so full. I know you must miss your village very much. I know you miss your husband and your family and your dolphin friend."

Kalah nodded, feeling a touch of homesickness. "I miss them, very true. But it is not so unusual to be apart from Makani right now. This is when he travels with the other men to the big island to see the volcano. She stopped. *"The big island,"* she repeated. Her eyes grew wide. "He is coming here!"

Kai looked stunned. "Makani is coming to this place? He is a time-traveler as well?" Her guardian wasn't expecting another visitor. He hadn't prepared! A vision was forming in Kalah's mind. She bowed her head and closed her eyes, going inward to understand. Then her eyes opened.

"An opening in time. We're going to be granted a brief opening in time to see the voyagers! They are coming this way, as they do every year." She clapped her hands. "It is a gift to us. It is a gift to Makani, too, in honor of his bravery. We will see each other!" She popped up from the chair. Then she abruptly sat down, closing her eyes again. "More is coming to me. I'm seeing more. There is something far greater going on here." She drew in a deep breath and released it, growing very still. To Hannah and

Kai it seemed that she left her body and was very far away. Kai could feel his heart beating. Something big was in the air. Very big. Kalah opened her eyes and a sweet light poured from them as she spoke.

"Great Father and Great Mother move closer together in their sacred dance," she said. She spoke as if she were in a trance. "With me came the power of the sacred feminine. The feminine needs strengthening in this time. The voyagers bring the power of the sacred masculine to ensure balance. For a brief period they will be in two places at once. When the sky opens and we see them, a shift will occur, a healing shift that will affect all life in this time. Only for a moment will they be aware of this. Then they will return to their journey and their own sense of time.

"It is all part of the plan. And I will be right back," she said, standing up. Her own lilting voice had returned. "I have to change my clothes." Hannah and Kai looked at one another, their eyes wide.

"More balancing of the planet?" Kai whispered after she hurried off. "How much more thunder and lightning can we take? Not to mention the wind!"

Hannah elbowed him. "Shhhhhhhh." A smile danced in her eyes.

"My dear, I'm quite serious," he said, feigning worry. "If our trees lose any more limbs in the storms we won't have any shade left! The woman comes with her own weather front! And now another boat-load is coming!"

"Relax. Things are calming down. It's actually beautiful outside," she answered, trying not to laugh out loud. She didn't want Kalah to hear and think he was serious. "We have all the shade we need."

"But her *husband* isn't here yet," Kai said, shaking his head. "He's probably the god of thunder!" He stopped. His face broke into a big smile. Hannah knew him so well. His joking was a cover for his great awe. Never had she seen him happier.

In her room, Kalah let out a little hoot of glee as she found the indigo cloth folded on a hanger. She wrapped it around herself. She put on the shell necklace, humming like a happy child. Then she reverently picked up the lamp and marched resolutely out of her room. She entered the kitchen, finding them still seated at the table. There was no question about who was in charge at this moment.

"Come," Kalah said, excitedly. "We'll go wait on the cliffs and watch the horizon." The three of them hurried out to the grass-covered cliffs, the older couple trailing just a little. Kalah moved quickly and with grace. Kai and Hannah glanced at each other as they walked quickly along.

"She is a woman in love," Hannah said softly. Kai took his wife's hand and gently kissed it. Watching the young woman walk to the water's edge to get a glimpse of her sea-faring husband had a profound impact on the man. His heart opened wide, like a door blown open by the wind. His wife looked and saw that his face was surrounded by light. He looked back and saw the same light around her. The three of them stood on the cliff, the warm wind blowing their hair. The big waves crashed and exploded. They watched the bright sun slip behind fluffy white clouds, its rays shooting out in all directions. Kalah held the lamp skyward and began to chant softly.

Kai bowed his head, his heart overflowing with feelings of deep honor. Hannah put an arm around his shoulder and stroked his hair. Her heart felt the joy of Great Mother. She realized that her heart was big enough to contain it. The sun moved out from behind the clouds. A single bright ray stood out among the others. It was full of color. It shot toward Kalah, making contact with the rainbow flame in the lamp. The little flame grew taller. Tones emanated from the lamp, tones that all three could hear.

"He is very close, now," Kalah said, her voice excited. "Let your eyes look out toward the horizon. Don't strain, for it is your mind's eye that will first see them. Closer now. Closer they come. I can feel them." Then she pointed. "Look! Can you see?" There was a flash of color just above the horizon.

"I see!" Kai shouted. He jumped up and down like a boy. "I see them!" He glanced at Hannah's face. Her eyes were wide with wonder. She nodded, but did not take her focus from the water. The three watched as the grand vessel and its billowing sail became more visible. They could see the powerful arms of more than 40 men moving with practiced precision. The craft was utterly beautiful, an aura of majesty surrounding it. The voyagers pushed through waves, bouncing back at times, then flowing forward again and lifting up on the crests. With great skill the men maintained the direction of their boat, sometimes flowing with the wind, sometimes against it.

"He's there! Makani! Oh, I see him so clearly," Kalah said. "Please hold this." She put the lamp in Kai's hands. Then she closed her eyes. She crossed her arms over her heart and allowed her spirit to rise out of her body, traveling across the sea to the boat like a soaring bird. "How beautiful they are," she thought as she moved toward them. She remembered seeing the men from this perspective in her dream. How grand they looked, so vulnerable against the backdrop of the churning sea, yet so powerful in their faith.

"Makani," she said to her husband, sending thoughts of love to him. He looked up at her. She felt the warmth of his love. She felt Nui watching and sending love as well. The elder had sensed Kalah moving near them. And then, a magnificent bolt of light shot through the sky, connecting the eternal and the timeless to this sacred scene unfolding on the planet. They all saw it. Time folded in on itself completely and a mighty presence pulsed through, charging the atmosphere with higher and higher levels of Great Spirit's love. Kalah had always known of Great Spirit's deep passion for the earth and its inhabitants, but nothing could have prepared her for the actual feel of it. She thought she would melt in the joy. She heard a voice, deeply feminine. "Reunion is sweet," the voice said.

She heard another voice, deeply masculine. "It is the only reason for the game of parting." Kalah looked at her husband, who now radiated a divine light. His powerful eyes locked with hers. The hands of Great Father touched him and his spirit was lifted up from his body. His soul embraced the soul of his wife. As this occurred, another explosion of light filled the sky, a light so dazzling that Kai and Hannah closed their eyes and bowed their heads as they stood on the cliffs. They felt themselves bathed in a vibrating energy that hummed up and down their spines, balancing their bodies, their minds and their spirits. They knew that they were forever changed. They basked in the rapture. It was a precious, glorious moment in which they felt the Oneness of all things. And it was a powerfully catalytic moment for the planet. A wave of purification and renewal was cleansing old wounds in all of the beings of the air, land and sea. The dolphins and whales paused in their swimming, recording the moment in the deepest parts of their brains. The birds felt cosmic winds lifting them higher.

Then, ever so gently, the portal was closed. Their sense of having individual personalities was returned to them. The voyagers were back solidly in their own time. Kalah's spirit re-entered her body and she spread her arms open like wings. The three of them watched the sea a while longer. Then the vision faded from view. It was a moment that each of them would carry in their hearts until they crossed over to the next place and merged again with the cosmos. The feelings of Oneness would settle into their cellular memory and dance in the energy surrounding them so that others would feel it, too, and perhaps be awakened to their original state. For several minutes none of them spoke or moved from the place. When it was time to go, Kai gently handed the lamp to Kalah and they walked back to the house. Kalah went to her room to pray. Mama Hanu's face appeared to her, beaming with happiness.

Then Hannah's face flashed through her mind's eye. She looked at the lamp on the table and knew what to do next. She stepped into the living room where the couple was quietly talking.

"Hannah, would you mind coming into my room for a moment?"

"Not at all. All you all right?" She stood up. Kalah nodded. They walked into the softly lit room and sat on the edge of the bed. Kalah reached over and picked up the lamp.

"It always burns so brightly," she said, gazing at the flame. "It never needs renewal." Hannah nodded, her eyes moist.

"It is fed by its parent, the great light that is our Source," Hannah said.

Kalah studied the older woman's face. She loved her eyes. They were green with flecks of yellow like a green turtle's shell. Then Hannah spoke. Kalah wondered if she could sense what was coming next.

"You know, Kai prepared himself for many years before you arrived. His own mentor, a great kahuna, told him that you would come. Kai's spirit traveled into the future one day and he saw your arrival. He knew just how it would be. He saw with the eyes of his spirit that you would bring this sacred lamp. He prayed for many months that he would be worthy to hold the lamp. If it had been very hot to the touch, he said, he would know that he was not yet ready. That is what he told me. That is how the lamp is protected from those who are not ready." She paused. "Is that what you know to be true?"

"Nothing like that was said to me," Kalah answered. "It never occurred to me that this lamp needed protection from anyone. Perhaps it does. Perhaps it does not. But I know for certain that you are very wise. It is no surprise that you were meant for Kai. I am so glad you are a part of this. You are such a comfort to me, Hannah. I feel like your daughter." Hannah reached out and put a hand on Kalah's shoulder.

"In my heart, you are."

"Kai is so lucky to have you for a wife."

"Kai says he was drawn to me because I am so grounded. Every sky-walker needs an anchor. That is the lesson he learned from his father and grandfather."

Kalah nodded. "Makani said something similar. That he is my anchor."

"Makani is a beautiful name. In this time it means the wind. What does it mean in your time?"

"In my time it also means the wind. An interesting name for an anchor, wouldn't you say?"

"Maybe it makes perfect sense," Hannah said. "How reassuring it must be, when the wind is the only thing under your feet, sky-walker!"

"Why yes, that does make perfect sense. Now I understand!" They laughed.

"And what does the name Kalah mean in your time?"

"It means several things. I was called bride, in honor of the marriage of the sacred feminine and sacred masculine. But as I am sure you already know, when the word is spoken it can be a call for release and forgiveness." Hannah nodded, looking toward the outer room where her husband sat.

"I think it is very telling that the same word, when spoken, means both bride and forgiveness," Hannah said. She grinned mischievously, but did not say more out loud. Kalah heard her thoughts. She understood that Kai had sometimes been a great challenge to her patience. She put her hand over her mouth, stifling a laugh. They sat quietly, gazing at the flame. Then she did what felt right.

"Here," Kalah said, offering her the lamp. "It is now your turn to hold it." A smile appeared. Then it drifted away from the older woman's face. Kalah saw her hesitation and sensed that fearful thoughts were holding her back.

"I haven't prepared myself," she said. "What if I'm not ready? What if it burns my hands? I'll be embarrassed." She shook her head a little. Feelings of unworthiness crept in. Kalah could see them move in as a cloud across her face.

"I think, Hannah, that you have been preparing for this moment your whole life. I think that your whole life has been a prayer. Here. Please take it. Please trust me."

Kalah again offered her the lamp. Its flame flickered and danced. "See? The lamp wants you to hold it." Hannah reached out and accepted it. The lamp settled easily into her palms.

"I will go sit with Kai while you sit with the lamp," Kalah said, slipping out. She found him in his chair, his head back and his eyes closed. A book rested on his lap. For a moment his body did not move. Kalah recognized that his spirit was traveling. She sat very quietly, her eyes closed, too. When she heard a stir, she opened her eyes. She saw him looking at her.

"I am so deeply honored by all this," he said.

She nodded. "So am I."

"You know, there was a time when my male ego would have balked," he said, nodding to the room where his wife sat. "I thought that I must prepare for years to hold the lamp. And perhaps in my case, that was necessary." Kalah realized that he had heard her conversation with Hannah, perhaps even witnessed the entire scene with his spirit. If so, clearly it was meant to be. His face was soft. Lines of age were disappearing.

"How perfect that she has prepared for this simply by being herself," he said. They heard Hannah humming. She was singing a lullaby. After several minutes she came back into the room glowing with satisfaction.

"It's your turn! The lamp calls you," she added playfully. She beamed at Kalah, who smiled back, marveling at the elder woman's great spiritual light. Kai stood up straight and walked toward the room reverently, his hands folded in front of him as if summoned by a great ruler. And as he approached the black bowl, the flame stretched up and danced. He sat on the edge of the bed, watching for a while. It hummed to him and in his soul he knew the melody. Softly he hummed along and when he did, the light grew brighter. He felt a vibration building in his heart. Another doorway to his soul was blowing open. With a rush, the winds of change came toward him. He listened. They spoke to him of healing and renewal. They spoke to him of shedding old ways, old skins, and of opening his heart even wider to more travelers who would cross his path. He listened for a long time and wept. Finally, he spoke to the lamp.

"Such a long way you've come," he said, wiping the tears from his face. "Such a long way you've come to help our tired world. Thank you. *Mahalo.*"

CHAPTER TWENTY-ONE

Winds of Change

Jolted awake from a dark dream, Sarah sat up and felt trapped. She grabbed her coat and went outside, but she couldn't shake the feeling. The night sky looked like a heavy canopy. Trying to free herself from a dream, she had the eerie feeling that the darkness had been thrown between the earth and heaven by a jealous demon trying to block God's light. Shivering, she found herself climbing the spiral staircase to the rooftop deck. There she looked up and declared to God with her heart and her thoughts that she wanted a miracle for her uncle. If God existed behind the canopy, as her weary mind now suspected, she hoped He could hear her. Then she remembered Porter's letter and her conversation with Minnie. Did she really want to wish Uncle David away from peace in heaven? Her mind jammed in confusion, like a computer with too many commands coming in at once.

"I don't even know what to wish for," she whispered. "Maybe it's actually better on the other side. "I don't even know what to *wish* for," she repeated plaintively. "I don't think I know how to pray anymore, Papa."

"Papa."

The word had slipped out from deep in her memory. It was her childhood name for God, the one she had used before religion taught her to fear her Maker. A strong wind swept in from the sea and she braced herself against the chill, wrapping her coat more tightly around her. Sitting down on the lounge chair she sighed and decided to put the whole miracle conundrum on hold. Wanting peace, she imagined herself on the deck of a cruise ship. The ship was headed for Hawaii. Palm trees awaited her. She would run away from it all and never go back to New York. She would call from a pay phone once she landed on Maui. That would be her first stop. She would explain to whoever was interested that she couldn't come back. She just couldn't. She would promise to send a forwarding address, once she actually got one. Until then, she would be on the move. She smiled, stretching her legs. That would be wonderful, except for one thing. She loved New York City. In a week or so she would call and announce that she wouldn't be staying gone forever. Not anymore. She was rested now. She thought about Gabe and figured he would be relieved by this change of heart. She imagined his smiling face, savoring the dimple on his left cheek and the kindness of his eyes. She thought about how he smelled when he held her, like warm spice. Maybe she could convince him to run away with her, just for a little while. Neither of them took enough vacations. She shifted in the chair, amazed at how relaxed she was starting to feel.

The wind grew more forceful. "Don't blow me off the roof," she told the wind. "I want to travel, but can I do it my way, please?" The wind responded by blowing harder. "Silly me for thinking I'm in charge." She tried to push her hair away from her face, but it kept blowing back. A beach towel flew off the rail and was blown into the yard. She stood up and opened her arms, allowing the wind to move around her body. It pushed through the fabric of her coat and her pajamas, touching her skin. Then she felt a warmth building on the top of her head. It shot down her spine, sending a jolt of pleasurable heat throughout her body. It was a familiar feeling. She leaned back and slid into the chair. Staring straight ahead, she saw two feminine hands holding a black bowl with the dancing rainbow light. Her eyelids grew heavy and her mind went into a deep sleep. Her spirit stepped out of her body.

"Kalah, you're back."

"I have a story to tell you. Come with me." Sarah saw that she was in a very different place.

"Am I awake?" she asked.

"Awake enough, my sister. Come."

They walked along a wooded path to the torch-lit place where Sarah had last found the circle of women. There were many women there, their hands moving as they quietly sewed. Her eyes were drawn to two figures standing away from the group under a large tree with roots above the ground. She saw Mama Hanu sprinkling dried herbs over a small fire.

"My beloved teacher," Kalah said. Sarah bowed to this woman. Then with joy she called out to Twylah, who was putting more wood by the fire.

"Why do I get the feeling that we've all met here before?" Sarah scanned the scene as she asked the question.

"We have," Twylah said.

"Wow. I know I must be asleep but this doesn't feel like a dream."

"It's not," her aunt replied, smiling. Sarah hesitated. It wasn't like her aunt to be so brief with her replies.

"Is that really you, Aunt Twylah?" She was starting to have doubts.

"Relax. It's me, honey, but I'm just so darned flabbergasted by what's about to happen that I guess the cat has my tongue, that's all." That was more like it. Sarah nodded. "Okay, it's you all right. Why don't we remember all of this when we're going about our day? It seems kind of important. You'd think I would remember." Her aunt nodded sympathetically. "It's too threatening. I haven't mastered remembering either. Mama Hanu has explained that

I can't help you remember until I remember, so now I'm very motivated." Kalah moved next to Sarah and put an arm around her.

"After tonight, you will help each other more and worry less," she said. "I promise." Mama Hanu was finished preparing the sacred fire. She wiped her hands and walked over to Sarah.

"Kalah is correct. Things will change after this night," she said. Her voice was reassuring. "As your teacher, Twylah will help you remember and understand. Now please sit down. I think you know where to sit." They had been standing in a circle with a cross dividing it into four quadrants. Each woman sat on a point of the cross, representing the four directions. Sarah intuitively knew the meaning of each.

Kalah sat on the point representing north, the direction of air and spiritual forces. Sarah was sitting on the south point, marking new births. Twylah represented the east, the place of wisdom and sacred fire. Mama Hanu was at the point of the west symbolizing the watery realm of the turtles and of the collective mind. Kalah looked at Sarah. "Mama Hanu received this story from the heavens and she shared it with me in preparation for our meeting." She brought Sarah's hand to her mouth and softly kissed it before releasing and folding her hands in prayer.

"Listen and hear with your heart," Kalah said. "This is the story of the first lamp, a gift of eternal love from Great Father to Great Mother and for all of their offspring to come. You are my twin flame, Sarah. That is why the story goes next to you and from you to the others of your time.

"We're twins?" As she spoke, light filled the spaces between them. Sarah blinked. She now appeared to be sitting on a cloud above the planet with Kalah next to her. They dangled their legs like angels. Kalah pointed to a great sea turtle swimming through the starry sky with the rainbow lamp on her back. They could see this being moving along in the starry sky while Sarah was given the story of the first lamp.

"I knew it," Sarah said when the parable of the first lamp had been told. "We haven't been given all the right stories. Jesus came to show us the way, but we've still gotten ourselves all confused. We've been tricked by ego. God is not a jealous God. He or She is pure love, pure generosity. Great Mother and Great Father reflect that truth. So should we. I feel like I've been asleep for a very long time."

"But now you are waking up," Kalah said gently. "Your world needs everyone to wake up. There is so much fear but it will be dispelled by the light of first stories such as this one. That's why it was given to you." Sarah felt herself being pulled back to the heaviness of her earthbound existence. She wanted to grab the cloud with her fingers and hold on. Even in this realm, she was fully herself, wondering how long she could stall.

"Kalah, wait. The next time we talk I have questions for you. Questions about red turtles and coconuts and the man who wears the necklace with the totems. I saw him. I left my body and traveled and saw him talking to you. I know that he is very important. And there is someone I think you should meet, Kalah. He is very important, too. Wait. Don't go. Don't leave me yet."

She felt the chair on the deck pressing against her back. Still, she fought to keep her link with Kalah. "He is my godfather! His name is Porter." To Sarah's surprise, Kalah replied before parting.

"Yes, I have heard of Porter. And Kai is the man you saw. He says that your Porter is a great kahuna. He is meant to help heal the planet. But he does not know it yet." With that, Kalah was gone and Sarah was back in her world under a canopy of black night that no longer looked heavy. Now it was just a thin veil.

Sarah sat up, pondering what Kalah had just said.

"Porter is a kahuna?" She burst out laughing.

CHAPTER TWENTY-TWO

Knowings

Sarah tried to get a hold of herself but the laughter kept fighting back. She put her hand over her mouth hoping to stifle the sound. It wasn't working. She felt like she was wrestling a drunken alligator. And the alligator was winning. She tried to steady herself by watching the brilliant sunrise. But waves of joy and surprise kept bubbling up and forcing their way out.

Inside the house, Uncle David rolled over in bed, awakening to the sound of helpless, nearly hysterical laughter. He thought he recognized the laughter as Sarah's. He heard quick footsteps, more half-stifled laughter and the sound of the door opening. Yes, Sarah was laughing. And at day break she was coming down from the roof. He turned to look at his wife, who appeared to be sleeping.

"I'm awake. I heard it too," she said softly. She opened her eyes and looked at him, a hand reaching over to caress his face. She did not yet remember tending the fire with Mama Hanu, but visions of a great flame danced in her early morning thoughts. And images of Sarah filled her mind.

"Happy laughter," she said. "What a great way to wake up."

David moved closer to her, wincing a little. He let the pain subside and wrapped an arm around her, kissing her forehead. "I would like to announce that this gathering is already a success," he said. Twylah studied his face, her eyes drinking in every nuance. Tears were forming in her eyes and she realized that for many days she had needed to cry.

"It's okay. Go ahead and cry," he said.

She shook her head. "I don't want to cry. I know better. When you leave me you will be in a better place than this."

"Some part of you does want to cry and will cry," he said, gently, wrapping her in his arms. "But let me tell you something. You're not getting rid of me. You of all people should know that I'm not really going away."

"I know," she said. "Somehow I know that more than ever. But this, this aspect of you I will miss." She squeezed him, wanting to melt into his body. She waited for the pain within her chest to subside. "This I will miss when you go to the other side," she said, gasping for breath as the words were released. Then the tears came and he held her.

"I know. I know," he whispered gently. "Me, too." They held each other for a while. Sounds began to fill the house. Their family was waking up.

"Breakfast," he said. "That's going to be a hungry crowd.

"Marianne is cooking this morning and James said he'll clean up," Twylah said. "You know my sister loves that kitchen. She'll be happy as a clam, particularly with her husband assigned to the dishes."

"All right, then I will tell you about my dream," David said, rolling over on his back. "It's kind of long, actually. You were in it. So was Sarah."

Twylah listened, amazed at the detail. She could not yet remember details of her night travel, but sensed that something important wanted to be remembered. In David's dream, Sarah had taken them to an island in the South Pacific. They met an older couple with a young foster child, a little girl with long black hair. The little girl did a hula dance for them. She called it "Sacred Turtle Hula." It was very intricate and very beautiful, showing how mother turtles made nests for their eggs. She told them they were good to protect the turtles around their beach home. She told David that there was a special turtle with a gift on her back. They should wait for this turtle. When they sensed it nearby, they would know that everything was going to be fine.

"It really will be fine," the little girl said. "In fact, everything is already perfect. David, you are whole." Then she grew up, right before their eyes. She was beautiful, with long hair like Sarah's. The two women walked away, looking from the back like twin sisters.

"You and I watched the two walk down a path into the jungle. They stepped into a hut," David said. "Then Porter stuck his head out of this hut. Somehow, we were not surprised to see him. The older man who was the girl's foster father suddenly appeared and took something from around his neck. He threw it toward the hut. Porter laughed and reached out a hand to catch it. He said, 'Got it!' Then he went inside.

"That's when I heard Sarah laughing," David explained. "I woke up. There was a good feeling in the dream. While I was there, it all made perfect sense. So what do you make of it?" Twylah was quiet. He studied her face. She was deep in thought, probably getting one of her *knowings,* he thought. Some angel, somewhere, was telling her something.

"What a gift, this dream of yours," she said, softly. "It's all true."

"What's all true?" he asked.

"Everything."

"We're going to Hawaii?"

"I don't mean in the literal sense," she said. "Perhaps we'll go to Hawaii someday, perhaps not. I'd say that Hawaii just came to you. Or rather, the spirit of Hawaii."

"I don't understand."

"I can't say that I completely understand, either," she said, searching the depths of her mind. "But that's what I hear from the other side. The girl spoke of a reality that is truer than this. And that girl is a real person, by the way. But I don't think she's really a child. She came through that way in the dream because of her innocence. She is in some way the true spirit of Hawaii, the spirit of Aloha. And she has a connection to Sarah. You should share this with Sarah." Twylah turned to him. "And I really, really like the part where the little girl says that things will be fine."

"I have a secret for you," he said. "Somehow I got ahead of you on this one. I already knew that."

She smiled. "I'm so glad."

They heard the back door opening and closing several times. People were coming and going. And Sarah was laughing again.

"Matthew, your flippers are awesome!" she said. "Ooops. I need to be quiet. Uncle David and Aunt Twylah are still sleeping." David rolled out of bed, opening the window. In this moment, he could move without pain.

"Good morning! We're awake," he called out. "Laugh away, dear lady."

He spotted his grandson, Matthew, with big webbed feet supporting long, skinny legs. His face was all but hidden by an adult-sized diving mask. He was dressed in the green bodysuit he had been given for his birthday.

"Good heavens, are we being invaded?" David asked.

A muffled voice came out from behind the mask. "Take me to your leader."

"That would be your grandmother. Come here, dear, you have to see this. Matt has morphed into an alien." Twylah looked out at the scene. Sarah was photographing Matthew as he walked in circles with big, floppy feet. He put his hands on his hips, mugging for the camera. Then he jumped in the pool. Uncle David put on his bathrobe and stepped outside, feeling the newness of the morning. Sarah kissed him on the cheek.

"I have an interesting dream to share with you," he said. "Let's take a walk on the beach later on."

"I'm in." Sarah sat and put her feet in the pool. With that, the circle of women came into her awareness. They were busy at work now, sewing a great quilt that sparkled on the table. She saw herself picking up a piece of red cloth and putting it on a deep blue circle.

"Red turtle at the center," she said. "The turtle is the heart of the sea." The other women nodded, smiling. She felt a hand on her shoulder and looked up. Kalah was there.

"Your mind can no longer keep secrets from you," Kalah said. "You are waking up. And you will remember everything. Trust this and make it true."

CHAPTER TWENTY-THREE

Trust Issues

Two children hovered over a plate of deviled eggs, a look of skepticism on their faces.

"Dad, what's this black stuff?" 7-year-old Annie asked.

"That's pepper."

"But the pieces are so big. It looks more like dirt."

"Nope. I was fresh out of dirt. I had to use pepper."

"You're silly, Dad."

"I'm silly? I'm not the one who thinks there is dirt on the eggs."

"Can we have some?"

"Sure."

Annie and her 5-year-old brother, Michael, reached up and grabbed an egg with each hand. They ran out to the back porch. Sarah glanced up, smiling at her niece and nephew. Her brother wiped off his hands and began massaging Sarah's neck and shoulders. She had left the pool to sit near him at the kitchen table. She was writing feverishly in her journal about sitting on a cloud with Kalah.

"Are you recording the brilliant conversation I just had with my kids?" John asked.

"I should. That's one I'd like to remember," she said, smiling.

"How are you doing with all this?" John asked, sitting down. "The last time we were all together Collin was with us."

"Better than I expected. But it's strange at times. I keep expecting him to walk around the corner. And that heightens my awareness about why we are here. I really miss him."

"I miss him, too," her brother replied. Their father walked in the house. He and Uncle David had been going through the fishing gear. He washed his hands at the sink, which was filling up with dishes again.

"Breakfast was two hours ago and here I am sniffing around for more food," he admitted. "I heard a rumor that you put dirt in the eggs, John. May I try one?"

"Help yourself," came the reply. "Annie's got a great imagination. But I wish she wouldn't slander my cooking. It makes me feel so vulnerable." He winked playfully at his sister.

"Are they just not used to seeing you in the kitchen, son? I'm sensing trust issues."

"Trust issues?" Sarah asked, looking up from her journal. "Now you're starting to sound like me, Dad."

"As a matter of fact I think I did get that from you. And you think I don't pay attention when you talk."

"Well I stand corrected," she said. "I must have trust issues."

"May I?" her father asked, reaching for more eggs. "Seriously. These are great."

"It's Karen's recipe," John said. "I used to eat them faster than she could make them. So she taught me how to make them myself. You can take the whole plate outside, Dad. I want to keep the troops happy until lunch time." Sarah saw her father pause to study the two of them.

"I like seeing you kids together. We need to get together more often. And I'll tell your wife I love the recipe." He took the eggs and walked out. Her brother stood up to tackle the dishes. She stood up and joined him at the sink.

"Just like old times," she said. "Let me wash. You dry. Did Karen tell you that we're taking charge of the Thanksgiving meal tomorrow? We thought we'd give everyone else a break."

"No," he said, "but that sounds like a winner. I'm about ready to throw in my apron."

"We're getting up at 5 a.m. to get things started. There's this huge turkey in the refrigerator down in the garage. Have you seen it?"

He nodded. "Yes. I found it when I was looking for beer. Biggest bird I've seen."

"Yeah, well that's where you come in. We'll need assistance with the heavy lifting. And Karen's setting the alarm clock, so you'll be awake anyway."

"Thanks!" He flicked her with the dishtowel. They finished and walked out on the porch. Twylah had stolen a quiet moment under the shady part of the porch. She was sitting in her rocking chair watching the commotion.

"May I join you?" Sarah asked.

Aunt Twylah patted the chair next to her. "Please do," she said. "Iced tea?" She poured from a pitcher on a small table.

"Thanks."

Sarah sipped the tea and surveyed the amazing scene. Light was everywhere, dancing off wet skin, shimmering in the air around them. She saw a soft golden light over her uncle, who was walking out to the beach with her father. She looked more closely at her father. Soft hues of blue and yellow were coming off his shoulders. There was a smoky white glow around his head. She felt an overwhelming urge to confide these things.

"Aunt Twylah, I think I've inherited the family tendency," she said.

"Which one?"

"It's like this. I've been seeing light. I see it around people, around things, even animals. Right now, I can see light dancing around everyone out there." Sarah looked at her aunt. "I see it pouring off your face. I see light streaming out of your eyes. It's very real. At this point, nobody could convince me that it's my imagination. Although when it first started I was trying to do that to myself. Maybe I've always seen it and was just blocking it out to fit in. Kids start doing that when they're old enough to read other people's reactions, right? They start denying what they can see."

Her aunt nodded. "You bet they do."

"Well, if I had it and lost it, guess what? It's back," Sarah said. "The light is back in the most persistent way. If I try to deny it, it gets around my denial. You know why? Because it's not really about me. I realize that, now. It's about something much bigger than me. It's not going to be stopped anymore. That's how it feels to me. Determined." She searched her aunt's face.

"Don't fall into that trap, now," her aunt said gently. "Don't search my face for a reaction. It's not about me, either. Whether I understand or not, whether I believe or not, it doesn't matter. You have to get used to holding firm in your beliefs. Please continue."

"Right." Sarah said. "So here I am, thinking I had hit rock bottom in my life, and suddenly life seems to have more meaning than it did before. In some strange way I actually feel more alive than I ever have before. Now I look back and wonder if I was asleep the whole time. I'm more authentically me. Does that make sense? Oops. There I go again. Looking for validation. Very bad habit."

"It's okay. You can't stop that overnight. It's deeply engrained in all of us. And the fact that your first instinct was to dismiss it only speaks to how you were raised. How we all were raised. But the fact that you have persisted in staying open, that you have allowed your curiosity and your instincts to work for you, now that gives me hope. You need to give yourself a lot of credit for that. I'm sure it hasn't been easy."

"It wasn't easy at first," Sarah said. "But now it is. Something is changing and not just in my life. It's big. Can you feel it?"

Her aunt nodded. "Something is changing," she said. "For those of us who are sensitive, our radar is picking it up. I think it boils down to this. Light is simply our original state before we came into matter. We come from divine light and we'll return to it. You could say that it's our parent. So why do we get so darned shocked when our parent shows up to see how we're doing? When it shows up to help us through the dark times?

"We take some comfort in the concept of returning to the light when we die. If somebody said to you, 'In heaven, everyone is surrounded by this beautiful light,' you'd nod and accept that without too much trouble. But most us of can't handle the thought that God is always around us. Maybe we don't feel worthy. Maybe we've made a mess of things and we don't want God seeing us at our worst. I don't know. We read in scripture, we hear in our churches, that God knows our names before we were born, that we have an intimate relationship with Him before we come to this place. Does it make sense that we get here and suddenly we're cut off, stripped of all the gifts we had before we came? Does that really make sense?"

Sarah shook her head. "It doesn't. But we're taught not to question the script that society hands us."

"That's exactly right," her aunt said. "It's a script that someone hands us as soon as we're old enough to read. I heard somewhere that if you talk to God it's called praying, and if God talks back it's called mental illness. I think that whole viewpoint is a form of cultural mental illness. Sometimes, in order to become sane again, you have to step apart from the crowd. I think that generations upon generations have been silenced with lies about a distant, angry God. Maybe that's the ultimate form of blasphemy, accusing God of being such a brutal parent. I'll be right back."

Twylah stood up and went inside. She came back with a worn Bible.

"This book is very precious to me," she said. "David gave it to me when we were first married. I still turn to it often, but there are things in it that make me wonder if something was lost in the translation. I have questions, but I have discovered a very simple solution."

"You have?"

"I talk to my Lord directly and ask for clarification," she said. "Our relationship is in the present. It's so simple and so natural that I'm probably a heretic in somebody's eyes. But that's not important. What's important is my very intimate and day-to-day relationship with my Creator."

Sarah was pensive. These were strong words, powerful words. They echoed what Porter had said. She had come to the right place. They were quiet for a while, their focus shifting to their loved ones who were now gathering to look at Uncle's David's catch. Sarah saw her father step back in admiration.

"I'm glad I'm here," Sarah told her aunt softly. "I'm sorry for the pain that this time brings, but a reunion was a great idea."

"Reunion," Twylah said. "I think that's what you and I have been talking about. That's what you're seeing Sarah, when you see those lights. If your senses are picking it up, if your heart is open to it, then you're in a more natural state than you were before. You are literally reuniting with a piece of yourself, the piece of you that has always been connected to God." Sarah turned in her chair and took her aunt's hand. They stayed that way for a while, holding hands and just being together. There was another question building inside of Sarah, the question of choice.

"Aunt Twylah, I need to ask your opinion about something else," she said, feeling a lump in her throat. "This might be the worst possible time to ask this question. But you know me well enough to know that this comes from the heart. Do you believe we have a choice about what happens to us when we get here? Are you familiar with the theory that as the offspring of God we are the creators of our own reality?"

"Yes, and in some way it's the only thing I can believe without losing my faith."

"Really? Boy, not me. When I read that recently, I just got pissed off. Big time. In fact, it triggered a brief melt-down." Twylah squeezed her hand and let go. She sighed deeply, looking back at her niece with compassion. "I can only imagine how that must have sounded to you," she said, shaking her head. "A woman chooses to lose her husband. Children choose to be hurt and abandoned and sick. What madness to even consider it, right?"

"And yet you believe it," Sarah said. "You actually take comfort in it."

"I don't think the part of us that we call our day-to-day personalities chooses those things," Twylah said. "But I think it makes perfect sense that our spirits, the eternal part of us, would find merit in these experiences, knowing that they are brief in the broad scheme of things. I don't think it is God's first choice for us, but for those of us who are not completely enlightened, it seems to be the way we've set things up."

"Then why don't we remember that we chose it? That would help so much."

"I don't know why we forget things, but I think that collectively we're starting to remember."

"I'm embarrassed," Sarah said.

"Why?"

"I threw a book across my apartment that was telling me the same thing that you are saying about choice. Somehow I can hear it now. It was a classic case of shooting the messenger, or in my case, throwing him in the air."

"Did it feel good to throw something?"

"It felt fabulous."

"Then it wasn't a total waste." They laughed. Sarah poured them both more tea. Sea breezes blew onto the porch, caressing their skin. She sighed. "But seriously. I'm still confused. "Wouldn't a loving parent stop a child from making bad choices? Are you saying that God would let us torture ourselves just to respect our free will?"

"No, I'm saying that God knows we are eternal beings who aren't really capable of dying. So if this is ultimately an illusion, then it's all a game to our very great spirits. It's not a silly game, mind you, but a big, important game, like the Olympics. They're called games, but they are serious stuff. Not for wimps. It's an arena for mastery."

"It has a nice ring to it," Sarah said. "I'm not really a hapless human. I'm a spiritual athlete. Or maybe life is like a super challenging university. Perhaps we've aced Easy Living 101 and we are now ready to sign up for a master's level course called "Keeping the Faith No Matter What."

"Maybe you even begged and pleaded to take that course, Sarah."

"Actually, I think I flunked it."

"I don't think so. You're asking very soulful questions, dear. You don't sound like a flunky to me."

"Thanks."

"You're welcome. This helps me, too. You have no idea how much. Just when I start to sink, something beautiful happens to lift me up again. Has your uncle told you about his dream yet?"

"No, we have a date for a walk on the beach. He said he has something wonderful to share with me."

"He does." Twylah was beaming now. It warmed Sarah's heart to see her looking so peaceful. Her aunt put her glass down and moved her chair to face Sarah.

"Next topic. Do you want to talk about what happened last night?

CHAPTER TWENTY-FOUR

And the Walls Fall Down

Sarah swallowed hard. "It was real, then."

"Yes, it was."

"I wasn't going to bring it up unless you did."

"I was waiting for you."

"I was stalling," Sarah said.

"I guess I was, too."

"Well, that was a nice fire you had going, Aunt Twylah. Not bad for a Florida girl who doesn't get much practice."

"Thanks. I had some serious help." They burst out laughing. They were quiet for a time. Sarah suddenly knew what she was supposed to do.

"I want to share the story tonight," she said, "the story that Kalah told me. Did you hear it? It seemed like she took me far away. But I could also feel you close by."

Twylah nodded. "I heard the whole thing. It heals me more than you know."

"And exactly why do you think we've been contacted by ancient Hawaii?" Sarah asked. The elder woman closed her eyes and stayed that way for a while. She looked as if she might have fallen asleep, but Sarah knew otherwise. She leaned back and tried to join her aunt's reverie, feeling once again that the universe was about to take things up a notch. Twylah opened her eyes.

"What I'm hearing is that walls are coming down. The walls of separation between us, or rather our *beliefs* about walls of separation are crumbling away. Illusions of time and space are melting, allowing two sisters with a shared purpose to share a beautiful story about eternal love. I don't think I really have to tell you that this is a very important time." Sarah nodded, smiling broadly and looking out at the sea.

"Your uncle was busy last night, too, although not in the way that we were. His spirit didn't leave his body, but he had an important dream. My guides have told me it was a vision dream, which means its essence was true. Much of it was highly symbolic, the way dreams are. But the people in it were real. In the dream you led us to Hawaii. We met people there who were very dear, very kind. A girl spoke of turtles, of a very special turtle in particular that would bring us some form of reassurance. According to your uncle's description, you seemed right at home in Hawaii. And your godfather was there."

"Porter? Porter was in Hawaii? Look at my arms. I have chills."

"Yes. It was a beautiful dream. David remembered it in great detail," Twylah said. "Listening to him, I was transported. Somehow the spirit of Aloha is reaching out to us. You know, Lemuria was in that area. It is called Mu by some. Human beings living there many thousands of years ago had not lowered their vibration, or experienced the Biblical Fall, to the extent that we now live with it. I believe the descent was a gradual process. Anyway, they were far less dense in body and mind, much closer to the original design for humanity. To be touched by the spirit of Hawaii is to be touched by the spirit of Lemuria. This is what I have been told. In my heart, I know it is true."

"I've heard about Lemuria," Sarah said. "Isn't it a place that sank to the bottom of the sea, just like Atlantis?"

"It had the same ending that took Atlantis, but in some ways it was a very different place," Twylah said. "Lemurians were said to be a much gentler people, more in tune with their intuition and their hearts. You could say it was a more feminine culture. According to the stories, Atlantis was a culture that revered the intellect over the wisdom of the heart. In other words, it was more masculine. They were both highly advanced civilizations. Legends say that Lemuria got into trouble by allowing too much influence from Atlantis. Maybe force was involved, one culture predictably imposing its beliefs on another as collective ego gained power. Or maybe Lemuria just lost its way and forgot its own strength. It seems like the same story plays itself out over and over again.

"I will tell you that reading about the ancient Polynesians is a great love of mine," her aunt continued. "In some way I feel that I know the place first-hand. They had a better understanding of their own spiritual power, including the power of the spoken word. They were masters of the story, masters of song. They were passionate healers, amazing mariners and gifted farmers. Your Uncle David is deeply fascinated by their extraordinary memories which they used to navigate the seas. They sailed the oceans with a level of precision that surpasses our understanding. Can you imagine going out into the Pacific Ocean, and returning to your tiny island like you were just pulling the car into a garage? Modern man has lost that type of intelligence and is dependent on navigational tools that the ancients didn't need. It seems like the more natural gifts we lose touch with, the more we have to invent things to replace them.

"They also used those incredible memories to store the wisdom of their culture within their own beings. The kahunas of story were living libraries. And they chose their words carefully because of the great influence they carried in shaping events around them. We could learn a lot from them. Our politicians could learn a lot from them. On second thought, maybe some of them already know too much."

The phone rang.

"I'll get it," Sarah said. She needed to jump up and move around. A warm heat was surging down her spine. She grabbed the phone and cleared her throat.

"Gordon residence."

"Sarah, it's you! Perfect!"

"Porter?"

"I was going to call on Thanksgiving Day, but I was getting a nudge to call you now. Is my timing good? Is everyone all right?"

"Your timing is impeccable! Aunt Twylah and I have been talking about light and love and Hawaii. And your name came up."

"I'm smiling. I can't wait to hear more about it."

"Our gathering is going really well, Porter. And things are getting more mysterious. I mean that in the best possible way. I have so much to tell you."

"When you're ready to share, I'll be all ears. But I'll be brief for now. I was reading something, and I thought of you. Kate gave me a book of poems. There's one by Rumi."

"I love Rumi!"

"Somehow I guessed that. Here's an excerpt that stopped me in my tracks. When I read it, a vision of you flashed in my mind, a vision of you watching the sunrise. I won't read the whole thing. I'm buying you the book for Christmas. Here is a little something for now. It's going to blow your mind. It says:

'Who gets up early to discover the moment that light begins? Who lets a bucket down and brings up a flowing prophet? Or like Moses goes for fire and finds what burns inside the sunrise? Jesus slips into a house to escape enemies and opens a door to the other world. Solomon cuts open a fish, and there's a gold ring. Omar storms in to kill the prophet and leaves with blessings. But don't be satisfied with stories, how things have gone with others. Unfold your own myth, without complicated explanation.'

"It goes on. I'll let you discover the rest for yourself. I thought of you when I read it."

"Porter, that's more astonishing than you know. Thank you."

"You are welcome, my dear lady." Twylah walked in.

"It's Porter," Sarah said. "Hey, Porter, I'm going to pass the phone around now. Love you. I'll look forward to reading more of that book."

"Okay," he said. "Big hug." Her aunt took the phone, smiling. Porter had a special place in her heart. Sometimes she called him Merlin.

"Sarah, your father is coming back toward the house," she called. "Why don't you give him a shout so he'll hurry it up and we don't cost Porter an arm and a leg?" Sarah hurried outside, her heart dancing to the words of Rumi.

"Dad! Porter's on the phone!" He nodded and stepped up his stride. Behind him Uncle David walked at a slower pace, surrounded by children who wanted to see the colorful fish he was bringing in. She noticed that David held the fish tenderly. She walked down the steps to join them.

"When we eat the fish, the fish becomes a part of us," he was explaining to the children. "So we have to say 'thank you' to the fish for filling our bellies." Sarah smiled. She knew that her uncle was no ordinary fisherman, but she had never heard him speak exactly that way before. She wondered if they would find gold inside the fish. Stranger things had happened. That evening, after a big dinner that included the fish, Sarah gathered the family around for storytelling time. She was going to talk about local turtles first, then share the story of the lamp.

"This needs to be a tradition," her brother said. "It feels like something big is in the air." Sarah nodded excitedly.

"Okay," she said. "Here's how the first story begins. This one will get us ready for the big story at the end. Are you ready?" Heads nodded around her. She looked at her uncle and smiled. Their walk together before dinner had been a continuation of the beautiful and mysterious. He had shared his dream with great enthusiasm and was astounded by the shared experience of his wife and his niece. He smiled at her now, his eyes happy.

"Well," she said. "To get us started, I want to tell you about some very special beings that live on our planet. Their ancestors lived during the time of the dinosaurs. They come from the deep in the dark of night with only one purpose in mind. They are big and they are quiet. Many people don't even know that they are out there. But they can come very close to the house. Do you know what they are?"

"Mommy turtles!" Annie shouted out.

"Very good! And they are looking for a safe place to lay their eggs. We have to help them." The turtle saga continued. The children were glued to their seats until the final moment, when Sarah described the babies pushing their way with brand new flippers to the coolness of the sea.

"Follow the moonlight!" Michael called out. "Don't get confused and come to our house!"

"Very good instructions," Sarah said, nodding. She took a long sip of water. "Now," she said, "does anybody need a break before the next story? I have one more and it is very special." Heads shook.

"We want more stories!" Michael said. He was curled up in his mother's lap.

"Good!"

She stood up, remembering how regal Kalah had looked when she announced the story of the first lamp to her village. How long ago that holy vision in Central Park now seemed! She felt heat on the top of her head, as if a very charged energy was flowing inward. Turning slowly in a circle, she studied the shining faces around her. "This is a great story," she said. "It's about a game of hide-and-seek and it's also about true love." She looked at her aunt and winked. Twylah winked back. They both felt a sense of oneness with everyone in the room.

From her brother's place on the sofa, the candlelight seemed to brighten as his sister spoke. The whole room was getting lighter. Others noticed it, too. It registered deep in their minds. They were all waking up and releasing their fears. Twylah looked around, seeing rows of angels seated around her loved ones. And as Sarah told the story of the first lamp, her aunt saw the light around the angels growing brighter. Behind them she saw a great doorway, an opening to another dimension. And a great light shone through the doorway. She was in awe. Heaven, it seemed, was simply in the next room.

Sarah joyfully brought the story to its conclusion. She told about how the game was a great success and how the brilliance of Great Mother and Great Father was enhanced by eternal love. Pondering this, Twylah's ability to see and understand also was enhanced. The sacred turtle of this story was the turtle foretold by her husband's dream, the turtle bringing them divine comfort and reassurance. It was the messenger. The story reminded her that her husband would only be away for a while. When they were reunited their love for each other would burn even more brightly. They would see each other in a new way, as if they truly were meeting for the first time. Feeling overcome with love, she saw a hand reach out from the light in the doorway, a beautiful hand. In it was a bowl with a light flickering inside. The light glowed with all the colors of the rainbow.

Sitting next to her, David saw the same vision. He was at peace. As his niece told the story of the cosmic turtle gliding easily through space, he had seen a vision of sea turtles swimming gracefully in the ocean. As he would later tell Sarah, he realized that human beings were a lot like sea turtles. On land, sea turtles were burdened by the heaviness of their shells. They moved slowly and with great effort. As his own body grew sicker, he would understand more about how those mother turtles felt on their way to and from their sandy nests. But once in the water, that was a different story. They were graceful and fast, moving with elegant ease. He understood how it would feel to shed his heavy body and swim in the vast blue sea of God's love. His heart opened and love poured inside. Soon, his heart would break open and he would be free.

CHAPTER TWENTY-FIVE

The Word

The plane ascended in an elegant line. Sitting in a window seat over the left wing, Sarah held an envelope. Uncle David had given a card to each member of the family as they filed out. She opened the card and saw a dolphin looking back at her. It was swimming in a light green sea, rays of sunlight illuminating the water around it. Behind the dolphin, huge pillars stood. They hinted of a sunken city. She recognized the style. Aunt Twylah had painted it. The dolphin looked completely real, as if it had simply paused from its exploring when the card was pulled out. In its mouth was a golden ring, a single key dangling from it. She turned over the card. Her aunt's name was printed on the back, along with the title of the artwork, "Key to the Kingdom."

She looked back at the front, savoring the images. Her eyes scanned the details, searching for clues. Twylah's art always had layers of meaning. She saw that the pillars were not in ruins. They stood free from their original structure, but they were in perfect condition. Etched on the pillars was an intriguing pattern. The markings looked like a flowing ladder curving around on itself. It reminded her of DNA strands. The lightness of the water indicated that the dolphin was not too far from the surface.

It appeared to her that the sunken city was moving toward the surface, as if the ocean floor were pushing it back up. She thought of Lemuria. An image of Kalah flashed in her mind's eye. She was swimming, heading for the sunken city. Her heart told her that Kalah had roots there. Her palms tingled. The plane bumped a little, making it hard to focus. She closed the card and waited for the turbulence to subside. Then she opened it again. Her eyes landed first on the printed words her aunt had chosen to go with the artwork. The words said, *"Look Within. The Kingdom Awaits You."* Uncle David had started writing just below these words. She swallowed hard and began reading.

"It was a miracle that we could all be together, Sarah. One of my favorite things about this get-together was the sound of your laughter. Never let anyone silence it. To me, it's the sound of triumph over adversity. Another high point was, of course, your storytelling, which actually inspired me to write these notes. I started writing them on Thanksgiving evening, after that incredible meal. Your stories reminded me of the power of the word, how we can stir each other's souls and why we need to. As you spoke, I looked around. The kids weren't the only cherubs in the room. All of you looked like angels. Your aunt saw a truck-load of them! That's what she said. I guess you could say I'm seeing the light, too. You called it 'that determined light' on our walk along the beach. Do you remember? That really stuck with me. It's not going to give up on us and I'm glad. When I saw the light on everyone's faces, I had the same revelation that you shared with Twylah. She told me what you said and how you realize that it has always been there. I'm betting that each time you share your experiences others will share theirs, too. Now that's what I call a chain-reaction worth starting! Speaking for myself, the old fisherman, I consider the story of the first lamp a big catch. A really big catch. It's going to feed a lot of people. I tend to think in terms of fish and food. Your aunt put it another way and I have to share her thoughts on the matter. Twylah said God is wrapping his kids (that would be us) in a big blanket. She said the blanket is made of the threads of our individual mysteries and that they're all coming together to make something safe and warm for us. That's an exact quote. I wrote it down so I wouldn't get it all scrambled up and say that God was wrapping us in a big fish. You know me."

Sarah burst out laughing. She apologized to the woman next to her, who smiled warmly. Uncle David had crafted that line specifically to crack her up. It would please him no end to know that it worked. She shook her head and continued reading.

"This will not be the last time you hear from me, so stop your worrying. (Yes, I'm talking to you, Sarah.) As I close for now, I feel inspired to give you a challenge, because I know that you love them. Find a way to write about all of this. Find a way to share the message of the lamp. To me, what jumps out loud and clear is the message of unbroken love. Your aunt and I are eternally grateful for that. Keep sharing that story and find your own words to describe what is going on. We all have gifts. Mine is fishing. Twylah's is painting and speaking to angels. Your gift is putting things into the right words. Let your gift shine. Love, Uncle David."

Her eyes danced over the words. She read the letter two more times. He had written small, filling every inch of blank space inside the card. But his words were big. And she liked the challenge. He was telling her to think big, to walk through her life in a big way. And she would do it. She knew she would. Things were starting to make sense. The hard places in her heart were melting. She remembered how an editor had once reminded her, "The pen is mightier than the sword." She was more cynical then, burning out quickly on newspaper reporting and feeling deeply inadequate against a barrage of world mishaps. In her eyes she hadn't accomplished a single thing with her pen. But she had never given herself enough credit. At the time, she had responded bitterly, coming from a place of deep emotional and spiritual fatigue.

"Forget the pen," she had told her editor. "Just give me the sword." Within weeks she was turning in her letter of resignation. But she wasn't really giving up. Collin had taken a newspaper job in New York City. Two months after they arrived she enrolled in Columbia University's social work program. She was going to shift her approach. She was going to figure out why things went wrong in the world, exactly how people's lives broke down. She would find the point of dissolution and try to make things right again.

But in truth, the joke was on her and she was the one who would be healed. It was a gentle joke that the universe was sharing, a healing dose of irony.

Because what she discovered along this new career path was how things went *right,* how people kept their goodness against all odds. Would newspapers report on that? If they could be convinced that readers wanted it, they would. This she knew from first-hand experience.

One of her last contributions as a journalist in Atlanta was to chronicle three good deeds done by total strangers within a short period of time. She had been the recipient of all three. In the first instance, a young couple on their way to an anniversary dinner stopped in the pouring rain to help her change a flat tire. By the time they were finished, all three of them were soaked to the bone. The umbrellas had been useless. Sarah remembered how bad she felt when she saw that they were drenched. They were dressed to the hilt. When she asked about their original plans, they explained that it was their second anniversary and they were going to celebrate. The young man stopped Sarah's apologizing, shaking his head and insisting that they had no regrets.

"If my wife were standing in the dark in the middle of a pouring rain, I would pray to God that someone would stop to help her," he said. "When I saw you, I realized it could have been her." His wife joined in. "I saw you first," she said. "And when I said, 'Stop! We have to help,' he didn't hesitate. He pulled right over. I knew he would."

"We can go out to dinner anytime," she added. Sarah cried tears of gratitude all the way home. The next two good deeds came quickly after the first and were not so dramatic. But they made her feel like a million bucks. In the second instance, an elderly couple discovered her wallet in a parking lot. She had just gotten paid and it was bulging with cash. They found her business card and called her immediately, insisting on bringing the wallet to her. When they arrived, they seemed even happier than she was. They walked away holding hands. The third good deed was simple and sweet. As she pulled her car up to a tollbooth, the cashier refused her 50 cents.

"The man up ahead of you paid," she explained. "He said that he looked in his rear-view mirror and thought you looked tired. He wants you to have a good day." She was stunned. Somebody on this notoriously busy road had noticed that she looked tired? Catching up with him, she waved, hoping that he would look in his mirror again and see that she was transformed. He gave her a "thumbs up." As he veered off toward an exit a few miles later, she passed and saw his face. He was not somebody she knew, but when he smiled at her she felt a kinship to this fellow highway traveler.

She was two weeks away from moving to New York. But she couldn't ignore these good deeds. They were simple, beautiful and totally uncalled for. What was the world coming to? What would she do with her cynicism now? That is just how she started her piece in the newspaper. It was entitled, "Is It Just My Imagination or Are People Actually Nice?" Readers responded beyond her wildest dreams, beyond the editors' wildest dreams. For several days, stories of kindness filled the Letters to the Editor page. There were so many that half of a section was devoted to reporting on them. The most dramatic were expanded upon by one of the paper's best writers. He talked to the readers who had shared these experiences and reported on their feelings of gratitude. As far as she knew, the Saturday paper still provided a space for readers to share their stories of good deeds.

"What if every newspaper did that?" she wondered now, looking back at her uncle's words. "And what if CNN reported thoroughly and regularly on the greatness of the human spirit, the earth-shaking news that most people are good and brave and creative?" The earth would probably move, she told herself. All of that good news, even one solid day of it, would do more to change the world than a year's worth of reporting about greed and hatred and violence.

"Note to self," she told herself. "Contact CNN. It doesn't hurt to ask."

The power of the pen. The power of the human voice. Her uncle was right. She didn't need the sword. Sitting in the plane as it soared through the cloud kingdom, she saw her life from a new perspective. She realized that she had never abandoned her mission to help change the world. She had just gone back to school. She got her master's degree in social work. But her ultimate degree, her ultimate mastery, came from a place called Brooklyn. Her experiences there, and the people who flowed through her life, were her most remarkable teachers. That is why she stayed.

The flight home seemed to take no time at all. She was still holding the dolphin card when the passengers were told to return their trays to the upright position. An hour later, she was leaving the airport with Gabe.

"You look great," he said, kissing her before she got in the car. "You look like you're at peace."

"It was beyond description," she said. "Forgive me if I can't talk about it all at once. I'm still absorbing it. But the bottom line is that Uncle David got his wish. His family came together and everybody had a great time. How's that for a miracle?"

Gabe nodded. "Just thinking about your family gathering has changed my perspective on dying," he said. "I find myself trying to figure out how I can recommend this to people. It shouldn't be so hard to put into words, but there are all these taboos about planning ahead when it comes to death. What I'd like to say is, 'If you have to choose between the funeral and a family reunion prior to the funeral, choose the family reunion.' Funerals are for the living anyway, so why not include the person who is getting ready to leave? The person you're going to be missing so much."

"Talk about a paradigm shift," she said. "That's a big one."

"Yeah, really."

They were quiet for a while. It started to rain.

"Are you leaving town for Christmas?" she asked.

"Not this year," he said. "How about you?"

"No, we had our family holiday. Nothing could compare to that, so we'll just savor the memories."

"You should have seen that Thanksgiving turkey," she added. "John carried it up a steep flight of stairs from the garage while he was half asleep. Karen and I stood behind him, just in case he started to fall backwards. It was huge, but very moist, I must say. Very, very moist." Gabe cracked up. His laughter startled her a little.

"What?" she asked. "What'd I say?"

"I'm sorry," he said, trying to compose himself. "It's just your description. 'Huge but moist.' I can't explain it. It just sounds really funny to me."

"Huge but moist? Why is that funny?"

He shrugged, chuckling a little. "Maybe it's the moist part."

"Oh. I think somebody has a really dirty mind," she said. "Is that what could be going on here, Dr. Freud?" He tried to give her an innocent look, which melted into more laughter. Obviously he needed the release. Perhaps he needed another type of release, too. As the laughter died down and he repeated "huge, but moist" two more times, it occurred to him, too. The shrink in him was having a dawning of awareness. Oops. He had given himself away. Freud would have taken Gabe under his wing and said, "You see, son. I was right. Everything goes back to sex."

Sarah patted his leg affectionately.

"I've missed you. Can you spend the night?"

"Thought you'd never ask."

"You can suggest it, too, you know. It's not all about me asking you."

"I know," he said, searching her face. He parked the car in front of her building.

"An open space. That's got to be a good omen." She elbowed him.

"Ouch." He took off his seatbelt and turned to look at her. It was time for another paradigm shift.

"Are you ready to be hotly pursued into the bedroom?" he asked, raising his eyebrows to look suggestive.

"Thought you'd never ask," she answered, leaning over to kiss him. "I like that coming from you, Mr. Huge, but Moist."

"No *you're* huge, but moist," he said. Their noses were touching.

"Watch it, buddy," she said, kissing him again. "Or you won't get any turkey tonight." She wrapped her arms around him, melting into the sweetness of Gabe.

CHAPTER TWENTY-SIX

Talking to the Shark

Pablo was back in the hospital. His condition was worsening. He had been admitted for a round of antibiotics to fight an opportunistic infection that was attacking his lungs. He was very pale and coughing a lot. But he was calm when Sarah found him in his hospital room, drawing with the hand that wasn't taped to an IV needle.

"Hi," she said softly. "I'm sorry you are feeling sick. Did your grandmother tell you that I loved the dolphin? You were asleep when I called."

"She told me," he said. "I thought about you the whole time I drew it."

"That makes me feel great. What are you drawing now?"

"A shark," he said, not looking up. He was tracing the edges of the shark in black.

"A shark?" She felt uneasy.

"Yes, that's what I'm seeing."

"You're seeing a shark? Where?"

"In my head."

"What's the shark doing?"

Pablo was quiet for a while. He coughed a little. She handed him his cup and helped bend the tip of the straw. He drank his juice.

"More?"

"No thank you."

Her wheels were turning. She was glad he was expressing himself. Who wouldn't think of predators when they were being attacked from within?

"Let me know if you want to tell a story about the shark."

"Okay." His grandmother walked in, greeting Sarah warmly. She kissed her grandson on the forehead and noticed the drawing.

"Another dolphin? That one looks a little angry."

"He's a shark and he is angry," he said, looking up at her. "He's angry because he's not getting enough to eat. But he's not bad. He's just hungry."

"I see," his grandmother said, glancing at Sarah.

She felt tongue-tied. Her little messenger of light was dealing with something angry and hungry. She wanted to grab a crayon and draw a spear, putting it right through the shark's heart. But this was about Pablo's feelings. And he didn't seem angry or afraid.

"I have an idea," Sarah said finally. "Let's ask the shark what he wants to eat and why he looks so mad. I see what you're saying. He does look angry. Let's ask him what he wants."

Pablo looked at her and the corners of his mouth went up a little.

"You're not afraid of it?" he asked.

"I'm not feeling afraid," she said. "But it's okay to be afraid. Do you feel scared?"

"No," he said calmly.

"Would you tell us if you were scared, Pablo?" his grandmother asked, stroking his hair, which was damp from the fever.

"I would tell you, Mommy," he said. "Okay. We're going to talk to the shark. You ask the questions, Miss Sarah. Talk to the shark." She drew in a deep breath and let it out. He held up the drawing so that she could face it directly.

"Mr. Shark. You look mad. What do you want?"

There was silence. The shark wasn't talking. Pablo looked at the picture, and then turned it back to face Sarah.

"Oh. I'll be the shark voice," he said, recognizing the problem. "I want to eat some fish. And I want to eat a boy," he said in a growling, raspy voice.

"You want to eat a boy?" Sarah asked, trying to conceal her uneasiness. "With all of the fish in the sea, why would you want to eat a boy?"

"Because he makes me *so* mad," the shark voice answered with conviction. Pablo coughed. His grandmother patted his back. Her eyes were serious and deeply focused. Mrs. Mendez nodded for Sarah to continue.

"The boy makes you mad? Tell me why," Sarah said, speaking with as much authority as she could muster. "You tell me, Mr. Shark, what's so upsetting about this particular boy? This is your chance to speak."

"He always gets in the way of things," the shark voice said. "When he swims in the sea all of the fish seem to get smarter. He's teaching them things. They learn ways to escape me. And because of him I have an empty tummy. I can't get a thing to eat. So I'm hungry and I'm mad. This is my part of the sea. It belongs to me and he has no right to be here. He has no right to teach the fish how to get away from me."

"I see," Sarah said, wondering how to lead Pablo away from the angry shark and what it represented. But the shark spoke again.

"Go away, boy! Get out of here right now and go far, far away and leave the fish for me to eat!" he said. They were all quiet. Sarah focused her attention on the shark. She wanted to stand up and order it right off the picture.

"No, *you* go away," she said to the shark with her thoughts. She caught herself glaring at the picture and struggled to remain calm. Pablo looked at her lovingly and the light around him intensified. She sensed his understanding and his compassion.

"I have an idea," he said, speaking in his regular voice. He put the drawing back on his lap-board and picked up a brown crayon. He added a boat. He picked up a yellow crayon and drew a sail. "There," he said, displaying the picture again. "The shark can't hurt me now. I'm going to sail to another part of the sea and give this shark some peace." He smiled, pleased with his solution. For the first time he was directly acknowledging that he was the boy in the story.

"Okay," Sarah said, trying to stay neutral. "You are going to help out this shark."

"Sharks have to eat, too," he explained. "That doesn't make them bad. But this one might eventually have to go to another place, too."

"Really? Why is that?" she asked.

"Because the fish in his part of the ocean are now very smart. They can still get away from him, even after the boy is gone. Maybe some will forget what they've learned, though. They might forget how to deal with the shark. You just never know. Maybe that's what the shark is hoping. We'll have to see how this turns out."

"So the boy taught the fish some important things," she said. "Would you like to bring the dolphin back?" she asked. "Dolphins can be good protection."

"I'll bring him back!" Pablo said happily. "Yes, he's swimming beside the boat. He's going to make sure the boy gets to the other place without a shark attack." The two women sat quietly as the dolphin manifested on the page. He made the dolphin pale blue with red and purple hues. It was a beautiful friend with loving eyes and a big dolphin smile on its face. He held it up and they applauded.

"Can you make another picture?" his grandmother asked. "Can you draw a picture that shows us the boy's new swimming place?" Sarah could hear in her voice that Gloria Mendez wanted a happy ending for her grandson, not just for the shark.

"I'll try, but I don't exactly know what heaven looks like," he said matter-of-factly. Sarah bit her lip as she looked at the older woman's face. His grandmother did not flinch. She did not seem surprised. Perhaps it was what she expected, Sarah realized.

"Whatever you draw will be absolutely perfect," she told her grandson. "I would love to see your drawing of heaven." She glanced over at Sarah.

"Me, too," Sarah said sincerely.

"I'll draw it today or tomorrow," he said, reaching to hug his grandmother. Sarah pulled the curtain around them and stepped away to give them privacy. Two more children with AIDS were being wheeled into the room. She saw that they appeared to be even sicker than Pablo. One was a little girl with blonde hair. The other was an older boy who could have been Pablo's brother. He had the same soulful eyes. Sarah greeted them softly and told their families that she would be back in a little while to see how they were doing. She walked into the hallway, a knot in her stomach. She felt torn. A part of her wanted to go into her office, shut the door and draw a shark. Then she would draw a picture of herself killing the shark with her bare hands. She imagined the shark's blood spilling into the sea.

But then she thought about her wise teacher in his hospital bed and she released the rage inside of her. Pablo had a plan for peace and a friend to travel with him on his journey. He didn't hate the shark. She wasn't going to dishonor this sacred moment by focusing on anything else. She headed for the chapel. It was empty, which was rare. She sat down and put her face in her hands, needing the release of tears. Then she wiped her face and said a prayer.

"Beloved Creator of all that is, please send us angels and dolphins to guide us home when the time is right," she whispered. "Actually, I realize that you have already thought of this, so I just want to say thank you. Thank you for loving us. Thank you for helping us to see your light. Thank you for making this place sacred ground."

CHAPTER TWENTY-SEVEN

Keys

She returned to her office and turned on the computer. Several e-mails called for her attention. She read the one from Porter.

"Will you be home tonight?" it asked simply. "I'd like to give you a call."

"I'll be home," she answered. "Looking forward to it." She picked up the phone. She called one of the hospital chaplains, a kind woman who was a veteran of hospital duty. Sarah always felt herself relaxing around Carol, who sometimes offered nothing more than her unconditionally loving presence when family members protested their sense of injustice to God. Sometimes that's all they needed to be reminded of God's unconditional love for them.

"Hi, Carol. Pablo is talking about heaven, now," Sarah said softly, leaving a voice mail. "He's talking about sailing there in a boat. I knew you'd want an update." She hung up, relieved to have shared this. Then she had an idea. She unzipped her backpack and pulled out a book. In it she had tucked Uncle David's card. She also found the conch shell she had discovered in Florida. She had meant to give it to Pablo right away. She took them to his room, peeking through the curtain to make sure she wasn't interrupting anything too private.

"Come in," they both said.

"I just had to show you something. My aunt made this card. She's an artist like you, Pablo. She likes dolphins, too." She handed him the card. His grandmother looked at it as he traced the image with his finger. She looked back up at Sarah, nodding with approval.

"It has a key to a kingdom in its mouth," Sarah said, leaving the nature of the kingdom vague. She didn't want to impose her own beliefs. "That's what the title says." Pablo's eyes grew bright as he examined the picture. He looked at it for a long time.

"What do you think about that?" his grandmother asked. "Isn't he a fine dolphin?"

"I think he's the king of dolphins," he said, finally. "The city sank but he found the key and he's keeping it for us. I really like this picture, Miss Sarah. I'm going to draw a dolphin with a key." She felt the air in the room grow supercharged, the way it had when she was preparing to share the story of the first lamp. She noticed the gold cross around his neck. He was touching it as he looked at the front of the card.

"Another key," she thought to herself. "They come in all shapes."

"I gave him that little cross last Christmas," Gloria said, following Sarah's gaze. "You know, honey, your cross is a gold key, too. That's why I gave it to you. It's a key to the kingdom, Papi." Sarah had not heard this knick-name before. She loved it.

"I know, Mommy," Pablo said. "We all have a key. They can have different shapes. But they all open the same door. They open the door to heaven." Sarah sat with them for a while. She gave him the shell, explaining that in ancient times the larger ones were used like a trumpet. He put his mouth to it and blew, making a humming sound. He laughed and blew again. His grandmother smiled. She was radiant.

"I'll come by later for the card," Sarah said. "My uncle wrote a letter inside that's very important to me. Otherwise, I'd let you have it."

"I'll color my own," he said. As she was preparing to leave, Carol walked in. Sarah noted to herself that this woman's light was so great it had preceded her through the doorway. Sarah thanked God for this vision and closed the curtain around them just as Pablo was pointing to the dolphin on the card. She found it hard to walk away. She wanted to stay and learn more about how to escape the shark. Willing herself to move on, she turned and walked into the hallway, bending down to sip from the water fountain. She felt a tap on the shoulder. It was Gabe.

"Can you join me downstairs?" he asked. "Somebody is asking for you."

"Who?"

"Mr. Sanders."

"Sandy is back?" she asked. "I thought he moved to New Jersey." He was a regular at Minnie's Café. He was also a former security guard for the Brooklyn Museum. He had been diagnosed with heart disease and retired to the Jersey coast.

"He did move to Jersey, but he's visiting his daughters and he got sick. He's not himself. They're doing some tests." Sarah sighed.

"Gabe, I know this is going to sound really strange since I work in a hospital and it's my choice to work in a hospital," she whispered. "But I'm tired of 'sick.' I'm tired of the word. I'm tired of the condition. I'm tired of being mad about it. And I don't know why I'm telling you this."

"Because it's true," he said. "Sometimes I get tired of 'sick,' too." They walked down the hallway. Waiting at the elevator, she looked around. No one was looking. She took his hand and squeezed it. He squeezed back. The elevator doors opened and their hands separated. Inside, they were alone again.

"Can I interest you in a trip to Hawaii?" she asked.

"Hawaii. That's thinking big."

"It's only about ten hours by plane. Ten hours to paradise. That's not so far to travel. I think Porter's going."

"He's going when we're going?" Gabe asked.

"So we *are* going, then," she said. "You just said 'when *we're* going.'"

"Heck, I guess we're going," he said. "Sounds adventurous. Even with Porter there."

"Especially with Porter there," she said. "You don't know the half of it."

"I'm getting a little confused," he said, feeling somehow that his fate had been sealed. "Has this trip already been planned?"

"Yes and no," she said as they stepped off the elevator. "I don't mean to sound cryptic. I'm sorry. Yes, I think it's meant to be. But I haven't planned anything and neither has Porter. I just feel it coming together somehow."

"I see," he said. "I have to admit, I've been craving palm trees."

"I think we'd have an incredible time," she said. She felt torn, wanting to tell him everything and not really wanting him to know. She would have to get off the fence eventually. But for now, she didn't know how. They walked into the crowded hospital room. Mr. Sanders' family surrounded him. He looked confused and agitated. Gabe said Mr. Sanders had insisted that he needed to speak with Sarah. Other than that, he did not appear to know where he was.

To everyone's surprise, he recognized her immediately.

"Sarah!" he said, as she approached the bed and squeezed his hand. She nodded to his wife and daughters.

"I'm sorry you're not feeling well," she said. "We've missed you over at Minnie's. Do you like living on the Jersey coast? I hear it's beautiful."

"I like living there, but I'd rather die here," he said, squeezing her hand. His chin quivered.

"Oh, Sandy," she said, seeing how scared he looked. "Does that have to happen during this trip?" She had not meant to sound glib, but her question seemed to tickle him and his face broke into a big grin. She saw the lights come back on in his eyes. He looked around at his family.

"Oh, okay. Maybe I'll schedule it for next time," he said. "I guess I haven't gotten my fill of retirement yet." Sarah looked at Gabe, who had been writing notes. His head shot up when his patient began speaking in clear sentences. Sandy laughed again. He sounded hoarse. His wife gave him some water.

"I knew you'd make me laugh," he said. "Even when I didn't know anything else, I knew you'd make me laugh. I've missed those lunches at Minnie's. Please tell her that for me." He did not seem confused anymore. Gabe cocked his head and studied his patient for a moment.

"Mr. Sanders, do you know where you are?" Gabe asked.

"Of course. Mercy Medical Center in Brooklyn, New York."

"Do you know the day of the week?" Gabe asked.

"Of course, don't you?" Sandy said, winking. "It's Monday. The Monday after Thanksgiving."

"Could you please tell me your full name so that I can write it on this form?"

"Nathaniel Adam Sanders, otherwise known as Sandy," the man replied. "I'm 67 years young and I have a beautiful wife, two daughters and two grandchildren. I know what you're doing, Doc. But I think I'm clearing up in my head."

"You had us worried, Dad," one of his daughters explained. "You weren't making a lot of sense. We got scared."

"I'm sorry, honey. I'm sorry. This is not a place for you. Go home."

"I'm not going home!" she responded. He reached for both of his daughters. They bent over the bed. He kissed them both. He turned his attention to the other side of the bed and kissed his wife. "It's going to be okay," he said. "I'll die another day."

He winked at Sarah. She sat with them for half an hour, hearing news of his life. Gabe slipped out as they were talking. Later, when they met at the hospital entrance to go home, he buttoned up his coat and helped her with her backpack. "I have to compliment you on contributing to your friend's turn-around," he said. "That was one of the more dramatic shifts I've seen in a while."

"That was probably just a coincidence," she said. "I mean I'm a total believer in the power of the mind-body connection, but I think in this case I just walked in at the right time."

"I'm going to have to disagree with you. He was transformed the moment you spoke to him. I went back later to double check and he was a new man. We did some more tests. He looked great. He was discharged late this afternoon. When I first saw him, he didn't even know his own name."

She studied his face as he spoke, seeing admiration. He was intent on conveying this and she stopped herself from interfering. "Even his color got better right away," Gabe said. "I certainly didn't have that effect." She shrugged.

"Okay. I'll take it. That makes me feel great. Really, I think it just helped that I wasn't buying into his conviction that he was about to die." She knew Gabe was a "seeing-is-believing" kind of guy. Maybe it had all unfolded that way for a reason.

"So we're going to Hawaii," he said, changing the subject. "When do we leave?"

"Let's plan something for real," she said. "And if you promise not to laugh at me, I'll tell you more about why it's so important to go to Hawaii. But you have to promise not to laugh."

"But sometimes you make me laugh," he said. "I can't promise."

"Well, then promise you won't scoff," she said. "No scoffing."

"Do I scoff that much?"

"Not so much lately," she replied. "Do *I* scoff at you?"

"You tease, but I haven't noticed any actual scoffing," he replied.

"Good."

He put an arm around her. "I'm sensing that there is quite a trip in our future." The wind blew hard. It was starting to bite at her exposed skin. She thought of the shark.

"Have you ever thought of serious illness as an angry shark?" she asked. "I'm trying not to hate sharks right now. I mean, I know they have to eat, just like the rest of us. I know they serve a purpose and they have a right to be on the planet."

"Are we still on the topic of Hawaii?" he asked.

"No, sorry. New topic. My little buddy is back. He drew a shark that wanted him to go away and then he came up with a solution. He drew a boat that would take him to another place. A place called heaven."

Gabe looked at her, his eyes moist. "We need Hawaii."

CHAPTER TWENTY-EIGHT

Lovers and Healers

They had just finished dinner when the phone rang. Sarah knew it was Porter. She had been worrying about how to update him without making Gabe think that she had lost her mind.

"Hi," she said to him.

"Is my timing good?"

"It's always good," she said. "Gabe and I were just clearing off the table. We've been talking about going to Hawaii." Porter hesitated, undecided about how much to say when she had company. She understood his silence. He understood hers. The pause continued.

"Well, the main reason I called was to tell you that I've sent two books your way, two books plus one deck of Mayan Oracle cards."

"I'm excited!" she said. "I need to put up a Christmas tree so I can put them underneath."

"You don't have to wait until December 25th to open the package," he said. "Every day can be Christmas, you know. It's a state of mind."

"Porter, are you in love?" she teased.

"Yes," he answered, surprising her.

"You are? Seriously?" She saw Gabe start to wash the dishes. The two of them had made quite a mess with the pots and pans. "Hold on a second. Please just relax, Gabe. I'll do those when I get off the phone."

"It's not a problem," he said. "It helps me unwind from the day." She turned on some music and kept walking toward the bedroom. Slipping in, she shut the door.

"I'm alone now," she said to Porter in a low voice. "Gabe and I have talked about a vacation to Hawaii, but he doesn't know about the other stuff. And I have no idea how to tell him. Maybe I'll never get up the nerve."

"I can call another time. I don't want to put you in an awkward situation."

"Don't go just yet," she said. "I have some things to tell you. I actually have a lot to tell you, but I'm going to write you a long letter. That'll be good practice for me. I have to find a way to write about these things. Uncle David gave me a challenge to start writing again. But before I go any further, let's re-wind here. You said you're in love. Is it Kate?"

"Yes," he said, sounding like mush. She tried to imagine his face looking smitten. She had always known he was a softy. It was pretty easy to imagine him being in love. "We're having dinner tonight," he said. "And... Are you sitting down? I'm going to pop the question!"

"Oh Porter, that is the best news!" she exclaimed. "I am so happy for you! Wow! Do you have a ring? What a dumb question, of course you have a ring."

"It's quite a beauty. Pearls and diamonds. I had it made for her. Her family imports pearls. She is half Japanese. Her mother is English. Her father was born in Japan and moved here after their marriage. She's an absolutely beautiful woman inside and out. I can't wait for you to meet her."

"I am just so happy for you," Sarah repeated.

"And how about you?" he asked. "You two are planning a trip? I won't jump to conclusions, but that sounds promising."

"I think it's promising. But I'm still scared."

"I know, sweetheart."

"I'm scared, but I don't want fear to win," she added.

"Amen to that."

"Porter, I have to tell you something right this minute before I pop, and then I'll let you go. I know it's a big night."

"I'm not in a rush at all," he said. "Remember, I called you. I've been eager to get caught up."

"Well, Kalah came to me in Florida in the most incredible way. She shared a story with me, and I shared it with everyone else. It was such a perfect story to tell our family at this juncture, when we might lose Uncle David. At least lose him in the physical sense.

"It was about the unbreakable bond of love. It was just so sweet, Porter, the way it all unfolded, and so grand. I felt an incredible presence watching over us. It was a magnificent presence and yet so gentle. The energy that filled the room was a true friend, but it wasn't Kalah. It was something even bigger than her. It filled the whole house with unconditional love. I know everyone felt it because everyone was glowing. The presence lifted all of us up."

"Amazing," he said simply. "In my words I would call that Christ Consciousness."

"I agree," Sarah said. "Christ Consciousness. The same words came to me while it was happening. And I know that this is going to sound a little strange to your ears, but along the lines of divine consciousness, Kalah told me that Kai says you are a kahuna."

"Say what?" he asked.

"Kalah spoke to me and she knows Kai, the wise kahuna in your dreams, and he says that *you*, my dear man, are a kahuna and a healer. But you just don't know it yet. He should know. He's the expert." Porter burst out laughing, reminding Sarah of herself.

"I'm sorry," he said. "I don't mean to laugh." Then he burst out laughing again. She truly felt for the man. She waited until he could collect himself. Finally, he got quiet again.

"Oh, my," he said. "Someone told Kalah that I'm a kahuna. God does have a sense of humor."

"Porter, it's *Kai.* It's your friend. The reason I know this is that he wears a necklace with two totems. One is a coconut. A *coconut.* Don't you see? The other is a red turtle. Didn't you say that the kahuna who was pelting you was named Kai?"

"Yes. Kai'ilo. It's Kai for short. But there's probably more than one kahuna by that name. I just can't believe it's the same man."

"Well, why not?" she asked. "I mean, what is the point of all these synchronicities if they're not leading us somewhere? Porter, she knew your name. Kai had *talked* about you. Given everything that's happened, it is far more likely that this is the same man. And if you don't stop fighting this, you're going to have a sore head."

He sighed. "You're right."

"By the way," she asked. "I think I have a general idea, but what exactly is a kahuna?"

"It's a person of great mastery. Kai is a marvelous healer and a natural psychologist. A kahuna can be male or female and have other specialties, too. They tap into the power of the universe, called mana. It's the same chi we talked about in Chinatown. These gifts of theirs can be used to build a magnificent canoe, perform a sacred hula or heal people on multi-dimensional levels. The native healers have always known what Western medicine is just beginning to discover. You can't really heal someone when you separate the mind, the body and the spirit. Much has been documented about the healing powers of some modern kahunas. Believe it or not, until fairly recently the Western-minded in Hawaii actually feared them, not because they were dangerous, but because they couldn't comprehend how bones could be mended so perfectly in a brief amount of time. Naturally, they feared some sort of sorcery. Stories abound of very loving healers being threatened with prison or large fines for practicing their sacred healing arts. When I was living there, I heard about one very revered elder woman who was almost jailed for a healing that some doctors considered impossible. That was their solution to a miracle staring them in the face on an X-ray screen. Throw the woman in jail!"

"Why does that not surprise me?" Sarah asked.

"The irony is that these same doctors probably considered themselves good Christians," he continued. "Would they have jailed Jesus for the same miracle?"

"Probably," she said. "The so-called rational mind often seeks to throw spirit in jail and toss out the key. I think the drama even plays out inside of us. I know it's a constant battle in me. But I'd never jail a healer who can fix broken bones. How can anyone do such a thing?"

"Fear," Porter said. "It will drive the human being to insane actions. I imagine that in Kalah's time, even the average person had abilities that we could call paranormal. To them, they were completely normal. We would be the strange ones for believing that human beings have so many limitations. To them, that would sound blasphemous."

"Wow," she said. "I can see why he called you a kahuna. You're having a very profound impact on me. Just listening to you now is unlocking some prison doors."

"I will accept that compliment," he said. "But I won't keep a straight face if somebody calls me a kahuna. Very few of the most skilled people in Hawaii will call themselves that. It's reserved for truly remarkable human beings."

"Now who is thinking in terms of limitations?" she asked.

"You've got me there. I guess I need to take my own advice. I've always had a hard time accepting compliments."

"But Porter, it's not just a compliment," she insisted. "I'm not into empty compliments and neither is Kalah. I think she says what she means. Besides, she was passing along something that Kai said. He has no reason to use that term idly, especially if it's such a special designation. You know, I think she lives with him now."

"Wait. Didn't Kalah say she lives in what we would call the ancient past?" Porter asked. "I don't mean to be dense. This is just a lot to take in."

"I'm almost positive that she's here right now. When she comes to me, though, I have such big things on my mind that I forget to ask about the details," she said. "But I did see her talking to Kai."

"You did? Did you have a vision?"

"A vision or an unplanned vacation," she answered. "I left my body in my sleep one night and flew to Hawaii." Oops. She had said that too loudly. She looked over at the door, wondering if Gabe had his ear pressed against it. Porter was quiet for a moment.

"Okay, now I've surpassed your tolerance for the strange and unexplainable," she said, feeling a little down. She remembered what her aunt had said and tried not to be so dependent on his reaction. But it was difficult. It was a lot more fun when they were humming along on the same wavelength.

"No, I'm the last person who's going to laugh at you," he said. "I believe you. I was quiet because my wheels were turning. We have to find him. There's a reason for all of this, like you said, and it would be stupid for me to ignore it. We have to find him."

This was more like it. Sarah felt like a little girl on Christmas morning.

"Yipppeeee!" she whispered loudly. "So how can we find him?" she said, warming to the challenge. "I could make a point to ask Kalah, but I never know when she's going to connect with me."

"I have my ways of finding people," Porter said. "I'm the cosmic pelican, remember? Kai might have settled down by now. When I knew him, he and his wife, Hannah, were traveling a lot between towns. Sometimes they would go into remote areas, too."

"Do you still have spy friends in Hawaii?" she asked.

CHAPTER TWENTY-NINE

Reaching Out

"I have one friend with good connections," Porter clarified.

"Is he a spy, Porter?" She whispered this, half hoping he would say, "Yes. Yes. My friend is a spy."

"I can't answer that," he said, a smile in his voice. "Does that answer your question?"

"Yes. By the way, don't you have to go now? Shouldn't you be getting all gussied up to propose?"

"We're meeting for a late dinner," he said. "And do you really think I'm going to hang up now?"

"Good. Just checking. So to review our plan, you are going to use your CIA connections to track down a gifted kahuna who has a penchant for throwing things at your head in dreamtime in order to impress upon you that you are also a healer with some important job to do."

"That about sums it up," he said.

"Have you noticed two, possibly three, levels of irony here?"

"Yes, and I love irony. That's why I'm having such a good time."

"Me, too," she whispered. She looked at the door.

"Give me a moment. I'd better go check on Gabe. I feel guilty that I left him with the dishes."

"Sure. We can talk more later on. Maybe next time I'll have some news about our plan to reconnect with our friend, Kai."

"I've never met him."

"Not in this lifetime. You say he wears a coconut around his neck?"

"He has one little coconut and one red turtle," she said. "The red turtle is key, but I'll talk to you about that another time."

"Oh, now that is interesting," he responded. "I didn't really catch that when you said it before. You think turtles are a part of all this?"

"Yes. Red turtles in particular. That's what the Hawaiians call the Hawksbill turtle. I looked it up. Anyway, the night I flew to Hawaii in dreamtime and was eavesdropping," she paused, shaking her head. "I can't believe I'm saying things like this. If Gabe's listening, he's probably calling 911. Anyway, that night I heard Kai explain that they are nearly extinct and that coconuts are part of the plan. Coconuts. *Your head.* Get it? I could swear he saw me."

"I see," Porter said. She couldn't see his face, but if there was such a thing as a poker voice he was talking in one. "Very interesting. Very, very interesting."

"Okay. Tell me quick. And then I know we both have to run. Why is the turtle thing so interesting? You're holding back."

"Well. It's interesting because Kate's last name actually means 'turtle' in Japanese. Her full name is Katherine San Kame. San means sun and Kame means turtle." Sarah dropped the phone. She winced when it hit the floor. Dizzy, she sat down. She picked up the phone, amazed that it was still in one piece.

"Sorry."

"Are you all right?" he asked.

"You're marrying a turtle?" she asked, rubbing her forehead.

"She's not an actual turtle."

"I know. I know. I can't think right now. I'm feeling spooked."

"Don't be scared," he said softly. "This is all pretty wonderful, don't you think? I mean how can you possibly feel alone in the universe with this going on? Remember the presence that you felt when you told the story to your family? You said it was the presence of a friend. You're safe." She was quiet. She felt a lump in her throat. He was quiet, too. He was very good at sitting with silence and not interrupting too quickly.

"So you're going to help turtles, somehow," she said, finally. "Is that where this is leading us?"

"If they need help, I think I'll probably end up being involved," he said. "After all, they're going to be my relatives after Kate and I marry." She smiled, but didn't respond. She was using her finger to draw a turtle shape on a suede patch of her quilted bedspread.

"That was a joke."

"I know," she answered. "My mind was still absorbing what you said about the universe. How we're not alone. How we're safe. It's becoming more and more important to me."

"It's a wonderful feeling, isn't it?" he asked. She heard deep emotion in his voice.

"It's the best feeling I've ever had," she answered. "Nothing can compare. Do you have one more minute?"

"I have several more minutes for you," he said, his voice tender.

"I have to read you something. Uncle David wrote it. He was quoting Aunt Twylah. I want to go in the other room and read it out loud so that Gabe can hear it, too." She opened the door, relieved to see that he did not have his ear glued to it. He looked deeply engrossed in a book. It was "The Disappearance of the Universe," by Gary R. Renard. "Thank you, Gary," she whispered to herself.

He looked up and smiled, not realizing that Porter was still on the phone.

"This book is strangely compelling," he said. "I've just been flipping through it, but if I understand the premise it implies that there's some sort of physics involved in the act of forgiveness. Like the whole universe is supposed to disappear when humanity reverses the effects of the supposed Fall by simply forgiving itself and going home! It's so 'out there' that it pulled me in."

"I know. It did that to me, too," she answered. "It's a brilliant concept. Hey, Gabe, speaking of brilliant, I've still got Porter on the line. I wanted to read something to him. And I'd like for you to hear it, too." She got the dolphin card out of her backpack and sat down on the couch. He put the book face down on the coffee table.

"Okay, here goes. Uncle David is writing about some mysterious things and he quotes Aunt Twylah." She studied Gabe's face for a moment and spoke into the phone.

"I'm quoting him: 'Twylah said God is wrapping his kids (that would be us) in a big blanket. She said the blanket is made of the threads of our individual mysteries and that they're all coming together to make something safe and warm for us.' Isn't that what we were talking about, Porter? Mysteries coming together." She glanced over at Gabe, who was watching her intently.

"A very wise woman, that aunt of yours," Porter said.

"I know. And you're a very wise man. And don't argue with me about that."

"All right, then," Porter said. "I'll call you when I have more news."

"Congratulations," she said to him. "Have a wonderful night with Kate."

She hung up. "Porter's going to propose tonight."

"Good for him!" Gabe said.

"Here," she said, handing him the card. "May I pull you away from the book for a moment? You can borrow it, by the way. I've already read it." He patted the couch. "Come sit next to me." He looked at the dolphin on the card.

"Aunt Twylah painted the scene on the front. Why don't you read what Uncle David wrote. Read it all, if you want. It will help bring you up to date on some things." He took the card, studying the drawing for a moment.

"I love this," he said. "The dolphin looks so real."

"I know. Like it could swim off the page," she answered.

"What is the symbolism of the key?"

"I haven't talked to her about that yet," she replied. "But the title of the painting is 'Key to the Kingdom.' I have a strong hunch that I know what it's about." She sat quietly as he read it, praying with a sincere heart that she would have the right answers for the questions she was certain he would have.

"Sounds like a mystical gathering," he said simply, after reading it.

She was surprised he didn't have questions. Gabe usually had questions.

"It really was," she said, feeling a little cautious. "Do you want me to tell you all about it?"

"Sure," he said, leaning back. There was a long silence. "Boy, you are really hesitating," he said, tugging at her hand. "You were excited about something and now your face looks completely blank. What's going on?"

"My face looks blank?"

"Kind of."

"I'm not sure why I'm hesitating. I guess I'm afraid you won't believe me."

"What's not to believe?"

"Um. The fact that I've inherited a certain family tendency to see lights, kind of like auras. And other things, too. I think it was dormant for a while, but now it's back. It's probably dormant in most of us. We all have abilities we don't use. You know, like we only use a small portion of our brains. You know that, right? I think you were the one who told me." Her voice was fading, her enthusiasm for sharing nearly gone. She sensed that Gabe was pulling away, though his facial expression had not changed. The room felt a little cooler.

"Gabe," she said, knowing she was grasping at straws. "How about if I tell you one thing from my life that you probably won't believe, and then you tell me something from your life that you think I won't believe. And we'll both try with all our hearts to believe each other. How does that sound?"

"Strange," he said, laughing. "What has gotten into you?"

"Did you hear what I said about the lights?"

"Well, sort of. You're voice kind of faded half-way through it."

"Okay. I'll say it again, only I won't let my voice fade."

"Good."

"Gabe?" she said weakly. She felt like a little girl.

He threw his head back and laughed. "What is it?"

"Have you ever wondered whether we only show people a tiny part of ourselves and keep the rest hidden away because it won't be acceptable? And in that case, have you ever wondered if we ever truly know each other?"

"Are you talking about us?"

"Yes. I guess I am. But I'm also thinking of the big picture. How we've been raised. What we've been taught to hide about ourselves and keep secret."

"Boy, now I'm really curious. You're going to have to tell me what went on in Florida! Did you guys have a séance or something and call in the dead?"

She looked him straight in the eyes.

"I'm going to tell you something very important and I'd like a little respect from you. This is not the time to make fun of me or try to shrink my head. Promise you won't do the shrink thing. You said it yourself. It was a very mystical gathering."

He smiled at her, a touch of cockiness still on his face. Sarah wanted to reach over and wipe it off. "I promise. I won't do the shrink thing. Sorry about the séance comment. Not appropriate." She studied him intently. And against her better judgment, Sarah began to tell Gabe about the light.

CHAPTER THIRTY

Perfection

A great being came to Kalah in a dream that night. He came as a man with a mask. He took off his mask and she saw her husband's face. She knew that he was a being of pure light. But it was comforting to see the loving image of Makani's face looking back at her. In her dream she was sitting in a small canoe searching the waters for Kei. The teacher came into the boat and sat with her. The little boat moved gently along.

"Sarah is going to ask for your help," the being said. "She's trying to open up to a man named Gabe. She wants to share her soul with him not just her life. But they have a big challenge ahead."

"How can I help?" Kalah asked. As she spoke, Kei swam up to the boat, resting her head on the side. The teacher reached out a powerful hand and stroked the dolphin's head. She made soft clicking sounds, looking up at him as he caressed her.

"When she calls to you, know that she is fighting painful emotions that need to be brought to the light," he said. "Gabe is going to challenge her to the core because he has difficulty trusting what he does not understand. His lesson is to rediscover his own deep desire to be intimately connected with the sacred, to embrace the mystery. And the lesson that Sarah will learn is that he actually reflects a wounded part of her own soul. Her mind is still looking for ways to beat down her spirit. Fear is cunning. She, too, will face the saboteur. They are not so different, Sarah and Gabe. Woman and man. But for a while it will seem that way. You will hear her cry out, and you will know what to do."

"This is far bigger than one man or one woman," Kalah said, looking down at the dolphin.

"Far bigger," he said. "Each time a woman is healed, each time a man is healed, the whole of humanity is brought closer to its original state, its original communion with Great Spirit. This is about achieving wholeness for the entire human race." She nodded, studying his face.

"I understand. When Makani and I were reunited for that brief time, I discovered what it was like to be in communion with my Maker. The joy cannot be expressed in human terms."

"Joy and pain are two sides of the same human experience," the great being said. "From my perspective, one is not superior to the other, but one is more natural than the other. Joy is more natural. Pain happens when the human being is deprived of joy."

She nodded. He patted Kei's head again. Then he took Kalah's hand into his. He heard her thoughts, her questions.

"Yes. It is all happening according to plan," he said. "Thank you for playing your part so beautifully. You hold the vibration of sacred innocence and spiritual power. Those who are open to it will begin to resonate with you until they, too, carry the same gift to others. And those who are not open will eventually change as well. Whether it feels like a gentle breeze or an earthquake is a matter of choice for them." He kissed her hand and disappeared. Where he had been sitting lay a white bird mask.

When Kalah awoke, the mask was on the bed. She looked at it and thought of Chief Ka-welo. She sensed that he was thinking of her. She closed her eyes and went deeply into prayer. She was given a vision. She did not see the chief, nor did she see Mama Hanu.

Instead, she saw a little boy who was drawing something. He was very pale. She knew that his body was sick. But his spirit was so powerful! It filled the room. He stopped drawing and looked at her. Instinctively, she handed him the bird mask. He put it on and was transformed into a brilliant being. She saw a doorway opening. He stepped through the doorway, turning to smile at her. Just before the doorway closed a dolphin swam through it, following him to the other place. She opened her eyes and gasped in surprise. The mask was gone. But the chief was now standing in front of her.

"Chief!" she exclaimed. "It is so good to see you!"

He put his hands to her face, smiling with a look of satisfaction. "I warm myself at the fires of your perfection," he said. He lowered his hands. Instantly he held two more masks. One was the red feather mask. The other was white. "Two are left," he said, holding them up. "The red one is for Sarah. The white one is for Gabe. When they wear these, there will be more balance. The prophecy will be fulfilled." The masks seemed to dissolve into his hands. "You will receive them when you need them. For now, the lamp is all you need. It is serving you all so well. I knew it would. It always has."

"The lamp!" she said. "It has hardly left the house since I arrived. Did it really come all this way to sit by my bed?"

The chief did not answer her question right away. "You have grown even more beautiful," he said. "You have accomplished so much. And yet you have hardly left the house since you arrived." She understood the comparison. The lamp did not need to do anything or go anywhere. It just needed to be the lamp and hold its powerful energy so that those around it would be returned to a higher vibration. The same was true for her.

"The lamp is something to look at and to hold," the chief said, his voice tender. "What it represents is far greater than itself. What it holds, what it represents, is every thing and every person on the planet. Do you understand?"

"Light exists in all matter."

"Precisely," he said. "Light exists in all matter. It is what you are. It is the essence of every being. Keep yourself centered in the light. In doing so you are holding the knowledge of the perfection of all things. With your simple presence, you are changing the planet. Is that enough for you?" She nodded enthusiastically. He smiled and turned to leave.

"Are you going now?" she asked, reaching for his powerful hand. She felt a little sad.

"We will only experience the illusion of separation for a while longer," he said. "Remember the story." He disappeared and she fell into a deep sleep. When she opened her eyes again she found Hannah sitting on a chair next to the bed.

"I was a little worried," she explained. "You seemed so far away. I'm sorry to intrude. I thought it would make me feel more at ease to sit with you and the lamp." As she said the last word, there was a flash of light.

"Look!" Hannah said. "It just changed!"

Kalah sat up, astonished at what she saw. Its flame had turned a dazzling white. The rainbow colors had been transferred to the bowl of the lamp. The colors seemed to dance on the surface of it, shimmering with life. Kai knocked on the door and stepped in, having had a premonition that this change was about to occur.

He knelt down in front of it. "I think this is a very good sign," he said. "A very good sign."

CHAPTER THIRTY-ONE

Gusts of Grief

Many miles away, things did not seem so bright. Sarah was suppressing a scream. After reading the letter from Uncle David, Gabe's phone rang. It was his roommate, Brian, explaining that his girlfriend had a family emergency. He wouldn't be home to take care of the dog.

"You can bring Haley here," Sarah suggested, feeling uneasy. Was he really going to walk away just when she was finding the nerve to open up? The situation felt vaguely dreamlike.

"Honestly, I'm too worn out to make the round-trip tonight," he replied. "I think I'm coming down with something. I feel really tired." She wanted to be big about it. A flu virus had been going around at the hospital. One of the first symptoms was deep fatigue.

"Okay, sure, get some rest," she said, trying not to sound needy. "But I don't like where we are leaving off. I was trying to explain the light that Uncle David was talking about and you were looking at me like I'm really weird. Now I feel uncomfortable."

"Of course you're not weird. But I guess I am a little worried."

"Worried about what?"

He sighed. "I'm concerned that things have gotten to be too much for you. I think you've had to deal with more than anyone should have to handle. You're probably on emotional overload. And Hawaii's a great idea."

"Oh, Gabe. Please don't call these life-changing experiences a sign that I need a vacation. It's so much bigger than that."

"Oh, I know it's bigger," he said. "Much bigger than that." He looked away.

"What are you saying?"

"If you really want to know, I think this has something to do with Collin. You're not over him. Trying to give your everyday life supernatural overtones tells me that you're having trouble letting go. Maybe you've created this experience to fill a void. You're a very intelligent woman. You know what the mind can do."

She felt a pang of fear. She had not even told him about Kalah yet. What if he was right? No, that was his fear talking. She couldn't let it become her fear.

"Let's stop for now," she said wearily. "Your dog needs you. And I don't want to say something I'm going to regret."

"You're mad. God, Sarah, the last thing I want to do is make you mad at me. I'm just trying to speak honestly. I'm giving you my gut reaction, but I'm not saying that I know everything."

"Well, I am truly relieved to hear that," she shot back. "For a minute there you sounded quite confident that your role was to ridicule my faith, and maybe to mock Aunt Twylah's faith and Uncle David's. And you would have to be quite the bold know-it-all to attempt that!" She heard rage in her voice. It bothered her to sound this way. She looked down. How could he ever believe that she was evolving when she sounded like a judge and jury?

"Look, I'm sorry," she said, looking at him sadly. "I'm not a good spokesman for what I'm trying to sell. I'm too easily provoked."

"I don't think you're trying to sell me anything," he said, reaching for her hand. "I think you got up the courage to tell me something very important, but it's not something I can relate to.

It doesn't sound real to me. I'd be lying to you if I said otherwise. Maybe we're having a left-brain versus right-brain argument. Maybe that's all it is."

"Or maybe we're having a half brain versus whole brain argument," she replied. He shrugged, looking weary. She kissed his cheek, feeling numb.

That is how they left it.

A full day went by. Sarah was miserable. Aunt Twylah's good advice about speaking her truth and trusting herself no longer filled her with confidence. She wanted to call her aunt but realized that this argument was a tiny problem compared to the prospect of dealing with Uncle David's illness. She called her mother. Her parents had been very receptive to Sarah's experiences. Since childhood her mother had respect and reverence for the unusual experiences of her sister.

"Mom," she said sadly when her mother answered the phone. "I tried to talk to Gabe about the things that happened in Florida. I tried to tell him about the mysteries of the light and how mystical and sacred life seems to me now. He says I need to take a vacation. A vacation! Like I want to be cured of this!"

"I guess I'm not surprised. From what you've told me, he's a great guy but his way of thinking is very different from yours," her mother responded. "Don't forget, you are changing very rapidly. A few years ago you would have been skeptical, too."

"I know," Sarah acknowledged. "A few *months* ago I would have been skeptical."

"And he hasn't seen what you've seen," her mother added. "That puts him at a disadvantage. Maybe his ego doesn't like feeling at a disadvantage. He's human."

"I know. But I don't want to hold back to make his ego comfortable," Sarah said. "I've been there and done that."

"You held back a lot for Collin. You thought it was the right thing to do as a woman and ultimately it didn't matter. It didn't save him," her mother replied. "You know a lot more about relationships than you used to." They were quiet. Sarah sat with her pain. Her mother ached for her daughter. Finally her mother spoke again.

"Remember when you were in the eighth grade?" she asked. "You were the fastest runner among the girls. Then they paired you with the fastest boy in your class and you won again."

"I was more surprised than anyone," Sarah recalled.

"You were surprised and you were worried. You were afraid that being faster than the fastest boy would turn all of the boys against you. You were starting to be very interested in the opposite sex. Something told you that you should have held back."

"I can still remember the feeling. I wanted to race him again and lose so that the other guys wouldn't laugh at him. Because even though he was faster than all of them, they were laughing at him because I won the last race."

"And do you remember my advice?"

"Yes. You told me to keep running, to run like the wind."

"That's my advice to you now. Be patient. Be kind. But don't hold back. Run like the wind if that's what you feel called to do. Gifts are given to us for a reason."

"Thanks, Mom. That's perfect."

"I'm so proud of you," her mother answered.

"I'm proud of you, too. You are a good Mom."

The conversation was a great comfort, but her sleep was restless that night. The next morning she had started her day determined to stay in touch with the grace that was so generously pouring into her life. Her determination lasted through lunch. She had eaten at Minnie's Café and savored the comforts of the place. Minnie sat with her for a while. She gave her a brief version of the family reunion, but didn't mention Gabe. Minnie knew she was holding back, but didn't press the issue. When Sarah didn't see Gabe in the afternoon, she felt herself weakening. She knew he was probably sick in bed, but fear began whispering to her. Gabe could never be her prince if he didn't even understand the easy stuff, this voice said. Didn't he realize how enchanted the world really was? What kind of sick game was he playing? It was a sneaky voice, pretending to be something that it wasn't. It gave her the creeps.

"Go away," she said. "This isn't a fairy tale and he doesn't have to be my prince." Now it was dinnertime and Gabe wasn't answering his phone. Had he lost respect for her? Her wiser self knew that she had spent too much time giving weight to his opinions about her spirituality. Still she felt tormented, realizing that this anguish actually had little to do with Gabe and much more to do with her relationship to herself. The pieces of herself were warring. She wondered if she had made any progress at all.

"Gabe? Are you home? Can I bring you some chicken soup?" she had asked on his answering machine when she got home from work. "Turn-about is fair play. I owe you some soup." She thought he would pick up when he heard her voice. He didn't. She convinced herself that it was over between them. That he didn't have a fever. He was actually giving her the cold shoulder. Fear fanned the flames of her anguish. The hospital was a big place and hiding was quite possible. She sat on the bed, hugging the pillow that was waiting to soak up the next scream.

"You know, it's not all about you," she lectured herself. "The man has a right to be sick and to ignore the phone." But worry and fear were building inside of her and a charged anger was pouring into the mix. Her feelings of helplessness were unbearable.

"This is really cruel!" she screamed into the pillow. "This silent treatment is the last thing I can take right now!" The phone rang. It was Gabe. She heard his voice on the answering machine. He sounded terrible. She grabbed the phone. "Hello?"

"Hi," he said weakly. "I think I'm being punished for scoffing. You asked me not to scoff, but I scoffed. You don't ask for much and I blew it. Now I'm sick as a dog."

"You didn't scoff," she answered softly, her anger dissolving. "You just told me what you think. It's not what I wanted to hear, believe me. But you were honest. Don't be superstitious."

"I'm always superstitious when I'm sick. I've been asleep most of the day. And I've had some pretty freaky dreams. I could use a glimpse of you. The bogeyman has been after me and he's pretty ugly." She wondered if it was the same one who had been taunting her.

"Chicken soup coming right up," she said. "Bogeymen hate chicken soup."

"Good. I'm glad you said 'yes.' But I won't let you stay. And no kissing," he said, hoarsely. "I'm not even going to hug you."

"Great. You really know how to make up."

"I don't want you to get sick. I'm probably wracking up ten more minus halos for inviting you over here and exposing you to this dreadful thing."

"Minus halos?" she asked. "What are those?"

"That's where you have to return some of the halos that you earned when you were nice. They're called minus halos."

"Gabe?"

"Yes?"

"Have you taken your temperature lately? That doesn't sound like you."

"It's the bogeyman. I'm trying to tell you that he's freaking me out!"

"I'll be over in a little while. But I have to say one thing before I come."

"What's that?" He coughed a little.

"The fact that I'm bringing you soup doesn't mean that you have to make nice and not argue with me anymore. I mean, of course we won't argue tonight. You're in a weakened state and I would have an unfair advantage." He laughed. "So, I'm coming over because I care about you. But you and I both know this argument isn't over. I'm standing my ground, Gabe, and I expect you to do the same until I convince you to do otherwise. Deal?"

"I'm not answering that question until my attorney is present," he said. "And Sarah?"

"Yes?"

"I missed you today. I missed you a lot."

"I missed you, too. I'll be over in a little while. Do you need something from the store? I can stop there, too."

"Liquids. I've gone through the juice. Brian is staying at his girlfriend's house. It was his turn to go to the grocery store, but he didn't get the chance. I advised him not to come home."

"You got it. Liquids. Anything else?"

"The Disappearance of the Universe," he said. "I'm hooked and I need some forgiveness."

"It's coming right up." She hung up the phone and sat down for a moment, wrapping her arms around herself. Maybe her timing hadn't been so great with Gabe. Predicting another round of arguing wasn't the best use of her social work skills. But in this moment she wasn't playing that part. She was standing up for herself. And she was very new at it. It would take practice to get the timing right.

When he opened the door he didn't look as bad as she thought he would, but he sounded terrible. He coughed the minute the cool air hit him.

"Soup," she said, handing him the bag. "And liquids. I'll put this bag down in the kitchen."

"Try not to breathe. It's hazardous in here."

"I'll do my best." She felt his head as she walked by. "Pretty hot. Are you going to the doctor tomorrow?"

"Well, the problem is that when I'm well enough to make the trip, I won't need him anymore. I'll be over the worst of it."

"But if your fever gets high you know you'd better call me or call an ambulance or something. No playing around with your health, okay?"

"Okay."

"Haley looks like she needs a walk," she said. The dog whimpered a little.

"I'm sure she would love a walk."

"Has she been out lately?"

"The neighbor walked her twice, but it's probably time for her to go out again."

"Let's go, girl." The dog jumped up, putting her paws on Sarah's thighs. She wagged her tail happily. Sarah got the leash and they walked around the block. Before they went back in, she knelt down to pat her head. She loved the dog's eyes. They were soulful. She was a mixed breed with silky fur the color of a red fox. She had the black nose of a German shepherd. Her spotted tongue implied a touch of Chow. Gabe thought there was also some Sheltie in the mix because she was so light on her feet. This unusual combination had created a beautiful dog with a winning personality.

"What a fine girl you are," she said, scratching the dog's chest. "You look after Gabe for me." She started to get up, then knelt down on one knee.

"Say, Haley," she whispered. "Could you do me a favor? When the time is right, could you take that stuffed toy of yours and give your master another whack or two on the head to open his mind? I mean, not right now. It wouldn't be fair." Haley licked her hand.

"Great," she said. "I knew you'd want to help. Shake on it." She held out her hand. The dog put her paw in it and they shook.

"Mission accomplished. She did her duty," she told Gabe as she brought the dog back inside. "It's getting a lot colder outside. I'm glad you're not trying to walk her."

"I really appreciate it," he said. He was guzzling juice.

She unzipped her backpack. "The Disappearance of the Universe," she said, handing him the book. "Read it and free your mind." He coughed when he laughed. Then she pulled out a surprise, handing him a stuffed dolphin. "I got it in Florida. It was going to be part of your Christmas present. But you need it now. Bogeymen hate dolphins."

"Ahhhh, thanks," he said. "I've always wanted one of these. I'm a Flipper fan from way back." She blew him a kiss. "I'm going to go now. My throat is starting to hurt just listening to you."

"Okay," he said. "Thank you from the bottom of my dumb heart."

She smiled, taking in the sight of him. His hair was a mess. He looked cute.

"It's not your heart that's dumb. Your heart's just waiting for your head to catch up." He shrugged. She knew he didn't get it, but she wasn't angry anymore.

"I'm really, really glad you called," she said. "I was freaking out a little. Actually, I was freaking out a lot. I'm ashamed of myself, but I thought you were avoiding me all day."

"I wouldn't do that."

"A part of me believes you and a part of me doesn't," she said. "That's my issue. You were right about one thing. I still have major Collin stuff to work through. But it's not what you think. I'm not holding on to him anymore. I'm just terrified of another abandonment."

"I know. Me, too."

"So we have to be extra careful not to make it happen because it's what we expect from the opposite sex, okay?"

"You are very right, counselor."

She paused. "And we also have to be extra careful not to go the opposite way and lose ourselves by trying to hold onto each other." He was quiet, looking at the stuffed dolphin. "Look, I shouldn't be talking about these things right now," she said. "It just keeps busting out of me. I think my true feelings have been waiting a long time for me to find my voice. Let me know how you're doing tomorrow. Will you call me at work?"

"I will."

She looked down at Haley, whose eyes were shining. Sarah detected a smile.

"Remember our plan," she told the dog. "But wait until the time is right." Gabe looked at Haley. Her ears perked up and she barked at him. He looked at Sarah.

"I feel outnumbered."

"You're perfectly fine," she told him. "It's all good. And you have your dolphin. Look on the label. I think they actually named it Flipper." He smiled, tossing the toy in the air. "This is mine," he told the dog, who was trying to jump up and catch it. "You've got your own toys."

She blew him another kiss. He blew one back.

"Love you," he said.

"I love you, too." She closed the door and walked outside, bracing herself against the winter air. She looked up at the dark sky. A few stars shone through the haze of city lights.

"Well, I talked too much. That wasn't my finest hour," she said to herself. "But I don't hate myself for it. That's progress." A street lamp flickered off and on in front of Gabe's brownstone. Then it grew brighter. The light seemed to extend itself across the sidewalk. She felt a beam of it on her forehead. It was warm, like a kiss.

"Thanks," she said looking up. "I really needed that."

CHAPTER THIRTY-TWO

The View from Above

Sarah was nudged awake by a buzz of excited energy. In her grogginess she realized she had company. Not one, but perhaps a dozen unseen beings were in the vicinity of her bedroom. This was not the circle of women. This was a gathering like none she had sensed before. From what she could feel, this "committee" had been brainstorming all night and was eager to convey its recommendations. She thought about Aunt Twylah's regular visits from those on the other side and figured this was also a part of the family tendency.

"You've had enough sleep! Get up and join us," these visitors seemed to call out. "Get up, we say! You have to start writing!" She felt a slight pressure on her chest, as if they had dispatched a friendly spirit dog to stand on her and lick her face. She tried to bargain for one more minute of sleep, but the energy around her was persistent. She could swear she felt something sniffing in her ear. "Is there cotton in here, or what? Aren't you getting the message?"

"Okay! Whoever you are, I'm up!" she said, rolling out of bed. "Today's the day. I'm excited, too." Saturday had finally come and she was free to start her project. Suddenly, it was all very clear.

She would meet her uncle's challenge by writing a letter to journalists, urging them to look at their addiction to bad news. The media was an industry that prided itself in being able to look in the same mirror that it routinely held up to others. Reporting on itself and having the foresight to question its own blind spots was an aspect of the profession that she had witnessed and admired.

As a former journalist standing on the outside and looking back at the industry, she knew she had something to offer. She would submit her letter to newspapers, asking that it be published as a guest column in the editorial section. She would also send it to broadcast journalists, hoping that even one person in a position of authority might be moved to look at the imbalances that were occurring. Given her experience in Atlanta, she knew it was a subject that mattered, if not to the powers that be, then to the public.

She made herself coffee and took a shower. She dried her hair, put on a little makeup, did a few stretches and turned on the computer. First, she would clear out the cobwebs and goblins. She had discovered that when she wanted to write something very important, it was best to start with a warm-up exercise: free-style writing. She gave herself permission to type whatever came to mind. It didn't have to be related to her project. Predictably, her inner critic jumped at the chance to talk. She typed what it said without judgment, having found that it was best to get these things out in the open so that she could move on. Like a court typist, she let her fingers record the words with little attachment to what the critic was saying. But sometimes it was hard not to laugh.

"How can you accomplish anything when you haven't figured out exactly what you want to say?" this voice asked. "And what about that half-gallon of water you were going to start drinking each day? How can you write something important when you can't even stick to your plan to drink more water? Have you weighed yourself lately? If you spend all morning at this computer you won't get enough exercise. I noticed that your pants were tight yesterday. You might be getting fat. You should really get out of here. Go outside and run a few miles. Then, and only then, can you write something that's worth reading. Hey, are you even listening to me?" the critic asked incredulously. "What makes you think you have something to say? Wait just a minute! Why are you typing this? Is this how you're starting your project? What's going on here?"

She paused from her typing and took a sip of water. She was going to let the critic hang itself with its own rope. She had discovered that if she kept writing what this absurd part of her mind was saying, sooner or later it would get bored with itself and go away. Yes, it had worked again. The critic was evaporating. It was taking less and less time to get rid of it. She smiled and closed her eyes. She needed to pray.

"Beloved Mother/Father God, it is true that I have no idea what I'm doing or where I'm going with this. I only know that it's important for me to give it a try. Thank you for your unconditional love, not to mention your sense of humor. I pray with all my being that I will stay attuned to your guidance and that when I stray or stumble I will be quick to correct my course. Thank you for the warm blanket of shared mysteries that are wrapped around us each day. Amen." She had released the critical voice and opened herself to divine guidance. Now she could begin. Her fingers seemed to know the way.

An Open Letter to Journalists,

My uncle the fisherman is a very wise man. I told him an ancient parable that had been shared with me, and he called it a 'big catch.' He said it was big because it would feed a lot of people with its light. By 'light' he means information that illuminates. The story is a simple, beautiful tale about the unbreakable bonds of love. In repeating it to my family during a recent reunion, I rediscovered the incredible power of the word. That story fed us better than our Thanksgiving meal. In time, I will find a way to share it with many others.

My point in writing now is to remind you of your own power as masters of the word. Within my family, great insights were birthed by a simple story about love. Within the larger family of man, there are many such stories unfolding, stories that not only have the power of illumination, but also the ability to inspire action and shift perspectives.

Now I know what you're probably thinking. What does that have to do with me? I'll bet you're feeling the heat of a deadline or juggling several of them, and you need to know if this is going somewhere. I know how you think and what kind of pressures you face. I used to be a newspaper reporter.

But if you have read this far and are willing to keep going, it's because the journalist in you is a lot like a fisherman. You both love a big catch. And your instincts might be telling you what that catch really is. It's that light, the one your customers are hungry for. You know they're hungry because they've been trying to tell you that they need something more. They need a more balanced diet in the news and information you are providing. They tell you every time they cancel their subscription or walk past that newspaper box without dropping in their quarters. They tell you when they change the channel and complain that television news is "all bad." And they tell you loud and clear when they turn the radio dial, preferring to listen to a song they've heard a hundred times or the honking sounds of road rage than the miserable details of another massacre or a political leader gone bad. This is a big problem. Here you are going to a lot of trouble to give people the news of what's going on in the world, and too many of them don't want it. That's got to be demoralizing for you, too. After all, the media is a service industry. Without it, a democracy cannot remain healthy. You are protecting our right to know the truth. It's a very challenging job with lots of obstacles thrown in your way by those who don't want us to know the truth. I know that a journalist's main mission is to shine the light on what's really going, to look beneath the surface of things and to push past illusions. It is a great impulse, but somehow it's gotten in a rut, a huge, mind-numbing rut. Yes, we need to know when human lives are being harmed or threatened. We need to know when political deals lack integrity and we need to know if something we're doing is making us sick. But the public also needs to know about the grand human actions and choices that we are capable of making. We need to know the details about how things take a sudden turn for the better, how things go right against the odds. We need this in the context of everyday life, not just as a side-story to your reporting on something terribly tragic, such as the destruction of the Twin Towers in New York.

I will tell you that when I reported on three good deeds directed at me while I lived in Atlanta the response was amazing. Never had I seen such reader participation, stretched out for several days, in the Letters to the Editor section. People wanted to say, and wanted to read, what was going right in the world. When they can get more of this in their daily diets of news, they will come back to you for information, information that is balanced and doesn't leave them feeling sick.

When I was a journalist, we tended to shy away from the so-called "puff pieces" of good news. That was our insecurity. We were afraid of being duped into becoming someone's spokesperson. But the point isn't to be cynical or to be overly optimistic. The point is to be balanced and fair and to get it right. What if this "lighter" news is out there changing the world and journalists are afraid to report that?

As a social worker in New York, I'm on the front lines. And I can tell you from first-hand experience that the courage, the resourcefulness and the mysterious tenacity of the human spirit have been working together to knock the socks off the cynic in me. You all have access to what I'm seeing – and so much more! Journalists can go anywhere and ask any question. You can ask NASA to show you what the most sophisticated cameras in the world are reporting back about our universe. You can ask physicists and mathematicians why their most recent discoveries about the building blocks of the universe are making them sound more and more like spiritual mystics. You can ask the medical volunteers who go to the world's poorest nations what drives them to leave their comfort zones. Ask them to talk about the impact they're making among people who might have otherwise feared or hated Americans.

Ask the brightest teenagers what they're cooking up for our future. We need to know. Together, these human developments are creating the biggest story that's out there. This is the news that your customers also need to make wise choices. We need it to feel hope. Don't be afraid to go into deeper waters.

Happy fishing! Sarah Anne Pierce

She took a long drink of water and pushed herself back from the computer. She was happy with her letter. She thought Uncle David would be pleased, too. And this was only the beginning. Deep in her bones she felt something even bigger on the horizon. As a tribute to her uncle, she would send the first letter to his favorite television journalist, CNN's Larry King. This veteran had the right idea before others did. At the risk of preaching to the choir she would send him her letter, hoping that he could use his influence and that something good would come of it. It didn't hurt to ask. She got up and stretched, wondering what to do next.

She looked at her watch. Gabe would be arriving soon. They had planned a simple day, something they both longed for. He would get caught up on his reading. She would work on her writing. Haley would make sure they got enough fresh air and exercise. For dinner they were having Sarah's homemade lasagna, which was already prepared and waiting to be put in the oven. If they could avoid butting heads, it might just be a perfect day. She went back to the computer and made a print-out of her letter. Then she sat down on the bed with her notebook and started listing all of the newspapers she could remember off the top of her head.

She stopped, feeling the buzz of more activity. Another idea was brewing. Rummaging in her closet she found an oversized atlas. She had gotten it as a gift when she renewed her subscription to National Geographic. She walked into the kitchen and put it on the table. She made another pot of coffee and put some muffins in the oven to warm. Then she opened the book to a picture of the entire United States.

There was a knock at the door. "That would be Gabe," she said, as if explaining to her unseen guests that they would be getting some company. She greeted him happily, giving him a long hug. He had brought his newspaper, his duffle bag and the dog. Haley sniffed around. "Smells good in here," he said.

"Muffins are warming up. Help yourself to coffee, too."

As he entered the kitchen he paused, looking at the map.

"What are you working on?"

"I'm working on my Christmas gift to Uncle David. In the letter he told me to do something that would bring more light into the world." She paused, shrugging. "It seems like the least I can do." He poured himself some coffee. She could see that he was intrigued. "So I've written an open letter to journalists, urging them to bring us a more balanced diet of the dark and the light," she continued. "I finished it just before you came."

"You've already written the letter?"

"I got up and wrote it this morning."

"You don't waste time."

"I'm trying not to. Uncle David might not have a lot of time. I don't mean to sound morbid. That's just the way it is."

"I think that's wonderful, Sarah."

"You mean it?"

"Of course I do. And the atlas, is that helping you visualize something?"

"Yes." She took a handful of pistachio nuts from a bowl by the phone. Carefully, she put one nut on each of the major cities. He laughed a little, which made her happy.

"Hey, you work with what you've got," she said, waving a pistachio. "This isn't the Pentagon. Here's the deal. I'm trying to help myself visualize how the newspapers and broadcast journalists are spread out across the country and what they accomplish from a broader perspective.

"Let's see, if I were a person in space looking down at Earth and I saw these nuts, I mean newspapers and television stations, spread out over the United States, what would I be able to see from that vantage point that the average Earthling isn't able to see? Sometimes it helps to think about things like that."

"I haven't tried that."

"I mean in terms of the big picture. I'm trying to think creatively." He walked over and stood next to her, scanning the scene. Haley came to the table and started sniffing. With quickness and stealth, she stole a nut.

"Haley! You just ate the Pulitzer-prize-winning Miami Herald," she said. Gabe put his coffee down and reached out.

"Give that to me, Haley." The dog looked worried but she wasn't giving it up. They heard a crunching sound. He gently opened her mouth and took out the remains of the nut. "I'm sorry. Your stomach is sensitive." He took a rawhide bone out of his duffle bag and held it out to her. She snatched it like an alligator and ran into the living room. Sarah joined Gabe by the sink and put an arm around him.

"I'm so glad you're here to help me stay grounded," she said. "I don't mean to get carried away. I just got an idea and wanted to run with it."

"Hey, it's a great idea. Your uncle challenged you to live your life in a bigger way and you're stepping up to the plate. You're starting with what you know. More power to you."

"I know it's a stretch to think I can actually change anything with a letter," she said. "But I really, really need to stretch." He put an arm around her and kissed her cheek.

"Go for it. Whatever happens, at least you know you did your part. And if you choose to use something inedible on that atlas, Haley won't interfere by eating any more award-winning newspapers. Speaking of papers, I'm going to go sit on the couch and read mine from front to back. I haven't been able to do that in a long time."

"Good!" She was happy that he was making himself at home. She took the muffins out of the oven. She offered him one, then handed him the whole plate.

"Don't leave these in the kitchen with me," she said. "Assisting with the evolution of mass consciousness tends to make me eat too much."

"We wouldn't want that," he said, whisking away the plate.

CHAPTER THIRTY-THREE

Back in the Business

She turned her attention back to the atlas. It reminded her of something, but she couldn't put her finger on it. She thought back to the letter she had just written, spinning one of the nuts absent-mindedly. Democracy. Keeping democracy healthy with the flow of information. Flow. Health. The word as light.

Each word led to another. She felt a beautiful concept blossoming inside of her, one that now seemed so obvious.

"This is like a map of the body's key energy points, but it's the body of our nation!" she said softly. "What we're really talking about is the health of our country, our world, really, and it depends on the flow of this… this information." She took a finger and ran it across the map, connecting the cities. "It depends on the flow of the word, the flow of the light. Words are the light. Words are energy. The energy needs to flow, like chi throughout the body!" That was it. This map reminded her of her dream in the acupuncturist's office.

"Oh, now I get it!"

"You get what?" he called out.

"Oh, sorry. Just thinking out loud about my project. I got a flash of insight." The thoughts in her head were humming, moving faster and faster until she could only capture a fraction of them. She was brimming with excitement. This was more than an impulsive idea, more than an idle exercise. It really meant something. She felt a tug and pull, as if she were a thread being positioned in a huge tapestry. The phone rang, startling her. She picked it up.

"Hello?" she asked, her eyes still scanning the map.

"Sarah? Hi, honey. It's Aunt Twylah."

Her aunt's voice sounded fine, but Sarah felt an ache in the pit of her stomach. Her first thought was about her uncle.

"Sarah, something took place this morning that I need to speak with you about."

"Is it Uncle David?"

"No, your uncle is okay for now. He's holding his own. No change there. It's Collin. I saw him. I spoke with him."

She was dumbfounded. She looked out into the living room. Gabe was reading the paper and scratching Haley's head. She felt torn. If she spoke to her aunt now, her day with him might go down the tubes. Gabe already felt threatened by the memory of Collin. How could she possibly have this conversation? And yet, how could she not have it?

"Sarah? Are you there?"

"Um, yes. Yes, I am." For a moment, she wanted to break off into two pieces. One part of her would ask her aunt if they could talk later. She would sit down next to Gabe and just breathe him in. She would focus on him and what a blessing he was in her life. Meanwhile, the other part of her would walk into her bedroom, close the door and ask every question she could think of. Her aunt's gifts also were a blessing. They were a gateway to something bigger than the eye could see. If only she could split herself in two. Unable to achieve this, she stood motionless in her kitchen.

"Oh, goodness. Here I go spouting off about Collin like he just dropped by for a cup of coffee. And if I'm reading you correctly, you have company. It's probably Gabe."

"Yes, yes, you are so right," Sarah said, fighting to stay centered.

"I'll call back another time. Please forgive me."

"No, please don't go. Gabe is reading the paper and I was just working on my Christmas gift to Uncle David. I have some time."

Hearing his name, Gabe glanced up at her, then returned to his paper.

She thought of a compromise. She walked into the bedroom, but left the door open. Shutting the door to talk in secrecy wasn't what she wanted to do this time. She was worried that this act had on some level contributed to their last argument, making him feel like an outsider when she was talking to Porter.

"Sorry for that long pause," she said, sitting on her bed. "Gabe is here but we're each doing our own thing at the moment. I'd love to hear more." Her heart was pounding.

"Well, to start with Collin said to tell you that what you are doing is a blessing. It's a blessing to those on your side of the veil and on his side," her aunt said. "He said he could see you working on your computer, writing a letter. A letter to journalists. You wrote that right from the heart, didn't you? And you got some very divine help with that letter. That's what he said. Could you feel it?"

"That's incredible. Yes, I felt divine guidance. I wrote the letter this morning and the words flowed right out of me. Uncle David was my inspiration. Did he tell you about his challenge to me?"

"Yes, he did. I think he got some divine help, too. He usually doesn't have that much to say when he picks up a pen."

"What else did Collin say?" she asked, her heart still fluttering.

"He said he would come to you directly. But for now he just had to say that your mother was right. You should keep running like the wind, Sarah. He knows now that you downplayed your writing abilities while he was alive. You were sensitive to his competitive streak. But he is adamant that you shouldn't hold back anymore. What you are doing is a very good thing."

"Thank you," she said, sitting upright. She felt a surge of excitement. "Does he think it will accomplish anything?"

"He didn't say and maybe he doesn't know. Those on the other side don't necessarily know more about outcomes than we do. Outcomes are tied to the free will of others. But he said something else that you'll find interesting."

"What's that?"

"He said he's back in the business himself. Back in the business of journalism. It seems that some very tired media muses have been told to take a vacation. He said he's part of a new bunch that's working on this same assignment you've been given, but from the other side. He's trying to infuse the industry with more light so that people will get the whole story."

"So this is a group effort!" Sarah replied. "I swear I woke up feeling like there was a meeting taking place right over my bed!" She winced and looked out toward the living room. But if Gabe was listening, he wasn't letting on.

"Honey, if there's one thing I know for sure, everything is a group effort. Well, I'm relieved that I didn't throw you into a tailspin. I'm going to let you go now. Your uncle sends his love."

"Wait. Was there anything else? I mean, did he say why?" Sarah stopped herself from completing the sentence. She still did not know why Collin had gone, why he had left so mysteriously.

"He wouldn't talk about that part. I got the feeling that it took a great deal of effort for him to make this appearance. The way he left us was deeply troubling to him, too. He was still hurting when he got to the other side, but he's better now. He does want you to know that he never meant to leave you. He thought it was important for you to know. I'm sorry. I almost hung up without telling you that part. Sarah, he said he wanted to put that fear to rest so you could move on."

"I understand what he's saying," she answered. "I've been wrestling with fear. It does have a tendency to get in the way." She stood up and looked out at Gabe. He had stood up and was putting on his coat. She could see that he was getting ready to take Haley outside.

"I'm going to let you go," her aunt said. "My instincts are telling me that this is a good place to stop for now. Please give me a call when it's easier for you talk."

"I will! And Aunt Twylah, the dolphin card is so beautiful. When we talk again, I want to know more about what inspired it."

"Lemuria is rising. That's what inspired it. That's what my guides are telling me," her aunt replied. "Funny how I painted that scene a year ago and didn't know exactly why. I just felt guided to do it. Now you have a visitor from ancient Hawaii who probably has ties to Lemuria."

"Amazing!" Sarah answered. "I'm so incredibly glad that you called me."

"Me, too."

"Tell Uncle David he'll be getting a copy of my letter soon."

"He'll love hearing that."

They hung up and she grabbed her jacket.

"I'll go with you. Want to make it a long walk? I could use the air."

"Sounds good to me. Was that your aunt?"

"Yes, it was. It rattled me a little at first. I was afraid it was bad news."

"But everything is okay?"

"Uncle David is holding up for now," she said, fumbling with her keys. She tried to lock the door, but her hand was starting to shake. He touched her gently on the shoulder.

"Was there more to that conversation than you feel like sharing? You looked so happy when you got off the phone. Now you're shaking. You look a little scared."

She shrugged, still trying to lock the door.

"You're in a bind, aren't you? You want to tell me more, but you're afraid to. I can see it on your face." His tone was gentle. She paused, looking up at him. Then she tried the key again. It went in and clicked. She turned to face him. She put her hands in her pockets and looked deeply into his eyes. She felt as vulnerable as a little girl, a little girl who didn't expect to be believed. She was glad they had been friends first. The friend in him was trying to reach out to her now.

"There was more. And if I share it with you, it will probably provoke another argument. Not because we want to argue, but because we're trying to be honest with each other. And we're discovering the places where we are very different, where we don't see eye-to-eye. We're also becoming more aware of our relationship scars."

He nodded. A smile flashed across his face, but his eyes looked sad.

"You do know that my aunt talks to spirits," she said. "I told you that a while back when your disbelief didn't hurt so much. That's why she called today. If I hold back on what we discussed, I realize that we could have an argument about that. It puts a wall between us. If I do tell you, you'll just think that she and I both have the same wild imagination and you won't be able to hide that opinion. I know you too well. I'll feel like you're patronizing me and I'll get mad. Either way, I'm afraid our plans might be down the tubes. So you're right. I'm in a bind." The subject of Collin hung in the air. She wasn't going further with it and neither was he. They walked.

"I don't know how this got so difficult so quickly," he said, softly. "We used to be good at talking. The romance is great, but this walking on eggshells is a surprise to me."

"Let's don't give up too fast. Can we drop it for now and just have a nice day? We both need a nice day." He nodded, taking her hand.

"Let's talk more about Hawaii. Is that safe enough?" he asked.

She looked at him with worry in her eyes.

"Another loaded subject?"

"Well, sort of. If I tell you everything."

"Boy. You sure have a lot going on."

"And I want to share every bit of it with you. I have no interest in keeping secrets from you. But I also don't want to fight. Too painful."

"And that's the rub."

"Yes. That's the rub, my dear man." They walked quietly for a while.

"Want to go dancing tonight after dinner?" he asked.

She looked at him. "I'd love to. But I didn't know you liked to dance."

"I've got a few surprises too. I've been practicing on the sly."

"Are you taking a class?"

"Yep."

She felt admiration. "When did you find the time to do that?"

"I took my first class while you were in Florida. Hey. You're working on your Christmas presents and I'm working on mine. But I couldn't wait to tell you. You gave me Flipper early. So you get an early present, too. Surprise! I can dance. Sort of."

"So you really like Flipper?"

"Are you kidding? He's got the power!" Having said these words, he threw his head back and laughed.

"What?"

"Flipper did it. He got rid of the bogeyman. I was starting to think he was trailing me again."

She reached up and gave him a kiss on the cheek. He was stranger than she thought. There was hope for them.

CHAPTER THIRTY-FOUR

Pablo

Mama Hanu was gathering flowers when she noticed the little boy surrounded by a bright light. He was sitting on a large rock overlooking the sea. He saw her and smiled, pointing out beyond the cliffs toward the horizon.

"Whales!" he called out. Mama put the flowers down and hurried to him. She recognized the language he was speaking. It was Sarah's. As she approached him, she saw that he was spirit. He had looked solid from a distance, but now that she was closer his form was semi-transparent. His eyes were the most substantial part of him. They were bright and full of wisdom. Pablo's physical moorings had been loosening as the disease took over his body. Now the ropes and chains of mortality had dropped completely. This gave his spirit unlimited freedom to fly across the vastness of many dimensions, allowing him to follow the long threads of his family lineage back to this place. Looking into his eyes, Mama Hanu felt a strong hunch that he and Chief Ka-welo were related. Like the chief, he was so wise that he had rediscovered his innocence.

"Your spirit has traveled a long way. You look very happy to be here," she said.

He smiled and nodded. She looked over the cliff to see the whales that had caught his attention. "How wonderful! It's a mother whale and her baby," she said.

"It seems like a long time since I've seen a whale," he said. "But when I was sick, I saw dolphins in my dreams."

"Dreams are very powerful," she said. "They keep us connected to the deep places that are still tied to our source." He watched her face as she paused and smiled. He looked out to sea. She sat quietly next to him. Her heart was brimming with love. After a while she told him so. She explained that it lifted her heart to see the greatness of his spirit and to know that he had deep roots in her village. He put his hand over her heart and smiled.

"I'm happy, too." He thought about his life as a boy. She saw the images flash through him.

"You know Sarah, don't you?" she asked.

He nodded and smiled in a way that reminded her of Kalah. The light around him intensified. "Yes," he said, pointing again to his heart. "She is in my heart now."

"So a part of her travels with you," Mama acknowledged. "She must feel this. I know it will help her. She is feeling the pull of her roots in this place."

He nodded.

"You know something? She is in my heart, too," Mama said, finally. "My heart tells me that she will come here, just as you have. I have seen a vision of this. You are like two great trees with tall branches and deep roots. And your roots are entwined, yours and Sarah's. They have led you here." He listened and a knowing seemed to spread across his face. Somewhere in his soul memories were stirring. She knew he was waking up gently. A great being, he was still tied to the heart and memories of a little boy. That is why he still carried the physical form of a little boy. "Is this the dolphin kingdom, where the king and queen of dolphins live?" he asked.

"You're almost there. Keep tracing the threads of your origins." He moved closer to her and reached out his hands, cupping her face in them. She basked in the sparkling love pouring from his eyes, knowing with certainty now that he was the chief's descendant.

"Thank you, Mama, for the story of the lamp. When Sarah told her family the story, my spirit was floating above my body. I heard the whole thing."

"I am so pleased that you know the story, and so pleased that Sarah has received it," Mama said with a full heart. Her thoughts moved to Kalah. Pablo followed her thoughts. He could see Kalah's face, which she now held lovingly in her mind's eye.

"I know her!" he said with excitement. "She gave me the white bird mask! I remember!" With those words there was a flash of light. Pablo stood up. There was another flash and he was transformed into an iridescent white bird. He rose into the sky and soared out over the water, heading further back in time. She moved closer to the spot where he had sat. She held her hand over the rock, feeling its energy dance under her fingers. Standing up, she called out over the water, telling the chief what she had heard and seen. In a little while, he was standing with her overlooking the sea. Together they collected stones and Mama brought shells and flowers. The chief produced a white feather secured by a small black lava rock. They placed these where Pablo had been. Then they prayed, giving thanks for his visit.

* * *

Asleep in her bed, Sarah saw Pablo rise up from his hospital bed and transform into a beautiful white bird. She awoke with a jolt and sat up, knowing that he had passed on. She got up, pacing for a moment. Then she knelt down and prayed that his grandmother would be comforted. Easing back in bed, she heard Gabe mumbling hoarsely in his sleep. She watched his lips move, lowering her head to hear what he was saying. "Pablo is gone," he whispered.

"I know," she said softly, realizing that he was talking in his sleep. "He's free now." She watched him. He looked so vulnerable and innocent, like a sleeping child. After a while she got back under the covers, staring up at the ceiling. Shadows danced as car lights peeked in through the curtains. She was already missing Pablo. But she knew that she would see him again. In the morning, she called the hospital and the news was confirmed.

"How did you know?" the nurse asked. "We didn't expect it to happen so quickly."

"I had a dream and I saw him as a bird," she replied honestly. "He was soaring across a dark blue sky. I can't explain it. I just knew what it meant."

"Thank you for sharing that image. I will hold on to that. You know, it's interesting that you saw him as a bird. His grandmother said that just before he went to sleep for the last time, he told her that he was going to find his dolphin friend. He was going to fly like a bird. He actually looked happy about it."

"I'm sure he was," Sarah replied. "No more time in the hospital."

"His grandmother asked him if he was going to turn into a dolphin and explore the sunken city. He had been talking a lot about that. He said that at first he would fly like a bird and then he would find the dolphins and turn into one. He also told her that he was going to become a famous artist."

"That's our Pablo," Sarah answered. "If we thought he was creative before, the possibilities are unlimited on the other side." They spoke a few minutes longer. She learned that his body had been taken to a funeral home. His grandmother would have it cremated and his ashes would be thrown out to sea. As she was finishing the conversation, Gabe walked into the kitchen looking for his shoes. Haley was following him, eager for their morning walk.

"Was that the hospital?" he asked.

"Yes. Pablo died last night."

"Oh," he said, pausing to absorb this news. "I'm so sorry. I know you worked closely with him. Did they actually call you to tell you that?"

"No, I called them. I had a dream that told me he had passed on."

"Really? Has that ever happened before?"

"No." She turned to busy herself, filling the coffee pot with water. "Don't be surprised if I have a good cry at some point in the day. Then I'm going to find a way to celebrate his freedom. Crying and celebrating. That probably makes no sense. I'm just glad he's not sick anymore. God, his grandmother must be heartbroken, even if she is glad he isn't suffering. We're happy, we're sad. We're happy, we're sad. It makes no sense."

"Feelings don't always make sense," Gabe said. Haley barked, telling them that the rest of their conversation would have to wait.

"Coming."

"Hey, you know what?" she said as he was walking out the door. "Last night in your sleep, you said the words 'Pablo is gone.' Can you believe that? You knew it, too."

"Seriously?" He looked confused. "I wonder how that happened." He shrugged and stepped out with the dog. She sat down, wondering why she wasn't crying. She thought of Collin and how he had died. She wondered what demons he had wrestled with that day. Perhaps he and Pablo would cross paths somewhere in the universe.

Gabe and Haley were walking back in just as the kitchen lights began to flash off and on. It surprised her, but she loved it, sensing that the world of spirit was being mischievous. However, the moving hands on the clock were unnerving. Slowly, the big hand began to move counter-clockwise, taking the small hand with it.

"Look!" she said as Gabe walked into the kitchen, staring up at the lights. "Look at the clock!" She looked at him, her eyes wide. If his expression could speak, it would say, "This place is possessed!"

"I'll go hit the circuit breaker," he said.

"I don't think that will change anything, but it's in the hall." He flipped switches but she was right. The lights kept flashing and the hands on the clock kept spinning.

"I don't know what to do," he said, sounding exasperated.

"It's okay. I have a hunch it's Pablo. This feels like something he would do to let us know he's okay."

Gabe sighed loudly. She turned to see him walk into the living room and land heavily on the couch. She could feel the tension mounting. Haley stayed with her, perhaps wanting to take her chances in the mysterious kitchen rather than being next to Gabe when he lost it.

"Whoever you are, you've got my attention," she said. "You can stop now." With those words things settled down in the kitchen.

"It's me." She heard Pablo's voice.

"I thought it was you."

"I'm sorry I scared Gabe."

"He's a big boy."

"I'm different now. And I'm not by myself," he said. "There are some huge angels here. I think that's why the lights went crazy. But the clock was me. I was showing you that I can move back in time. And forward, too. It's like a big circle."

"Wow!" He sounded older, but still so innocent. Little had changed since they spoke in his hospital room.

"And guess what?"

"What?"

"I found dolphins. They are very wise, Sarah. But they are also a lot of fun. And they like to be tickled." She bit her lip, trying not to laugh. If she let go now with the joyful laughter that was brewing in her belly, her fate would be sealed. Gabe would take it as a sign of insanity.

"Thanks," she said. "That's really good to know."

"Bye for now. I'm going to see my grandmother."

"I'm so glad you came for a visit."

Then he was gone. She wanted to jump up and down with excitement. Instead, she stood frozen in place, afraid to turn around and see the look on Gabe's face.

CHAPTER THIRTY-FIVE

Spinning

"My God. I heard every word," he called out from the couch.

Her heart sank.

"Look, it's not what you think. I wasn't talking to myself."

"I know you weren't. When I said that I heard every word, I meant that I heard Pablo, too."

"You did?" She ran into the living room, landing on the couch next to him. "You heard Pablo? That's incredible, Gabe!"

"I wish I could share your excitement." He was pale. He rubbed his face and she could see that his hand was trembling.

"So now you're worried that you've gone crazy," she said. "Look, I know what that's like. When these things first started happening to me, that's exactly what I thought. I wasn't happy about it. Not one bit."

"Yeah, I can't say I'm happy about the fact that I'm hearing voices," he answered. "Maybe I'm so desperate to understand you that I'm falling into your strange fantasy world."

Sarah stiffened. "My strange fantasy world? You can still call it that when you heard it, too?"

He rubbed his temples with his fingertips.

"I feel dizzy," he said. Her anger faded and she felt a deep compassion for him. This must be how she looked to Kalah in Central Park. This must be exactly how she sounded.

"Look, who really knows what's going on?" she said softly. "But it doesn't feel threatening. Why don't you lie down? Would that help?"

"No, I think it'll make me nauseous." He stood up, holding his stomach. "I should go."

"But why?"

"Because I don't know up from down right now."

"And you're supposed to leave because of that?" she asked, her voice pleading. "Do you expect your patients to get up and walk out when they don't know what's happening to them?"

"So you do think something's wrong with me."

"No, I don't. Not at all."

"You just compared me to one of my patients. I don't see people when things are going well in their lives. I see them when they're feeling crazy." She sensed that he felt out of control.

"Let me get you some water," she said. "Please don't go. This is the worst possible time to get up and go." When she came back, she was relieved to see him still sitting on the couch.

"Thanks," he said. "I feel like I'm dreaming. I'm definitely ready to wake up."

"Believe me, I understand. More than you know. Something is definitely going on. It's so big it feels unreal. Do you know what I mean? Like my mind can't get a handle on it at all, but my other senses are picking up something. It's so hard to describe, but it feels like there's a presence around us, a comforting presence." She stopped. "I don't know whether to keep going or shut up now."

He shrugged. "If you can explain this to me, I'll feel better," he said. "I'm listening." She rubbed her forehead, wondering where to begin.

"Let's see. Well, this experience doesn't surprise me because things have been happening in my life that you would probably call paranormal. Remember that day in the hospital lobby when I called out to you? Something flew by. It was bright. And then I started seeing things differently after that. I started seeing lights around people, and other things, too. I'm feeling self-conscious. You're looking at me like I'm a nut. I know you're skeptical. But I've talked about these things with Porter and my aunt and uncle. Even my parents. Nobody has seemed too shocked by it. I think these are spiritual events. Deep inside of me I know that's what they are, Gabe. The words I'm saying are falling flat. They don't do justice to what I'm feeling and what I've been seeing."

"Now wait a minute. The clock going haywire is a spiritual event?" he asked, his voice cracking. She heard sarcasm mixed with panic. Again, she saw herself in the park.

"I think the clock and the lights were responding to something unusual, something supercharged that was happening around us," she said. "Aunt Twylah said the walls of separation are coming down. She means that in the best possible sense. The fact that you heard the same things I did, the fact that you knew in your sleep that Pablo had died, well, that tells me she's right. I felt afraid at first, but now I'm at peace with not understanding it all. My instincts tell me not to be afraid. But a few weeks ago, I had a different reaction. That's why I understand yours." She touched his hand.

He was quiet, looking down.

"I got through it because I had people to discuss it with," she said. "When Porter understood where I was coming from, I knew I was on solid ground. So many people are keeping their own mystical experiences a secret but when you start talking about them others start talking about them, too. I guess I just want to be that touchstone for you. I want to tell you that I get it, that you're not crazy. I think we're all waking up. Maybe we've been sleep-walking our whole lives."

He didn't respond. She tried to catch his eye, but he wouldn't look at her. Her forehead was starting to hurt. He had put up a wall and she was banging her head against it. "Look, I was talking about this because I thought it would comfort you. But if you really want to go, I won't push this anymore," she said finally. "It's not what I want, but do whatever you have to do to feel safe."

"It's not that I don't feel safe," he protested.

"Really? You look totally spooked."

"I was spooked for a minute because it took me by surprise."

"I understand."

"I just don't like feeling this confused."

"I hear you."

"I have a Celtic grandmother, or I had one, who saw spirits and lights and stuff."

"Really? Your family had an Aunt Twylah?"

"Yes. She wasn't treated very well by the rest of the family. She died when I was a kid. She'd actually get a kick out of this. I loved her a lot but at my house it was dangerous to buy into her beliefs. She was probably the most spiritual person among us but some people considered her a nut. I'm a psychologist, for God's sake. A mental health professional who just heard the voice of a dead child. Celtic granny or no Celtic granny, I'm not thrilled."

"I know. Hearing voices can be a very bad sign. I won't argue with that," she said. "But I think we both know we are not psychotic. Look, you have said that when it comes to mental health, an occasional shake-up is usually better than a neurotic attachment to a tired old way of viewing things. Remember?"

He looked up at her, studying her face.

"See there? I really do listen to you," she said. "In fact, those very words helped me get through some confusing times recently. You were helping me and you didn't even know it, because I remembered what you said. You said that people who are otherwise healthy but in a rut psychologically need a little chaos in their lives. Chaos is almost always a part of creativity and growth. It's better to shake things up, than to let things stagnate. That's what you said."

"Using my words against me. Very clever," he said tersely. She was shocked by the sudden change in his tone.

"Do you really think I'm against you?"

"I'm feeling a little backed into a corner, that's all."

"By me? Or yourself?" she asked. "Maybe it's that bogeyman thing. You're not in control and you don't understand. So it feels like something sinister must be happening." He looked at her, a flash of anger in his eyes. She had hit a nerve. Not a great move, she told herself.

"You think I'm rattled because I'm not in control? I never realized that you considered me a controlling person. Only one other person has ever called me a control freak. She and I are divorced now."

"Gabe, what just happened here? You are not a control freak! I happen to think you are incredibly flexible. I'm not trying to insult you and I'm not your ex-wife!"

He stood up. "Why are you so angry right now?" she pleaded. "Help me understand what you are going through."

"I don't like being badgered." She felt these words like a blow to her gut.

"Gabe, I'm just trying to talk to you. This is how you make a living, for God's sake. Do you consider yourself a nag when you're talking to your patients?"

"Once again, you're comparing me to one of my patients. But you don't think I'm crazy. Make up your mind." His tone pierced her heart.

She tried again, searching for some sign of the Gabe she thought she knew so well. "Do you remember what your motto was when we were first friends?"

"No," he said flatly.

"Your motto was, 'Keep it real.' You said that if people kept things real between each other, there would be a lot less mental illness in the world, particularly depression. I thought it was brilliant in its simplicity. That's why I'm trying to stay real with you now."

He rolled his eyes. "Nice try."

"Just go," she said standing up. "This is deteriorating. I'm not going to engage in a fight with you just so that you can feel tough and manly and on top of things again. Please go home and cool down." He paused. She could see that he was teetering. He threw up his hands. He gathered his things, the dog slinking around him looking miserable. He paused before putting his hand on the door.

"I don't know what to say."

She fought back tears. "Me neither. Too bad, huh? Like you said, we used to be so good at talking." He started to walk out. She wanted to reach out to him, to pull him back.

"Gabe," she said before he closed the door.

He turned and looked back in.

"Yes?"

"The Lord is my shepherd. You wrote those words in a card when I found out about Uncle David's cancer. Remember?"

"Yes. So?"

"What did that mean to you?"

He shrugged. "It meant that we're not alone during the dark times. That someone will lead us to the light again."

"That's how I took it. It's beautiful and poetic, but it's also true, isn't it? We both know that." He didn't answer.

"I just want you to remember that. It's something we both agree on," she said. "We're focused on our differences, but we do have plenty of common ground. We're spiritual people and we have a healthy sense of curiosity, too. I think it's such a waste of a great mystery if we dismiss all of this because we don't understand it. The scientist in you must be dying of curiosity, Gabe. Admit it! This has been an incredible day!"

"Right," he said blankly, starting to shut the door again. She felt defeated. He looked through the crack and saw her starting to cry. He came back, leaving Haley in the hallway. Now she felt angry.

"Oh, is this what you wanted? You wanted to see me cry so that you could be big and strong and save the day?"

He threw up his hands. "Hey, I'm sorry."

"Just go. You won't be saving the day today. Believe it or not, Gabe, a power greater than your ego actually does exist."

"Look," he said. "You told me to go. So I was going. Then you start reciting scripture on my way out. I come back in and now you tell me to go again. This is whacky."

"I wasn't reciting scripture! That's a cheap shot coming from you. I was searching for common ground and trying to salvage this day. I was reminding you of something you wrote to me about a higher power leading us. I know those weren't empty words when you wrote them. You have beliefs."

"Yes, I believe in a higher power," he said. "But the electrical system going haywire is not my idea of a higher power. Hearing voices is not my idea of a higher power. That's crazy stuff. It does not comfort me. It upsets me!"

"Gabe, it was Pablo! He's not one of the four horsemen of the apocalypse. He's an angelic little boy. He was talking about dolphins. He was talking about tickling dolphins!"

"I know. I heard. But if heaven is behind this, I just can't see it. It's not my idea of how a higher power makes itself known."

"Oh, I see. There *is* a higher power but it has to follow your rules about what it can and cannot do? It can only manifest in ways that don't rock your boat? Give me a break! From what I'm seeing today, anything at all would rock your silly little boat. And if somebody ever needed a shake-up, it's you, buddy! I hope every light in your apartment flashes all night long! I hope every clock goes haywire! And I hope that's just the *beginning.*" He walked out and slammed the door.

She picked up a pillow off the couch and threw it with all her might at the closed door. Then she retrieved it up and marched into the bedroom. She put her face in the pillow and screamed.

CHAPTER THIRTY-SIX

Reflections

Kalah heard Sarah's scream.

She had been taking an early morning walk along the beach with Hannah and Kai. Watching the sunrise and the majestic way it illuminated the sky, she realized that it was the perfect time to tell her hosts the story of the first lamp. They had discussed many important things during the weeks since she arrived. But until now, she had not been guided to tell them the story as it had been told to her. She realized that this perception was, in the larger sense, quite misleading. Since all beings are connected, Kai and Hannah had, on some deep level, already felt the message of the story in their hearts. Still, they urged her to speak it out loud.

Just as she finished, Sarah's scream flashed like sizzling lightning into her mind. She stopped, feeling a surge of adrenalin. Kai heard it, too. But it had less of an impact on him. As an experienced healer, he knew these screams and the inner battles they signified. He guessed that Kalah's spirit longed to leave her body and head directly for the source of trouble.

"Come," he said, extending one hand to Hannah and the other to Kalah. He led the women to a clearing on the rocky shore.

Removing the towel from around his neck, he spread it across the ground and motioned for them to sit down.

The three of them held hands in a circle.

"This is the challenge," he said calmly. "It usually comes when there is a tremendous down-pouring of spiritual light. Sarah has embraced the story. Now her ego will want to fight. It is fighting for all things temporary." He turned to Kalah. "You, too, are feeling challenged. I have watched you grow in maturity and mastery. When I listened to the power in your voice as you shared the parable of the lamp, I knew the saboteur would come."

"But that scream was *Sarah's.* It wasn't the saboteur," Kalah said, feeling disoriented and confused. She was struggling to recall the lessons of the past, the lessons of Makani's struggle. But her mind was going blank. "Sarah is not the challenger. She is a woman in pain."

"She is not the challenger, but fear is testing her, trying to discern the strength of her faith. And you think you should help her. I can feel you trembling. If you get pulled into this, it will make it more real than it needs to be. For both of you." Kalah closed her eyes, praying for wisdom. She felt love pouring from Kai and Hannah as they continued to hold her hands.

"Do you trust her?" It was Hannah who spoke now. Her voice had become deep. "Do you trust Sarah's ability to overcome this? Do you think she can do this without your intervention?" Kalah considered the question. Memories of Makani's writhing body flashed threw her. She released them. His battle was over. He had won. Her thoughts returned to Sarah. She sensed in her strength equal to her husband's. She knew that the greatest gift she could give Sarah was to acknowledge her spiritual strength.

"Yes, I trust her ability to overcome this challenge. From what I have seen, she is a great spiritual warrior. She has faced more challenges than I will ever know in my lifetime and with very little preparation. I trust her ability to meet the saboteur."

"And yet the sound of her anguish stirs something deep in your soul," Kai said. "It stirs your own fears."

She looked at him, wide-eyed. Until he had spoken these words, her fears had not been acknowledged. Now they fluttered to the surface like moths coming toward the light. In her mind's eye, she could see their dark wings. Her heart began to beat rapidly.

"How did you know?"

"Because I have been there. I have faced my own fears. It is the most sacred work of a kahuna. It is the most sacred work of any human being."

She bit her lip. She realized that Sarah did not need her as a rescuer. How then, would the saboteur challenge her now? Pain was brewing deep inside her gut. Again, she heard a scream. This time, it was not Sarah who screamed. It was Mama Hanu. Her entire body lurched forward and she put a hand over her heart. Kai saw this.

"Try to stay grounded," he said, his voice calm but firm. "Try not to leave your body, Kalah." She fought the pull. But it was profoundly difficult. Never had she heard Mama Hanu sounding so distraught. Kalah closed her eyes.

"Beloved Creator, let me see with the eyes of my spirit," she prayed. "What is happening in my village?" Her prayer was answered and she could see. Many of her people were gathered around the shore. Kei had beached herself. It appeared that she was dying. "No!" Kalah broke away from them. She stood up and ran toward the sea. Tears of grief poured from her eyes.

"Something has gone wrong! It is time to go back!" she called out to them, her arms opening plaintively. Blind with pain, she turned and kept walking into the water, as if she could somehow reach her dolphin friend in this way. She held her hands up, like a small child reaching up to a parent. "Take me back now! Please!"

"Kalah, it's not time!" Kai called out. "Don't try to go back now! It is not the right time, I assure you!" She turned around.

"But how do you know?" she asked. "How do you know that? It is not your friend who is dying on the beach! Kei is in trouble!"

Kai got up, wanting to run to her, to put his arms around the grieving woman and comfort her. "Kai, do you have faith in her?" Hannah said, pulling him back. "Do you trust her ability to overcome this challenge?" He looked at her, his eyes wide. He nodded.

"Then calm yourself," she said tenderly.

"Thank you," he said, sitting down. "Let us pray."

Together they sat, heads bowed, as Kalah stood in the water, struggling against fear.

"Somebody must do something!" she called, still reeling against the image of Kei on the wet sand. She closed her eyes and watched Makani and the others as they poured water on the dolphin and tried to get her to move back toward the sea. She saw the dolphin looking deeply into her own eyes. Across time and space, their hearts had made a connection. But what was this she was seeing? Mama Hanu was shouting, but she was shouting for them to leave the dolphin alone! Chief Ka-welo was there. His face looked calm. He was doing nothing! Kalah put her hand over her mouth, suppressing her own scream. She knelt in the water. The waves rocked her. Sharp rocks scraped her knees, but she didn't feel it. What could this mean? Her heart told her beyond a doubt that this was not a false image conjured by the saboteur. She listened to the whispers of the ancestors, pushing past fear into her awareness. "Look within," they told her. "Look within yourself."

Of course! She should have known. If Kei was taking this drastic action, she was doing it in the service of the light. She looked back at Hannah and Kai, who were deep in prayer. She stood up, staggering a little from the shock of her experience and led herself back up to shore. She knelt down beside her guardians. Hannah reached out for her, wrapping an arm around Kalah. Kai moved closer to the two women, hovering over them protectively.

"Tell us what you see, dear one," he said.

"I see Kei stranded on the beach," Kalah said, choking back sobs. There was no time to lose. She knew she had to grasp this lesson quickly. "And I see that she is showing me my own fear. I am afraid of being stranded here. It is not my home. If I stay too long, I will die. That is how I feel deep inside. I'm sorry. I love you both. But I am afraid of being stranded here. I can feel it now. I have denied my own fears."

Kai nodded. He fought back tears.

"How could you not have fear?" he asked gently. "You are a human being so far from your home." The tears were released and rolled from his eyes as he spoke. Hannah stroked Kalah's hair. "All this time, you carried that fear with you, not wanting to acknowledge it," she said. "And yet, it could have been a dangerous fear, one that blocked your trust and brought you harm on your travels back through time. Or it could have lured you home prematurely, before the prophecy was completely fulfilled."

Kalah nodded. "Kei knew this. Our bond has remained strong during my travels. In her love for me, she is showing me my own fear. I am afraid of dying in this place. I am afraid of being beached here. And Mama Hanu knows it, too. That is why she stopped the others from forcing her back out to sea. My friend was helping me."

"Thank you, Kei," she whispered. "You are very brave." She put her face in her hands, praying for strength. Then she closed her eyes and went into the deepest part of herself, the place where the saboteur had been hiding. She sensed a simmering anger, but understood what was behind it and did not deny it. The saboteur was simply that part of her that did not trust her Source. If she acknowledged this aspect of herself but did not give it the weight of a real threat, it had no power. Suddenly enlightened by love, she spoke to this shadowy being within her.

"It will be all right," she said. "Come away from the shadows. You are nothing more than a frightened child. You are such a furious, frightened child! But I will no longer disown you and banish you from the light. You are a part of me and I love you unconditionally. Fear, I honor you as my teacher. You have opened my eyes still further. Enemies are illusions. They are like frightened children. They only beg for release from the darkness and for understanding. They long for reunion with Great Spirit but fear punishment instead. There is no need for that. Come into the light."

As she spoke the dolphin returned to her family in the sea.

CHAPTER THIRTY-SEVEN

Soul Searching

"How did Mama know?" she asked Hannah and Kai when she had collected herself. "How did she know what was happening and why they should not interfere?"

"Because she knows how to listen," Kai said simply. "The same force that holds this world together and directs the course of the planets will speak to those who are willing to hear. She knows how to listen."

Kalah's thoughts returned to Sarah, who was also learning how to listen and how to see.

"Sarah will be arriving soon."

"And her godfather, too," Kai said. "Porter, the sleeping kahuna."

The women laughed.

"And just how do you plan to wake him up?" Hannah asked him.

"Oh, that's being taken care of. I've been very busy in dreamtime. Somewhere in Texas, he is. His ears must be burning."

This was, in fact, the truth. Porter sat with Kate on her back porch, pulling on his left ear lobe. "Someone must be talking about me. This ear tingles."

Kate smiled.

"It's probably my parents."

He looked at her.

"Do you think they approve of our wedding plans?"

"I'm sure the thought of their daughter radiantly happy as she marries the man of her dreams is something they can live with. I wish they could come, but Dad's health isn't good. You and I are both good storytellers, though. We'll paint them a picture when we see them again."

"You're incredibly beautiful," he said, his feelings overtaking him.

"Thank you. Being in love does that to a woman."

"I feel like I'm dreaming. I never expected this to happen to me," he said.

"Why not? You're charming and handsome. Why should you be left out?"

"That's the very question I used to ask myself, but I never got a good answer."

"So when are you going to tell Sarah that you and I are taking early retirement and going to Hawaii?" she asked. "Or maybe she already senses that. Isn't she the one who insisted that you honor your dreams and realize that you had a role to play with the sea turtles?"

He nodded. "I think she'll be excited, but not terribly surprised," he said. "I'll call her a little later. I don't know why, but I have a strong hunch that she and Gabe are sharing a very important time right now."

"Love is in the air there, too?"

"I believe so. And if it doesn't rock their boats too much, they might just make it."

* * *

Sarah was, in fact, adrift on a rocking boat and feeling seasick. The vertigo had swept over her right after Gabe left. She looked at the letter she had printed out earlier in the day. It seemed like a decade had passed since she felt so inspired, and now she wondered, "How on earth did I write this?" The afternoon had been emotional agony, her fears filling her and rocking her with a fury. But she had gotten through it, clinging to her faith in God like a kitten clinging to a tree limb during a thunderstorm. In time the storm subsided. She had been this way before. Storms always passed. She had survived far worse than an argument with Gabe. Later, sitting at her kitchen table, she idly shuffled the deck of Mayan Oracle cards Porter had sent her. Something about these symbols spoke to her, triggering flashes of insight each time she handled the cards. She pulled one at random and saw the image of a lightning bolt resting in her hand.

She had pulled this one before. She opened the book to refresh her memory about what it meant. It read:

"You are a planetary transformer. Awaken to your vast potential!"

"Hah!" she snorted. "Lightning. How appropriate. I feel like a gnat on a hot power line. If I wake up anymore I'm going to be toast." She realized that she sounded just like Gabe. Why had they fought? Probably because they were so much alike. The book beckoned her to read on.

"In receiving this lens, you are being asked to transform the collective reality constructs of this planet by expanding your own limiting belief systems. By their sheer force, the collective energy and thought forms of all human beings shape reality into what we perceive. What we call reality is actually a collective dream field, a holographic reflection of our shared beliefs. As you process your own personal experiences of apparent separation, pain, fear, denial, judgment and limitation, you bring healing and integration not just to yourself but to all of humanity. Your personal

changes affect the collective reality of the entire planet. In fact, all your dreams, visions and beliefs have an impact on the collective dream field. By simply embodying the consciousness of love, you help to realize the miracle on Earth."

She took all of this in, realizing when and how things had gone wrong. During the course of their heated conversation, she had let her love slip away. She had replaced it with fear. It was pretty obvious that Gabe had done the same thing. Love had turned on a dime, transforming into anger and even hatred. It was a truth that she could not deny and did not feel compelled to deny. She had heard it said that hate is not the opposite of love. Indifference is the opposite of love. How true, she thought. She knew she would mess up again, many times. But at least she could put her finger on a part of the problem.

She looked at the letter to journalists with fresh eyes. She needed to get busy. There would be plenty of time to wallow in self-pity when she and Gabe crossed paths again. Or when they didn't. She got out a Christmas card and addressed it to her aunt and uncle. The first letter would go to them, along with a couple of books she thought they would like. Thinking about them, she felt a sudden, compelling urge to call her aunt. But she resisted, not wanting to trouble them with her own morose tale of feeling misunderstood by her boyfriend. Instead, she put the lightning bolt card squarely in front of her computer where she could see it. If there was a better symbol for the meaning of Christmas, she hadn't seen it. She thought about the bright light of baby Jesus and the intense spiritual authority of the man, Jesus, who urged humanity to practice the most powerful act of all, the sacrament of forgiveness. Forgiveness. It was an art form she had not yet mastered. She discovered that despite her spiritual growth she was still in the trial-and-error phase when it came to that sacred act.

For despite her intention to remain loving, and Gabe's deep longing to reconnect, their egos were hard at work building a case for prolonged separation. It took them six phone conversations, four lunches and three coffee breaks to fully make up. These conversations were spread out over two tumultuous weeks.

During that time she sought the counsel of her mother, her godfather, her two best friends and Minnie, who prayed with her, fed her and offered her some simple advice. While her mother again had urged her to "keep running like the wind," Minnie counseled her simply to "keep carrying the torch. Hold it high in the darkness. It's your purpose." In one bizarre dream, these two images melded together. She saw herself as an Olympic torch-bearer running into the sunset. Gabe followed pitifully in her dust, carrying a flashlight that kept blinking off and on. The next night, she dreamed that she was in a hut on top of the world. Somebody torched the hut and she had to go running outside, her rump toasted. Seeing Gabe at work the next day, she tried not to suspect dreamtime arson. But the lingering sensations of running from a flaming hut almost set back their relationship rebuilding.

Through it all, she was determined not to abandon her relationship with Kalah. But she was not consciously connecting with her, either. She wondered if the drama with Gabe was crowding out her new teacher. She went to Central Park and sat on the bench where she had first heard Kalah's voice. Her heart had called out to her friend, but she did not get a response. She tried again, imagining Kalah in her mind's eye.

"Are you still there?" Sarah called out with her thoughts. In truth, she already knew the answer. The young time-traveler was a part of her now. Whether she answered or not, she believed in their bond. This was huge progress. She turned inward, listening with her heart. This time she heard the soft whisperings of confirmation.

"I have faith in you."

Sarah put her hand over her heart, smiling. "Thank you."

The critical voice in her head had been weakened, forced to acknowledge that Kalah was real. But it still lingered, looking for a vulnerable moment. It found another approach. "Give it up," this side of her said. "Kalah's got her own life. She can't be bothered with your petty problems. You should try to live a normal life and be grateful for a man like Gabe." For a moment she imagined herself married to him. But to her shock, the thought actually made her queasy. Her fears, grasping at anything now, began telling her that she would have to make a choice between being close to a man and being authentically her self. This was, perhaps, one of her biggest fears and the fight with Gabe only reinforced it. She couldn't confide it to anyone. She was afraid it sounded prideful, this new urge to stand in her power. But in meditation and prayer she came to the conclusion that it was not prideful at all.

She wanted only to reconnect with the gifts available to her at birth, to know what God really had in mind when he made children in His own image. She was coming to believe that true spiritual power, the innocent connection with the Divine Parent, was something children were born with but were taught to fear by adults. They, too, had been taught to fear their potential. She realized that if she were going to reclaim her birthright and encourage others to do the same, she would have to be a little bull-headed at times about being herself. If it got on someone's nerves, so be it. With time and practice, she hoped she would become less annoying.

She was beginning to understand that finding her own strength meant working through the mixed emotions bubbling at her core. Advice from family members and friends was extremely helpful. Friendship and solace felt great. But nobody could fight her battles for her. Nobody could pluck this struggle from her life without robbing her of a chance to grow. When she realized this, she understood that Kalah was giving her room to do her soul work. It wasn't a weakened connection. It was part of the divine plan. When it was time to hear from her, Kalah would come in loud and clear. So she met the challenge and went deep inside herself, determined to find the answers. Should she pull the plug on her relationship with Gabe and focus on truly getting to know and love herself? Or should she fight her fears and try to build a new life with him? Wasn't true soul work done on the level of everyday life, particularly in the context of relationships?

Were those even the right questions? Maybe she was missing the point entirely. Surely heaven had weightier matters for her to consider than whom she should date and whether she should ever remarry.

I'm realizing that we don't have to die to go to heaven, she wrote in her journal one night. *And we also don't have to die to go to hell. Heaven definitely knows where I live. That much is clear to me now. And so does hell. Which one I step into is entirely my choice. But even if we choose heaven, she continued, at what point do things start feeling, well, heavenly? So far, it's been a mixed bag. Oh, I get it. I'm the mixed bag.*

CHAPTER THIRTY-EIGHT

Honorable Struggles

During those times when she and Gabe were trying to talk it out, she struggled to understand her fears and how she had equated his lack of understanding with a red flag that abandonment was imminent. Reluctantly at first, he began to open up and acknowledge that his behavior had actually been highly rejecting. He had gone on the offensive, he said, because he felt foolish when he didn't understand what was going on. His ego told him he was foolish. And he fell for the trap.

In a second conversation, she explained what she had realized about herself. For much of her adult life she had squelched her voice, particularly if it would rock a relationship. She had chosen silence over being alone. But the closer she got to Gabe, the more she craved total honesty between them. She had grown fearful of secrets. Collin obviously had kept a few. Without this experience, she might not have been so insistent on Gabe understanding the deepest mysteries of her existence. But now, it seemed crucial that he know.

"My own advice about keeping things real was good and I want to stand by it," he acknowledged. "I knew that was true when you were saying it. I just didn't like being reminded to take my own advice. I was already feeling stupid."

She listened intently to him as he described a deeply wounded sense of self-worth brought on by an unexpected divorce. On some level, he confessed, he expected to be judged again and found "not good enough." No just by Sarah, but by God as well. With great embarrassment, he finally admitted what had been so obvious to her. A part of his surliness had to do with feelings of jealousy toward Collin. If Pablo was around, Collin might be close by.

His recognized that his fear of the unknown was a scar from the religious battle that raged within his own family. His grandmother, Nana Gwen, was in the minority as she fought to keep Celtic mythology and mysticism a part of spiritual life within her extended family.

"Everyday life was so holy to her," he explained, looking pained. "She saw God everywhere, in nature, in others and in the simplest rituals, such as baking bread. I'd hear her blessing the dough and praying before she put it in the oven. She was a devoted Christian, but ironically, my father's side of the family treated her like a heathen, particularly because she talked to spirits. Somehow the fact that she believed in eternal life after the body had fallen away was a sign that she had fallen from grace and was going to hell. Go figure. To my Dad's side of the family it was probably the work of the devil. They missed the whole point of her very loving life."

Sarah listened, her heart making a connection between the Celtic way of life and the Aloha spirit of Hawaiians. Both had such a strong and innocent connection to God and to the original plan for humanity, she thought. And yet both were overpowered by supposedly superior belief systems that seemed more fear-based.

"When I reacted to what was going on in your kitchen," he said, "I kept seeing my paternal grandfather pointing angrily to the Bible. 'Show me where it is,' he would say to Nana Gwen.

'Show me where God gives His blessing to this.' That's what I was hearing him say."

Tenderly, Sarah tried to talk through this spiritual dilemma with him.

"But they didn't have clocks and electric lights when the Bible was written," Sarah said. "So God used burning bushes. We don't have that many bushes in New York City, not enough for everyone who needs a spiritual message, so other things are used. Burning bushes, blinking lights. What's the difference if it helps us wake up? And just think how confused Ezekiel must have felt when he went up in that flying thing! But clearly he was loved by God. What would Grandfather Mahoney do with that event if it happened today?"

"Ezekiel went up in a flying thing?" Gabe realized that he needed to reread the Old Testament. It sounded vaguely familiar.

"A flying chariot of fire or something to that effect. You can only imagine how odd that must have felt. The Bible is chock full of normal people going through paranormal events. But you know, the Bible wasn't written yet when all of this was happening to them, so they had to trust their hearts and their direct connection to God. And the angels were constantly saying, 'Be not afraid! Be not afraid!' They weren't saying, 'Be afraid. Be very afraid by all of this weird paranormal stuff!'"

She felt good about this argument, but Gabe was having trouble letting it sink in. Maybe it was no use fighting about things that people were taught before they were old enough to question authority. The only things they could truly agree upon were that they cared for each other deeply and that these matters should not drain all of their energy. They both had other important things to do. People were depending on them. Fear was courting them both, but they knew they couldn't give in to the pull.

Sarah fought mightily to keep her focus and mailed out letters to newspaper editors and broadcast producers. She started to research red turtles, ancient Hawaii and the legacy and practices of kahunas. Slowly, what she took in was helping to purge old paradigms and clogged pipes in her head. She gave a presentation to fellow social workers, challenging them to engage in paradigm shifts about how to help grieving clients. She talked to them about the healing nature of grief and the differences between dark nights of the soul and clinical depression.

"People don't always need to be rescued during these dark nights," she said to the group. "In fact, I think that when we interfere too much, we rob them of something sacred. What I'm learning is that very often, they simply need to know that their struggles are very human and completely honorable. And sometimes all they need from us is a sympathetic ear, someone willing to hear their stories. I believe that this can, in many instances, ward off depression." She had gone out on a limb with this semi-mystical discussion of grief, but her meaning was understood and her presentation was very well-received. Others had been thinking about the same things, they told her.

The highlight of this period was her final home visit with Gloria Mendez, with whom she wanted some healing closure. Gloria presented her with one last drawing created by Pablo. He had drawn another ocean scene, but instead of fish and dolphins there were hearts floating on the water. Some were red, some were purple and some were blue. Some of them reminded her of turtles. Other hearts looked like boats. A bright yellow sun looked down from above, smiling. Love was everywhere.

Gabe came over on Christmas Eve, grinning like the Cheshire Cat. Among the treasures he had selected for her was a red silk lei. He put it around her neck.

"We haven't talked about Hawaii lately," he said. "And this might not be the right time. But whether I go with you or you go without me, I want you to know that I respect your right to make this journey. I've watched you doing your homework about the culture. I've seen the joy on your face when you discuss these things. If you don't do anything else in the coming year you need to immerse yourself in Hawaii. So I'm giving you enough frequent flyer miles to get there and back, first class. Whatever happens there, it's going to be really important. That much I know."

Sarah burst into tears.

"Oh, my God. That is so perfect. You just gave me the perfect Christmas gift. And it's not so much the sky miles, it's the spirit in which you gave them to me." She gave him a huge hug and a long, deep kiss. Then she handed him his gift.

"For you," she said, a twinkle in her eyes. "I hope you like it."

"Such a big box, but it's so light," he said, shaking it.

"I'll give you one hint. It floats."

He opened the box to find it filled mostly with glittering gold tissue paper. Reaching around, he fished out a tiny toy boat.

"Oh. It's my silly little boat," he said a little hesitantly. She winced.

"No, Gabe. That's not what this is about. Keep looking. I think you'll find that we were on the same wavelength." Inside the paper, he found an envelope. Opening it, he found a gift certificate for a boating excursion. She had bought him an opportunity to swim with dolphins off the coast of Bimini.

"You and wild Flipper and wild Flipper's family," she said, beaming like a child.

"You are kidding me!" he said, looking at the brochure. "Where did you find this?"

"Cruising on the net."

"This must have been expensive," he said, his eyes wide.

"No, not really. You have to get yourself down there, though. I hope you have more frequent flyer points."

"I do."

He put his arms around her, looking deeply into her eyes.

"Well, I guess we might as well get married, he said. "We're like an old married couple planning separate vacations."

"Who said anything about separate? We're not finished discussing Hawaii are we?"

"I know. I guess I just needed to hear that."

He hadn't heard about Kalah yet, but she hoped that his Celtic grandmother would start preparing him from the other side. "You know, Nana Gwen, I have realized that you and the Hawaiians have a lot in common," she had whispered in the dark, hoping that she was within hearing range. "They aren't afraid to be mystics. They see God in every day life. They're more trusting with their faith. Do you see where I'm coming from? Could you work on him for me, please?" She didn't remember that in dreamtime Nana Gwen was a part of the circle of women, and that she was busily working with them to mend the wounds in their psyches.

Porter called the next day, excited about a video she had sent him, a documentary called "Red Turtle Rising." It was filled with the wisdom of Hawaiian elders. It described the challenges of those trying to protect turtles. Watching it was final validation that he needed to do something important with his life, something that had to do with helping sea turtles. He now had the time and the financial means to help those in Hawaii who were searching for solutions. He and Kate knew that it was something they were meant to do together.

"Seeing those baby turtles pushing with their flippers toward the moonlit sea made me want to get on the next plane to Hawaii," he said. "If I had known this is what Kai wanted he wouldn't have had to throw coconuts at my head. By the way, my source has located him."

"He has?"

"I'm going to write my old friend a letter telling him the gig is up," he said, laughing. "I know what he wants, or at least I think I do. Honestly, I can't wait to see him again."

"So you really are a part of the plan to help turtles!" she said, feeling exhilarated. It was hard to keep from jumping up and down.

"Well, I always did want kids."

"*More* kids. I am your first turtle. Always remember that."

"That you are, dear. That you are."

CHAPTER THIRTY-NINE

Pieces of Cloth

Turtle descends, pushing with ease through watery space.
Shafts of sunlight point the way.
Through ancient eyes that knew the dinosaurs,
She sees ruins that sit on the floor of the sea.
Great pillars crafted by the hands of man, inspired by the dreams of God.
They will rise to meet the sun again.

Sarah paused. In her mind's eye she saw the great ruins of Lemuria. She picked up her pen again.

Turtle circles the sunken city, a stirring in her soul.
She turns inward to receive the sight of the ancients.
A lamp appears, resting in beautiful hands.
She hears the beating of a heart, then the beating of two,
As the Beloveds meet once again.
Now she calls out to the dolphins and the whales,
Those who kept the sea from sinking into incomprehensible silence.
She calls from her heart with a story to share.
The darkness has found its source. The vessels know their course.
And I, turtle, have found my voice.

Now the floor of the sea moves with the deep contractions of birth.

Great pillars crafted by the hands of man, inspired by the dreams of God

Prepare to meet the sun once again.

She paused again, sighing deeply at the imagery that flowed effortlessly through her pen. How beautiful, she thought, to be a voice for Turtle, a voice for the hopes of Mother Earth. She felt like a scribe. Feeling a shift, she continued to write, putting her own voice on paper.

Kalah came to me in a dream last night. She told me that the time of the turtle has arrived. She spoke to me of a prophecy. The darkness will find its source. The vessel will know its course. The turtle will find her voice. For my own small part, I believe that the darkness within me is moving up toward the light. Like the child who has kept her secrets under the bed I have been afraid to truly know myself. But that is changing. And I believe that the vessel is the human body and also the ego, the thing we call the personality. I feel the pull of my destiny, like undercurrents of soul guiding me toward something far greater than anything I could imagine for myself. And finally, I believe that the turtle will gain a voice. Many people will come together to tell her story. Porter can be a voice. Kate can be a voice. Maybe even I can be a voice. I don't know how turtle's story will end, or what difference we will make in the big picture, but with Kalah and Kai guiding us, how can we go wrong?

She stopped and closed her journal. It was time. Hawaii was calling.

* * *

Across the continent and across the great Pacific, two researchers in Honolulu watched a radar screen as a hawksbill turtle made her way around the island of Maui. A small satellite transmitter rested securely on her back, illuminating the course of her travels.

"So that's where she goes," the female researcher, Rose, said to her co-worker, Ricky. "She's faster than I thought." With those words, a flash of light filled the room, causing the two to step back from the display screen.

"What was that?" Rose asked. "Did we overload something?"

"I don't think so. The system's still up. And it wasn't lightning," Ricky said, looking out the window. "The sky is blue. That was incredibly strange."

They looked at the screen. The pulses of light that tracked the turtle's journey had somehow changed. The two moved closer to the screen.

"Speaking of strange," Rose said, her voice trailing off. "Get a look at this."

Pulses of light were forming spirals on the screen as the satellite continued to track the voyage of the red turtle. The universe, it seemed, was having a grand time with the tracking device, giving them a picture of what the turtle could see as light spun like little tornadoes in the emerald sea. Cutting gracefully through the water with her great flippers, the turtle smiled to herself and followed the long shafts of sunlight to the great ruins of Mu. Her ancestors had seen much in that place.

* * *

Porter opened the letter with the Hawaiian postmark.

"Kate! This is it. A letter from the World Turtle Trust!" he called out. He pulled the letter from the envelope.

"We get to join them for the egg laying!" he said happily. "This is it, honey. In a short while we'll be witness to a birthing ritual that was taking place when dinosaurs walked the earth. We'll be part of group that protects the nests after the mothers lay their eggs. We'll see the hatchlings running out to sea! And this is just the beginning. Look at this list of possible projects for us. There's so much we can do right off the bat."

"Wow," she said, reading the letter over his shoulder. "This is fantastic. They need grant writers. I can do that. They need brochures to educate the public. And speakers."

She kissed his cheek and ran a hand lovingly through his thick hair. "No more sore head for you! No more coconuts."

"Are you sure you want to do this?" he asked.

"Are you kidding? What else could possibly make us happier right now? We're going to look back and wonder what took us so long to do something truly meaningful with our lives. Better late than never, I guess."

"We might be roughing it at times, but something tells me that when we get into it, we're going to feel like two of the luckiest people on the planet."

"Especially if we can make a difference," she said, wistfully. "If we don't, we'll be witness to our own folly. I sure hope we're not going down there to chronicle the death of a species."

"Kate, I'm willing to do whatever it takes to keep that scenario from unfolding. I mean, whatever it takes," Porter said, surprising himself with the forcefulness of this vow. She came around to him and put her hands on his face.

"So you're on board, 100 percent?" he asked, already knowing the answer.

"I am. Or my name's not Katherine Sun Turtle," she said.

"Soon it will be Sun Turtle-Hudgins," he said, taking her hand. "It doesn't have quite the same ring.

"What does 'Hudgins' mean, anyway?" she asked. "Have you ever looked it up?"

"It means, 'he who swims with sea turtles,'" he replied. She pinched his nose playfully. "If you lie, this will get bigger and bigger," she teased.

"Red turtles have pretty long beaks. Is that what you call them, beaks?" he asked, rubbing his nose. "I have so much to learn. Have you noticed that I kind of look like a turtle? I mean around the mouth and nose?"

She cocked her head and didn't answer. He kept reading the letter, his anticipation building. At the bottom was a hand-written note. He read it out loud to Kate.

"Mr. Hudgins, I read your letter with excitement. We need you. Your passion for this will only be heightened when you get here, that much I can assure you. I believe that you have been touched by turtle magic. Once you are touched by it, your life will never be the same. Welcome aboard."

It was signed, *"Rose."*

* * *

Sitting at his computer, Gabe studied the details of the Christmas present Sarah had given him. A chance to swim with wild dolphins! He jumped from one web site to another, gathering information about the area around Bimini. One thing gave him pause.

"Well, I'll be," he said, shaking his head. "She's sending me to the heart of the Bermuda triangle!"

He picked up the phone, not wanting to miss an opportunity to tease.

"Thanks a lot," he said, when she answered. She could hear the smile in his voice.

"What?"

"You're trying to get rid of me. I should have known it was too good to be true."

"What is too good to be true?"

"My Christmas present. You're sending me into the Bermuda triangle."

"Well, yeah," she said, feeling a little sheepish.

"You knew about that?" he asked, a touch of genuine concern in his voice.

"Well, I did. But I dismissed my worries because you are a man of reason."

"Oh."

"Or *are* you?" she asked, sounding devilish.

"I'll have to get back to you on that one."

"If you *do* come back," she said, "from the Bermuda triangle, I mean." Sometimes it was hard not to tease Gabe, the so-called man of reason who was one of the most superstitious people she'd ever known. "And if you don't come back, I'll comfort myself by knowing that you're down there shrinking some dolphin heads and having a grand old time on the lost continent of Atlantis. It's all part of my dastardly scheme to make a believer out of you."

"You win. I believe you. Don't send me there to make a point."

* * *

Somewhere nearby, in a dimension not so far away, the women who gathered around the sewing table began to giggle. The eldest, whom the others knew as Mama Hanu, laughed out loud, the joy of it all filling her being.

"She's a funny one," Mama Hanu said. "She reminds me so much of Kalah." The others nodded. "And she's a sky-walker, too. Did you know?"

Aunt Twylah nodded as she handed a spool of golden thread to Nana Gwen.

"I'm working on my grandson," Nana said. "He's got great potential, you know."

The others agreed.

Outside of Gabe's window, he saw a magnificent red sun peaking through tall buildings as it settled toward the horizon. The day was done. He watched as darkness embraced the light. They were one.

CHAPTER FORTY

The Visitor

The temperature had dipped well below freezing throughout the night. Frost collected on the windows of Sarah's bedroom, making lacey formations that looked like tiny frozen starfish wanting to come in from the cold. Sarah saw them threw blurry eyes. It was Sunday and she was in no hurry to get up. With one hand, she reached around for Gabe. Then she remembered that he had slept at his own place. She grabbed a pillow and wrapped her arms around it, turning away from the window and the first rays of light. She heard a noise that sounded like a footstep.

"It's just Haley," she told herself. Then she remembered that the dog wasn't there.

"Sarah, it's me."

Her heart jumped. Rolling over, she saw him. He was nearly transparent at first, but his form grew more solid in appearance. He was surrounded by a soft white light.

"Collin?"

"Don't be afraid," he said. He looked like an angel. Her heart was beating hard. She sat up and pulled a pillow to her chest, holding it there like a shield. He saw the gesture and reached out a hand to her.

"I didn't come to frighten you," he said. "I came to comfort you."

"I know," she whispered softly. "Aunt Twylah said you'd come." He smiled. She reached her hand toward him and their fingertips met. She felt a current of energy running from his fingers to hers. It filled her with peace.

"I miss you," she said. "I miss our life."

"Me too." He looked down.

"Come closer," she said, patting the bed. A lump was forming in her throat. He moved toward her and sat on the edge. She noticed that the bed was pressed down by the weight of him, as if he were flesh and bone. He was quiet for a moment. He seemed to be collecting his thoughts.

"I know you have questions. You deserve answers. There was a time when I thought I could never face you again. I was a wreck when I got to the other side. My spirit was battered."

"What happened, Collin?" Tears rolled down her face.

"Well, you were right. My death wasn't really a suicide, although I'm the one who went through the motions of killing myself."

"I don't understand."

"I was murdered. Murdered with thoughts of hate. I would never have believed it was possible while I was alive on your side. But it is."

"Who hated you?" she asked incredulously. "I thought everyone loved you. You know how much I loved you."

He nodded. "I always knew." The light around him intensified.

"Then what happened? My God, Collin, *what happened to you?"*

"I was keeping a secret from you. You know I was traveling more. I had volunteered to work on an investigative piece about a cult. The group's leaders were using very aggressive brainwashing tactics. I was told it could be dangerous, but I didn't really believe it. I was cocky and didn't see myself as vulnerable. It turns out that the situation was far more sinister than I could have imagined. While the leaders professed spiritual values, their actions were entirely ego-driven. And I mean ego in the darkest sense of the word. That is the true anti-Christ, Sarah, and it can appear in anyone who has confused faith with the fear-based drives of the ego. These drives are often shrouded in spiritual sentiments but they have nothing to do with the love of Christ. They are all about hatred, projection and control. What I understood just before I lost my sanity was that I had asked too many questions and made the wrong people angry. I became the victim of a sustained and very organized psychic attack. It was done long-distance and went on around the clock until I cracked. When they finally got inside my head, it all happened very quickly. I didn't even have time to ask you for help. I was too crazed at that point. Too far gone. I became convinced that I was a bad person who deserved to die. I was blinded to the love all around me. That's how it works. My will crumbled and I obeyed their command, committing an act of murder against myself. Like I said, I would not have believed it was possible unless I had gone through it. Maybe that's why I went through it, to learn and join the response from the spiritual side."

"Who are they? They need to be punished!"

"They have been dealt with. In the spiritual realm, they were allowed to experience their own hatred turned back on themselves so that they could learn the lesson of their actions. You might call it karma. There was no return of malice in this lesson, only an opportunity to learn. Their group was shattered. It's over. You don't need to trouble yourself with them."

"But Collin, they will never be charged with your murder," she protested. She realized that her hand had curled into a fist and was pounding the bed.

"There is justice, Sarah. Don't be consumed by this. It just doesn't matter any more, not compared to the important things that are ahead for you."

"It doesn't *matter?* It matters to me. I was hurt terribly by your death. So were a lot of people."

"I know it doesn't make sense to you right now. Someday, when you're on this side, you'll understand what I mean. For now keep your focus on the light. Your focus determines how your energy will be used and what you will manifest. You have a job to do, a very important one. The fact that you weren't stopped by all of this speaks volumes about your strength and your faith."

"My faith," she said, "has been sorely tested."

"I know, Sarah. But the darkness didn't win, did it? Say, you have a book on your shelf. It's one of your favorites, 'Vision,' by Ken Carey. Remember how you wanted me to read it, and finally I did? I loved it. It surprised you how much I loved it."

Sarah looked over her shoulder toward her book shelf and nodded. It made her heart ache to remember how much they loved to share their favorite books. They challenged each other to see life from different vantage points. He had helped her grow in ways that he couldn't imagine.

"When I'm gone, open it to page 17 and read the middle paragraph out loud. It will help you to hear it read out loud."

She struggled to take in everything he had said. It seemed important to step out of her pain and see the bigger picture, to get something good from this. That's why he had come. She realized that his visit was a gift. "The bottom line is that you haven't completely vanished," she said. "And that's good news."

"No. I'm alive and well in another realm. And let me share a secret with you." His tone was playful now. His quirky grin returned. "Now, I don't want you to take it the wrong way," he said.

"What?" she asked a little apprehensively. "Don't tell me you've already remarried."

"No, silly. I'm not even dating." She smiled, wiping tears from her face.

"No, the secret is this. Where you are right now, the realm that you're in, well..." He paused, shrugging a little apologetically. "Well, that's as dead as it gets."

"It's *what?*"

"The dimension that you're in, Sarah, the third plane, the material world, whatever you want to call it, that's really and truly as dead as it gets. I know it sounds strange. But that's good news, right?"

"Not if you are telling me that I'm dead!"

"No, I'm telling you that there is no death," he corrected. "When you're on my side of the veil you feel even more alive than when you are on that side. You have more freedom. You have more knowledge, a lot more knowledge. You remember things that you had forgotten, like the fact that death is an illusion. And you don't have to floss your teeth to prevent tooth decay. No traffic, either. That's all I'm saying." He laughed a little. His eyes were bright.

"Thanks."

"That was supposed to make you smile."

"Maybe you should have put it another way. Now, I feel dead."

"No, you don't feel dead," he said, laughing. "You can't fool me. You're just having a good time playing with me."

"Yeah, you're right. It's fascinating really, when you think about it. I can't wait to share the news."

He shook his head, smiling with amusement. "Here it comes."

"I'm serious!" she said, laughing. "I can't wait to spread the word. Hey everybody! Paradigm shift! If somebody's got to play the role of the dead in this vast, multidimensional universe, we're it. You don't actually get to join the un-dead club until you go to the other side!" She rubbed her eyes, which were now crying happy tears. "But seriously, Collin, I think we all secretly remember that on some level. We're playing a game of hide-and-seek with ourselves, aren't we?" He nodded. She paused. "I miss our talks. We had such a good time."

He stood up, the glow of laughter still shining in his eyes.

"Yes, we did. And on that note, I have to leave now," he said. "As time goes by, you will think of me less and less. I feel your heartache, but later, on my side of the veil, we'll get reconnected. By the way, I think there's actually another marriage in your future, if you want it."

"You mean Gabe? It feels really strange dating someone if you're watching, Collin. I don't think I can do that."

"I'm not really watching. It doesn't work like that. And I'm not going to make any predictions. I never said anything about you and Gabe getting married. I mean how many times have you gotten mad at me for telling you the ending to something?"

"Right. You never told me for certain that it was Gabe."

"But I will tell you this, because I can't resist," he said, flashing an impish smile. "You need to buckle your seatbelt, Sweetheart, because you are going to have quite a day. Just remember, though. It's all good. I always loved it when you said that to me. And guess what? You were right." He stepped back, fading a little.

"Don't get into any more trouble," she said.

"I won't. And don't you forget to keep your focus on the lamp."

"Hold on. Come back," she said. "You *know* about that?" She was shocked. "You know about Kalah?"

"Darling, it's headline news on my side," he said. "We're just waiting for the headlines on your side to catch up. I love you, Sarah. Love is eternal."

With that he was gone.

"Of course he knows about Kalah and the lamp," she said, softly. "Duh!" She got up and reached for Carey's book, opening to the page Collin had given her. She sat on her bed and read it out loud, hugging a pillow as she spoke the words:

"There is no cause that justifies fear, and there is no work motivated by fear that in any way contributes to a better world. Those who are motivated by fear, no matter how they justify such motivation to themselves, are working to keep the world in darkness. Action motivated by fear brings sorrow just as surely as the sowing of any seed brings the harvest of the same. Love can cry, love can care, love can initiate action to heal the infirm and uplift spirits, but love does not react in anger. Love does not nurse resentment or entertain vengeful passions. Love recognizes no injustice save one: the injustice of denying the Creator of Heaven and Earth communion with the human soul."

Collin was right. It helped. She sat for twenty minutes replaying what he had said. She looked at the clock, trying to remember whether Aunt Twylah and Uncle David went to church. As if on cue, the phone rang. It was Uncle David. His voice was raspy and he coughed for a minute before he could get a full sentence out.

"Uncle David, how are you?" she asked, her heart aching. "Believe it or not, I was just thinking about calling you."

"I believe it. I think I dreamed about you and Hawaii all night long. That's why I'm calling. We're mailing you something to take on your trip. Twylah tells me you're going to Porter's wedding next month."

"That's right. Is it something you want me to give him?"

"No, this isn't for Porter. We're mailing him a wedding gift this week. No, this package is for your friend Kalah. It's the original painting of the dolphin with the key. Twylah said she knows why she painted it now. Kalah has to take it home with her."

"Wait. She's going home? And she needs to take an oil painting? Okay, that's just weird. I'm starting to think this whole morning has been one long dream."

"I'm telling you, Sarah, Twylah's guides started talking to her this morning when I was trying to describe my dreams and I could barely get a word in edgewise after that. They said Kalah's going to leave something important here. And she needs to take something back with her when she leaves. And you're supposed to give it to her. That's what the wife and her transparent friends have announced, and you know I've given up trying to argue." He tried to laugh a little. It made him cough.

She was speechless.

"Sarah? Are you still there?" She moved her lips, but she couldn't speak. She tried again. Nothing would come out. Her eyes started to burn. She made them blink. Tears streamed down her face. She heard her uncle speak to her aunt.

"I think she's in shock. I should have let you tell it. You were right. Me and my bull-headedness. There's no sound coming from her end but I think she's still on the line."

"Let me talk to her, dear." Sarah's mind started to clear when she heard her aunt's voice.

"Sarah, are you there? Have we totally shocked and confused you?" Sarah cleared her throat. Her vocal cords released their paralysis and slowly started working again. "Um. I'm sort of confused. And a little shocked. And slightly mystified about how I'm going to get a painting to Hawaii without completely wrecking it, not to mention how Kalah's going to get the painting back through time and space.

"Oh, and Collin just paid me a visit. In fact, he woke me up. Other than that, I'm fine, Aunt Twylah. Just fine." Her aunt started laughing. In fact, it was one of her more raucous episodes of laughing. She heard her uncle asking, "What in the heck's going on, woman?" Then Sarah started laughing, too. She laughed until her stomach hurt.

"Oh, let me catch my breath," her aunt said finally. "I needed that. So, where do we begin? Collin's visit?"

"Well, I thought that was incredible, but after hearing Uncle David talk about sending the dolphin painting back to ancient Hawaii, I think his visit was actually pretty normal stuff," Sarah said. "He looked great. He made some fascinating points about the anti-Christ, cleared up a few mysteries about what he was up to before he died and made a prediction about my future without really telling me anything. Then he was on his way."

"That's usually how those things go," Aunt Twylah said nonchalantly. "They tend to unload a lot of information and move on. It's bizarre at first but after a while it's just as natural as anyone else dropping by. You'll get used to it."

"Hey," Sarah said. "Do your guests ever tell you that this place is as dead as it gets?"

"Honey, *all the time.* Some of them really like to rub that in. Maybe it's payback for us referring to them as dead."

"Maybe. It sure shifted *my* paradigm. So how's Uncle David?"

"He's holding his own," her aunt answered with some neutrality. "His dreams were spectacular. I told him it sounded like he went on another spirit journey, but before we could even finish discussing it the guides started yammering at me and it was like a convention in here, everybody trying to get the floor. To sum it up he saw you at Porter's wedding and he saw the man, Kai, the one that Kalah is living with..."

"Wait a minute. You know that for a fact? Kalah is living with him?"

"Yes, dear, that's what I'm told," her aunt answered. "And Porter knows it, too, now. Seems he used a trustworthy old connection. You know what they say: Once a spy, always a spy. Apparently this other man is on a spiritual quest, too, and Porter trusts him completely. And apparently Kai knows about all of this and thinks the whole thing is ironic and very funny, Porter the sleeping kahuna using his CIA connections. At least that's what my sources say." The words rushed past Sarah in a blur. She was still stuck on the first part.

"Wait. You know that he was in the CIA? And how long have *you* known?" Her aunt forged ahead, not giving her a direct answer.

"Anyway, he was able," her aunt continued, "to not only verify Kai's address, but also to get some declassified photographs of an ancient city that sank to the bottom of the sea. Of course you and I both know that it's Lemuria, which explains a lot about why Kalah is contacting you now."

"It does?" Sarah answered weakly. "And why were the photos classified? It's just showing some ruins, right?" Her voice sounded very far away, even to her. She felt herself leaving her body and drifting somewhere above her head.

"Are you with me, Sarah? Have I shocked you again?"

Sarah's body jumped a little and she got back inside of it. Her mouth was extremely dry. She poured herself a glass of water at the kitchen sink. Her aunt called her name a couple more times, relieved that she could at least hear swallowing sounds coming from her niece.

"I'm here," she said. "I'm here. I think you're going too fast, though. My head's spinning. I'm still trying to visualize Kalah with an oil painting. Will it even make sense to her people? Will they know what a key is? Isn't that like tampering with the past or something?"

"Past, shmast," her aunt said. "They've got more sense than we do. They're descendants of an advanced civilization. They build sea-faring boats. They might not work with the same raw materials, but the concept will make sense. Don't you worry. God has the copyright on the story of humanity. So it's all subject to God's tinkering and revision. Anyway, time is an illusion. Albert Einstein said that, you know."

"So I hear."

"And that's why the photos were classified, dear. The ancients knew it, too. Some of them knew how to get around time. That's apparent from some of the ruins. There are carvings of a place that looks like New York City. I'm told there's quite a bit of detail. But don't worry yourself about that right now, Sarah. Getting back to the painting, David saw you in his dream, delivering it to Kalah in Hawaii. It was in perfect condition. You'll take it on the plane. It's not really that big. It'll work."

"But really, Aunt Twylah, can't you just Fed Ex it or something? I just don't trust myself."

"Nope. You have to take it. That's the way it's got to be. Trust yourself."

"And you say that Uncle David actually saw me giving it to her?"

"Yep."

"Okay then. I won't worry." Her thoughts jumped to Porter.

"Now then, did you say Porter has photos of the sunken city?" Sarah asked this question a little cautiously.

"That's what the guides say. They're all abuzz. Actually, they're way ahead of us."

"That's what Collin said. I had never thought about it that way, but they get excited about things, too."

"You bet they do. To them we're just neighbors. What affects us affects them. We're all children of God. Bodies or no bodies."

"Makes sense."

"I hate to stop now," her aunt said. "But your uncle wants to go to church. I thought we should wait until later to call you, but he was so excited he couldn't stand it."

"I'm so glad he's excited," Sarah said. "Love you."

"Love you, too." They hung up.

Sarah realized that her head hurt. She put the phone down and it rang instantly. Startled, she let out a little shriek.

CHAPTER FORTY-ONE

Twists and Turns

"What now?" she asked the ringing phone. "What do you want?"

It rang again. She picked it up.

"Hello?" Her voice sounded tense.

"Sarah, it's Porter."

"Hi," she said, taking in a deep breath and letting it out.

"Did I call at a bad time?"

"No, this is a perfect time," she said, wrestling with a sudden urge to scream.

"That doesn't sound very convincing."

"I'm sorry," she said, her voice cracking. "But I talked to Aunt Twylah and I already know what you're going to tell me and I don't know if I can handle it."

He was silent for a moment. "You know about the pictures."

"Yes."

"And that frightens you."

"Yes!"

"Why is that? I thought you'd be excited. One of the platforms was built in the shape of a sea turtle! And that's not the half of it. I have so much more to tell you about all of this."

"I think I know already. Someone from that time traveled to New York City. I guess that's probably Kalah. Maybe there's a depiction of her talking to me with my hair standing on end and a wigged out look on my face." She paused to imagine this. "I would actually find that kind of funny if Collin hadn't come by first thing this morning to tell me he was actually murdered and that I'll probably get married again."

"That's a lot to take in. It's not a pretty picture," he said. "The murder that is."

A wave of knowing suddenly washed over her. "You know about how he died, don't you? Why have you been holding out on me?"

"I didn't want to," Porter replied, sounding guilt-ridden. "I couldn't leave it alone. I knew your hunch was right. So I talked to some people who could get to the bottom of it. I knew the real story when I called you in Florida, but it didn't seem like the right time to tell you and anyway, your aunt begged me not to. She wanted Collin to have the chance to tell you himself."

"Wait a minute. How did my aunt know? Did you tell her?"

"No, Sarah. Your aunt has higher connections. She doesn't need me or agents of the United States government to find out what's going on." She sat down on the floor and put her face in one hand. He could hear her crying.

"Oh, honey. None of us meant to hurt you. I wanted to respect your aunt's advice. But I've been so eager to validate your intuition about his death. He never meant to leave you. Very few people who take their own lives really want to leave the people they love."

"So you do know it's a cult? A creepy, psycho cult?" Sarah asked, a sob bursting out of her.

"Yes. A *former* creepy, psycho cult. It no longer exists."

"But the evil that was behind it still exists."

"The *fear* still exists," he said. "The ego's fear of God creates that particular form of brutality. And yes, it will pop up somewhere else. That kind of fear is abundant in our collective consciousness and it will find an opening somewhere else." She noticed that he repeatedly chose the word "fear" and avoided her reference to evil. She remembered that Porter had shocked her recently by saying that he no longer believed in evil, just consciousness in the dark waiting to become the light. Her mind had a hard time discerning the difference. But for now, it didn't really matter. She felt his unconditional love pouring over her as if the distance between them was meaningless. It was deeply soothing, but it did not dispel her inner turmoil. Only she could do that.

"Porter, it's just too much," she said, crying. "I mean, every piece of news I've gotten today has in some way been highly illuminating. But I'm just not equipped to handle this. Not all at once."

"Yes you are," he said gently.

"No!" she insisted. "I am *not* equipped. Do you hear me? *I am not equipped!"* She practically shouted the last four words. It was an odd declaration coming from her, particularly since she could feel heavenly love all around her. She thought about Minnie and her sometimes grouchy response to being filled with the light and love of the Holy Spirit. She was glad that she had warned her about this.

"I hear you," Porter said, tenderly. They were quiet. He let her finish crying without hanging up. She put the phone down for a minute and blew her nose. Then she put it to her ear and spoke to Porter calmly, feeling like herself again.

"I'm so sorry."

"For what? For being human and feeling overwhelmed?"

"I really want to hear about the pictures. My God, it's incredible. But my mind is so tired," she said. "Profoundly tired. I feel like I've been watching a Twilight Zone marathon."

"I think that when the time is right, this is all going to make you extremely happy."

"Me, too."

They said their good-byes and hung up. A few moments later the phone rang again. She looked heavenward and prayed that it would be a simple matter.

It was Gabe.

"Hi," she said, a little edgy. "I hope you're not going to say anything weird."

"Well if that isn't a twist," he said. "What's going on?"

"I just really need to have a normal conversation," she said, her voice pleading.

"I just called to tell you we have dinner reservations for New Year's Eve. Is that too weird?"

"No, that's not weird," she said. "That's good. Where are we going?"

"We've inherited some tickets for a dinner cruise around the New York harbor. My roommate and his girlfriend got another offer and they already had the reservations. I hear it's quite an experience."

"Love it," she said. "Are you coming over today?"

"Well, is it safe?"

"I think so. But I can't make you any promises."

"I'll risk it. I miss you."

"Good," she said, feeling happy. "I was hoping you'd say that."

"Oh, and by the way," he said. "I made my reservations to Atlantis, I mean to Bimini, today. I'm going in March. Want to come and get lost with me?"

"Don't toy with me, Gabe."

"I'm sorry. I couldn't resist. I've been doing a little research. The whole Atlantis thing is really intriguing. Once I started reading about it, I couldn't stop. Can you just imagine if it was all real? If humanity really became incredibly advanced but lost its bearings somehow and sank its own civilization like a battle ship? I mean, what does that open up for us in terms of understanding our own history?"

"I'm right there with you. It's mind-blowing to me, too. I knew you were a man after my own heart."

"That I am," he replied. "That I am."

* * *

Sarah slept peacefully in Gabe's arms. Haley was at the foot of the bed making soft snoring sounds and kicking a little in her sleep. Gabe looked up at the ceiling, wondering about colorful shapes dancing in a circle of light. His thoughts shifted to Hawaii. Sarah was waiting for an answer about whether he would accompany her there. He couldn't explain the barrier that seemed to stop him from committing.

The subject was dropped for the time being. It didn't ruin their New Year's Eve celebration on the cruise around the harbor. In fact, the evening had become one of the most moving experiences of their lives. He recalled the details: Close to midnight, the boat headed for the Statue of Liberty. The captain came on the intercom, telling them that they would soon be coming to a stop at the statue's base. It was freezing outside, but coats were quickly grabbed and most of the excited group headed outside to the boat's bow. Approaching the great icon, the crowd became silent. The awe was palpable. Sarah watched other boats moving toward the statue. In each instance, a wave of reverent silence washed over the merrymakers as the boats pulled up and silenced their engines. Standing around them were people from every part of the globe. They were unified in this one moment by the image of a very grand woman shining her light in the night.

He recalled their whispered conversation as they waited. What was it about this powerful figure, with her torch held high that seemed to touch everyone the same way? "It's the Great Mother," she had whispered. "Look at everyone's faces. Can you see the child in them?" It was true. Shifting in bed, he now mulled over the scene on the boat. They had all been reduced to little children wearing the same expressions of innocent wonder. He remembered her gentle words.

"At times like these, I think I see what God sees," she said softly when they had gone back inside the boat. "We are all one being."

"You mean one family?"

"No, actually, I mean one being," she said. "What if there's one big Christ Child and all of humanity is it?" And then, he recalled, Sarah had changed the subject. "I think you'd love Hawaii."

"I know. I can't explain my resistance. I recognize that it's there. Can you be patient with me a little longer while I try to figure this out?"

"Of course," she had answered. "Maybe I'm meant to go by myself this time."

Sleeping now, she moved a little in his arms, bringing him back to the sweetness of their shared bed. Her saw her lips move. "Uncle David," she whispered. "Why have you come?" In dreamtime, she was sitting at the table with the circle of women. Mama Hanu sat on one side of her. Her mother, Minnie and her Aunt Twylah were also seated at the table, as was Hannah. They had been laughing and talking. The women were having a grand time talking about all of the exciting things that were to come. It was here that they all understood the grander scheme of their lives. Only in her so-called wakeful state was she burdened with the problem of forgetting.

Aunt Twylah was pulling a long golden thread through a patch of white linen when Uncle David walked into the room. He had a look of deep peace on his face.

"Uncle David," Sarah said, softly. "Why have you come?"

But as the words left her lips, her heart already knew the answer. Her uncle had completed his journey and crossed to the other side. Twylah stood up and embraced her husband. Their forms seem to merge for a moment, then separate again.

"Everyone, I have an announcement to make," Aunt Twylah said. "David would like some of his ashes scattered in Hawaii. It looks like I'll be joining you after all." Uncle David nodded and bowed a little. He seemed to take a moment to look lovingly at each woman's face. Then he looked at what they were sewing.

"The earth," he said simply.

"We are mending what has been torn," Mama Hanu said. "We have been sewing for many lifetimes at this round table. Sometimes there is a rip while we are working and we must begin again. But there is a plan for its completion and we are very close now."

"Your round table effort has been valiant," he said. "May your needles and thread be more productive than men's swords. Certainly, they will be more creative." Sarah saw the nobility in him, then. His tired body, the costume of the fisherman, seemed to roll away, revealing an even brighter persona behind it. He put his arm around his wife. "You are my hero," he said to her. "Always remember that, my lady." He kissed her and looked around the circle at the beautiful feminine faces smiling so lovingly upon him. "I will see you in Hawaii," he said. With that, he was gone.

Sarah opened her eyes from her sleep, knowing in her heart that Uncle David had passed on. She also knew that he would be with them in Hawaii. He was no longer too sick to travel. She felt Gabe's eyes on her. She looked at him. They held each other without speaking for a while. A street lamp illuminated their faces.

"Uncle David has passed," she said. A tear rolled down her cheek. Before she could wipe it, Gabe reached a hand to her face and gently touched the wet place on her face. He nodded in understanding, trusting her knowing. She moved closer and he wrapped his arms around her, feeling her tears on his chest.

"I'm happy and I'm sad," she whispered.

"I know," he said. "Me, too."

She heard the gentle thumping of his heart. After a while, they both drifted back into dreamtime. Neither Sarah nor Gabe would consciously remember that as their spirits slipped out of their sleeping bodies, they had been released from the bondage of the body to go swimming with Uncle David and a large family of sea turtles. For a moment, their forms melted into the vast waves of the great cosmic sea, giving them great joy and peace. Then they took shape again as individual human beings and individual turtles. It was the stuff of mystics and quantum physicists, this dreamtime adventure. And it was only the beginning.

CHAPTER FORTY-TWO

The Call

Porter was studying a photograph of a hawksbill turtle when the phone rang. It was Sarah's mother, Marianne.

"Well hello, there! Happy New Year's Day," he said. "How are you?"

"I've had better days, Porter. I'm afraid I've called with some pretty rough news." He stood up, suddenly feeling a need to pace. A sense of sadness washed over him. Before she could get the next words out, he knew. David had passed in the night, she explained. It was a relatively peaceful death at home. Twylah held him in her arms for his last breaths. In a sense, it was unexpected, even though he was extremely ill, she told him. David seemed to rebound for a while and had actually spent his last day out on his boat, fishing. That night, he told his wife he felt his spirit slipping away.

"She didn't beg him to fight it," she said. "She sensed he was ready to move on. He told her he was ready to swim in the sea again, and she knew what he meant. Did Sarah tell you how he had an epiphany while we were in Florida? He was thinking about sea turtles coming to shore, and he had a moment of feeling as if he were somehow one with that experience."

"No, she didn't tell me," Porter said. "But please share it. It sounds like something I need to hear right now." Porter sat down and picked up the photograph of the turtle.

"Well, he thought about how hard it is for the turtle to walk on land. She drags her heavy body ashore and fulfills her purpose, then she goes back into the sea, where she's swift and graceful. He told us that he was filled with a sense of peace when he really thought about that, how there's a time to be struggle on earth and a time to glide in the sea again. He knew that he wouldn't be dragging his body around forever. When he died, he would be swift again."

Porter looked up at Kate, who had walked in the room in the middle of Marianne's story about David. He swallowed hard and reached a hand out to her.

"I can't tell you what a comfort that is," he said into the phone. "I guess we're all like that. Coming onto the earth for a purpose, then slipping back into the waves again."

"So true. And I don't really care whether David has flippers right now, or wings, as long as he's happy." Porter smiled, and then laughed. He couldn't hold it back. It reminded him of something Sarah would say.

"Forgive me for laughing," he said. "But that tickled me."

"It tickles me, too," she said, her voice sounding lighter. "And I'll bet it really tickles David, wherever he is. Twylah doesn't expect him to come back to her right away, as a spirit, I mean.

"She says that they usually rest for a while when they cross over. Knowing David, though, he's probably gone fishing."

"I hope so."

"Well, I have one other reason for calling and I'm afraid it's going to sound strange, but here goes," she said. "James and I are on our way to Florida. There will be a big memorial service there. A lot of people love him. But Twylah had asked that the whole clan not come down again, only those who won't be able to make it to Hawaii for your wedding. What I mean is she wants to honor one of her husband's last requests. How should I say this? She wants to bring David's ashes with her. To your wedding. I mean not to your wedding, exactly, but on the same trip." She let out a deep breath. "There. I said it."

"Of course. Absolutely. I can't tell you what that means to me," Porter said. Kate was sitting next to him now. He took her hand and kissed it.

"I only hesitated because it sounds like we're bringing a funeral to your wedding.

"I think it's perfect," he said. "And I think Kate will agree. I know it's a dumb question, but how is Twylah?"

"She is both heartbroken and relieved, relieved that his suffering wasn't greater. My sister had a lot of time to prepare herself and a lot of time to hear why her husband didn't fear death. But she is missing him and their life together. That is going to be challenge for her and for all of us."

"It is," he said, sighing deeply. Tears welled up in his eyes and rolled down his face. He saw from Kate's expression that she felt a sense of urgency now to know what was going on. "It's David. He passed early this morning," he whispered to her. She nodded. Porter cleared his throat to speak again.

"What can I do to help?"

"Just being on the other end of the phone means more than you know. I know Twylah and Sarah would also love a call from you, but there's no rush. We've all been on the phone this morning and I think everyone's pretty exhausted at this point. Sarah's having a hard time with Twylah's insistence that she not use more of her vacation time to come back down to Florida right now. Those two are very close, and I know Sarah wants nothing more than to get on the first plane for Tallahassee. James and I are going, and we're taking Sarah's brother, because this will be his only chance to honor his uncle's passing in a formal way. So that just increases Sarah's feelings of being left behind.

"It's not meant that way at all. I think I really understand where Twylah's coming from. She told Sarah that what will take place in Hawaii with David's ashes is so profoundly beautiful that it will erase any doubts that Sarah had about staying back and not coming to Florida. And she wants Sarah to keep her focus on the miracle that she is living out right now, with Kalah. You know about her, right?"

"Yes, I do," he said.

"Anyway, you've known Twylah a long time now and when she gets like that, with a very clear and unwavering sense of what should come next, she's calling on her divine guidance and we try to respect it even if we don't always understand it."

"I know what you mean," he said softly. He looked at Kate. She put her head on his shoulder. They spoke a little while longer about David and his life, then said their good-byes and hung up. Porter put his arm around his fiancée.

"I'm sorry," she said. "That's so tough."

"He was an incredible man," he said. "As genuine as they come. Apparently he had a special request before he died. He asked that some of his ashes be scattered in Hawaii. He had become attuned to the mysteries playing out in Sarah's life." He told Kate about David's epiphany regarding the sea turtles march to land, then their freedom when they returned to the sea.

"Marianne and James want to bring Twylah with her when they come to Hawaii next month. And Twylah wants to bring the ashes then. She called to ask our permission."

"Of course. But why do they need our permission?" Kate asked. "We don't own the state of Hawaii."

"I guess they think we own the experience of getting married there next month."

"Well, I don't even think we own that," Kate said. "A wedding is a community's experience, not just a couple's experience. Our loved ones will be around us and that includes David."

"Thank you. Thank you for being so grand."

"There's something incredibly sacred about joining the two ceremonies," she said.

"I agree," he said. He wiped tears from his face. "If returning to God isn't the ultimate experience of love, I don't know what is."

They held each other for a little while.

"Do you need to call Sarah?" she asked.

"I'm going to wait until evening. She's dealing with a lot, and I think she needs some peace and quiet more than anything else. I'm sending her my love. Sometimes words just get in the way." They sat together for a while, not speaking.

"What are you looking at?" Kate asked finally, taking the picture from his lap.

"This is a very special turtle," he said. "This is Miki. You can't really see it from this picture, but she has a small satellite transmitter on her back. She's helping to tell the story of where hawksbill turtles go when they're not on the shores of the Big Island laying their eggs."

"Where does she go?"

"Well, sometimes she swims to the waters around Maui," he said.

"Smart girl," Kate said.

"One can only imagine what she sees."

He pulled the underwater photos of the ancient sunken ruins out from under the collection of turtle photographs. She gasped. "I hadn't seen this one yet. A turtle-shaped platform!" she exclaimed. "What do you imagine they used it for?"

"Maybe the holy sacrament of marriage," Porter said. He pulled out another photograph, this one showing the remains of a building.

"Beautiful," she said. "I wish I were a dolphin. I'd live there."

"Or at least use it as a honeymoon suite," he said. Her reply surprised even him.

"You know, Porter, this place looks strangely familiar to me. I mean really, really familiar. Something tells me that you and I have already been there and done that."

CHAPTER FORTY-THREE

Questing

Sarah went through a stack of books, looking for the ones she would take on her trip. Gabe looked on from the couch.

"The Mayan Oracle," she said, holding it up. "Porter sent it. Remember? It comes with these cards. They have symbols on them. Here, pick one." She stretched and handed him the deck, grinning. Sometimes she just needed to have a little fun with him.

"Just draw any card?" He asked.

"Go ahead. See what the cards have to say to you today. Don't be a chicken."

"All right then," he said a little defiantly. He shuffled and drew a card. It was a cross with a circle around it. It said, "Adventurer's Quest."

"Show me what you picked," she said. "Oh, that's a great card! That's one of the first cards I ever picked." She handed him the book. "You can read up on it. You'll find its explanation about mid-way through the book.

"What does it say?"

"Just read it. It's not spooky or anything."

He flipped through, finally finding the symbol in the book.

"It says it's the symbol of the mythic call," he said. She watched his face as he read, thinking to herself, "Could it be any more obvious that you're supposed to come with me to Hawaii?" But she kept quiet.

"I'm sure you think this means I'm supposed to go with you to Hawaii," he said.

"Impressive. Have you taken up mind-reading?" She pretended to be half-interested in his card, studying the cover of another book.

"No mind-reading. But I do know how you think."

She pretended to ignore the comment and held up another book.

"Did I tell you the funny story behind this one? You'll love this," she said. "I got really mad at this book awhile back. It was during my 'creature' phase. You know, my meltdown."

He cocked his head, looking puzzled. His expression said, "Let's see. Which one?"

"My *first* one," she said. "When I screamed. I threw it across the room and eventually tossed it in the trash. It's actually a very good book, but it hit a nerve that day. So guess what Aunt Twylah and Uncle David sent me for Christmas, among other things? The same book! Is that wild or what? It's like somebody was watching me trash the thing and gave Aunt Twylah an idea for a practical joke."

"You never told them you threw this book in the trash?"

"No way. Too embarrassing. To them, books are like people. You don't throw them in the trash because you disagree with them." He took it from her. "I wonder what actually prompted them to pick this particular book for you."

"Well, there's probably a very logical reason why they gave it to me. It talks a lot about the concept of choosing our life experiences before we're born. You know, in order to grow in the spiritual sense. Aunt Twylah and I got into a conversation about choices when I was down there. I asked her if she thought we actually picked our life experiences as wisdom-seeking spirits. And she really surprised me with her answer."

"Did she say she believes that? Even with everything going on in her life?"

"She totally believes that," Sarah said. "In fact, it's the only way she can truly keep her faith when she sees bad things happening."

"But isn't that like blaming the victim?" he asked. "How can you tell the victim of a tragedy that they chose it?"

"Well, I think if you're smart you won't try to tell them that while they're in pain," she said. "That's where this author went wrong with me. Although I guess you could say it was my choice to buy the book."

"But it still sounds off to me," he said earnestly. "Why would we choose to suffer so much? I mean illness is one thing, but what about helpless children who are abused? I can't accept that it's their choice."

"I can't quite get my mind around it, either," she said. "But Aunt Twylah thinks that from the perspective of immortality, this is like a big university. Or the Olympics. Only the bravest and the strongest among us choose the biggest challenges. I'll tell you one thing, though. The next time I go into a hospital room where someone has been diagnosed with a serious illness, I'm not about to say, "Congratulations. You've been selected for God's Olympics!"

"But you know," Gabe said, "look at how that moment of unexpected humor was so transforming to Mr. Sanders. Do me a favor, for possible research purposes. If you ever find it appropriate to say something like that, try to keep some good notes on their responses. I think you might be surprised. Maybe it's just what they need to hear."

"And if you see me with a couple of black eyes, you'll know how the research is going."

"Well, I could see that kind of reminder possibly being helpful to me, if I ever start feeling sorry for myself," he said, surprising her. "But I still can't imagine applying that theory to child abuse. What could be the lesson there?"

"I can't say, Gabe. Maybe it's the ultimate lesson in unconditional love and compassion. Or maybe it's about something so far above my head and yours that there's no point speculating. This is probably all a big dream and when we wake up we won't care about it that much. We'll just see God smiling at us and saying something like, 'Good morning, sleepy head. How about breakfast?' Or something to that effect. That makes more sense than anything. Dreams feel real when we're in them but the people watching us dream usually aren't terribly concerned because they know it's not real."

He shrugged. "I can't imagine a loving God letting us suffer, even with a bad dream. But I can imagine a loving God letting us grow."

"Well, I'm taking this book to Hawaii," she said. "It's a long plane ride and I'll be a lot less inclined to throw it inside the plane if it makes me mad. All I know is, it came back to me for a reason. I'm supposed to get something out of it. Or maybe this is the book's revenge. Everybody I know will start sending me a copy. Did you ever see the Twilight Zone episode, at least I think it was the Twilight Zone, where the guy kills a spider and a bigger one comes out of the drain? He kills it and washes it down and a bigger one comes, and then a bigger one, every time he tries to get rid of one."

"It reminds me a little of obsessive-compulsive thinking," he said. The painful thought keeps growing and coming back with a vengeance. It wants to be dealt with, not washed down the drain."

"Yep. Good analogy." She looked at the book cover and thought about choices.

"You know, I just remembered how my Mom stopped herself when her thoughts got too negative and repetitive," Sarah said. "She'd say, 'Duchess, it's time for the lampshade.' Duchess was our dog."

Gabe cocked his head. "Go on. This sounds interesting."

"Well, a friend of hers is a veterinarian, and she told Mom that dogs often absorb our emotional turmoil and act it out. Mom had taken Duchess to the vet because she was biting fur off of her leg. And Mom says, 'Okay, Julie. Tell me what my dog is trying to tell me with this fur-biting business. Because she's starting to look like Sarah's ratty old teddy bear. I might have to rename her Patches.'"

"And her friend says, 'Well don't be too hard on yourself. Maybe she just has an allergy.' But while they were measuring Duchess for one of those silly collars that look like a lampshade, she was talking to my Mom and finally she says, 'Marianne, you seem really anxious. Are you obsessing about something?' And Mom admits that she has been kicking herself over and over again about something she wished she hadn't said. And they figure out that whenever my Mom was chewing on herself about something, Duchess starting chewing on her fur. So when she felt it coming, those repetitive thoughts, she'd say, 'Duchess, I feel a lampshade coming on.' And that would usually snap her out of it. She'd imagine herself wearing the lampshade and that would crack her up."

"Vets should be paid more," he replied. "Julie pinpointed your Mom's problem while she was taking care of the dog."

"Funny how that works." She watched him. His attention was drawn back to The Mayan Oracle book. He saw her watching him, and smiled sheepishly, closing it.

"You can read more. I know you want to," she said. "Your secret is safe with me." He laughed.

"Okay, smarty. Your turn. You pick one," he said, handing her the deck. She shuffled elaborately and drew one. "Oh, my gosh.

The same one you got," she said, holding it up. "See? Adventurer's Quest!"

"Fascinating," he said. "I wonder if this means you should consider going to Hawaii."

"Very funny." She sighed. "Look. I know it's not my place to tell you what to do, but it just feels like you're supposed to go with me, Gabe. I'm not going to say it anymore. I just had to get that off my chest." He scooted across the floor, sitting next to her. He put an arm around her and kissed her. She kissed him back. She loved his kisses. After a while, she pulled back, studying his face. It was so full of tenderness.

"I'm not rejecting you," he said. "Believe me, it's a huge sign of growth that I don't feel rejected by your desire to do something amazing that has nothing to do with me."

"How do you know it doesn't?" she asked. "Maybe it has a lot to do with you."

He shook his head. "It doesn't. And I'm fine with that. Really."

"But you like Porter a lot. And this is his wedding, Gabe."

"It's more than that. You were feeling a call to go to Hawaii before Porter decided to get married there." She nodded.

"True," she said. She had never told him the details about Kalah and Kai. She had only told them that there were important people she was destined to meet there, one of whom Porter had met years before. But Gabe was becoming more intuitive, and for that she was grateful. Perhaps he was right. Perhaps he was not meant to go with her. She picked up another book and handed to him.

"Oh, man," he said. "'The Kabbalah.' It's the book of Jewish mysticism."

"Porter gave that to me, too. Now he's reading 'A Course in Miracles,' which was scribed by a New York psychologist, Helen Schucman. It is said to contain the words of Jesus. Basically, according to her, Jesus is saying he was misquoted a whole lot and he wants to set the record straight. Porter said the scribe wasn't a mystical person at all. She was just great at taking notes when somebody spoke. Apparently she was bewildered and sometimes even upset by what was coming through her yet certain that she was supposed to take it down and share it. He said the central message is forgiveness, including self-forgiveness. He said the book really rattles his ego's cage. The voice coming through has such profound spiritual authority. But he keeps reading a little every day because in his heart he knows that Jesus really is the author."

Gabe whistled in admiration. "Boy, I'd sure like to join his book club."

"He's been on a true spiritual quest," she said. "And I'm reaping some of the benefits." He continued flipping through the book.

"I wonder what the word actually means," he said.

"What word?"

"Kabbalah."

"I don't know. Is it in the glossary?"

"If it is, it probably says, 'Hello, dummy. If you don't know what the word means, you shouldn't be reading this book,'" he said, flipping back to the glossary. "Oh, now this is interesting," he said, stopping at a word.

"What?"

"This word. You say it a lot in your sleep."

Sarah's heart did a flip. Suddenly the air felt supercharged and goose bumps were forming on her chest and arms. She felt the angels of synchronicity moving closer. "What word?" she pressed.

"Kallah," he said. "You say it a lot. I've been meaning to ask you what it means."

She swallowed. "It's in the glossary? What does it say?"

"Well, it means bride," he said, studying the definition. "Kallah means bride in Hebrew. But when you're sleeping, it sounds as if you are calling someone by name."

"The word means bride?"

"Yep." He showed her the book. "See right here?"

She looked down at it, then back at his face. "When I'm saying the name, I'm talking to someone I'm going to see in Hawaii. I have no idea how her name is spelled, but the similarity between the two words is probably not a coincidence. I'm starting to think that nothing is really a coincidence."

"Interesting. You're going there for a wedding, and you're going to meet someone whose name means 'bride,' at least in Hebrew. It definitely doesn't sound like a simple coincidence."

"It's a long story," she said. "For another day."

"Wait a minute, I'm remembering the story of the brides and their lamps," he said. "Jesus referenced the Jewish wedding tradition in a parable, remember? You know, Sarah, you also talk about a lamp in your sleep."

"I do? I say all that?"

"Yes. These things are linked. Bride. Lamp." She swiveled around to face him, no longer concerned about hiding her flushed cheeks. Was this the time to tell him?

"You're right," she said. "Kalah and the lamp, they go together." She was on the verge of pouring out the whole story, when Gabe's eyes brightened.

"I remember!" he said. "The parable of the virgins and their lamps! The wise one keeps oil in her lamp, so she's prepared to go with her bridegroom when he arrives. And then there were the so-called foolish ones who weren't ready. They let their oil run out. It's the parable of readiness, staying spiritually ready for the return of Christ."

Another wave of goose bumps rippled across her skin. It wasn't the story she was going to tell him, but it struck a chord and resonated deeply inside of her. The similarities were too great to ignore. And too beautiful. Was Kalah here to remind them to be ready?

The story she had told of the first lamp, it was a parable. It was the kind of story that had meanings within meanings. And it, too, told of beloveds coming together. She felt the familiar warmth of spiritual grace washing over her.

"Thank you," she said gently to Gabe. "Thank you for reminding me of that story in the Bible." He glanced up at her, smiling, then returned to the glossary.

"You're welcome," he said. "But I think that you're the one who jogged my memory." She sat quietly for a while, pretending to be absorbed in the stack of books. When she glanced over her shoulder from time to time, Gabe had gone back to shuffling the deck of Mayan cards and flipping through the book to discover their meaning. He no longer looked embarrassed.

"Look," he said, holding up the same card. "It keeps showing up. And I'm really shuffling the deck well."

"Porter told me it happens sometimes."

He re-read the meaning of the card. "I didn't catch this the first time. It sounds like what you and your aunt were talking about."

"It does? What does it say?"

"Well, it says that if you pull this card you're being asked to rewrite your life script in a more mythic way. It says, and I quote, 'Remember also that what appears to be tests and trials in your life are actually priceless gifts and teachings. By looking at your life as a grand adventure, you know that these lessons offer opportunities to grow.' It also says here that you are being drawn into an initiation."

"I can't argue with that," she said. She pulled another book from the stack, flipping through it and pausing to look at the pictures. She suddenly felt as though they were two children playing on a mound of sacred treasures. She felt the presence of Nana Gwen, pleased with this turn of events. She also sensed that Kalah was nearby.

"This one is also a fascinating book. It's about the ancient roots of sacred hula dancing. Did you know that men were the first hula dancers? It requires so much skill and strength to perform it properly, that warriors were actually selected from among the best dancers. Women joined in later and gave it their own feminine quality."

"I guess that makes sense," he said, "when you consider that some of the best football players take ballet. And I hear that the military teaches tai chi to its soldiers now."

"They do?" she asked.

"It's all about balance," he said. "Balance and agility. Are you going to learn to hula dance in Hawaii? Social workers need balance, too. And agility. They need a lot of it." She gave him a look and shook her head.

"I can't imagine anyone having the patience to teach me," she said. "And besides, my hips are rusty." She stood up and walked into the kitchen. "Thirsty?"

"Yeah. How about some water."

"Coming up." Before she could turn around from the refrigerator, she felt him approaching her. She felt his hands on her waist. Slowly they slid down to her hips. He kissed her ear, then her neck. She turned around to kiss him.

He took the glass of water and placed it on the counter.

"I don't think these are so rusty," he said, touching her hips again. "You would look incredibly beautiful doing the hula." She kissed him again.

"Remember now, the hula is sacred," she said.

"I know," he said, tenderly. "Very sacred." Then he led her to the bedroom and closed the door behind them. Haley whimpered and scratched on the door for a moment, then settled down, resting her chin on her paws. Sarah unplugged the phone and made true love to Gabe.

CHAPTER FORTY-FOUR

Sky-Walking

Kalah and Hannah sat on a blanket overlooking the sea. Tomorrow their guests would arrive. The air around them was charged with mana. The light from the sun had an added radiance, a sparkle that neither of them had seen before.

"Love is in the air," Kalah said. She wiggled her feet. "Can you believe it is finally happening?"

"I shouldn't be surprised, after all these years of living with Kai. The extraordinary has become the ordinary. But this is a whole new level of miraculous. You know, it's like our waiting has been a time of gestation, like those final months before a woman gives birth. On the surface of things, we've been rather still. But on another unseen level, there's been an incredible amount of activity and growth."

"I love thinking of it that way," Kalah said. "The stillness that is not really still. It is a lot like pregnancy." She rubbed her belly. "Soon," she said. "I hope it's soon."

Hannah looked uncertain. "You're not... now, I mean."

"Oh, no. Not yet. But this time next year I hope to have our first." Hannah felt a deep tug in her heart. It was another reminder of how much this young woman had put aside to come to their world. Kalah watched her, sensing what she was feeling.

"It has been an honor," she said, "to be of service here with you."

"Thank you, dear. Though I can't imagine what it's been like for you to be so far from home." They looked out to sea. The spout of a whale caught their attention. Hannah leaned back on her elbows, admiring the scene. "I imagine that when you are home, the view isn't so different when you're looking out to sea. It will help me when you're gone, to know that what you see is not so different from what I see."

Kalah smiled. "I like that."

"I'll miss you more than you know," Hannah said. "You're like a daughter to me now."

"I'll miss you, too." She paused, searching her heart about what she next wanted to say. Yes, it seemed like the perfect time.

"I would like to share something with you," she said. "I had a vision about you and Kai. I think it will make you very happy."

Hannah sat up, looking at Kalah. "Please share it."

"This time next year, you, too, will have a child."

"A child? Oh, dear, sweet Kalah. You see all this gray hair? Do you have any idea how old I am?"

"You and Kai are going to adopt a child." Hannah looked stunned.

"I'm not sure I can comprehend the two of us becoming parents at this stage in our lives. But I'm open. Having you here makes me realize just how open I am."

"The child's spirit is powerful, but there is much darkness in her life right now," Kalah said. "Darkness that I can barely comprehend. There is a reason that this child will come into your life. She has the spiritual power to become a great leader. But this power will need direction, the kind of direction that you and Kai can give."

"Kai as a father. In his seventh decade," Hannah said, laughing. "I suppose we will call ourselves the child's adoptive grandparents. That sounds more appropriate."

Kalah shrugged a little. "Maybe. You are both quite ageless. It is your mana. But if you want to see it that way, I can tell you that grandparents play a big role in raising the children of our village. The older these elders are, the more they are considered experts in what a child needs. What this little girl needs is to be reconnected with her Hawaiian roots. That is why she has chosen you."

"She has chosen us?" Hannah asked.

"Yes. The three of you have chosen each other, much like we have chosen Porter and Sarah to be a part of our lives."

"And this child," Hannah asked, "Where is she now?"

"She is in a home where she is mistreated," Kalah said.

Hannah winced. "Oh, I can't bear to think of that."

"I am sorry. If I have caused you pain, I have told you too much. But let me put it another way. The girl is in a home with great lessons in bravery and when she comes to you her bravery will be a shining light in your lives. You will be her teachers and she will be yours. When her roots to this land are restored, she will feel her power and she will use her big heart to reshape this world."

"Good. I'll hold on to that. And you are certain Kai will go for this? You've seen it?"

"Oh, yes. On some level, he is already preparing himself for the challenge. In passing your wisdom on to her, you both are ensuring that the spirit of Hawaii will thrive. It will be a dream come true for both of you."

"Amazing."

"So I will have a child and you will have a child, and there will be more turtle babies floating in the sea," Kalah said. "My heart is so happy."

"You know that for sure? About the turtles?"

"I feel it more than I know it. The winds are shifting. It is their time again." She fell back on the blanket, looking up at the sky.

"I feel Sarah's heart more and more. In some ways it is light and full of joy. But there is also some heaviness."

"Well, Porter told Kai that her lover, Gabe, isn't coming."

"He's not?" Kalah was very surprised. "She pulled herself up on her elbows, still looking up at the sky. "But I think he *is* coming."

"Well, someone needs to tell him."

Kalah was very quiet for a while. "Maybe I will," she said, finally.

"What's that?"

"Maybe I'll tell him he's coming." She sat up and with a finger drew the image of a turtle in the sand. A strong gust of wind blew from the sea. Their hair blew freely in the wind. The sand drawing was not disturbed.

* * *

The day had come. Sarah was packed and preparing to call a cab. The painting of the dolphin with the key had arrived from Florida well padded and wrapped. She tucked it under one arm. Aunt Twylah was right. It carried a powerful spiritual punch. But the painting was smaller than she expected. She handed Gabe a typed itinerary of her flight information and the address where she would be staying.

At the bottom was Kai's address and phone number. Porter had suggested that she give it to Gabe so that he could contact her if he wished. It seemed surreal to see it all written down, as if she were about to step into another universe that actually had a forwarding address. She watched him fold the paper carefully and put it in his pocket.

"I'll walk out with you and help you call a cab. You're sure you won't let me drive you?" he asked.

"No, it's okay. You're doing me a bigger favor if you'll wait for the plumber. I really appreciate it." The kitchen sink had mysteriously backed up. No amount of tinkering with a variety of sharp objects seemed to clear the blockage. A cab appeared as soon as they walked down the steps onto the sidewalk. He helped her in, kissed her tenderly and closed the door. She smiled at him and he saw the unconditional love in her eyes.

"I'm a moron," he said to himself, walking back up the steps. The previous night had been full of dreams. His Irish grandmother had appeared, showing him scenes from their time together when he was a boy. He watched himself sitting at the kitchen table eating oatmeal while she pounded dough to make bread. She was telling him a story about sacred trees, trees that were bridges between the earth and the sky.

"Do trees have feelings?" he asked.

"Yes, they feel many things."

"Do they get mad at people?"

"I don't think they feel anger," she said. "But I do think they feel pain."

"Then I won't climb them anymore."

"You can climb, boy. Keep reaching for the sky." The scene faded. Another took its place. They were sitting together at the same table. Now he was an adult.

"Why do you fear Hawaii?" she asked.

"I didn't know I was afraid. I thought I would just be in the way."

"In the way of what?"

"I don't know."

"Remember the stories, Gabe. When you were a child I told you the old stories for a reason."

"I want to understand, Nana. Help me understand."

"I've already told you everything I know," she said. "Now I have a question for you. Do you want to be a sleep-walker or sky-walker?"

"Sky-walker? What does that mean?" She didn't answer his question.

"Your heart knows. Join your lady. Join her in Hawaii." Now Sarah was gone and he was sitting on the couch feeling like a failure. But how could he change his decision because of a dream? It just wasn't rational. The phone rang and he got up to answer it. The answering machine beat him to it and he heard a woman's voice. He picked up the receiver just as she was explaining on the message machine that she was calling on behalf of broadcast journalist Larry King.

"Hello," he said cautiously.

"I was calling for Ms. Pierce. Is she there?" the woman said.

"No, she just left for the airport," Gabe said. "I'm her boyfriend, Gabe." At times like these he wished there was a more mature term for his relationship with Sarah. The woman explained that Larry King had been taken with her letter. He liked the challenging nature of it, and wanted to use it as a way of introducing a segment on the public's opinion of American journalism.

"Amazing."

"It's a great letter. Very thought-provoking," the woman said. "I'd like to speak with her directly. Can she be reached later today?"

"She's on her way to Hawaii. But I can give you the phone number where she'll be staying."

"And you didn't go with her?" the woman said, suddenly getting personal.

"Right. I'm not the brightest man in the world," he said, suddenly feeling talkative. "I've chosen instead to make my own journey deep into the center of the Bermuda triangle. I'm doing a documentary on how men get tragically lost, and why they won't ask for directions. I mean that in the cosmic sense."

She laughed. "That's really funny. I think you just made my day." This response cheered him up a little. At least he was serving some useful purpose. He gave her the number and they hung up. He sat down on the couch and scratched Haley's head.

"Tell me again why I didn't want to go to Hawaii?" he asked the dog. She rolled over and turned her back to him. "Don't tell me you're mad about it," he said. "What's it to *you?*"

The phone rang. "That's probably the plumber, saying he's lost. Let's see, he's only two hours late." He picked up the phone.

"Hello. Pierce residence."

The voice on the other end came through like a soft breeze. He felt a rush of warmth across his skin and a tingling from head to toe. He sat down in a chair, slightly off balance.

"Hello, Gabe. This is Kalah. I'm calling you from Hawaii."

"Yes, I have heard your name," he said, feeling stunned.

"Gabe, as they say in your world, I will get right to the point. I don't know if Sarah has told you why I am here. But I have traveled very far across the vastness of time and space to help fulfill a prophecy. I know that she is coming here. I'm calling to tell you that you are supposed to be coming to Hawaii, too. Maybe you do not realize this, but your presence here is important. It is important to a lot of us. I tried to speak with you another way, with my thoughts, but you blocked me. So I thought this device might work better with you. Will you come?"

"Yes," he said, hearing himself answer with great certainty. "I'll make arrangements. I'll come." He looked at the piece of paper with Kai and Hannah's address.

"You know exactly where to come, then?"

"Yes," he said. "I will leave tomorrow." Somehow he was certain that he would get a flight, get permission from work and that everything else would fall into place.

"Thank you, Gabe," she said, a smile in her voice. "I am so happy! We will see you when you arrive."

"Yes," he said simply. "Yes, you will see me. When I arrive." He sat down, feeling stunned. Somehow as this woman spoke he could hear his grandmother's words coming through. He wanted

Nana Gwen to be proud of him for making the right decision, even if it was in the eleventh hour. And he knew that she was. He could feel it. Haley walked into the kitchen with the stuffed blue bone in her mouth.

"You found it. I thought it was lost," he said. "Well you can put down your weapon, girl, because I'm going to Hawaii!"

He reached down to take it from her. She pulled against his hand, making it a game. Finally she dropped it at his feet. As she did, he heard a strange gurgling sound. It was coming from the sink. He got up to investigate. The sink had suddenly cleared and a small whirlpool was forming as backed-up water flowed down into the drain.

"Well, I'll be. It fixed itself. I guess we don't need the –"

There was a knock at the door, which sent the dog rushing toward it, barking loudly. Reaching down to hold her collar with one hand, he opened the door with the other.

"Hi," he said. It was the plumber.

"I hear you have a clog," the man said, studying his work order. The drain made a final loud burping sound.

"It seems to have cleared up."

"Oh. Well, I'll still have to charge you for coming. I have come a long way."

"Across the vastness of time and space?"

"Excuse me?"

"Never mind. How much do we owe you?"

CHAPTER FORTY-FIVE

Flying Together

It seemed that the flight to San Francisco went by in the blink of an eye. Sarah slept much of the way, dreaming that the sunken continent of Lemuria was rising up, pulled closer to the surface of the water as the plane passed over. In the dream she heard the rumbling of the ocean floor and saw ancient structures being pushed upward toward shafts of sunlight. Then her attention was drawn to the white sand on the sea bed. There, she saw a golden anchor. It was shaped like a six-pointed star, a Star of David. Attached to it was a golden thread that went up to the sky. She woke up. Reflecting on the dream, she remembered an article that she had read about the Star of David. The article claimed that the symbol was older than the ancient Hebrew culture and that it could be traced back to time of Lemuria.

"Interesting," she whispered. Her eyes closed and she drifted back to sleep. This time she saw her uncle. He looked strong and at peace. Still, she was overcome with feelings of missing him.

Her spirits were lifted when she saw her parents and Aunt Twylah at their designated meeting spot. She kissed her parents, handed the oil painting to her father and opened her arms to her aunt. Her aunt burst into tears. Sarah took a deep breath and absorbed her sweet, familiar perfume.

"Here I am falling apart already," Aunt Twylah said, wiping her face. "I'm sorry. I thought I had done all of my crying."

"Not without me," Sarah said. "You can't finish your crying without me. We were long overdue for a good cry together."

They all settled on another plane. First class felt luxurious. It was a good time to be spoiled. She placed the painting in an overhead bin just above her head. Miraculously, it was empty and stayed that way except for the painting. Her parents sat in the aisle next to them. Aunt Twylah urged Sarah to sit by the window. "So I can't see out," she explained.

"All we'll see is the ocean," Sarah said.

"That's why I don't want to look. Where are we supposed to land if we have trouble?"

"On the water. But we won't have trouble. I have never felt so certain. Think of this plane as a giant spear thrown by God. It has only one option and that is to land in exactly the right place. And remember, the painting is with us and Uncle David already told you that he saw me handing it safely to Kalah. So think of it as our little insurance policy, Aunt Twylah."

"Thank you. That puts it all in perspective." She squeezed Sarah's hand. "And thank you for not thinking I'm crazy for sending the dolphin painting to New York and having you carry it all this way. It just had to unfold this way. Someday it will all make sense to you. You'll look back and say, 'Oh, now I get it!'" The plane hit some turbulence. Aunt Twylah looked at Sarah and made the sign of the cross.

"I'm not usually this nervous," she said. "I don't know why this is bothering me so much."

"It's fine," Sarah said. "When I'm nervous you are there for me." Midway through the flight, when the food trays had been taken away, the two women started talking in earnest. They weren't in the rocking chairs on Twylah's porch, but they might as well have been. Everything else seemed to melt away.

"I'm sorry that Gabe wouldn't come. I'm very surprised," her aunt said.

"Me, too. I thought he just needed some extra reassurance that he was wanted there. But now I think he really believes that he is supposed to stay back."

"Maybe he did it for me," Aunt Twylah said. "Maybe he stayed back because David's not with me and he didn't want me to feel this widow thing so much by being a third wheel."

"That's something I hadn't thought of," Sarah said. "Knowing him, it's plausible. But then again, I think he had his mind made up even before that. It's almost like he knew Porter was going there to get married, but he still felt somehow that it was a journey Porter and I were supposed to make together. It makes no sense to me, but he came really close to saying that a few times."

"Well, I think you and your godfather are definitely on a journey together, wedding or no wedding. You two have been on a journey since you were a baby. You're like a daughter to him. You always have been. You stole his heart the minute he saw you."

"He really wanted kids and he would have made such a good Daddy," Sarah said. "You know, I feel like I already know Kate. I think she's going to blend right into our family. Don't you?"

"She's part of the circle."

"The circle?"

"The circle of women. They were nearby when Kalah told you the story, remember?" Sarah studied her aunt's face and saw the scene in her mind's eye. Yes, Kate had been there, too. It was true. Somewhere in dreamtime they had already met.

"I have chills," Sarah said. "I remember now. The morning Uncle David, passed I was sitting right next to her at the table. She had introduced herself as Kate." She looked over at her parents to see if they could hear. They were both reading. "Yes, it's all coming back. Uncle David referred to it as a round table, making a reference to King Arthur's table."

"I have the same memories about his visit there," Aunt Twylah said. "And when I woke up he was struggling with his last breaths. I put my arms around him, and..." She stopped, fighting back tears. Sarah reached around and put her arm around her aunt.

"I love you so much," she said. "I love you both so much."

"I love you, too," her aunt said, hoarsely. "Our round table. We have replaced swords with needles and thread. You know, your uncle was so proud. I could see that."

Twylah rested her head on Sarah's shoulder and dozed for a while. When she stirred again, she saw that her niece looked very deep in thought.

"A penny for your thoughts."

"I was just thinking more about the round table and King Arthur," Sarah said. "And it made me wonder about Porter. Why do you call him Merlin?"

"Because he's magical."

"I think I'm the last to catch on about that. I've had such a limited view of him."

"No, I have to disagree. I think you've always sensed his depth. You know that inner critic of yours need to go soak her head." Sarah laughed out loud.

"But seriously," Aunt Twylah said. "You've asked a good question and I'm going to give you an answer that I wouldn't give anyone else. Because I know you'll understand. Porter is like Merlin because he's gained so much of his wisdom and spiritual light, from his time in the cave. I don't mean a literal cave. I mean the dark places of our society. He's walked in those places. Like Merlin, his spirit caught fire and grew to such brightness because of his time spent walking through the cave. Merlin even told the boy Arthur to seek the grail in the depths of the cave, you know. Not all of the stories tell it that way, but the one I love the most points Arthur toward the crystal cave, where he'll come to know his own soul once and for all. When the darkness is understood and transmuted, it feeds out light like nothing else can. It's the ultimate, richest fodder. That's what I believe."

"The grail," Sarah said, thinking about the Mayan card of the quest that she and Gabe had drawn. "I can definitely see Porter on a quest for the holy grail. I can see him playing both parts, Merlin and King Arthur."

"I think we're all playing those parts and more," her aunt replied. "We're the wise wizard and the wise child and the warrior and the wise fool. Every day of our lives we're probably working through those roles."

"Even as women," Sarah said. "When it's not so obvious that we're the warriors or the wizard."

"Especially as women. Your uncle saw what we were doing at that table, didn't he? He saw it very clearly."

"Mending the earth," both women said in unison.

"And mending the atmosphere around the earth," Sarah added. "That's not a job for sissies. And speaking of strong women, I hear that Porter has been so bold as to choose a bed and breakfast inn right on Pele's territory. Pele, as you probably know, is the goddess of volcanoes."

"That she is. The goddess of fire and the goddess of passion," Aunt Twylah said, winking. "I'm glad they arrived two days ahead of us. They can get some lovin' underway without wondering if we're listening."

"I heard that," Sarah's father said, laughing. "What was Porter thinking, booking us all at the same hotel?"

"He was thinking that we'll only be there for a few days, then they can pick up where they left off," Aunt Twylah whispered loudly. Sarah was glad for the noisy vibration of the plane, although she noticed a couple of passengers chuckling.

"Who's marrying them?" her aunt asked.

"Kai. The man who was hitting Porter's head with coconuts in dreamtime. Did you hear about that?" Sarah asked.

"Yes, you told me. If that doesn't beat all. You know, you and your godfather are cut from the same cloth. Eccentric yet grounded, innocent yet brilliant."

"Aunt Twylah, I'm flattered, but I'm not brilliant. And I'm not innocent, either."

"Inner critic, go soak thy self," Aunt Twylah whispered, dismissing this protest with the wave of a hand. "We're all brilliant and innocent as children of God. You should work on that because in the future you're going to help others with their self-esteem issues. Look at that! There's an angel in the aisle. She just showed up and she's standing in front of that empty seat. She wants you to understand this and believe it."

Sarah peered around her aunt, looking for the angel. She didn't see one.

"Don't worry," her aunt said. "Your inner critic is blocking her, but after this trip to Hawaii gets going that little gremlin of yours will be making some travel plans, if you get my drift. My critic needs to take a hike, too." Sarah laughed.

"But really now. Your parents sitting over there are brilliant, too, for matching you up with Merlin. He's the perfect spiritual mentor."

"Spiritual mentor," Sarah repeated. You know, it seems like I have been blessed with quite a few of those lately."

"You are one, too."

Sarah looked puzzled. "I think we are all teachers for each other," her aunt continued. "I believe it's actually part of God's grand design. Here's how I see it playing out. God sends us all down here with our little cosmic parachutes and says, 'Okay, kids. You look out for each other down there. And if Miss Twylah over there starts forgetting some of her wisdom, well Sarah, why don't you ask her a good, tough question and help her remember it. And if Sarah's inner critic starts working over-time, why Twylah you can throw some cold water on it.'"

"You are so good for me," Sarah said, "so very good for me, but so very bad for the critic."

"Stick with me kid. We'll melt that sucker down."

* * *

Porter, the man who would be both Merlin and king, was standing radiantly with his bride-to-be when they all landed at the airport on the Big Island. Kate was, indeed, one of the women whom Sarah had seen in the dreamtime circle.

"I already know you," Kate said, as if reading Sarah's thoughts. They hugged. Sarah loved her instantly.

"Have you seen Kalah yet?" Sarah blurted out as soon as Porter approached her for a hug. She saw that he was surrounded by light. "You look completely transformed."

"No way would I go over there without you," Porter said. I have talked to Kai on the phone. They know we're waiting for you. They don't live too far from our hotel."

"Porter, I can't believe we're talking like this. I mean we're talking like it's an everyday thing that we're going to connect with Kai and Kalah." They walked toward baggage claim, pulling away from the others to talk a little.

"I mean, look what I'm holding," she whispered. "It's Twylah's painting but it was her mission to have me bring it all the way from New York. She sent it to me so that I could bring it across the country. It is a part of the plan, she said, even if its journey with me is symbolic. Symbolic of what, I don't know yet. Anyway, I swear it must have some kind of force field around it. I was skeptical about carrying it on two planes, but nothing came close to bothering it the whole way here. Eventually it goes back home with Kalah, to the past! When she gets there, the paint on it will not have been invented yet!"

"Don't run this through the left side of your brain," Porter replied, shaking his head in amazement. "That's my advice because that's how I'm dealing with it. In fact, if you really want my advice, don't run it through your brain at all. Let your heart handle this one."

"Works for me," she said.

"I hope you're taking notes," he said, as they walked toward the others. "You have a story to tell."

CHAPTER FORTY-SIX

Miracles

As soon as she laid eyes on her, Sarah knew that Kalah was miraculous and her mission was divine. Kalah heard her thoughts very clearly and said tenderly, "You, Sarah, are the miracle."

They stood facing each other, their eyes locked and their hands clasped while their circle of loved ones looked on. Porter stood with his hand over his heart. Aunt Twylah rested her head against her sister's shoulder, watching a soft light settle over the two women. So many paths had led to this place. To everyone involved the moment was timeless and eternal.

Sarah and Kalah spoke to each other with their thoughts. Kalah sent blessings from everyone in her village, telling Sarah that she, too, was their daughter and that they knew her well. Standing in Kalah's presence, Sarah did not need to ask why or how this could be. She accepted it as truth. She knew that someday she would understand more. But for now, this sense of being loved and accepted was all that mattered.

"You are my sister," Sarah said with her thoughts. "My family is also your family." Then they opened their arms and embraced. Spontaneously the group broke out in applause. The two women bowed and laughed. They hugged again. The rest of their day was strikingly normal and relaxed. All of the women eventually found themselves gathered in the kitchen, chatting like old friends. The men sat outside on the porch, talking about matters both sublime and funny. Porter was a good sport as Kai teased him about the dreamtime coconuts.

"At least they were small," Porter said, rubbing his head.

"I was just trying to wake you up. I wasn't trying to kill you."

"Well it did the trick," Porter answered. "At least I hope it did."

"I think it did," Kai said. "You're here. The turtles are glad of that."

Eventually, all conversations inside the house, and outside, turned to life changes and sea turtles.

"My house has already sold and Porter's is on the market," Kate told the women. "It's a great house. I think it will sell in no time. After the honeymoon, we'll go home and get our things in order and start transplanting our lives. It's all happening very fast in some ways, but in other ways it's just not fast enough. We're ready to get on with it."

"It's a big change, moving to Hawaii," Hannah said. "And leaving your jobs and so many things that are familiar to you." She looked over at Kalah, smiling. "I've never made a move that big, or even a trip that big. My life has centered on this place. I've always lived in the same time zone."

"You're right, it is a big deal," Kate acknowledged. "Some things I will miss. Some people I will miss. But we both realize that we don't have forever, at least not on this planet. And we feel that we have wasted many years on things that aren't really important. So we want to make up for lost time. I have a strong hunch that Hawaii and the sea turtles are going to help us with that. We'll be helping each other." Kate was standing between Aunt Twylah and Sarah's mother. They were slicing pineapple and putting ham on a plate.

"Kate, you are so perfect for Porter," Sarah said. "I've never seen him look so happy."

"We're a good match," Kate acknowledged. "A good blend of East and West. We keep each other balanced I think." She looked down, suddenly taking on the girlish excitement of a bride-to-be. "Not to mention the fact that he's handsome and sophisticated and I'm crazy about him." The others nodded, smiling.

Outside Porter was sharing similar feelings with the men.

"She stole my heart in about three weeks," he said. "First it was the books. Then it was the cooking. Then it was..." He lowered his voice, "those eyes." Sarah's father slapped him on the back.

"Congratulations, Porter. It took you long enough."

"I was just being picky."

"Obviously. But that's good. She's got beauty and brains and she's wild enough to go on an adventure with you to save sea turtles. I'd say that all of that was worth the wait."

"She feels very passionately about the turtles too," Porter said. "She's not just doing it to accommodate me. Believe me, she's a strong lady. If her heart wasn't in it, she would tell me. But she's ready to do what it takes, personally and financially. We both are."

"The turtles need your energy, and frankly they need your money, too." Kai said. "There's so much more that could be done if people would invest in them."

"Well, neither of us have ever had children," Porter said. "And I've been lucky financially. So I've got this money sitting in the bank doing absolutely nothing useful, except making other bankers feel good. It's the college fund for the kids I never had. I was a little sad about that, until now."

"You will find that as you part with it, you will be rewarded in ways that you cannot begin to imagine," Kai said. "Don't get me wrong. Having lots of money in the bank must be a good feeling. But watching a baby turtle hatch, and knowing that you had something to do with helping it survive, well, that experience has a richness that is far beyond what money can buy. Imagine a piece of your own spirit swimming out there with that turtle, because that is what's taking place. You help the turtle and the turtle gives you something in return."

"I am so ready for that I could cry," Porter said, sincerely. "In fact, I think I'm actually about to cry right now." He swallowed hard. "That's embarrassing."

"You're among friends," Kai said. "And I promise. No more coconuts." He tousled Porter's hair as if he were a young boy. "Here, I want you to have this. It's a peace offering." Kai took off the necklace with the totems and put it around Porter's neck. Porter fingered the little coconut.

"Actually, I wish you had started pelting me a lot sooner," Porter said. "What took you so long? My God, what if I had missed my chance?"

"I wouldn't let that happen," Kai responded. "I respect your free will, but letting you miss the boat was never an option."

Later in the evening, Kalah gathered them together and told them the story of the first lamp. Even those who had heard it before were enraptured. Then each of the guests spent some time alone with the lamp as it sat by Kalah's bed. It was her idea. Sarah went last, not wanting to feel rushed by someone else waiting for a turn. Porter went just before her. They met in the hallway.

"It's beyond words," he said softly.

"I feel a little nervous. Will you come back to the room with me for a moment?" she asked, looking up at him. He let her lead him back by the hand.

"Oh my God," she said, her eyes widening as they entered. She dropped to her knees. "It's real."

"Yes it is." She looked up at him and saw a man whose full glory and spiritual power was just beginning to manifest. She searched his radiant face.

"You're changing. I can see it. That's what it does," she said, looking back at the lamp. "It brings out our true light and beauty. It shows us who we really are."

He nodded. She could see the dancing flame of the lamp reflected in his eyes as he got down on his knees beside her. He folded his hands in prayer.

"You know," he said softly. "Kai said it changed a while back. The bowl was black lava rock and the colors in the flame were like a rainbow. Then something shifted, and the rainbow hues were transferred to the bowl itself. The light became pure white."

"Really?" she asked. "Does he know why?"

"He told me that it was transformed when the collective consciousness on the planet built up a critical mass and went through a major spiritual shift," he said. She studied the bowl, shimmering with colors that seemed to move like streams of water across the rough surface.

"I understand," she said. "Somehow I understand. The rainbow has always been a symbol of reassurance emerging from the storm clouds and dark skies. The flame was rainbow-colored when our souls were bright and beautiful but our physical lives were in heavy darkness. Now, the light of our souls is finally pouring into our physical experience on this planet. Our bodies are changing. I can see it on you and the others here. Everyone looks younger, lighter. And the lamp shifted to reflect that. Now, the body of the lamp is colorful and bright, too. White is the color of unity. The white light of the flame symbolizes everything coming together." Porter put an arm around her.

"You are my smartest child," he said, a smile flashing across his face. Sarah smiled back.

"Hooray! I finally got to give one of the big answers," she said. He gave her a squeeze and stood up.

"I'm going to leave you alone with the lamp for a while," he said. "Everyone else has had some time alone."

"I love you, Porter."

"I love you, too, honey." He slipped out, shutting the door behind him.

"I love you beautiful lamp," she said.

After a while, there was a soft knocking on the door. "Come in."

It was Kalah.

"Kalah! I'm so glad you are here! I didn't mean to disappear," Sarah said. "I lost complete track of time."

"That's understandable. The lamp comes from a timeless place. The others will be driving to the hotel in a while. The traveling has made them tired. I wanted to spend time with you before you leave for the night. They have assured me that there is no hurry. Kai will drive you back." Sarah nodded enthusiastically. They sat across from each other on the floor, folding their legs like little girls about to play a game of clapping hands.

"This lamp," Kalah explained, "will stay here after I go back. It will stay with Kai and Hannah for a period of time in thanks for having me here. Then they are free to pass it on. I believe it will go next to Porter and Kate, enhancing their journey with the sea turtles. And then it will be passed on to you. You will know when it is the right time to pass it along. I have complete faith in you.

"And I will tell you this, Sarah," she added. "The one who receives the lamp from you lives here in Hawaii, on this very island. She is a brave child who will grow into a powerful woman. The two of you will meet someday and form a bond. The wisdom of the lamp will guide you both. It will guide this woman back to my time."

"Thank you," Sarah said, "I'm speechless."

Kalah nodded and smiled. "I know how you feel. This has been amazing to me, as well. Now, I have something to give you."

She took off her necklace. It was made of small, conch-like shells. She put it around Sarah's neck. "They are like trumpets.

These shells are small, but they herald great news. Mama Hanu gave this to me when she was satisfied that I had reached a high level of spiritual awareness. I give it to you, now, as a token of your own wisdom, Sarah. Can you feel its power?"

"Yes."

"More importantly, can you feel your own power?"

"Yes. I can."

"Good. Now then, close your eyes. I have something else important to share. Your world needs to know this somehow." Sarah closed her eyes, feeling so light that she thought she might lift from the ground. Behind closed lids, images began to unfold, images of life in Kalah's time. They were being transmitted without spoken words in vivid flashes of sound, color and understanding.

Sarah smiled, her eyes still closed, as she saw Kalah dancing on the sand as Makani pretended to chase her with a rope. She saw Kei and the other dolphins, and a multitude of sea turtles, swimming with Kalah and her sisters. And she saw Mama Hanu. She saw and felt that this wise woman who had guided Kalah since childhood to the wonder and magic of this very moment. In time, these images slowed but their impact remained, touching her deeply. She saw the pillars of the sunken city, the ones on Aunt Twylah's painting. Pulsating strands of DNA wrapped around them. She felt a shift within herself, as if her own physical evolution had just taken a giant leap in order to keep up with her spiritual growth. Like the body of the lamp, her own vessel was changing.

"Use your voice," Kalah said, gently squeezing Sarah's hands. "Use your own words to tell the story of events that are unfolding. Human beings need to trust that the original design for humanity was the most intelligent one.

"Anything that has been done to mar this design can be undone. It *will* be undone," Kalah added. "When there is more balance between the mind and heart there is more spiritual power. Intuition is then restored as the chief navigator, the one who knows how to follow Great Spirit's course. When this takes place, the world will not feel so lost. It is the way of Aloha. It is the way of the ancient people. They knew where they were going and where they came from." Kalah paused, looking deeply into Sarah's eyes. "We come from the place of Great Spirit.

"My sister, you and I have both learned that the story of fear is the story of a lost child. I learned that lesson on this journey. It is a great gift to me. You have learned the lesson as well. Human beings' hearts will open, and they will forgive themselves once and for all, if they understand the story of this lost child who is welcome home to heaven anytime. Remind them of this. It will be the most important thing that you ever do."

"I promise you," Sarah said, feeling deeply inspired. "I will tell them this story."

CHAPTER FORTY-SEVEN

Fulfillment

Wedding preparations were unfolding. The women, rested now, agreed on a girl trip to the goddess Pele's chief residence, a nearby volcano and the beautiful national park land around it. Then men stayed back to plan the evening's feast, which would include people from around the island, some of them sea turtle scientists and advocates. Musicians and caterers came early to begin setting up. Torches were erected around an area that had been cleared for dancing.

"If you come back this afternoon and we're not here, it's because we need to go into town and pick something up," Kai said. "A package. It's a big one, so we all have to go."

"It's our surprise guest," he whispered to his wife. "We're picking him up at the airport. Do you think we should go ahead and tell her?" He looked over at Sarah.

"No, if she seemed more upset about his absence I would tell her now," Hannah said. "But she's happy as a clam being with Kalah. I'm glad they've had this time together. Maybe it was all meant to unfold this way."

"In talking to Porter about it, I think Gabe and Sarah had to discover that they could give each other room and still feel secure," Kai said. "That was a huge lesson for them. Once it was learned, the situation was free to shift in a new direction. Kalah just helped nudge that along."

"Yes, she has a real knack for doing that," Hannah said. She kissed Kai, reaching up to touch his face affectionately.

"Hold that thought," he said, also responding to the tingle of romance in the air. "Hold that thought for later." He looked around and saw that nobody was watching. He gave her a smooch and a light pat on her behind. "You look beautiful, by the way." It seemed that they were all feeling and looking younger. The women, in particular, were reflecting the joy in their physical beings, all of them glowing.

And then they were off, Hannah driving their big car with gusto. The windows were rolled down and their hair was flying. She turned on the radio, no longer worried about shattering Kalah's focus, and found one of the few stations not bothered by the immense energy given off in the volcanic region.

The scenery was unlike anything the mainland women had ever seen: Impossibly lush rain forest scenery suddenly giving way to Martian-like rocky terrain. Then the rain forest would emerge again, thick and healthy. Then more rocky plateaus and cracked, steamy ground.

"The goddess loves the greenery and the heat," Hannah explained. "Both reflect her moods."

"This is so humbling. I feel like I'm watching the planet's physical evolution," Sarah said.

"You are!" Kalah said. "The planet is still evolving."

"As we speak, honey," Aunt Twylah said. "Make sure your seatbelts are buckled. It's going to be quite a ride." Sarah's mother let out a laugh and waved her hands as if in protest. "Now, slow down. Some of us would just like to take a leisurely drive through paradise without spinning off the planet." The car was filled with raucous laughter. The women returned to find that the men had left for their errand, but a tight-knit group of Kai and Hannah's friends were still working around the house, preparing for the night's party and the next day's wedding ceremony. Most of the work was done before the women could lift a finger. It was late in the afternoon when they heard the sound of the car on the gravel driveway.

Sarah looked out the kitchen window.

"It's them," she said to her mother and aunt, who were sipping iced tea. "Wait a minute." She looked out the window again, straining her eyes past the glare to see who was with them. "They have someone. It's Gabe! My gosh! Gabe's here!" She let out a squeal like an excited child and started to bolt out the door.

"Do I look all right?" she asked, stopping and smoothing her hair. The others nodded excitedly. She ran out the door.

"You're here! I can't believe this!" He was uncurling his long legs from the back seat when she approached. He pulled himself out and wrapped his arms around her. With all tension drained from his face he looked more serene than she had ever seen him.

"This place is incredible. I feel like I'm on another planet," he said. He kissed her and held her face in his hands. "I'm sorry I'm late. But there's no place that I would rather be." She looked over at the other men, who were trying not to be obvious about watching. "Thank you," she said. "Whatever you did to get him here, *Mahalo.*"

She turned to Gabe, "That means 'Thank you' in Hawaiian."

"It wasn't us," Porter said, carrying Gabe's suitcase toward the house.

"They aren't the ones who got me here," Gabe explained. "They picked me up at the airport. But it was mostly Nana Gwen. She told me what you've been trying to tell me for months now. The man in me was trying to resist, but the boy in me still listens to my grandmother. And it didn't hurt that she had some serious help from Kalah."

"Kalah?"

"Yep. I was sitting at your apartment feeling like an idiot as soon as you left, but still wanting to think I had done the right thing by staying back. I started remembering a dream I'd had the night before, actually a whole string of dreams. Nana Gwen was reminding me of what she had tried to teach me while she was alive. It was so vivid, like flash-backs. Then she started talking about the present, basically kicking my behind in her own gentle way. And like a cosmic one-two punch, I get a call from Kalah and she told me why I had to be here with you. That part was not a dream. I was awake and waiting for the plumber. Oh, and I think Kalah might have unclogged the drain, too." Sarah shook her head in disbelief.

"She actually picked up the phone and called you?"

"She did. She said she tried to reach me telepathically but I was blocking her. That sounds like me, doesn't it? Good grief, Sarah. Why didn't you just tell me she had traveled across the vastness of time and space to help fulfill a prophecy? I would have come sooner." Sarah laughed so loud that she almost fell over. She practically knocked him over, which made him laugh. Finally, they collected themselves.

"Oh. Did Larry King's office call you?" he asked.

"Yes."

"Can you believe that? I mean wasn't that a little too easy?"

"I had help from some heavenly muses," she said. "And anyway, why should everything be so hard? I'm so tired of hard things." This time the snort came out of his nose. She looked at him.

"I heard that! You have a dirty mind."

"I didn't say anything at all. I'm completely innocent, you lusty woman." They were nearly at the house. She stopped and wrapped her arms around him.

"Maybe I am a lusty woman." He whispered something naughty in her ear and they almost fell on the ground again. The others were now unabashedly spying.

"They are so darned happy they're drunk," Twylah announced with satisfaction. That night they all partied in perfect Hawaiian style. Drums, flutes and guitar sounds punctuated the evening. Kai had arranged for a pig to be roasted so that his guests could get the full flavor of a real luau. Kalah gave Sarah and Gabe wooden spoons with pasty purple poi root mashed to perfection.

"Taste it," she said. "You'll think it's really *different*, but the night should not go by without you trying some of it."

Sarah licked her spoon right away, but Gabe, the more cautious one, hesitated, sniffing it a little. "No poi, no dessert," Kalah said playfully, the lilt in her voice full of fun. He ate it.

"No fair," Sarah said, pouting a little. "You'll do anything she says. What's your secret, Kalah?"

"Well, when I ask him to do something, I visualize the outcome I would like, which is the same as asking for the highest good. It doesn't always work, of course. Everyone has a choice. But with him I've been getting a good response. I sense that he's eager for a little direction."

"I'll have to try that. If I can get the hang of it, he'll be putty in my hands," Sarah said. Gabe heard that.

"I don't think so, whatever you're saying," he said, finishing his poi. "And anyway, you like a good challenge. I'm not going to make it too easy for you. No way."

"See there," Sarah said. "He's Mr. Putty with you. Maybe it's your dress. Where can I get one?" They were teasing now like sisters.

"I have one for you that is almost like this," Kalah confided. "Hannah and I picked it out for your ceremony tomorrow."

"I'm in a ceremony?"

"Yes, you are. You both are," she said, nodding toward Gabe. "If you choose." A strong breeze blew off the water. They looked up, watching the tall, regal palms blowing in the wind.

"This is everything I have ever dreamed of," Kalah said, her eyes shining. "This is not just amazing and mysterious to you. I am, as they say in your world, blown away!"

"I need to ask you something," Sarah said. "When we first met, you told me I was a miracle. Why did you say that?"

Kalah paused, going back to that moment. "Time-travel is a great mystery and a great miracle to me, even though I have been raised to know of it and trust it," she said. "I am a sky-walker not because I understand it with my mind, but because I trust in the deepest reaches of my heart that Great Spirit does. So in that sense, my journey is about choosing to trust, choosing to let myself move in the service of the light. Your journey to get here also involved trust and a desire to be in service of the light. In that respect, we are very much alike.

"But I have been raised in a time and place that makes it easier to trust," she continued. "I have had my challenges, but I have not been filled with the illusions of separation and limitation that plague your time. So in that sense, my journey here is much less of a miracle than your journey. Each of you who came to Hawaii is miraculous to me because you have chosen this path against great odds. That's what I meant.

"You will understand so much more about this miracle tomorrow, when Kai speaks," Kalah added. "There is so much more to say. But it is like fine, rich food. Small bites are easier to digest."

CHAPTER FORTY-EIGHT

Union

The day unfolded like a fairy tale, as all wedding days should. Porter was the handsome king marrying his queen near a cliff overlooking a turquoise sea. Kai, an ordained minister, officiated with gentle authority.

Kai talked to them about the great love of Great Father for Great Mother and reminded them that a lamp of love must always burn in their hearts to honor the first marriage of divine lovers. With great feeling and tenderness, Porter spoke directly to his bride about the great respect he had for her balance and kindness. He pledged to seek her guidance and to offer his own as a loving and loyal mate. Kate responded with a poem that had blossomed in her mind as the gathering of women walked through Pele's world the day before.

"I will tend the garden of your heart, Beloved, and you will tend to mine," she said, her words resonating with grace. "I will nourish your visions and you will nourish mine. Together, we will watch our creations flourish and flow. We will feed the body of this planet, great mother turtle carrying us on her back. And she will feed our spirits, giving the gift of knowing our true selves. Together the two of us will ride, sometimes on turtle's back, sometimes gliding on the wings of a bird, surveying the gardens and forests and the rivers and oceans of God's love. When there is soft rain, we will drink it up. When there are storm clouds we will accept the gift of their purification. I take you as my husband in the land of rainbows. We are the children of the rainbows."

Kai beamed with pride and nodded. When they were through he breathed in deeply and looked heavenward. Then he lifted his arms and opened them wide as if to embrace not only the couple, but the entire gathering as well.

"Children of Hawaii," he said, "some of you blood kin to this land, some of you adopted into our great family in the spirit of *hanai*, we will walk together on the path that lies before us. It is the path of Aloha, the path of the heart. Porter and Kate, with the love of this land surrounding you, I now pronounce you man and wife. Porter, you may kiss this beautiful woman!" The newlyweds kissed, smiles of joys lighting their faces as their lips met. The gathering of loved ones moved closer, showering them with hugs and kisses. Gabe hugged Sarah, rocking her in his embrace. "I can't imagine missing this. Thank you. Mahalo." He kissed her.

"You're sexy when you speak Hawaiian," she whispered. He kissed her again.

"Mahalo," he repeated. "Mahalo, mahalo, mahalo."

As the day wore on the happy gathering prepared for the next rite of passage in the day's extraordinary schedule. At sunset, Uncle David's ashes would be released to the wind and sent out to sea. Then another ceremony would follow, one that would bring a prophecy to completion. To those gathered, it was a mystical dance of life. Great feelings of knowing washed over the people basking in the love of Kai and Hannah's home. Releasing a need to plan and to feel in control, the guests moved to the rhythm of things greater than themselves.

As dusk rolled in, Aunt Twylah stood flanked by Kai and Hannah as they prepared to throw her husband's ashes. The sun dropped gently as if lowering itself into the sea. Its golden light was mirrored in the faces of those watching. A great whale rose from the depths of the dark blue sea and shot a white plume of water into the air. As this took place, David's ashes were released to the winds of eternity. Twylah waved to the whale as she tossed the ashes. She rested a hand over her heart.

"I love you, darling!" she called out as she faced the sea. "I release you from my needs. But I hold your love here. I hold the gifts you have left me. You are free now. Free to enter any form you choose." She paused and swallowed hard. Kai put a protective arm around her. When she spoke again, her voice had regained its strength.

"Thank you for sharing your life with me, David," she called out. "I know you are watching us. I can't see you right now, but I can feel your love." When the last of his ashes had been carried away by the wind, the gathering of loved ones stood watching and listening to the pounding of the mighty waves upon the cliffs. The waves were picking up power now. The sky was growing a darker shade of blue, shifting to indigo, and the first of the stars were shining. Hannah led the group inside for a light meal and some rest. Aunt Twylah was nurtured and supported during this time of reflection, release and thanksgiving.

There was one more ceremony and eventually it was time to prepare. Sarah and Kalah slipped back into the room with the lamp. There was more to share, more to discuss about what the rest of the evening would bring.

Kai brought out two flashlights and asked Gabe to join him on a walk along the road that led to the sea. The final ceremony was a ceremony of the heart. It was important for him to know that Gabe did not feel coerced about participating.

"So, you had strong women asking you to come to Hawaii," he said. "Still, you have a free will equal to theirs. You could have refused. You did hesitate. But in the end, you chose to come. What brought you here?"

Gabe told Kai about his grandmother. "I call her Nana Gwen. Even now, when I say that name, I feel like a young boy, a boy who is asking question after question. In my family, her mystical viewpoints were usually scoffed at. But we had plenty of time together when I was little. She told me stories with lessons.

"My biggest regret is that I didn't learn more from her while she was alive. The night before Sarah left, Nana Gwen came to me in a dream and asked me why I was afraid of Hawaii. I wanted to argue and tell her that I wasn't afraid. But on some level, she was right. I was afraid of what would happen to me here."

"Does this place feel foreign to you? Do we seem like strangers?" Kai asked. "Because I need to prepare you. It could get stranger. At least in your eyes."

"No, it's not that," Gabe said. "This is a magnificent place. A part of me simply believed that Sarah was on a spiritual journey that didn't apply to me. I also think I was scared of not being hunkered down on my home turf, like that would put me at a disadvantage somehow. I didn't want to admit it to myself, but I was afraid of feeling vulnerable with Sarah. I was afraid of falling completely in love with her. But it's too late. I've already done that. Staying home won't save me now." Kai laughed.

"But no, Kai, when I travel I'm looking for adventure and discovery," he added. "I'm not interested in swimming pools and suntans. When I actually build up the momentum to pull away from work and leave home, I'm looking for a big experience."

"Then you've come to the right place."

"Why? What's going to happen?" Gabe asked, intrigued.

"That's a fair question, but I'm not going to give you an answer yet. I'd still like to know more about what led you here. What did you experience when Kalah called?"

"Well, her phone call stunned me to the point that any remaining resistance melted away. When she spoke, it felt like she was speaking to me on many levels. Her voice sounded familiar, too. I can't explain it. It was a voice that I've heard before."

"I'm sure that's the case," Kai said.

"She's powerful."

"Yes, she is. And so is Sarah. And apparently, so is Nana Gwen. You really didn't stand a chance, did you son?"

"No sir. I didn't." They sat down on a large rock and were quiet for a while, staring up at the stars. "My grandmother asked me an interesting question," Gabe said. "In the dream, she asked me if I wanted to be a sleep-walker or a sky-walker. When I woke up, I knew without a doubt which one I wanted to be." Now it was Kai's turn to be intrigued.

"She used the word 'sky-walker?' Had she ever used that term with you before?"

"No."

"Then she must have met Mama Hanu."

"Who is that?"

"She is Kalah's teacher in her village. Mama Hanu lives in what we would call the distant past. She is helping with the transformation of our present, but she is also working to change of part of her own past. Change can work both ways. There is a sunken continent not too far from here. Its restoration is a part of the plan. But that's a story for another day." He studied Gabe's face. "I sense that you are surprised but that you understand what I'm saying. You believe that I'm telling you the truth."

Gabe nodded. "I believe you," he said sincerely.

"You were looking for a big experience, and I think you're ready for one," Kai said with approval.

"So can you tell me now, what I can expect tonight?" Gabe asked.

"Yes. And I want you to know that at any point, you have a right to decline. This is about choice."

"Does this experience involve leaving the ground?"

"Not that I know of, at least not for you. Not this time," Kai said. Gabe's eyebrows shot up.

"But you never know," Kai added. "There might be a few surprises for me, too."

With that, Gabe was told everything that Kai knew about the final ceremony. As they spoke, the dolphins and the whales caught their words on the wind and the sea turtles were drawn from the depths of the sea to hear the completion of the prophecy.

CHAPTER FORTY-NINE

Children of the Stars

Everyone rested. Time seemed to stop. After a while, they were filled with peace and the energy to complete the next step. Torches were lit and they were called outside. Kai had changed into a fresh white linen shirt. Kalah had changed into her indigo and white dress. Sarah wore a red Hawaiian dress with white flowers embroidered into it. It was the most beautiful dress she had ever seen and she knew that it had been selected with great care. She gently touched the shell necklace resting against her skin and looked up at the flickering stars.

When Hannah walked outside with the ancient lamp, flanked on one side by Sarah's mother and on the other by Aunt Twylah, Sarah felt as if her heart would burst with wonder. Enchantment pulsed through the gathering. She reeled slightly, feeling a little dizzy. Kalah gently touched her arm, steadying her.

Kai produced a spear that had been resting on a nearby stone fence. He raised it to the sky, singing an ancient Hawaiian prayer. Then he plunged its tip into the ground, a wave of great joy washing over his noble face.

"Today, new trees are planted," he said. "New life will take root on this land."

He opened his arms to again embrace the gathering. Kalah moved next to him, suddenly holding two exquisite masks in her hands. They seemed to have materialized from the supercharged air. One was made of red feathers, the other made of white. They vibrated softly in her palms.

"Sarah and Gabe, will you come to the center of our circle?" Kai asked. They stepped forward. Kalah handed her the red mask and gave Gabe the white one.

"With these masks, your true nature will be revealed," Kalah said. "For the hidden reveals the truth. This is the gift of renewal that I bring to you from my time." The wind gathered and blew with great strength off the water, whispering to them of great forces at work. The great Mother Earth herself, working in her own way, sent up a mighty rush of love through the soles of everyone's feet, speaking to them of her delight. They were energized.

Kai nodded to the couple in the circle. With reverence, they put on the masks. Their bright eyes sparkled from behind. They held hands and stood to face Kai.

"Sarah, you stand here tonight as a representative of every woman in this time," Kai said. "For we are one. Separation is an illusion that we will learn to see through. Do you accept this role?"

"I do."

"In doing so," he continued, "you are being asked to take back your power, the creative power of the sacred feminine. You are wearing the red feathers that have come to be reserved for the male aspect of our collective being, red feathers designating royalty, authority and power. In wearing this mask and claiming its essence for the feminine, you are helping to mend a deep rift and heal the collective consciousness of humanity. You are forgiving yourself and all who participated in this wounding of the feminine. Will you take this lesson into your heart and share it with others?"

"I will. Yes, I will."

Kai flashed a big smile, his eyes conveying his happiness. He turned to Gabe.

"Gabe, you stand here tonight as a representative of every man in this time. Separation is an illusion that we will learn to see through.

"Do you accept this role?"

"I do."

"In doing so, you are being asked to take back your innocence, the innocence of the collective masculine. You are wearing the white feathers of purity that have come to be reserved for the maiden bride and the pure spirits among our collective being. In wearing this mask, you are reclaiming the innocence with which all men are born. You are washing clean the soul of the collective warrior. You are forgiving yourself and all who have participated in this great wounding of the masculine. Will you take this lesson into your heart and share it with others?"

"Yes. I will." Kai closed his eyes to pray. Then he opened them again.

"Sarah and Gabe, in standing here with us tonight and participating in this great ritual of ancient Hawaii, a ritual of *kala,* which is both forgiveness and release, you are adding your mighty spiritual weight to the great forces at work in our universe. These forces are aching to see the energies upon this planet healed and balanced. All of you here tonight, will you carry this moment in your hearts? Will you accept your heritage as children of the rainbows, as children of the great winged beings? Will you accept your right to soar and be free?"

"We will," they all said together. The winds blew and they felt a powerful force surround them.

"In doing so, you are participating in a shift that will give new direction to the planet. As a collective vessel, we now sail on bright waters. I ask you to forgive yourselves and all who have participated in the wounding of this planet and of humanity. It is the most important thing you will ever do. Look ahead and decide what your role will be. You are helping to redirect the course of human history. You have the power to do this. Everyone has the power to do this. Believe it and honor it." He looked around at the shining faces smiling back at him. Then he looked back at Sarah and Gabe.

"You may remove your masks, which are yours to keep. Reveal your true nature. You are children of the stars. From now on, you will carry that vibration." They took them off, holding them over their hearts and standing to face on another. To all who were watching, they radiated the essence of Great Mother and Great Father, two lovers who had played a game of separation, then beheld each other as if for the first time.

Kalah marveled at this. Then she spoke.

"My sisters and I searched and found these feathers in the land of my birth. We were sent on an errand by our chief. We did not really understand. Now I understand. Chief Ka-welo is a man of wisdom. There was a third mask. It was given to the one you knew as Pablo." Sarah and Gabe looked at each other in amazement. "I urge you to find your own rituals and in your own unique way practice the great art of forgiveness and renewal."

Kalah put her fingers to her lips and paused to collect herself. Waves of emotion were building inside of her. She looked around at each of them. Then she raised her hands toward the heavens. She drew in a deep breath and released it.

"Tonight, a prophecy has been fulfilled. My heart is bursting with joy. The wedding that has blessed us is a treasure that I shall hold in my heart to the end of my days. Porter and Kate, two great beings who have found each other, you will create much beauty together. Aloha.

"Twylah, your husband now reclaims the freedom of pure spirit. He asked that his ashes be thrown here not only for his own pleasure, but to draw you, his beloved wife, to the comfort of this place. Thank you for allowing us to share in this great ritual of love between husband and wife. Marianne and James, you have brought forth into this time a time-traveler and a storyteller who will help guide her brothers and sisters back to the path of innocence. She would not have risen to this challenge had you not believed in her. You, too, are part of the plan. Mahalo!

"Sarah and Gabe, you have chosen to walk the path of healers, healers of yourselves and of others. Healers of the planet. The rite of passage in which you have participated is cause for rejoicing in the heavens. Take these masks into your home and into your hearts. Create your own rituals of healing and renewal. The world is hungry for balance, the sacred balance between the mind and the heart, the masculine and the feminine. Aloha." She looked heavenward, then back at the gathering. "All of you are descendants of the star people, the great winged beings. It is now your wonderful task to blend your own creativity with the creativity of Great Spirit. My dear friends, have fun with this. Have fun!" Her sweet smile seemed to light the evening, outshining the moon. She paused and continued.

"There are three pieces to this prophecy and they have been sung to me since I was a child. Each and every one of you has participated in its fulfillment. As a result, each of you has been gifted with a new torch in your hearts and a higher vibration. Hannah, Kate, Twylah, Marianne and Sarah, you are now charged to spread the light and you will do so quite naturally wherever you go. Kai, Porter, James and Gabe, to you I say the same. You are the light wherever you go. And you will transform the darkness. For our lives are the darkness and the light. You cannot know one without the other. In your hearts, the darkness has come to know its Source. Like a child basking in unconditional love, it runs now to its parent, the Great Light. All darkness is transformed by the light when it recognizes that it is loved by the light.

"The prophecy also reminds us that our forms are the vessels that carry this light. As a collective vessel, we strengthen ourselves and now shift to a new course. As mariners of the universe, we will be guided by the stars. We can float on the waves of time and space, or we can *merge* with the waves, flowing into the great cosmic sea of God's love. We are the vessel and the waves. David understood that." She looked at Twylah. "He experiences it now."

"And our story," she said, "looking around at the faces smiling back at her. "Our story is told by the one who is silent." She focused now on Sarah. "One day you heard a voice, an inner voice reminding you to speak up. Do you remember?" Sarah nodded.

"I heard it, too," Kalah said. "It was your voice, not mine. I was with you even then, hearing the words that you stifled, the wisdom that you were afraid to speak. But you have reclaimed your spiritual power and that includes your voice. You will meet others who are also choking back their own wisdom. Collectively, your once silent thoughts will now be heard."

Kalah had more to say, but she waited. It was time for her to feel the arms of those she had come to love so much. Everyone took a turn holding her and breathing her in. Finally, they collected themselves and stood back. She folded her hands prayerfully and began to speak again.

"Great turtle," she said. "The last line of the prophecy belongs to human beings and to her." She looked at Porter and Kate. "Great Turtle, symbol of Mother Earth, finds her voice every time a new heart is moved to tell her story. In the end, you see, her story is our story and her destiny is ours. Like the turtle, we are the offspring of Spirit, delving deep into the great sea of consciousness and arising in material form. In this realm, she has agreed to hold the sacred resonance of this watery planet within the plates of her shell. She holds the vibration of its original innocence. You can see it in those precious ones, her babies, as they push from their shells and run toward the moonlit sea. We cannot help but smile when we see this, for we are seeing ourselves through the eyes of Great Spirit. We are just this innocent.

"This mythic role she has played, it has been a burden at times, for the collective consciousness of humanity has created great forces that whip and challenge the wisdom she holds. But she is so loved. What happens to her happens to us. In the spiritual sense, she has carried us on her back since the creation of time. Now we will carry her to safety. Together, we will sing a new story and the planet will be mended. Along with us, it will wake up from the dream and feel the loving embrace of Great Spirit. We are safe. "Thank you," she said, looking around. "When we meet again, beloveds, our light will shine even more brightly." She blew them a kiss and was gone.

CHAPTER FIFTY

Flames of Lemuria

The day will come when there is nothing left to forgive and celebration with your sisters and brothers is in order.
Gary R. Renard, "Your Immortal Reality"

Their bodies lurched forward, as Makani's had done, when she ceased to stand before them. As predicted by the circle of women, a ripple of joy shot across the time-space continuum as a new skywalker joined Kalah.

Sarah landed softly on the sand next to her. They looked heavenward in time to see a flaming spear soaring across the starry sky. With it came an explosion of light that for a moment turned night into day. They pointed and danced like children. In the water, the dolphins jumped.

"I had a feeling you would be close behind," Kalah said. She put an arm around Sarah's shoulder and they looked out to sea. Then she turned to speak again. She put her hands on Sarah's shoulders.

"There is another story that is told in our songs, a story about the eighth flame," she said. "In your first vision of me in my village, you saw seven bright torches, the offspring of the great fires of wisdom from the land of Mu. But there is an eighth flame, the great flame of redemption. It is a feminine force, and her name is Ra-Mu. This is a piece of that eighth flame." As Kalah spoke the last words an orb of light appeared in her hand. "I knew, Sarah, that it was in you all along."

She brought it upward to Sarah's astonished face. "It is time for you to understand. You were once a sacred vessel for the ancient fire of Ra-Mu. You lived on a continent your people call Lemuria." Sarah was speechless. Kalah's eyes were dancing. Sarah shook her head. "I don't understand. Kalah, I'm from *New York.* Well, not originally. But what does any of that have to do with me?"

"In time, you will remember. You will remember all of it and you will tell it in your stories. You will teach me from your own perspective about the sacred vessels and the great flame of redemption. And I will fill in other pieces from my own journey and together we will both tell a new story. Our hearts will beat with joy as we share the good news of redemption. Our drums will call to the others."

"Then I will see you again," Sarah said. "Or perhaps we will never be apart."

"Yes to both. And know this. Whether you walk the skies again or keep your feet firmly planted on the ground, you will always be close to the light that Great Father shared with Great Mother. If need be, the stars will come to you, Sarah. They know their own and they will come to you." Sarah's heart felt that it would burst.

"You were making us ready for His return," Sarah said, "for the return of the Ultimate Beloved. You carried the lamp to us, like the turtle did."

"And now you are a great being like the turtle," Kalah responded, "as is every human being who brings the gift of light to those who are waiting. Great Father as the sun is returning to Great Mother as the earth. They are fulfilling their own story.

"He brings light to matter, infusing the planet with love. Mother greets him in readiness to help with the shift in awareness. All of her children hunger for this shift. Feelings of loss will change to feelings of love. This will manifest in your life. Many hearts and hands will work with you, in your world and my world and all of the spaces in between. The circle of women will continue. I came to help prepare you and to learn my own lessons of forgiveness and release as well. Like you, like everyone on the planet, I am a teacher and a student."

Sarah nodded. The two hugged, and she felt the tug of her own time pulling her back. But one more question burned inside of her, a practical question. Kalah heard it before she spoke it out loud. She suppressed a giggle.

"Kalah, I have one more thing to ask before I go back."

"Yes, you do."

"Did Gabe and I just get married?"

"No." Kalah shook her head kindly. "No. In my opinion, it is best for all concerned if the wedding ceremony is not a surprise to the man and woman." Sarah let out a sigh of relief.

"I agree completely. I will see you again." Then as quickly as she left, she was returned to the gathering of loved ones standing outside Kai and Hannah's home. Only Kai knew what had happened. To the others, Sarah had never left.

* * *

Kalah paused. She saw her dolphin friend.

"Oh Kei. It was amazing! Come back tomorrow and I'll tell you all about it." She looked at the light in her hand, the flame of pure radiance that had been drawn from Sarah's heart. She pressed the sacred light against her own heart, joining their souls in the sacred task of redemption. Then she turned and ran up the hill to the waiting arms of those who knew her best. They were standing expectantly at the family altar when she arrived, admiring the dolphin painting that had preceded her. It had disappeared from Kai's house and landed precisely where it was intended to be, glowing by the fire.

"Ah! The flying dolphin," the chief said with joy as it materialized in front of him. "This is perfect! And you," he said to Kalah, "you are the second flying dolphin to arrive here tonight." She laughed and threw her arms around Makani, who seemed to envelop her and rock her with his whole being. She was home. Chief Ka-welo nodded to the painting.

"This painting is for your next journey," he said.

"My next journey? But I just got home!"

"Not now," he said. After you have your first baby."

"Do you hear?" She looked at her husband. "Baby comes first." He nodded, wiping tears from his face. They walked home, with Mama Hanu holding the painting. She would stay with them until morning. The winds were blowing harder now, and it smelled like a soft rain would grace their night. Finally, Kalah was unable to contain her curiosity any longer.

"Where will I go next?" she asked the chief.

"You will go in the other direction," he said, "along the thread of time to the past. You will see the people you have come to love." Her eyes lit up.

"And you will deliver this to Mu's great hall of art," Mana Hanu said, her fingers caressing the painting. The elder woman felt the resonance of Twylah and of David, who had crafted the frame. "The dolphin is a symbol of Mu's original innocence and it will be a reminder to them as they make their choices."

"A reminder of what?" Kalah and Makani asked in unison.

"That they have the answer, the key. They must not throw it away as the shadow of another civilization comes upon them," Mama said. "They know the way of the heart and the way of the right path. The past is being retold, you know, as is the future. It is all in motion and quite a wonderful story, but one for another day."

"I will tell you one thing now," the chief added. "The great being known as Pablo, he will greet you in the halls of Mu. He exists in that time as their master artist, the one who will be the guardian of this painting. If they forget about their strengths, he will remind them."

That night, Kalah slept peacefully in the arms of her husband, basking in the bounty of his great love and gratitude. She dreamed of a red bird feeding babies in a nest. Makani watched her, his heart full of love.

* * *

Sarah, too, felt the love of her man as she relaxed into his arms. The divine marriage of the sacred male and sacred female still shimmered and moved within them, clearing away guilt and fear that had lodged in their hearts like stones. They had lingered outside to admire the stars in the vast Hawaiian sky, more stars than they had ever seen. As they watched the indigo sky Sarah and Gabe saw several stars that stood out among the rest, a cluster of seven pulsing orbs. With awe they watched as these love lights moved toward them, precious gifts from the Beloved, carried earthward on the backs of great beings. The lights would guide them home.

THE BEGINNING

Epilogue

I remember Lemuria.

I do not remember the sinking time, although I know that others do.

My mind recalls the peace of the place: blue skies over white temple domes and suns adorning great stone urns.

The urns held the wisdom of our ancestors and this wisdom looked like dancing fire. I remember seven urns in all.

When I was a child I danced around the urns and felt the flames smiling at me.

Wisdom loves a child. This was particularly true in Lemuria.

As I am pondering these things I now recall the eighth flame. It represented the spirit of redemption.

Yes, somewhere deep in my core I remember that dancing fire. It was a feminine force and we called her Ra-Mu. She was the true spirit of Lemuria.

How could I have forgotten, even for a moment?

I can see myself very clearly now in my mind's eye. My hair is long and black. In the light of the sun it also has shades of red and blue. Some said they saw rainbows in my hair, but I would tell them, "Look into my eyes. That is where the rainbow lives."

In Lemuria my heart could fly right through the walls of my body, high into the sky! It returned as fire in the night. As a woman I came to know that I was a great urn holding the fire of the ancients. At the bed of my earthly death, they said the eighth flame had danced inside of me, and I had danced inside of her. I would like to know if this is true.

Kalah, dear Kalah, you have opened the place in my heart that was sealed by a heavy stone. I have looked into your eyes. That is where the rainbow lives. I have listened to your heart, and I have heard the compassion of Ra-Mu.

From the journal of a modern time-traveler

Made in the USA